OUT OF THE ASHES

NEW YORK TIMES BESTSELLING AUTHOR
L.A. CASEY

Out of the Ashes
A Maji Novel
Copyright © 2017 by L.A. Casey
Published by L.A. Casey
www.lacaseyauthor.com

This book is licensed for your personal enjoyment only. This book may not be re-sold or given away to other people. If you would like to share this book with another person, please purchase an additional copy for each recipient. If you're reading this book and did not purchase it, or it wasn't purchased for your use only, then please return to your favorite book retailer and purchase your own copy. Thank you for respecting the hard work of this author.
All rights reserved.
Except as permitted under S.I. No. 337/2011 – European Communities (Electronic Communications Networks and Services) (Universal Service and Users' Rights) Regulations 2011, no part of this publication may be reproduced, distributed, or transmitted in any form or by any means, or stored in a database or retrieval system, without prior written permission of the author. The scanning, uploading, and distribution of this book via the Internet or via other means without the permission of the publisher is illegal and punishable by law. Please purchase only authorized electronic editions and do not participate in or encourage electronic piracy of copyrighted materials. This is a work of fiction. Names, characters, places, brands, media, and incidents are either the product of the author's imagination or are used fictitiously. The author acknowledges the trademarked status and trademark owners of various products referenced in this work of fiction, which have been used without permission. The publication/use of these trademarks is not authorized, associated with, or sponsored by the trademark owners.

Out of the Ashes / L.A. Casey – 1st ed.
ISBN-13: 978-1546433187 | ISBN-10: 154643318X

For those who believe there is life beyond the stars.

CHAPTER ONE

The Earth is dying.

Overpopulation, natural disasters, illnesses, world wars, a breakdown of government and law, and as of late, global warming have *all* been a deathly combination to my precious world over the past few centuries. The latter has been the worst of all to deal with. The Earth's ozone layer has depleted so much, it's practically non-existent, and it's causing nothing but death and destruction in its wake. Crops aren't growing, animals and people alike are dying at a rapid pace, oceans and rivers are drying up to form deserts, and it's getting nearly impossible to be outside without the UV rays from the scorching sun causing severe burns.

Since the year 2005, my beloved planet and race have been fighting a losing battle for survival. Nine point nine billion people out of a ten billion population have perished in the past 110 years. Nine point nine *billion*. Roughly, 100,000 people scatter the Earth's surface, and that's *it*. After 200,000 years of procreation, that small and still dwindling number is all we have to show for it. That number now defines us.

For the first time in existence, human beings have been declared an endangered species.

We have joined many other species in becoming endangered,

and because of that, we are more vulnerable than ever. Five days ago, our species' status was broadcasted to the cosmos, and the Maji touched down on our exhausted planet four days later. That worried me greatly. Either they were close to our planet when the announcement went out, or they had unrivalled space travel speed to reach us so quickly.

In the year 2002, it was discovered that humans were not the only intelligent lifeforms in the universe—far from it. Including humanity, 233 known extra-terrestrial species lived in the cosmos. Several of them were hostile, several of them were peaceful and wished to co-exist, and several of them wanted to be left alone.

The greatest discovery in mankind's history would quickly break the foundation of human life as we knew it. Back in that period, religion to billions of people wasn't just a concrete faith; it was a way of life. With the news of other life in the universe, it unravelled many people's beliefs and, for the most part, wreaked havoc and destruction. Holy landmarks were attacked and destroyed, leaders of all religions were slaughtered, and that was only the beginning of the terror humans would unleash on the Earth.

Around the time of the extra-terrestrial discovery and breakdown of religion, an advancement in science and medicine caused a massive breakthrough that created its own point in history. Prosthetics and blood and organ donations quickly became a thing of the past. Scientists discovered ways to *grow* new organs, create new blood types, replenish others, and *attach* augmented limbs to living tissue and have every human host accept it as part of their anatomy.

Scientists took up the vacant role of creator and decided to play god. They wrote DNA codes as if programming a computer instead of a live person. 'Build-a-Baby' became an 'it' thing for people with enough credits. Once an egg from a female and sperm from a male were donated, a scientist could design the DNA structure of the newborn based on the specific requirements from the parents. You could decide what your child would look like at every age of their life. You could eliminate all natural flaws and choose enhanced limbs and organs if you wanted your child to excel at something like sports. They could even enhance the percentage of useable brain to literally make people smarter.

Soon after that advancement, robotics and technology made its grand mark on the world. Androids were the new cell phones, hover cars were the new bicycles, holograms were the new video calls, and retina scanners were the new thumbprints. The world rapidly changed into a truly presidential digital and robotic era.

Aliens were real. Robots were real. Augmented humans? *Very* real.

All of it became the norm, and after a while, something else caught everyone's attention because nobody could miss it. The sun began to die, and with it, so did the Earth. Not even the smartest of humans could figure out a way to protect our planet, and that was when the chaos *really* imploded.

It was currently the year 2115, and sadly, things had only gotten worse. With the Earth's current fragile state, an unexpected visit from a new species had everyone on edge. Well, more on edge than usual. The Maji's intentions for humans and our planet were unknown. For me, a twenty-three-year-old woman with no family, friends, or protection other than my two bare *original* hands, the not knowing was terrifying.

The Maji were the *only* reason I was so close to Command Central, and why I was out past curfew. Being out past curfew didn't exactly make me a rule breaker since law broke down forty-odd years ago, but a person was still likely to be shot on sight if they were caught sneaking around after dark, *especially* at my region's Command Central.

Over the past month, it had become the new World Base of Operations since the whole continent of Asia was wiped out in a terrifying set of quakes that, quite literally, shook the Earth. Once that incredible mass of land broke apart and became a huge crater on the

Earth's surface, those who were able scrambled together and reformed their military force.

The World Base of Operations had been set up six times since I was born, and like the other times, it was destined to fail, too. Though it was unreliable, it was desperately needed. Without the WBO, the Earth's trading posts would be no more, and as of right now, the trading posts were the only way the people of Earth were being fed, hydrated, and getting medical care. Without the trading posts, we would all be dead in a few short weeks.

Or less if the Maji decides to gift us death sooner.

I shook my head at my defeated thoughts. My father would turn in his grave if he heard the cowardly words that ran through my mind. He raised me to be strong, to be a survivor, and never to quit when things got hard or give up when hope dwindled. He taught me that my life was a gift, and no one in the universe could take it from me without a fight. It was mine and mine alone.

'Keep on keepin' on, baby,' he would say with that teasing crooked smile of his and a thriving glint in his ocean blue eyes.

My eyes, identical to my father's, glazed with tears at the thought of him, and I quickly wiped them away before they had a chance to fall. I missed my father dearly. I missed my entire family dearly. My remaining family members had succumbed to the Great Illness seven years ago that wiped out ninety percent of the Earth's population. I had been sixteen when my father and cousin died, and every day since had been a tremendous struggle.

I was born in an era when playing tag and going to school were things of the past. I wasn't born in a hospital or even somewhere that could be called home. I was born on the roadside while my parents, uncle, and four cousins were making the tough journey to relocate somewhere that would provide us with a better chance at life. But that dream was not to be. My mother died during childbirth, and I almost didn't make it either.

At the time I made an appearance, every mass of land on Earth was already deemed a war zone, and civilian casualties outnumbered the military's. I only knew of the beauty that the Earth once beheld through the vivid tales from my father and uncle, as told to them by their father, and through the occasional picture I stumbled upon. My childhood was not all pretty pictures and captivating stories, though.

Instead of playing with my cousins or getting an education as I grew up, I was being taught to hunt, skin, and prepare game. How to filter dirty water to make it drinkable, and how to tell edible leaves and berries apart from the poisonous ones. How to clean and dress a wound to keep infection away, how to move without being seen, and how to fight as good as a grown man. How to store the meat for travel so it wouldn't spoil, and how to use weapons. I was taught how to survive.

Even though I was grateful for my upbringing and thankful for the family I had, I knew I was all alone on a dying planet with nothing but my thoughts for company without them.

Now and then, I'd come across other travellers, and I'd trade with them and even have an intelligent conversation here and there; but people, in general, were not to be trusted. Most of the men and women I met would either try to rob me, capture and sell me, enslave me, rape me, or kill me. 'Try' being the keyword. I had never killed another person—I came close more than a few times—but I had maimed quite a few. I had never felt an ounce of guilt for the things I'd done, though, because I was left with no choice. It was maimed or be maimed. Kill or be killed. Survival was all that mattered ... no matter what you had to do.

Humanity had died long before the Earth began to.

Focus, Nova.

I climbed the stairs of a long-abandoned building a few hundred metres away from the WBO and made sure to keep all noise to a minimum. Even though I did my best to go undetected, I knew my safety measures would prove futile if any augs were nearby. Augmented humans were the *ultimate* security system. The truly amplified augs had all their senses upgraded. If they detected me and wanted to find me and kill me, they would do so without breaking a sweat. There was no stopping an aug that wanted to kill. The Great World War that took place eleven years ago proved that.

I was twelve when it began.

I was in the woods with my four male older cousins—Jarek, who was twenty, Tala, who was eighteen, Zee, who was sixteen, and Sammy, who was twelve like me (only, he was a few months older). His mother—like mine and like a lot of women who birthed children without medical care during the war—had died in childbirth, too.

We were hunting deer and brought down a hundred-pound buck that had us grinning from ear to ear. Most days, we'd catch rabbits, badgers, and whatever else we could snag in our traps, but a buck as big as the one we brought down was a rare thing indeed. To make matters even better, it was *my* arrow that pierced the creature's left eye and ensured our family would be eating well for the next two weeks. It also gave me bragging rights that I was *definitely* going to cash in on. In a family of primarily males, bragging rights were a big deal.

Not long after we brought down the buck, we heard screaming.

With all thoughts of our prized buck instantly forgotten, we readied our weapons, and together, the five of us ran from the woods. Ten minutes later, after the heart-wrenching screaming had stopped, we entered the clearing where we were staying. It was a survivalist camp and just one of many we'd come across over the years. But instead of children playing, women cleaning cloth on washing boards and preparing meals, or the men patrolling the camp's border and weapon training in the practice ring, they were all lying dead amongst pools of blood and dismembered limbs.

I spotted my uncle first. I saw his trademark brown cap that he loved clutched in his bloodied hand, and when I scanned my eyes up to his face, I couldn't stop the scream that tore free from my throat. His eyes had been gouged from their sockets, and his mouth was wide open as if he was silently screaming, even in death. My cousins tried desperately to shield both Sammy and me from the massacre before us, but they stopped when I told them what I saw. Sammy was the first one to break from our group, ignoring our protesting as he ran towards his father.

We all screamed in horror when a motionless blood-covered body on the ground suddenly stood, and like an android, it turned and grabbed Sammy by the throat and lifted him from the ground like he weighed nothing. With shaking hands, I scrambled for my bow that I had let fall when we entered the camp. I drew an arrow from my quiver and aimed it at the *woman* who was strangling my cousin.

I sucked in a breath, and a scream died in my throat when she twisted her hand, the hand that was around Sammy's throat, and a loud crunching sound echoed throughout the deathly silent clearing as she broke my cousin's neck. I promptly dropped my bow and arrow and puked all over the ground. I turned back in time to watch her release Sammy and to see his lifeless body drop to the ground with a *thud*. My screams became audible and rose even louder when Jerek and Tala both rushed forward, armed with their daggers, and speared the woman to the ground.

At first, they tried to restrain her, but she was hell-bent on trying to kill them, so with no choice, they began to stab her in her chest and her stomach … but she acted like she couldn't feel it. Only then did I notice the skin of her right arm hanging off, and I saw the mechanics underneath it. I screamed at my cousins that she was augmented. It was hard to tell an augmented person from a human, and we had never had any reason to fear them … until that day.

Zee and I were wrapped in each other's embrace, and we roared when arms came around us. We struggled and fought against the hold until we heard the voice of the owner. It was my father. I was so relieved he wasn't amongst the bodies that I was almost sick again. Through our sobbing, we had rapidly told him what happened.

How we heard the screams, how we found the camp, how an aug had killed everyone, including Uncle Joe and Sammy. Without needing more information, my father cocked his aged gun and aided Jerek and Tala in killing the crazed woman.

Augs were a hell of a lot stronger than us humans, but they *could* die.

I thought it was the end of it, that the nightmare was over, but it had only just started. All the commotion had attracted two more people to the clearing, and I knew they were augs straight away. It wasn't only how they looked on the outside, but the dead look in their eyes gave them away too. My cousins and father fought them off, but Jerek and Tala were injured during the fight, and though I tried my best to stop the bleeding, they were injured so badly that they both died. Tala had winked at me before he died, and Jerek told me to take care of Zee and my father. I promised him I would. Both Zee and I were like robots following their deaths; we heeded my father's orders without speaking, and we were numb whilst doing so.

My father managed to find a working handheld radio on a dead body of a patrolling member of the camp, and together, we held our breaths and listened to a broadcast from the watchmen who informed us that augmented humans were to be shot and killed on sight by civilians and military personnel alike. The collective chip embedded in every augmented human's brain—a chip required to deliver updates to an augmented person's upgrades—had been targeted by a terrorist group. The code for every augmented human had somehow been rewritten, and it had turned the augmented humans into an army.

The beginning of the Great World War was officially announced at the end of the broadcast. The war had only started, and already, my uncle was dead and so were Jerek, Tala, and Sammy. That left only me, Zee, and my father. We weren't allowed time to grieve our loss before my father had us pack our bags to the brim of what could be carried, and we evacuated the area. We weren't allowed to bury our loved ones, and we barely even got to say goodbye.

Our already hard lives were about to get a *lot* harder.

Flashes of my dead cousins and uncle covered in blood entered my mind, and then images of my sickly pale and unmoving father and cousin took centre stage. It made me sick to think I broke my promise to Jerek when my father and Zee died in my arms from the Great Illness. I failed them; I failed my entire family, and I always believed that my walking the Earth alone was my punishment from the Almighty.

I closed my eyes, forcing the images of the war from my mind. The war had only lasted a few weeks—just until the virus uploaded to the augmenteds' collective chips could be rewritten—but within those few weeks, hundreds of millions had been slaughtered. Within those few weeks, families had been torn apart, and a divide in mankind had been created.

Originals—the nickname for humans without augmentations—were on one side and the augmented were on the other, and to this day, that divide still stood tall, waiting for the other to step out of line.

I focused on my task and thought calming thoughts to bring down my elevated heart rate. I didn't want to make it easy for any augs who took up work as watchmen. My current heartbeat would only act as a dinner bell to them. I focused on the building that could just as easily kill me as any aug. The roof, most of the walls, and parts of the floor were missing from the structure, so I needed to watch my step and look out for animals and people who could sneak up on me and attack.

With an arrow in one hand and my trusty self-made bow in the other, I crouched down and moved towards an open space in the wall and looked through it. Bright white spotlights lit up the WBO; it gave away many of the positions of the patrolling watchmen on the forty-foot wall of the building. I curled my lip in disgust at the sight of them.

Watchmen were worse than any mindless man, woman, or rabid

animal. They were the humans with great power and could decide your fate with the snap of their fingers. There used to be a thing called the 'court of law' where those accused of crimes could go and fight their accusations for their freedom, but not anymore. If a watchman decided you were guilty of something, then you were guilty. No ifs, ands, or buts about it. They were supposed to be protectors of the innocents and a beacon for a new law and order, but many of them were monsters in uniform. To me and many others, they were the root of all evil.

I'd take my chances with a pack of feral mutts before I'd *ever* trust a watchman.

My head was low as I scanned the perimeter. I glanced at my surroundings every few seconds to keep an eye on things before I'd return my attention to the WBO. My eyes searched the dark night sky for drones in the air, and when I saw none of the flashing red lights, I breathed a sigh of relief.

Drones were a nightmare to deal with, in general, but at nighttime, they were *always* going to cause the death of someone. They scanned everywhere for the heat signature of a living being. It gave up people's positions to the watchmen even if they were hiding in the most unlikely of places. A traveller I met hours before told me that the power link for the drones and all operating weapons of the WBO had been shut off when the Maji arrived. No one knew why, and if someone *did* know, they weren't letting the information slip.

Normally, I wouldn't care. Normally, I wouldn't break away from the rules that have kept me alive all these years, but I had a gut feeling I *had* to come to the WBO and see for myself what was happening.

So far, my gamble was turning out to be a complete waste of time … until something happened. I startled when a patch of dark a thousand or so metres to the left of the WBO compound lit up suddenly. I sucked in a choked breath. A few smaller spacecrafts came to life and lifted from the Earth's surface, ascending to the starlit heavens, but that's not what amazed me.

The mother of all spacecrafts was sitting in the newly lit up area, and it was *huge*. I had never seen an alien spacecraft up close before. When I was younger, I saw a few of them from a great distance as they descended from space and docked at one of the many trading posts stationed across the planet. This spacecraft, however, was the largest I had ever seen. I could not believe the sheer size of it, and when white lights began to flash across the hull, I found myself staring at it, my mouth agape with awe.

I was, by no means, an expert in vessels not of this world, but I had listened to my father discuss them from the moment I could understand him until the moment he died. Growing up, manmade craft engine halls were like a second home to me. I knew the ins and outs of your typical spacecraft and its engines. I wholeheartedly knew the functions of a destroyer vessel and what made up the interior and exterior of one, and this craft was most *certainly* a destroyer.

Being an engineer had been my father's trade since he was twenty. After years of hard work, he had been promoted to chief engineer for many different crafts from the Earth's military fleet when they were docked. He was so good at what he did; he even assisted the aliens with their mechanical problems when they docked at one of the trading posts. Because of my father, I understood spacecrafts, and I appreciated them, which was why this very one blew me away.

It was easily five thousand metres long, and from what I could see, the only colour anywhere on it was the blue glow of the reactor core—the heart of the spacecraft. That very reactor powered sixteen *massive* drive assemblies that would propel the ship at what must be an unmatched speed. Ten dorsal turrets mounted particle projection cannons in pairs, lending what I knew would be excellent firepower. Eight monster plasma blasters were on either side of the nose of the craft and a heavier alpha plasma down its centreline most certainly permitted the ship to deliver blistering damage to anything unlucky enough to be caught within firing distance ... and those were just the weapons I *could* see.

If only you could see this, Papa.

Again, my eyes watered, but I rubbed them until the stinging threat of tears subsided. Apart from being in love with the crafts, my father was a space fanatic or 'space freak', as I liked to tease him in my younger years. He loved the other species and was fascinated with them. Their differences, their similarities, their history, their culture—everything. He loved it all. He was part of a small faction of humans who believed the other species had a right to exist just as we did. He always said, "No planet or race lays claim to the universe; it lays claim to *us*."

My father was a wise man, and if he were with me, experiencing a spacecraft of this magnitude up close and personal, he'd be beside himself with happiness. The emotion I felt at that moment distracted me, and that distraction was about to cost me dearly.

When I heard softly creaked movements close by, I jerked away from the crack in the wall, reached back, withdrew an arrow from my quiver, and readied my bow. I heard a gruff curse then the sound of heavy footsteps began to pound up the stairs of the building I was in. It caused my heart to slam into my ribs as it thrummed in my chest.

Watchmen.

"Civilian female at HQ," a muffled voice said. "No signs of any augmentations on the scanner, but she is armed and dangerous. Alert the Maji of a possible attack."

Alert the Maji? My brow creased with confusion. *Not alert the watchmen patrol?*

I took aim, steadied my breathing, and like a reflex, I released an arrow when I saw the head of a watchman breach the hole in the floor beneath the stairway. Not a second later, the arrow penetrated his exposed eye socket, and he dropped onto the stairway with a thud. It was only as my arrow pierced his skull that I realised he hadn't worn a helmet, and he had no protection against my weapon.

A yelp was heard after the watchman dropped then vile cursing followed.

"She *kill't* him!" a deep voice bellowed. "That fuckin' whore kill't Kiker!"

The reality I had just killed a person did not sink in. Instead, stomach-churning fear did. If they weren't going to kill me before, the watchmen surely would now that I had killed one of their own. I sucked in a breath, and with rapid speed, I released another arrow in warning. I didn't wait around for the second watchman to call for backup or to come after me. I turned, and without thinking, I jumped from the first floor of the building. I turned mid-air and landed on my left side, almost instantly falling into a roll as I tumbled down the side of a ditch.

Searing hot pain vibrated through my body, but I couldn't pause to soothe away the aches because I had to get moving. I pushed myself to my feet with my right arm when I realised my left one was burning with pain and wouldn't move. I looked down at it and saw the joint was clearly dislocated and the bone was possibly broken at the elbow. White dots splashed across the back of my eyes, and I had to close them to get control.

Don't think about it.

I opened my eyes, reached for my bow and quiver, but then abandoned them when I saw they were in pieces and scattered around the ditch. I used my right hand to hold my left arm against my body as I scrambled up the mud bank and ran like the devil himself was on my heels. I bit down on my lip when each step caused excruciating aches to tear through my arm. Twice more, my vision was spotted with white dots, but I forced myself to continue running as the area lit up with spotlights, betraying my position. Sheer determination to get away was the only thing that kept me moving, but it wasn't enough.

Less than a minute after I jumped out of the building and began running, I was tackled to the ground from behind.

A scream of agony tore from my throat as fresh pain surged through my body, mainly from my left arm. I was flipped onto my back, and a quick glance downwards gave me a revolting picture. The bone of my forearm had snapped in two, and a prodding piece stuck out of my skin for all to see. All doubt was wiped from my mind—it was *definitely* broken. I turned my head to the side and promptly puked up my stomach contents. Not a second later, I was pulled to my feet by my hair and forcefully shoved. I stumbled backwards away from the watchman who tackled me. I looked up at him and saw he was pointing an old-fashioned handgun at me.

"This is for Kiker!"

I closed my eyes and awaited my release from this prison sentence many called life.

I'm coming home, Papa.

A *bang* rippled through the air, but surprisingly, it was the gurgled male scream that startled me and caused my eyes to open. The watchman who was about to take my life was on his knees before me with a large gaping hole in the centre of his chest. It smelled like his flesh was burning, and from the slight puff of smoke that rose from his wound, I'd say a plasma blaster made the hole. I switched my gaze to his face and felt the blood drain from my own. His dark, panicked eyes were focused on me, but his mouth was agape, and blood was spewing from it like a river.

"Help," he choked out around the thick liquid before he fell forward.

I jumped backwards as his face smacked off the ground with a sickening *crack*. His body twitched once, twice, then his movements ceased. I thought he was still breathing but quickly realised the hyperventilating rasps weren't coming from him; they were coming from me. I lifted a shaking hand to my mouth and covered it as I stared down at the now dead watchman.

I swayed from side to side as my pain and shock became too much for me. I focused my blurring vision dead ahead and made out six dark figures walking toward me. Six *huge* figures. When they stopped a few metres from me, they stared at me, and me at them. They were fully clothed in a black armour of some kind, and it only made them look that much more intimidating.

The man in the front said something in a language that didn't sound of this planet, and without thinking, I stammered, "Wh-what?"

The man grunted and turned to his right and spoke to the person behind him in that same strange language.

"No," the man behind replied in strained English. "We've practiced for weeks; you have not. You need to learn how to speak the human languages to make this mission easier, just until we fit them with translators of their own. Do what I told you to do. Repeat what your translator says through your comm, and the female will understand you like you can understand me right now. I'm not responding to you anymore unless you use this particular human language."

With a defeated sigh, the large man turned back in my direction.

"I sa-said," he rumbled in a bizarre accent as he switched to an extremely choppy version of English, pausing every couple of words as if he was trying to form them as he spoke. "What 're … you 'oing … out … 'ere?"

After he had spoken, he removed the mask that covered his face. The now well-lit area shone brightly on his face and revealed all I needed to know about him to be terrified. He had vibrant *grey* skin, dazzling *violet* eyes, and menacing *sharp* teeth with gold caps on them. That was the moment I dropped to the ground like a sack of potatoes and began tumbling into darkness.

"Why do fe-females … 'eep 'oing … dat 'round me?" the Maji asked with a tired sigh.

Without missing a beat, the other voice said, "I *told* you that you were ugly. How many human females must faint at your feet before you realise that?".

CHAPTER TWO

I f I was safe, I usually woke to silence. If there was a sound, no matter how minimal, it usually had a bad outcome for me. Today, I awoke to humming, soft singing, and beeping. Loud, constant, annoying beeping. I opened my eyes, and when a damaged concrete ceiling didn't come into view, I began to panic. I tried to sit up, but I couldn't. I looked down at my body and saw I was in a white gown of some sort with thick black straps covering my arms, chest, and lower legs, pinning me to the spot.

Oh, my Almighty.

My heart slammed into my chest, and I began to hyperventilate as I struggled against the ties that bound me to the unexpectedly comfortable ... bed. I paused in my struggle and looked down once more. I blinked, surprised at what I found. I was on a *real* mattress and not one that was years old, flat, insect infested, and caked with dirt. A *clean* white linen sheet covered this one, and it had a *lot* of cushion in it. It felt incredible as if I was lying on a soft cloud.

The comfort astonishingly calmed me down and gave me my bearings to scan my surroundings. My jaw fell open when the room I was confined to registered. It was clean—*really* clean—and undamaged. It had all its walls, and the floor and ceiling were intact. It disturbed me greatly because I had never seen any place so pure and beautiful; it was somewhere that didn't look it was dying. I had never seen anything like it.

The shock from taking in the beauty of the room was quickly replaced with worry. Many questions ran through my mind.

What's going on? How did I get here? Where is here? Why am I strapped down to a bed? Is that somewhat fresh smell coming from me?

I stared down at my arms and legs, and I couldn't believe when I spotted clear patches of skin. Usually, my skin was so caked with dirt it was hard to tell the colour of my skin but not anymore. Someone had gone to great measures to clean me. While they had done a good job, I could still see patches of dirt and catch the faint stomach-churning twang of stale sweat. I *knew* my hair hadn't been washed, considering how itchy my scalp still was. I wondered who cleaned me, but my thoughts on the matter suddenly fled, and my body tensed when I sensed I wasn't alone. I had heard humming and soft singing when I awoke, but those sounds were now mute, and for a moment, I wondered if I had imagined them. That was until I looked to my right and saw it.

A Maji.

The Maji staring at me from across the clean room was clearly a woman. I could see her skin was a vibrant grey, the irises of her eyes were the most eccentric colour of *pink* I had ever seen, and her hair was as white as the sheet was I lying on. She was huge in stature and leaner than anyone I had ever seen. Apart from those differences, she looked completely human. That was the part that freaked me out the most. She was very similar to a human woman, and I didn't like it.

I need a weapon.

"Oh, my Almighty," I whimpered when the woman slowly approached me.

I had to crane my neck back to look up at her when she neared me. She must be at *least* six feet tall, give or take a few inches.

"Be still, female," she said, her voice surprisingly gentle. "I mean you no har—"

I screamed before she could finish her sentence.

"Female," she repeated, her features contorting in dismay. "I implore you to be calm. I mean you no—"

The centre of the wall across from me opened like a hidden door and in stepped another Maji. He was even taller and broader than the woman trying her best to quieten me. He had different coloured skin; it had more of a blue hue to it than grey. His hair was tight to his head, black as darkness, and his eyes were blood red with streaks of silver in a pattern like lightning strikes. I lost my calm all over again. I began to scream even louder than before, and it caused the female Maji to plug her ears with her fingers. The man did the same, and he had a look of pain on his face.

"Silence!" he bellowed after a few seconds.

I clamped my lips shut and ceased breathing altogether.

"Mikoh," the alien woman *snarled*. "You're scaring her!"

She *actually* snarled at him, and the sound reminded me of a vicious animal I'd normally encounter in the woods.

Mikoh lowered his hands from his ears. "She was scared before I entered, or was she screaming for another reason?"

"Leave." The woman growled, her posture rigid. "She is *my* charge, and you being here is making my introduction to her more difficult than it needs to be!"

Mikoh lazily grinned, and it caused me to scream again because he had gold caps on his ... *fangs*. Not mythical vampire kind of fangs, but fangs that would do a hell of a lot of damage to someone's throat all the same. It was weird, but the fang observation made it concrete in my mind that I *definitely* couldn't refer to them as man and woman anymore because they most certainly *weren't* a regular man or woman. They were male and female.

They were *aliens*.

Mikoh quickly stuck his fingers back in his ears, and so did the alien female, but she was glaring at Mikoh, not me.

"This is *your* doing, you intolerable fool!" she hissed at him.

Mikoh laughed, and the sound was almost human, only it had a lot more gruffness to it. I stopped screaming because I ran out of breath, but also because I wanted to hear the exchange between the two Maji who eyed each other with such obvious distaste.

"Must you blame everything on me, Surkah?" Mikoh asked, still grinning. "Surely, the little alien is terrified of *your* face, not mine."

"Leave!" Surkah shouted and threw a sharp object at him, but he ducked, easily avoiding it.

I momentarily wondered where she got the sharp object. I also wondered if there were more so I could avail of one and use it to defend myself if I needed to.

"I'll do so happily!" Mikoh snapped back at Surkah. "If the little alien attacks you, do *not* cry for my help like you did when the tiny Earth rodent entered your quarters yesterday!"

"I didn't cry for *you*," Surkah mocked. "I cried for *anyone*, and it wasn't tiny; it was the size of my foot! It could have *killed* me."

Mikoh laughed, ducking again when Surkah threw something else at him, then left the room quicker than he'd entered. I shook my head, feeling like my eyes and ears were betraying me. I wondered if I had imagined things, or did I really just witness two Maji arguing with one another? It seemed like an awfully human thing for them to do, but that was impossible. Other species weren't like humans. They were just ... different.

I blinked and looked at the female who was now watching me with more interest than before. She made no attempt to talk or move closer to me, and I felt better because of it.

"Please," I whispered when I was sure she wasn't going to move. "Don't kill me."

Surkah frowned, furrowing her thick white eyebrows. "I wish you no harm, tiny one."

Tiny one?

"Why am I here then?" I asked, trying to keep my composure.

My heart was beating so fast it felt like it would burst. It was then that I noticed the beeping I had heard earlier was louder now and faster. It began to hurt my head.

"You were injured." Surkah shrugged as she pressed the machine next to her, silencing the beeping. "I mended your injury, and now I'm tending to you because you're still unwell. You're in my charge, and it is my duty to care for you."

"I was injured?" I questioned.

Surkah nodded slowly. "Badly. You lost a lot of blood, and I feared your bones would not set and mend correctly when you were brought to me. I healed them as best as I could then I tended to your minor wounds, bathed you briefly, and dressed you in a wrap made for humans ... though, I think it is too small for you."

I was relived she had been the one to bathe me, but I didn't linger on that thought long because confusion gripped me, so I closed my eyes and thought. Hard. What was Surkah talking about? She said I was injured, but how? *How* was I injured, and how on Almighty's Earth did I end up in a *Maji's* charge?

Think, Nova.

I remembered scouting the WBO, and I remembered being attacked by watchmen. I ... I killed one of them and fled from the other, only I didn't get far. I opened my eyes when my memories resurfaced. The watchman to intended to kill me was instead killed by the huge Maji with violet eyes and sharp teeth. I fainted, and they brought me to Surkah for treatment, but why?

Why would they want to help a human?

I looked down at my arm and stared at my virtually unmarred skin. I vividly remembered my radius sticking out of my flesh and a deep, jagged slice in my skin surrounding it that pooled with blood. I touched my skin carefully and pressed gently. There was no pain. There was no anything. Not even a mark.

"How?" I asked, my voice raspy. "It was dislocated, and the bone poked through—"

"I healed it," Surkah cut in. "That is what I do. I am one of the healers aboard that is assigned to humans."

Healer?

"So ... you're like a doctor?"

"I do not understand." Surkah frowned, her forehead creasing. "The word 'doctor' does not translate into Maji language."

"Um, a doctor is a person who cares for the injured and sick."

Surkah considered this. "That is what I am, but we use the term healer."

"Well ... I ... Thank you for ... *healing* me."

I didn't understand how she did it, but I was grateful nonetheless.

Surkah smiled, and I was pleased to see she didn't have fangs like Mikoh. Her teeth were sharper than mine were, but they weren't scary or something I'd stop and stare at. I silently thanked Almighty for that.

"It is an honour to tend to you, tiny one," she said, and she sounded very ... excited. "You are the first human I have healed, and I am very happy there were no complications. While you were resting, I scanned you with my *lissa* because I feared your biology would differ greatly from Maji and that our medicines, or my ability, would have no effect on you, but to my delight, I discovered we're *one hundred percent* compatible. I cannot believe the results; it is truly a gift from Thanas that we came here. My shipmaster and my people will celebrate greatly with the news."

What in the fresh hell is she talking about?

I had a whole bunch of similar questions floating around in my mind, and I didn't know which one to ask first. Instead of voicing them, I kept flicking my eyes from Surkah to the section of the wall that opened before. I heard a noise outside, and I tensed. I was so scared Mikoh would re-enter the room.

I really need to get free and get a weapon.

"Why are you fearful?" Surkah asked, gaining my attention. "I scent it on you."

Excuse me?

"What did you just say?" I asked, baffled. "You *smell* my fear?"

"Yes," she replied, sniffing the air. "Fear has a sickly sweet scent, and you reek of it."

These aliens can smell fear?

"Well ..." I swallowed. "It's just ... I was kidnapped."

"By who?" Surkah growled. "I will break their bones in places they won't mend correctly."

The animalistic noises she made silenced me.

"Speak, tiny one," she pressed. "Who kidnapped you?"

I blinked. "*Your* people did."

Surkah gasped and placed her hand over her chest as if I'd physically wounded her.

"We did not abduct you," she stressed. "My people *saved* you."

I looked down at the straps that bound me to the bed and then back up at Surkah. She winced.

"Those bindings are for your protection as well as mine. We weren't sure how you would react when you awoke. The shipmaster ordered the restraints."

The shipmaster?

"Okay," I said, trying to understand her point of view.

"Surely, I would not have healed you if we meant you harm?"

I bit my lip. "Well, other species have kidnapped men, women, and children from trading posts and sold them into slavery on other planets, and they didn't harm them as to not... devalue them. I guess I'm just worried about something like that happening."

And about you eating my flesh.

I had heard all sorts of horror stories over the years about the aliens, and the worst one was that some aliens enjoyed eating human flesh while blood still flowed through their veins. The thought terrified me.

I really needed a fucking weapon.

Surkah's eyes blazed with anger. "No one will kidnap *or* harm a human whilst Maji take hu—I mean rebuild Earth."

Her slip of tongue didn't go unnoticed by me, and it only made me even *more* wary of her. She was lying to me, but I didn't know why. To avoid drawing attention to the fact that I knew she was lying, I played dumb.

"Rebuild the Earth?" I repeated, tilting my head to the side. "I'm sorry, but what do you mea—"

"Surkah!" Mikoh's voice shouted from outside the room, gaining both our attention. A second later, the wall opened, and Mikoh stood in the doorway but didn't enter the room. "The shipmaster requests an update on your scan of the human. He disapproves of you unlinking your comm from the system and so do I. I *told* you I need to be able to contact you at all times when I am not in talking distance. Our comms provide that, so why must you disconnect?"

"Because I don't like having male voices inside my head twenty-nine hours a day!"

Twenty-nine hours a day? Comms? What on Earth are they talking about?

"We aren't just *any* males, though," Mikoh said, his eyes focused solely on Surkah. "Just give me the update, and I'll pass it onto the shipmaster since you won't reconnect. He is giving me a sore head."

Surkah did something that surprised me then; she squealed.

"It is a *positive* result, Mikoh."

Mikoh's jaw dropped open. "Truly?"

"Truly," Surkah gushed. "Humans will be our salvation."

"That's earned a huge *what* from me," I cut in, feeling great unease about the conversation happening before me.

Mikoh locked eyes on me, and I tensed when he leisurely ran his eyes over my form. I didn't like how he looked at me; it reminded me of a wolf and how they would stare at their prey before they gobbled them up.

"Are you *sure* we're compatible?" he asked Surkah without looking away from me. "She is very small."

What the fuck does that mean?

"My *lissa* does not lie; human female internal organs are very much like our females in function. They'll benefit from our medicine, and the essence of a mating bond would even *extend* their lifespan. I'm positive."

"I'm going to throw out another *what* here if anyone is interested?" I said, my eyes wide with confusion.

Mikoh switched his attention from me to Surkah, and he stared at her with disbelief.

"I'm not convinced," he said gruffly.

I might as well be invisible.

"What else would you have me do?" Surkah demanded of Mikoh. "My *lissa* does *not* lie. You know this, Mikoh."

What the hell is a lissa?

Mikoh closed his eyes for a moment, and when he reopened them, he said, "I've sent for the shipmaster. He will be here momentarily; we will await his decision on the results."

"As you wish," Surkah said through gritted teeth.

Mikoh backed out of the room then the doors began to close, but before they shut completely, his electric red eyes flicked in my direction, and he winked. A second later, the doors closed, sealing him from the room.

"Stubborn male," Surkah grumbled to herself before turning her attention to me. "Are you well, tiny one?"

Her voice was so clear and well-spoken that for a moment, I felt dazed at the soothing calmness it provided.

"I have so many questions."

"Ask away."

You got it.

"How can you speak English so well?" I asked, blinking.

She tapped on the section of skin behind her right earlobe.

"While you were sleeping, I inserted a tiny translator into the *kornia* section of your brain. There is no translation for *kornia*, but it is a region of the brain. I feared it would take a long time to work, but as we can hear each other clearly, it is working perfectly."

I touched the spot behind my ear, but I felt nothing.

"So right now," I began, "do you hear English or your own language?"

"When you speak, I hear Maji language, and when I speak, you hear human language. Your *selected* human language anyway. I cannot believe there are so many. There is only one Maji language."

I exhaled. "That is crazy. I don't hear anything other than perfect English when we speak."

Surkah smiled. "The translator makes it possible."

"I loosely understand that, but what I *don't* get is the Maji who … saved me from the watchman. They spoke English, a choppy version, but it was English, and I understood that. I didn't have this translator in my head then."

"It's hard to explain, but the Maji would have thought their words, and through their comms, the translator would relay the message to them in your language, and they would just verbally repeat it. It is the reason it sounded odd. The Maji were just repeating the words since your language is foreign to us. The males informed me that it is difficult to make the correct sounds when speaking your language because their tongue moved too much. They're trying, though; even now, most of them are talking in English, Spanish, and Italian to those without translators to try to … fit in. Many have practiced on our journey here, and others for even longer."

What is a comm, and how can the Maji silently communicate with it?

"I'm so confused."

"About the translator?"

"About everything."

"Ask more questions," Surkah encouraged. "I will answer them as best as I can."

"Okay ... what is a comm? Mikoh said you disconnected your comm from the system, and you just said the males who saved me used their comms to speak English to me."

Surkah tapped behind her left earlobe.

"Comm is short for communicator," Surkah explained. "At birth, a Maji has his or her comm inserted into the *vixer*. I am also aware the *vixer* has no translation in human language, but it is simply another name we have for a certain region of the brain. After insertion, a comm remains dormant until our tenth year and then activates. We Maji use a greater percentage of our brains compared to humans. Our comms grow with us like an extra organ. With it, we're all connected to a system that connects *all* Maji. Of course, the higher your rank in our society, the more access you have within the system. Mine is restricted on Ealra —my home world— and on board the *Ebony*—that's the name of this ship. I am only allowed access to the medical wing, its equipment, as well as the life pods in case of emergency evacuation. Mikoh and the shipmaster are the only Maji I can contact and who can contact me, but I was tired of listening to them give me orders and telling stupid jokes, so I disconnected myself from the system. I'll reconnect later, but for now, I'm enjoying a non-crowded mind."

What. The. Fuck.

"I've never heard of anything like that before in my entire life," I said, amazed.

Even our augmented humans couldn't mentally talk to one another, not that I knew of anyway.

"Is it strange?" Surkah asked, seemingly amused at my shocked reaction. "I have never given it much thought. It is part of the Maji way and always has been."

"This is a lot to take in."

"I am sorry; I thought humans were educated in other species."

"We were aware of other species, but we were never allowed to be thoroughly educated beyond what the Earth's government wanted us to know. Knowledge is power, and that is something our government doesn't want its citizens to have."

"That is a great shame."

You're telling me.

"Where *is* the Earth's government?" I asked, frowning. "Why am I not with a human doctor right now?"

Surkah licked her lips. "It is not my place to say."

That was another red flag in my mind, so I tried to steer away from the topic of Earth's government until I wasn't strapped down to a bed. Surkah had healed me, but I knew it wasn't out of the goodness of her heart. No one did something for no reason; there was always a reason for someone to help someone else, and there was also always a price to pay. Surkah was being kind and answering my questions, but I knew it was just to keep me calm. I was in this room for a reason, and I didn't want to stick around to find out what that reason was.

"So," I said, changing the topic. "Why did you say you didn't like to have males in your head twenty-nine hours a day? Why that number?"

Surkah raised a brow. "Well, a typical day on Ealra is twenty-nine hours long."

Woah.

"It's only twenty-four on Earth."

Surkah smiled. "I am aware."

Clearly, her kind was aware of Earth if they were here. That brought me to my next question.

"I'm confused as to why you are here, and why you think humans are the salvation to Maji, *and* about how humans and Maji are compatible. What does all that mean exactly?"

"Well—"

I jumped when the doors to the room opened once more, and instead of Mikoh standing there, it was a different Maji. A tall Maji with grey skin, violet eyes, and menacing gold-capped teeth. It was *him*, the Maji who saved me from the watchman. He had on the same uniform as Mikoh, but my alert state allowed me to notice what I hadn't noticed about him before. He had cropped black hair, and on the section above his ears, the hair was tightly braided to his scalp, keeping the hair from falling forward into his face. His eyebrows were dark, thick, and nicely positioned above his large eyes. His jawline was so sharp it could have cut something, and on his neck, a jagged white line peeked out from underneath his jumper top.

Oh, my Almighty.

"Greetings, Shipmaster," Surkah said as she closed her fist, placed her right arm on the left side of her chest and bowed her head. When she looked up, the shipmaster nodded, his lips turning upwards at the corners.

"Greetings, Surkah."

His voice was *super* deep.

"My *lissa* garnered positive results from my scan of the human, and they're better than we could have ever possibly imagined."

The shipmaster's eyes seemed to light up with curiosity. Those hypnotic eyes flicked to me for a moment then switched back to Surkah.

"Mikoh informed me ... It is a definite match?" he questioned.

A match of what?

"Yes. It is a hundred percent match," Surkah beamed, sounding giddy. "We have succeeded in finding our primary objecti—"

The shipmaster suddenly said something in a strange language that cut Surkah off. She frowned and glanced at him then me and back again before nodding once.

"What was *that* about?" I asked Surkah. "Why couldn't I understand him?"

"Because I momentarily disabled your translator so you could not understand me." *He* answered instead.

Oh, shit. That didn't sound good. He didn't want me to know what they were talking about, and I didn't need to be educated in their species to know that was bad news for me.

"Why?" I asked him, without looking at him.

"That is none of your business."

His clipped answer caused me to tense.

"I don't understand *any* of this," I said, feeling helpless. "Why am I here?"

"It will be explained later," Surkah assured me. "You need your rest. Your wounds are healed, but your body still needs to recover from the blood loss you sustained."

I nodded but said nothing further as I turned and stared at the Maji shipmaster who was staring right back at me. His stare was unnerving but captivating at the same time. He looked from me to Surkah and frowned.

"You seem tense, sister. Are you well?"

Surkah is the shipmaster's sister?

"I am troubled." She sighed. "She feared she would die by Maji hand or become a slave. I assured her we wish for peace with humans, but she remains unconvinced."

You're damn right I remain unconvinced!

"Surkah speaks the truth," the male rumbled. "Humans need not fear us. We are here to help."

So you say, you huge son of a bitch.

"Okay," I mumbled.

Surkah made a sound of displeasure.

"She does not trust us," she said. "Her fear stinks the room."

The shipmaster nodded. "I can scent it, but it is to be expected after her … ordeal last night."

I've been out the whole night?

"We were informed that no human citizens come close to your World Base of Operations," the shipmaster said, interrupting my thoughts. "But you came very close last night … why?"

I hesitated in replying, and this prompted the shipmaster to say, "Be truthful."

I pondered on that request for a moment. I wasn't sure what would happen to me if I told the truth. Would they hand me over to the watchmen? I looked at Surkah.

"If I tell the truth, will you keep your word that you won't allow any harm to come to me because I'm a human?"

"Yes," she replied instantly. "Human females are just as important as Maji females now. No male or female of my people would allow any harm to come to you. You are ... precious."

Why are humans so damn valuable to this species?

"Okay," I said slowly before looking back at the shipmaster. "I came here because a trader I met told me that the power was down at the WBO and that the watchmen had retreated to the wall. I wanted to see if that was true."

"A very risky move," the shipmaster commented.

"Every move I make is risky," I countered.

He raised a thick brow. "I've noticed."

"In case you *haven't* noticed, Earth is currently in a global civil war. There is no law, no order, no humanity, and now, the sun is affecting things. Earthquakes happen nearly every day; just last week, I had to hike hundreds of miles to avoid flooding so bad it would consume a five-story building in hours. Things are ... falling apart here. It's why your arrival has everyone even *more* on edge than usual."

"If what you say is the truth, then we have arrived just in time."

"What does *that* mean?" I asked, flustered.

Every time one of them spoke, it only resulted in more questions, and it was pissing me off.

"Rest," the shipmaster responded. "We will converse when you're stronger."

"I'm not sure humans *get* much stronger," a voice said from the door, earning a menacing growl from Surkah.

I turned my head and stared at Mikoh, who was leaning against the door panel with his massive arms folded over his broad chest. He winked at me, which earned another growl from Surkah. He looked at her, puckered his lips, and made kissing sounds, and when she advanced on him, the shipmaster moved into her path. He was grinning like a fool.

"Please do not maim my second in command, sister."

I mentally stored the information about Mikoh's rank. Surkah kept her focus on Mikoh; her lips curled up and her teeth bared at him.

"I won't cause permanent damage," she hissed. "I'll rip open his thigh and leave it to heal naturally. *That* will make him rethink bothering me in the future."

Mikoh laughed, and this caused the shipmaster to sigh.

"Mik, she *will* harm you," he informed his second in command.

"Only because I won't hit back," Mikoh teased. "We *all* know that Surkah just wants to get her hands on me and on a region close to my cock as well. A coincidence? I think not. You're not hiding your lust for me very well, my *intended*."

Surkah roared and knocked the shipmaster's arm aside to charge at Mikoh.

With wide eyes, I watched as he pushed away from the wall and took up a defensive stance with a sadistic grin on his face. He caught Surkah the second she jumped and crashed into him. They both moved incredibly fast, but Mikoh was faster, and within a couple of seconds, he had Surkah spun around and pressed against the wall with her arms pinned behind her back. Mikoh had her legs spread apart and had his knee between them to prevent her from kicking him. One hand held both of her wrists at the base of her spine, and his free arm was pressed on the base of her neck to likely stop her from using her head as a weapon.

"Do you feel better?" Mikoh growled low.

Surkah growled back, and she sounded meaner than he did.

"You won't be aware of when I harm you," she warned him, her voice gruff. "I swear I will *kill* you."

I glanced at the shipmaster and jumped when I found he was watching me. His gaze was intense yet curious at the same time. I couldn't break eye contact until he did. He turned from me and looked at his sister and his second in command and just stared at them with obvious interest. I could have sworn I saw him smirk a little, too.

I looked back at the pair and jumped when Surkah let out a vicious roar that was quickly silenced by Mikoh. He leaned in and *bit* her neck; I watched as his gold-capped fangs and other teeth sank *into* the flesh of her neck. Surkah let out a cry of what was obviously pain, but Mikoh didn't retreat; he simply held still with his teeth in her neck. I could hear him growling, and I felt horrible for Surkah because her cries had turned into whimpers. It reminded me of the sound a dog would make when they were hurt and needed help.

I didn't care for Surkah, and I *knew* she was lying to me, but she had saved my life when she healed my destroyed arm. And it was for that reason alone that I concluded my anger at seeing her hurt was out of genuine concern for her. It would probably prove me a fool in the long run for trying to help an alien, but I couldn't stand by and watch her be attacked. I just couldn't. Anger gave me the courage to struggle against my ties, but I could not break free. The material rubbed against my flesh, and it stung like hell. When I pulled too hard, it began to chafe my skin.

"Help her!" I ordered the shipmaster.

He looked at me and blinked as if he forgot I was there.

"No," he said nonchalantly.

"*No?*" I repeated incredulously. "She is your *sister,* and he is hurting her!"

"He is *disciplining* her for attacking him and threatening him with death."

"Disciplining her?" I repeated, dumbfounded. "He is abusing

her, you fucking *idiot*." I looked at Mikoh and shouted, "Let *go* of her, you big bastard!"

This made the shipmaster laugh, and I didn't know why.

I jumped when Surkah let out a cry again, but it was only because Mikoh had retracted his teeth from her. I raised my eyebrows when he licked at the bite wound that *he* caused. He didn't move an inch; he stayed put and continued to pin Surkah in place as he cleaned her wound like an animal.

"Hey!" I shouted again. "I'm going to get free of these ties, pick up the nearest object to me, and bash you over the head with it if you don't get away from her right now, you piece of shit!"

The shipmaster laughed again, and so did Mikoh, but he quickly refocused on Surkah and asked, "Okay?"

She nodded once, and a few seconds later, Mikoh released her. She spun away from him, keeping her head low as she returned to my side. She fussed over me while I glared at Mikoh who she was obviously, and rightly, now afraid of.

"You're an asshole!" I hollered.

Surkah clicked her tongue at me. "It is fine."

I jerked my head in her direction. "It is *not*! How *dare* he put his hands on you in that forceful way and then to *bite* you and make you cry? He *is* an asshole."

"It is our way. I challenged him, so he reacted," Surkah explained. "He was declaring his dominance, tiny one. He didn't hurt me; he'd never hurt me. I am female; I have no physical chance of harming him while he is at full health, and he knows that. He was letting me vent my anger, and when he'd had enough, he forced my submission."

"I'll declare *my* dominance and force *his* submission by putting my foot up his ass!"

This caused both males to burst into gleeful laughter, and I even caught Surkah hiding a smile. I didn't understand any of what was happening, but I was spitting mad.

"You're not fearful anymore," she said happily.

"No," I agreed. "I am angry because he hurt you."

Surkah shook her head. "He did not."

"He bit you, and I heard you cry. Don't lie to me. I know what I saw and heard."

"His bite has already begun to heal," she said and showed me the teeth marks that now looked like day-old red insect bites instead of fresh wounds, which freaked me out because there was no natural way they could have already healed that fast.

"And my cries were of annoyance because I cannot best him. It hurts for a few seconds, but that is just to get my attention. He was warning me that his patience had worn thin and I had better stop fighting, or I *could* get hurt."

I didn't understand how she dignified what he had done.

"Do humans not fight a lot when they need to let off steam?" she asked when she saw my expression.

"Not most," I replied. "We take a walk or something. If a human man harmed a human woman, he would be looked down upon and classed as weak. Well … that *used* to be the way."

Before everyone started killing each other.

"Females are precious to us," Mikoh angrily growled. "We would *never* harm our females, no matter what they do. A female could try to kill me, and my only objective would be to restrain her so she wouldn't harm herself. Surkah is my *intended*; I'd die before I bring her harm."

He said that word 'intended' like it meant something important.

"What's intended mean?"

"They're to be mated soon," the shipmaster replied to me, his voice encircling me like a warm blanket.

I looked at Surkah who was busying herself with a machine next to me.

"You're *marrying* this guy?"

She glanced at me. "What does *that* mean?"

"Is he going to be your husband, the person you spend your life with?"

"Oh," she said then nodded. "Yes, Mikoh has been my intended since my birth. When I am of age in four more moon cycles, we will be mated."

What. The. Hell?

"Wait just a second," I said as I tried and failed to sit upright. "*Who* decided he would be your intended if he has been that since your birth?"

"My father, of course," Surkah said with a smile. "Do human fathers not pick their daughter's intended?"

"No," I said, managing a snort. "We pick our own. Arranged marriages are a thing of the past. Now that I think of it, marriage is a thing of the past, too."

"Oh, well, our males can pick who they want and so can females, but many prefer their fathers or eldest brother to choose for them. The females do have a say just in case she does not like the match, but a rejection is rare. They trust their father or brother to pick them a good male."

I raised my brow. "Do *you* have a say?"

"Yes, but Mikoh has always been my intended. All the people know it, and if I now decided against the pairing, no other male would mate with me because of his position. That, and Mikoh would kill them if they touched me."

Mikoh's growl of agreement made the shipmaster chuckle.

"I don't understand," I said, terribly confused. "I thought you didn't like him. From how you both interact—"

"We don't like one another," Surkah cut in. "But he is still my intended, and that won't ever change. In four more moon cycles, I will belong to him."

"Like property?" I asked on a gasp.

"No, not slavery." Surkah giggled. "He cannot force me to do something I do not wish to, but he will be the lead Maji in our homestead. He will make the decisions and so forth. I will be his female, and he will be my male."

It was hard to digest that.

"That is *so* different to the human way."

"Really?" Surkah quizzed.

I thought I saw concern on her face, but I wasn't sure.

"Yeah," I said. "Our women are very independent, and if a man ordered us about, he'd be dropped so fast his head would spin."

"I do not understand your words," Surkah frowned. "You would harm him?"

"No." I chuckled. "But if my husband ordered me about and treated me like anything less than his equal, I'd leave him."

Surkah gasped, and I could have sworn that the Maji males did, too.

"You would *leave* your intended?" Surkah asked, and I could have sworn she had a hint of horror in her tone because it was plastered all over her face.

"Well, yeah. Long before the war, humans got divorced, separated, or just disappeared all the time. It's not a big deal; people change their minds."

"Not Maji," Surkah said firmly. "We mate for life."

Nothing is for life.

"What if Mikoh cheated on you with another woman?"

"I do not understand."

"What if he had sex with another female?" I clarified.

Surkah blinked. "That would be impossible. His loyalty would be to me, and my scent would be imprinted on him from our first mating as he would know going into the mating that I am his intended. He would open his senses to me and encourage the mating scent. He would never want another female because he physically would not be able to respond to her sexually; another's scent would irritate him, and he would become aggressive towards a female. He would not harm her, but he would force her submission until she learnt her lesson. We may not like one another right now, tiny one, but once we mate, we will never part, not until death."

"That is ... crazy."

"Is it?"

I nodded. "It sounds like your species has a chemical bond with your partners."

"What does that mean?"

"Well, when Mikoh ... mates with you, he'll become addicted to you ... your scent ... right?"

"Well, yes, and I to him."

Yep, so different from humans.

"So do you all wait until you mate before you have sex?"

This prompted another laugh from the males and an eye roll from Surkah.

"No," she said. "We can share our furs with another until a mating."

"Then how does the intended thing work?" I questioned. "Why hasn't Mikoh become addicted to another Maji female?"

Surkah shrugged. "None were his intended."

"Yeah, but what *if* he got addicted to another Maji female?"

"Then *she* would be his intended because he would not be able to part with her, but as that has not happened, I remain his intended. Sometimes a bond happens without knowledge, but most of the time, a male or female will feel the connection to their intended and *will* the bond to occur. Mikoh already feels a strong connection with me, so our bond will snap in place fast; it can happen before we share furs if it's strong enough. Besides, if Mikoh found another intended, my father and brothers would kill him for dishonouring me since *he* made the offer to be my intended when I was born."

I widened my eyes as I looked at Mikoh.

"How old are you?" I quizzed.

I knew he wasn't human, but he looked twenty-five years old, if even that.

"Two hundred and three," he answered.

My jaw fell open. "Get the fuck out of here."

"No." He frowned. "You cannot make me leave."

I laughed at him because he took what I said literally, but also because I was shocked and amazed by their lifespan.

The shipmaster nudged him. "Sera said their lifespans are greatly shorter, so she is probably surprised at your age." He switched his eyes to me and asked, "How old are you?"

I shrunk under his gaze and murmured, "Twenty-three."

"You're a *minor*?" Surkah asked, her surprised lacing around her words.

A minor?

"No, on Earth and especially during these hard times, anyone aged thirteen and up is considered an adult. I've never known anyone to live past sixty-five years. *Many* years ago, some humans could live to one hundred years of age but not anymore. If you make it to sixty now, then you're considered really old."

My father had made it to fifty-nine.

"Maji are minors until our fortieth year," Surkah informed me.

Holy Almighty.

"So you're nearly forty?" I asked, my shock obvious. "Forty *years*?

Surkah nodded.

"Forty Earth years?"

"No, Ealra years. Your orbital period is three hundred and sixty-five days for one year; ours is seven hundred and thirty-four days for one year."

One Ealra year was *two* Earth years. That meant Surkah was *eighty* Earth years old.

Holy crap.

"You look *incredible* for forty. Seriously, you look like you could be eighteen."

Surkah smiled widely. "Thank you, but forty is very young in

Maji culture."

I gestured towards Mikoh. "So you can't marry him until you're an adult?"

She bobbed her head. "Mikoh does not want to mate me until I am at *least* one hundred years of age. He thinks I am too young right now, but I cannot share sex with another male unless he is my intended. Mikoh does not wish me to be in pain, so he has agreed to mate with me as soon as I am of age."

"You're going to have to explain that," I said with a shake of my head. "Why do you want to get married straight away?"

"Because I fear the pain of my *uva*."

"Your *what*?"

Surkah gleefully laughed. "This has turned into a schooling lesson on the Maji way."

The males chuckled while I waited for an answer.

"When a female Maji reaches adulthood, her *uva* activates. It means her body is now able to carry offspring."

"Oh!" I said excitedly at finally understanding something. "You mean you'll hit puberty? That means your body creates new hormones that help the growing body and enables a woman to bear children."

"Then yes, my *uva* is to us what your puberty is to you. Does your puberty cause your body to hurt when you don't share sex?"

I frowned. "Uh, no."

"You're lucky!" Surkah stated, her brows furrowed. "We females feel pain if we do not have sex after our *uva* activates. It is why our females are so sexually active and why our males have a high sex drive to tend to our needs. Only pregnancy sates the *uva*."

"So you're telling me that when you and Mikoh get together, you will have sex … uh, share your furs, like horny animals every single day until he gets you pregnant? Pregnancy will be the only way to sate the *uva*?"

Bright purple bloomed on Surkah's cheeks, and she dropped her head which earned a deep chuckle from Mikoh, but he said nothing as not to embarrass her further.

"That is not the wording I would use, but yes."

"How many children would you bear if this is the case?"

I couldn't imagine being in pain and the only way to make it go away was to have sex and get pregnant.

"I'm am the sixteenth child in my family," Surkah said with a shrug. "But I know of a family with twenty offspring; originally twenty-three, but three of them died due to illness when they were infants."

Wow.

"I am my mother's last child. That is why Mikoh chose me. I am the only princess amongst our princes."

Wait a minute.

I stared at Surkah. "You're a princess? Like a real *royal* princess?"

She nodded.

I'm talking to a real-life freaking princess.

Surkah asked, "Are *you* a princess?"

I laughed. Hard.

"No, I am a commoner of my people … a peasant to some. Our royals lived behind big walls in a life of luxury. They have lived off the planet since the Great World War. No one knows which galaxy or planet they went to when they abandoned us."

Surkah wouldn't look me in the eye, but Mikoh and the shipmaster did. They almost glared at me, like I had said something I shouldn't have about my royal family.

"Sera has informed us of the activities on Earth."

"Who *is* Sera?"

They had mentioned the name several times.

"A human who has been with us many years. She has taught us about your people, but I must be honest, I don't listen to her often. Therefore, I am fascinated with your explanation of your people and your ways. It sounds different because you have really experienced it."

Oh.

I looked at the shipmaster. "So you're a prince?"

He nodded.

I looked at Mikoh. "Are you important like them?"

His lips twitched. "No, I am the shipmaster's *jra* when he travels."

"His what?" I quizzed.

"There is no translation," Mikoh replied, "but it's a titled word for something you might call a protector or guard."

"He is also his best friend," Surkah informed me. "They are always together … like a mated pair."

Both males hissed at Surkah, and it made her laugh.

"I will remember all your words when we're mated," Mikoh warned her.

She rolled her eyes. "Punishment for me means punishment for you, too."

"I will endure it to teach you a lesson, *young one.*"

Surkah chuckled again, not bothered by Mikoh's growl of annoyance.

"What does he mean?" I asked.

The longer this conversation went on, the more I found similarities between the Maji and humans, yet I didn't know how to feel about it.

"He does not like my attitude because I talk back to him a lot." Surkah grinned.

"You talk back to *everyone* a lot." The shipmaster snorted. "Mother and Father have spoiled you."

"They like me best," Surkah teased with a big cheesy smile.

Her brother laughed but didn't disagree with her.

"Are you close to all your brothers?" I asked her, noticing the look of admiration her brother gave her.

"Of course." Mikoh snorted and answered me instead of Surkah. "She is the princess, so they adore her. All the people adore her. She is precious to us."

My lips twitched. "That's really cute."

Surkah blushed again. "I wish they would not fuss over me or treat me differently. It is why I like being out in space so much. My brother allows me free rein on his ship whereas back home, I'm inside a lot for safety."

"For safety?"

"She is the *lone* princess to our royals," Mikoh said, and his tone indicated he thought I was stupid. "Our disloyal Maji would take her without hesitation. Males outnumber our females ten to one. Our females are *always* protected, especially Surkah."

"Because you're a royal?" I asked her.

"Because my firstborn son will lead our people when my father steps aside or passes on to be with Thanas."

I gaped at her. "What?"

"What?" she repeated and laughed at my expression.

"Well," I began, "the firstborn son sired by the king and queen in the human royal family is the next leader."

Surkah nodded. "I'm aware, but that is not the case for Maji. If no daughter is born, then the title of Revered Father goes to the firstborn son, but if a daughter is born, the title of Revered Father goes to *her* firstborn son then to *his* daughter's firstborn son and so on. We have a long lifespan, so waiting for me to reach age and conceive is no issue. My son will likely reach my brother's age or older before he takes the throne."

I flicked my eyes to the shipmaster's, noting he looked the same physical age as Mikoh.

"How old are you?" I asked, shyly.

"Two hundred," he answered.

In Earth years that meant he was *four hundred* years old.

Wow.

I looked at Surkah. "That is why you can only have sex with your intended? In case a random male got you pregnant?"

Surkah nodded.

I looked at Mikoh. "Is *that* why you asked for her to be your intended? So your son would eventually lead your people?"

He narrowed his eyes at me and growled, but he relaxed when the shipmaster cut him a look and muttered something to him that I couldn't hear.

"It is my *honour* to be Surkah's intended. To be considered, let alone be granted permission by her father and have the approval of *all* her brothers is the greatest compliment any male could receive. They're confident in my abilities as a warrior to protect her and as a male to care and provide for her and our offspring. There is no greater honour that could have been bestowed upon me."

Aww.

"Why'd you bicker with her then?" I questioned.

Mikoh grunted. "Because she has a big mouth and annoys me just to amuse herself. She has done so since her tenth year."

Surkah smiled, not denying the charges against her.

"Do you annoy all males?" I asked her, grinning too.

I hoped they thought all my questions and now my grinning meant I was relaxing around them. I needed them not to be wary of me; I'd never escape otherwise.

Surkah snorted. "No, Mikoh would kill them."

"Why?" I asked, shocked.

"Because she is *mine*," he growled. "If any male that wasn't her father or brothers spoke to her, I'd reach the edge in seconds."

"The edge of what?" I asked.

"Of sanity," Mikoh replied, curtly.

I looked at Surkah, my brows raised in question.

"The edge is a term we use when a Maji has gone past the point of rational thinking and is acting on instinct alone."

Riigghhhtttt.

I looked at Mikoh. "You *clearly* have anger problems."

The shipmaster laughed and so did Surkah; even Mikoh's lips twitched.

"So that's why you're posted outside this room," I said in understanding. "And why you keep popping in? You're guarding her?"

Mikoh nodded. "We just tell the Hailed Mother my assigned job of *jra* is to protect Kol *and* Surkah just to appease her. She loves all her sons, so their safety matters just as much, but Surkah is my only real charge. Kol does not need protection; it would be an insult to his Elite status to suggest otherwise."

I assumed the Hailed Mother was the title of the queen—Surkah's mother.

"Who is Kol?" I quizzed. "And what is an Elite status?"

"*I* am Kol," the shipmaster replied. "And being an Elite means you're a highly skilled warrior and part of the Guard that protects the people. It is the highest status a warrior can obtain. To be a member of the Guard is an honour."

Oh.

I couldn't look the Maji in the eye—his gaze was too much—but I allowed my mind to repeat his name over and over.

Kol.

I cleared my throat. "Well, I'm Nova. It's … nice to meet you all."

"That is a stupid name," Mikoh informed me.

Surkah grabbed a little black object from the top of a machine next to her and threw it at his head. He avoided it easily but couldn't dodge the elbow Kol rammed into his side. Mikoh growled and rubbed the spot.

"*Iamui!*" he bellowed at Kol.

I looked at Surkah. "What does that word mean?"

"It is an insult that does not translate well," she whispered. "It means waste canal."

An asshole.

I snorted and looked back at Mikoh, who shoved Kol and demanded, "What was *that* for?"

He sure didn't talk to Kol like he was his prince.

"What is our mission?" Kol rumbled, his glare terrifying.

Yeah, what is your mission?

Mikoh straightened up. "The mission is perfectly fine. She—"

"Doesn't like you because you're being insufferable."

"I apologise," Mikoh grunted to the shipmaster, not to me. "It is because of Surkah's presence; I'm growing ... impatient to have her."

I looked at Surkah and saw she rolled her eyes.

Kol clapped his friend on the back. "Four more moon cycles and she is yours, my friend."

"*That* is when my lifelong prison sentence begins," Surkah whispered to me.

The others heard her whisper, which told me how good their hearing was. I laughed when Kol had to restrain Mikoh, who looked like he wanted to paddle Surkah's ass. She grinned at him, and amusement flashed in her beautiful pink eyes over his annoyance. She clearly liked pissing him off, and he wanted nothing more than to rip into her because of it.

"You have a beautiful smile," Surkah said to me.

I blushed. "Thank you."

"I am glad you are no longer scared—"

"*Iamui!*" Kol suddenly bellowed, cutting his sister off. "That broke the skin!"

"It was payback for your elbow. I think you cracked a rib!"

I screeched when a ground shaking roar filled the room. I jerked my head in the direction of Kol and Mikoh and was horrified to find them both on the ground, beating the ever-loving shit out of one another. I'm talking hard punches, kicks, headbutts, and it even looked like there was some *biting* going on. I could have sworn I saw red liquid smeared on Kol's arm.

Did Maji bleed red?

My instant reaction was to flee and protect my life but being bound to the bed meant I couldn't move a muscle. My heart pounded against my chest as fear and worry consumed me. Before I realised what was happening, my eyes rolled backwards, and I began to lose consciousness.

"Nova!" Surkah gasped.

I felt a hand on my head. A delightful shiver ran the length of my body, and a relived sigh left the one touching me.

"She is fine," Surkah said, exhaling a deep breath. "She just ... fainted."

I heard Mikoh's humourless laughter.

"And you say humans are the salvation of us Maji?" he sarcastically asked. "Watching us grapple has caused her to lose consciousness. They're *not* meant for us."

I practically felt Surkah's growl.

"Sister," Kol rumbled. "Watch over her. She is going to need all the rest she can get if she is to stand with us ... and Mikoh, if you bite me again, I will break your nose in a place it will not heal correctly."

"Your sister has a better chance against me than you, friend."

"One more word, Mik. That is all I need."

"Look at the bright side, my *prince*, the human fainted out of fear this time and not because of your ugly face."

I heard more roaring, Surkah's sighing, and the sound of my own heart beat before I blacked out completely.

CHAPTER THREE

When I awoke, the room was not bright anymore. There was light, but it was dim, and it was quiet. Too quiet. I lifted my hand to my face and rubbed the crusted sleep out of my eyes. I lowered my hand back to my side and released a gratified sigh. My body felt so relaxed, and I knew it was because of the bed I was lying on. I smiled and lifted my hand back to my eyes and rubbed at them again. I paused mid rub, though, and opened my eyes to look at my hand.

It's free.

I quickly sat up and lifted both of my arms and bent my legs. The black straps that tied me to the bed earlier were gone, and they left no marks on my skin, even though I had struggled to get them off. I looked around the room and found it empty. No Surkah, no Mikoh, and no Kol—the mysterious shipmaster I couldn't bring myself to look in the eye for more than a couple of seconds. I turned to my right and let my legs dangle over the side of the bed. I gripped the bedding and carefully lowered myself to the floor.

I was extremely surprised to find the floor of the medical room was heated. I had heard that the rich and powerful had heated floors and walls to protect them from the soul-splitting cold on Earth during the harsh winter months, but I never expected them to feel so wonderful. A shiver ran up my spine, and a sigh of delight left my lips.

This feels good.

I shook my head and focused on my main objective. I needed a weapon, and I needed one *now*. My eyes scanned the room, and I could see nothing that I could use to defend myself. I shifted my stance and momentarily lost my balance. I accidentally bumped into my bed, causing a thudding noise. I jumped when a bright light suddenly filled the room. I squinted, looked up, and saw the door to the room was open, and … Mikoh was standing in the way.

"What are you doing?"

Lie, Nova.

I swallowed. "Stretching my legs."

Mikoh flicked his eyes to said legs, and I wished that the gown I was wearing was longer.

"You have stretched them, so get back into bed."

"Don't give me orders."

The words were out of my mouth before I could stop them.

Mikoh took a threatening step forward, and before I could think of anything else to say, I jumped onto my bed. Mikoh laughed at me and leaned his shoulder against the doorway panel. He watched me with obvious amusement while I watched him with fear. He was huge.

Seriously. Fucking. Huge.

He was taller than Surkah was, and she was a giant herself. He the same height as Kol, who towered over his sister with ease. I fully assessed Mikoh while he was silent. His eyes were blood red with licks of silver streaking through, his skin was a pale blue, and his hair was jet black. Mikoh's hair was cut short, tight on the side and a little long on top. Just like Kol's minus the braids. His uniform was black, and the armour plates were a shiny black, which told me they were a solid material of some kind. He didn't have a gun in a holster; instead, he had silver dagger blades strapped to his thick thighs.

He scared me to death, and he knew it.

"Are you tall for a human?" he randomly asked me.

I raised my eyebrows at the unexpected question.

"No, I'm not. I'm considered short by most."

Mikoh nodded in understanding.

"You're defective. I assumed something was wrong—"

"I'm not defective," I angrily cut him off. "Some human women are as tall as Surkah, and some are shorter than I am. It is the same with human males. We all come in different shapes and sizes. Don't discriminate."

Mikoh features hardened. "Your tongue is dangerously close to being cut off."

I stared at him, not knowing how to respond to his threat, but then he laughed and confused me even more.

"What is your problem?" I asked. "Why do you hate me?"

He furrowed his brows.

"I don't hate you ... I just don't trust you."

"You don't trust *me*?" I spluttered. "*I'm* the one who was kidnapped by your people, and now I'm being held here and ordered to stay in this bed by you. Who shouldn't trust who here?"

Mikoh lips twitched. "You're fierce for such a little being."

I narrowed my eyes. "If you call me little one more time, you'll be sorry."

This caused Mikoh to laugh. Loudly.

I heard a little commotion outside the room, and I watched as Mikoh leaned his head back and looked down the hallway to see what was making the noise. Whatever he saw caused him to sigh.

"It is too early for you to be growling at me, *darling one*."

Not what the sound came from but who, and I had a good idea who that person was.

"I have tended to my other charges alone, yet I find you *here*. It is barely sunrise, and you're bothering Nova *again*," Surkah's voice bellowed in a low tone. "I don't care that she is the only human who does not whimper in your presence. You can't bother her just because she impresses you. You're asking to be attacked by me, Mikoh."

Mikoh is impressed by me?

He laughed gruffly. "I'm *always* asking for you to attack me."

"You're being improper."

"I'd say my thoughts for you are surely *proper*, my intended."

"Step aside, you insufferable male."

Mikoh laughed merrily but did as requested. Surkah entered the room, wearing the same navy uniform she wore the last time I saw her. She smiled when she saw I was awake, and she crossed the room to the side of my bed.

"Your colour has returned to your face."

Memories flashed through my mind.

I felt my cheeks stain with heat. "Yeah, um, sorry about the whole fainting thing."

Normally, I prided myself on how tough I was, but even I could relent to my body shutting down in the situation I was in. Stress could do crazy things to a person, but to me, it rendered me unconscious.

"Do not apologise; it is my brother and Mikoh who should apologise to you for fighting in front of you when they *know* you are not accustomed to the Maji way ... and weak from blood loss."

I waved my hand. "It's okay."

It wasn't okay at all. It still totally freaked me out, but I wasn't about to tell the Maji that.

"It's not," Surkah said with a huff. "We want humans to feel safe with us, and their behaviour did the opposite of that."

I looked at Mikoh when he sighed from the doorway.

"Surkah's right. I apologise."

Surkah spun to face him. "What did you just say?"

"You heard me," Mikoh said with a roll of his eyes.

"I did." Surkah nodded. "But I want to hear you say it again."

"Aggravating female," he grumbled before he turned and left the room.

Surkah turned back to me as the door closed, and she had a big smile on her face.

"That felt good. He has never once admitted that I am right about something."

I snorted.

"How are you feeling physically?" she asked as her eyes scanned over me.

"Great," I replied. "I feel well rested for the first time in a long time."

"Are you hungry?"

As if on cue, my stomach rumbled in response, and Surkah chuckled.

"I wanted to have food brought to this room, but the shipmaster would like for you to be immersed into the population aboard the *Ebony*, so you aren't confined. And as you're not wounded any longer, you will no longer need to stay in the medical bay."

My heart jumped, but I made sure to keep my expression worried instead of eager. I didn't need Surkah suspecting that I was planning to escape the second I got a weapon and the chance presented itself. Getting out of the medical room would surely open me up to many chances.

"Um," I said unsurely. "I don't know."

Being in a room full of humans was *not* something I ever wanted to be a part of, but being in a room full of humans *and* Maji even more so. There was no way I could escape if eyes were all around me. Especially Maji eyes. They didn't seem to miss a thing, and I hated that.

Surkah placed her hand on my shoulder. "I will not let anyone harm you, Nova."

I didn't trust Surkah. I knew she and the other Maji were up to something, but I felt conflicted because she didn't seem to be malicious. My gut told me she was the genuine female she appeared to be, but I couldn't overlook that she and the other Maji were keeping something from me.

"Okay," I said softly.

"Oh, and I want you to know that I disagree with what Mikoh said yesterday. Your name is beautiful."

My lips twitched. "You're very sweet, thank you."

"He can be very … difficult to deal with."

"I'm sure you're putting that mildly," I deadpanned.

"Maji is a male dominant race, so it's ingrained in them to be stubborn, I guess."

"I kind of feel bad for you since you have to marry him."

"Do not feel bad. Mikoh is a dominant male, but a male's mate is *really* the Maji who is in charge. When Mikoh and I mate, he will do everything in his power to see that I am happy, and he will grovel when I am not. If he makes a decision I am not happy with, he would only do it once it's for our family's best interest."

That drew a surprised laugh out of me. "That sounds like human men, the grovelling part anyway."

Surkah smirked. "Males will use mating as a way to make us forgive them. We love touching one another and need sex often, so when a female is upset with her mate, he will go to great lengths to be close to her and be sweet and gentle. Females have so much power over her mate; she is his heart, so he will do just about anything for her."

My heart fluttered.

"That's romantic," I said. "In a weird, sexy kind of way."

Surkah giggled. "I was once told a story by my eldest brother, Ryla, that I think you would enjoy. Nearly forty-two years ago, my father *greatly* upset my mother because he missed a planned meal with her. It was the four-hundredth year since their mating, and he missed it. Ryla told me she cried a lot, and it distraught him and my other brothers who wanted to beat my father for bringing her pain.

When he got home, and he realised the day, he went almost as white as your skin. He tried to make it right, but Mother refused to talk to him for three whole weeks. She withheld sex from him—even though she needed sex for release so she wouldn't feel discomfort, she somehow stayed strong. My father took it as a respected male and waited for her permission to touch her, but still, she refused. The final straw for my father was when my mother smiled at other males during the monthly banquet meal between the royals and the Guard. He dropped to his knees before her in the great hall, in front of *everyone*, and begged her forgiveness because her smiles were only meant for him, and he hated that another could receive them. He poured out his heart to her and told her there was no other female he would rather spend all his days with. They conceived me that very night."

I smiled widely. "I like that story."

"Me too; it reminds me that when I want to throttle Mikoh, he will treat me like that too. Soon enough, I will become his whole life, and he will become mine."

I eyed Surkah. "I know he is your intended and has been forever, but do you *want* him to be?"

She didn't reply to me with words, but instead, she blushed, and that was a clear answer to me.

"You *do!*" I gasped. "You like him."

Her blush darkened.

"Do not tell him," she pleaded in a hushed whisper. "He would never let me forget it."

"I won't say a word." I beamed.

"Do you think he is attractive?" she asked then quickly added, "I will not be angry with your answer."

The thought of the Maji being attractive never crossed my mind, but I didn't think of Mikoh when I thought of what I found attractive in a Maji. I was thinking of Kol with his tall, muscular body, his strong jaw, high cheekbones, plump lips, and his large, hypnotising violet eyes. Yeah, the Maji was an attractive species, and Kol was hotter in ways I never knew were possible.

"I think he is very attractive," I said to Surkah, switching my thoughts to Mikoh, "but his attitude needs a *lot* of work."

Surkah laughed merrily. "I tell him that often. He is too serious."

"And sarcastic."

Surkah nodded, smiling wide.

"I really like this," she told me. "I have been waiting for my brothers to mate so I could have a sister-in-mate to talk to. It can get very tiresome in a family full of males."

"I haven't had anyone to really talk to since my father died, but before my family passed away, I was surrounded by men, so I understand how you feel."

Conversation with my father had only been short and sweet after Zee died, but for the two extra days I had with him before the sickness claimed him, I talked to him all the time even though I knew he probably couldn't hear me. Him just being there was enough.

Surkah reached over and pressed her hand on top of mine, startling me from my thoughts.

"I hurt for you, Nova." She frowned. "I feel pain just thinking about my father passing. I cannot fathom my life after him, so I truly hurt for you."

Don't cry.

I cleared my throat. "Thanks, Surkah, but I'm okay. I'll see him again someday."

"How?" she quizzed.

"In Heaven," I said.

"I've never heard of a planet called Heaven. Is it recently discovered?"

"It's not a planet, but my father is there."

"Is he not dead?"

"He is."

"Then how will you see him again on a planet that does not exist? I am very confused."

I laughed.

"Heaven is a belief," I informed Surkah. "I believe my father is with the Almighty in Heaven. It is a very old belief on Earth and—"

"Oh!" Surkah cut me off excitedly. "Your Almighty is to you what my Thanas is to me. He is the keeper and protector of Maji. When our bodies die, our spirit goes to be with Thanas to assist him in protecting the people."

I smiled widely. "Yes, that is exactly it."

"Then I agree that you will see your father again someday." She patted my leg. "Come. I will show you to the cleansing unit and how to work it. I'm sure you wish to get clean before we go and eat breakfast."

I tried not to appear too eager at the possibility of getting clean.

I winced. "I bet I smell bad."

Surkah shook her head. "You smell better than when I first met you. I had to *really* scrub you down with rags."

The female widened her eyes the second the words left her mouth, and purple stained her sculpted cheeks. I laughed loudly at her slip of the tongue.

"Don't be embarrassed," I told her. "I know I smell bad, and trust me, I've smelled this way for a *long* time. It is hard to come across a working cleansing unit back on Earth. The ones that do work require payment to use them, and I have no credits to my name nor did I want to sell my body to be clean because then I wouldn't feel clean no matter how hard I scrubbed my skin."

Surkah stared at me with wide eyes.

"You've ... You've had a hard life, Nova."

I didn't think my life was hard, just certain aspects of it.

"I've had it hard on most days, but I'm still alive and kicking. That's got to count for something, right?"

"Right."

Surkah got me to my feet from the bed and walked across the room with me to the far side of the room. I had no idea what she was doing until we came a few steps away from the dead end when, out of nowhere, the wall automatically opened. I jumped, and Surkah laughed at me. I entered the room with her and found it looked *nothing* like a cleansing unit on Earth. First of all, there was no knobs, buttons, or even a showerhead. It was just an empty corner.

I looked at Surkah. "Where is the cleansing unit?"

She laughed once more and stepped into the space where the unit would usually be. As soon as she stood still, the ceiling opened above her and a huge chrome showerhead lowered. I looked at Surkah when she said, "Put your hand on any part of the wall, and it will automatically start the unit. The temperature of your body will be scanned as soon as your hand touches the wall, and the unit will adjust the water temperature to your perfect setting. For hair and body wash, you say, 'Cleanse,' and a small amount of it falls with the water but provides a huge amount of product when cleaning. When you're finished, press your hand against the wall again, and it will turn the unit off."

"That's ... amazing."

Surkah didn't look like she thought it was amazing, but she humoured me by smiling widely.

"The wash gel has restorative properties in it," she mentioned. "It will aid your broken skin in healing. We made that adjustment when we brought you humans aboard; many of you have really bad skin conditions, and tiny pests that live in your hair, but one use of this medicated wash gel will aid your skin greatly, and it will kill the pests."

"That's even *more* amazing!"

When Surkah left the room, I stripped down and stepped into the unit. I followed her instructions and pressed my hand against the wall. I jumped when water began to fall onto my head. It reminded me of the time I stood under a waterfall; only the water was perfectly heated. I groaned as my ideal setting of heated water matted my hair to my head. I spoke the verbal command for some hair and body wash, and I smelled it the second it fell. It reminded me of a mixture of fruits that used to grow on Earth.

Surkah mentioned she had cleaned me when I arrived aboard the craft, but she barely got off a couple of layers of grime because the dirt was still caked into the creases of my skin, and I still stank to the high heavens. My hair was tangled in clumps, and where my fingernails and toenails weren't chipped or broken, dirt was packed under them. Sections of skin were dry and flaky while other areas had open sores from the dirt. I was so grateful for the healing properties of the wash gel because my skin was an awful mess.

On a personal mission to be clean for the first time in a long time, I lathered my skin and hair with the suds and used a rough version of a sponge that was on the floor to scrub my body clean. It took a long time, and that was mainly because I was using my fingers to detangle my hair. When I was grime free, and my skin was raw from scrubbing, I turned the unit off then stepped out and yelped when hot air began to blow down on me from above. I was surprised by the automatic dryer, but I stood still until my hair and body were free of water droplets. It took less than a minute to fully dry me, and it didn't even burn my skin!

When the dryer stopped, a small section of the wall opened to reveal a mirror and a cabinet. I stared at my reflection for a few minutes, shocked at how different I looked. I looked younger, fresher ... healthier. Focusing on the cabinet, I opened it and found a bunch of items. I opened a few bottles, but I had no idea what the products inside did, so I steered clear of them. I did gasp with delight when I spotted a small pair of scissors. It was the first weapon I had come across, and I was thankful for it.

Finally, I won't be helpless if I need to defend myself.

Next to the scissors was a large hairbrush. Looking almost brand new with all its bristles, it helped greatly in my effort to detangle my long brown hair. It took a further ten minutes, and a lot of my hair had to be cut from my head with the small scissors when certain clumps couldn't be detangled. My scalp burned like a bitch from the scrubbing and detangling, but I was so pleased when the brush eventually slid through my hair from root to tip with ease.

It was the first time in a very long time I was able to achieve that.

The surprises didn't stop there either. I spotted funny looking nail clippers, and I took my time to clip all my finger and toenails. I picked up a small jar that had little sticks with soft blue padding on the end of them; the padding smelled nice, but I didn't know what they were supposed to be used for. I tried to use a small cloth to clean out the water in my ears, but when I couldn't get inside, I used the little sticks, and they worked like a charm. I was positively giddy with excitement when I spotted a brand-new toothbrush. Like everything else, it was bigger and weirdly shaped, but it was perfect. I didn't need any paste on it to clean my teeth because when it was wet, the tops of the bristles glistened with a mint-scented gel. It was a strong possibility that I spent longer brushing my teeth, gums, and tongue than I did showering.

When I wrapped myself in a gigantic towel that was softer than any fabric I had ever felt before in my life and gripped my scissors, I re-entered the room I had slept in and blinked when I saw a small bundle of clothes placed on my bed.

I changed into the clothes provided for me, though I wondered where the Maji got them in my size when they had just arrived on Earth two days ago. It amused me that I was wearing a similar uniform to the male Maji—only mine was dark grey, and I had no armour plating like theirs did. It was soft and easy to move around in. It had pockets in the pants too, so I safely tucked my scissors inside a pocket and patted it. There was no underwear and no shoes or socks, so with a shrug, I walked over to the doorway. When it opened, I hesitantly stepped into the white hallway and straight away noticed the silver and black pipes that ran along the ceiling. I knew they had an important purpose, but I couldn't help but marvel at how pretty they looked against the white background that surrounded them.

Sudden growling gained my attention. I turned my head and blinked at Mikoh and Surkah who were facing off just outside the med bay room. She looked like she would rip his throat out if she was given the chance.

"Uh ... hi."

Surkah looked at me and beamed, but Mikoh continued to stare her down.

"Thanas, you look excellent, Nova," she practically sang with joy. "So ... clean! You smell wonderful! And your hair is so beautiful. I have never seen such a pretty shade of brown before. Your clothes fit you perfectly, too."

I blushed something fierce as I looked down at myself then at Surkah and said, "Thanks. I've never had clothes without mending patches on the worn sections. I love them."

She beamed at me and then looked back at Mikoh. "Excuse us. We're going to break our fast *alone*—"

"I'm accompanying you both."

Surkah stomped her foot on the ground after Mikoh cut her off, and it caused my lips to twitch. She might be almost forty years old, but her action just made her appear like the teenager she looked.

"I want to go on my *own* with Nova. I *never* get to spend time alone with another female."

"I won't speak or engage in anything you both do, but I'm accompanying you both. Your safety is my number one priority."

"*Please.*"

"This is not up for discussion, female."

"Mikoh."

"Surkah."

"My *intended*," she growled softly and stepped closer to him, putting her back to me. "I will be *very* thankful if you grant me this."

Mikoh sucked in a deep breath, and I momentarily wondered where Surkah's right hand went to until I heard Mikoh's struggle for breath. I grinned and looked down as I scuffed my toes against the heated floor, trying to give them as much privacy as I could without walking away.

"My female," he hissed. "The answer is still ..."

I muffled a giggle with my hand when his answer was a groan instead of a word.

"What is your answer, *my* male?" Surkah purred.

She purred like a cat.

"Thanas damn me, but it's ... no."

Surkah stopped whatever she was doing to Mikoh, and I heard his strangled whine of protest as she dropped her hand and shoved past him. She was pissed at his decision, but to be honest, no one looked more annoyed than Mikoh at the current moment. It meant his hanky-panky was indefinitely cut short.

I pretended not to see Mikoh adjust the front of his pants for two reasons. One, because it was private and he didn't need me gawking at him. And two, because the outline of his penis was shockingly large. He didn't trust me as it was, so I didn't want him to think I was a pervert too.

"Shall I lead the way?" he asked Surkah through gritted teeth as he mockingly bowed.

When I moved to her side, she grabbed my hand and tugged me along with her. I had to jog to keep up with her long strides. I heard Mikoh's low chuckles as he followed closely behind, but he said nothing further. We walked down long hallways, passing by a few males who were dressed in the same uniform as Mikoh and had serious expressions on their faces. I jumped when two of them lifted their right arms over their chest, roughly pressed their fists against their bodies, and bowed their heads. I looked at Surkah as she walked by them without so much as a glance their way.

Weird.

I moved closer to Surkah when we entered a large mess hall lined with tables and chairs. Maji occupied the left side of the room, and human women were on the right side. There were faces everywhere, human and Maji, but only the Maji stood, put their fists over their chests, and bowed their heads. Again, I looked at Surkah. She had told me she was a princess, but at that moment, I fully grasped that she really *was* a freaking princess.

I found it cool, but that emotion was wiped away when I took in the Maji. There were so many of them, and they were all so big, muscular, and damn tall. If they decided to kill every human in sight, not one us would stand a chance.

Surkah suddenly turned to face me when she inhaled.

"What do you fear?" she demanded.

I hated her heightened sense of smell.

"It's just crowded in here, but I'm fine. I promise."

Big. Fat. Lie.

I had to remember that my fear gave off a scent she could easily detect. I also had to suck it up. I couldn't afford to become an annoying burden to the Maji; I didn't want any extra attention from them. I sat with Surkah and Mikoh and was surprised when a male brought us three trays of food. I noticed he pointedly ignored Surkah and gave her tray to Mikoh. As a matter of fact, every male in the room made it their business to look away from our table. A few of them even moved tables to get further away from us.

"You weren't joking about no other male looking at you," I mumbled to Surkah.

She chuckled. "They might be curious if Mikoh wasn't here, but they fear him."

"I can't imagine why," I said dryly.

Surkah snorted, Mikoh grumbled to himself, and I grinned.

Surkah dug into her breakfast, but Mikoh didn't. He looked at me like he was waiting for me to start eating before he would even consider beginning. I was hesitant because I had no idea what I was about to consume, and I didn't know if I *wanted* to know. There was a thick-cut, dark brown piece of meat of some kind with a white sauce over it and what looked like mashed potatoes but was a little creamier and was blood red. My instincts told me not to eat it, that it could be laced with drugs, but the rational side of my brain told me the Maji didn't need to go to great lengths to knock me out if they wanted to. Another quick glance around the mess hall told me the food was fine because other humans were happily eating it.

With an emphasis on the *happy*.

"It's good," Surkah said when she saw I wasn't eating. "The other humans have said, and I quote, the 'nicest food ever.'"

My lips quirked as I picked up my funny looking knife and fork. I cut up some of the strips of meat into small bites and gathered some of the red mash and white sauce onto my fork and tucked it into my mouth. Flavour instantly burst over my taste buds, and I couldn't help but groan. It was *so* good.

"The nicest food ever?" Surkah asked, a teasing grin playing on her lips.

I bobbed my head, making her and Mikoh chuckle. She and the human women were right; it *was* the nicest food ever. Granted, I only ate what could be grown in bad soil or whatever small, malnourished game I could catch and kill on Earth, but even on my hungriest of days, food never tasted as spectacular as this.

I cleared my plate in minutes, and I looked at Mikoh when I felt his eyes on me. He had nearly finished his own food at this point, but his focus was back on me and not his food. I didn't get a chance to say anything to him because he suddenly stood and walked over to the food buffet. The males who were queuing up for food moved aside when he approached. He gathered more food on a tray and brought it back over to me. He silently put it in front of me and removed the now empty one.

"Eat," he said gruffly after I thanked him.

I continued eating because I was still very hungry. I managed to clear three-quarters of the food piled tray, but that was the best I could do without becoming violently sick and throwing up everything I just ate.

"Thank you," I said to Mikoh once more.

He nodded, still eating, but he was clearly tense.

"He does not like that you were so hungry," Surkah said to me, seeing my confusion at his attitude.

"Oh," I said. "It's okay. Being hungry is pretty much a permanent thing on Earth for common folk like me."

Mikoh growled but said nothing.

"Females are fed first on Ealra," Surkah explained. "If there was only enough food for one, it would go to the female. If the food was in short supply, males would refuse to eat anything until our hunger was sated first."

My chest warmed, realising Mikoh did just that. He waited for me to begin eating before he even considered touching his own food, and I knew even though he wasn't my biggest fan, if we were stranded and there was only enough food for two people, he would make sure it went to me and Surkah. I didn't like that I was seeing him in that light. I wanted to keep Mikoh and the rest of the Maji under one category: dangerous.

"That's really sweet," I said and looked at Mikoh. "You get angry easily, and you have a *serious* attitude problem, but I think you're very sweet."

He glared at me, and it made me smile.

"I'm still hungry," Surkah suddenly announced. "I think I'll get seconds, too."

She got up and headed towards the buffet, and of course, Mikoh was right by her side. I chuckled, shook my head, and turned back to the table, startling when I found I wasn't alone.

"Hello, little one."

Kol was sitting across from me with a tray of food in front of him, and his eyes locked on mine.

Where the hell did he come from?

I gasped. "Majesty Kol ... I mean Shipmaster Kol ... I mean ... Shipmaster."

Kol's violet eyes shone with amusement.

"You may call me Majesty Shipmaster Kol if you wish. That will be interesting to hear."

I knew he was teasing me, and my cheeks heated because of it.

"I'll stick to shipmaster, thank you very much."

His lips twitched. "You have used a cleansing unit."

I blushed. "You can smell the difference, huh?"

"And see it," he replied, his eyes rolling over me *slowly*. "Your skin is so clear, and your loose hair is framing your face. I like it. I have never seen that shade of brown before."

I swallowed and said nothing further.

"Has my sister informed you of the changes today?"

"Uh-huh," I mumbled. "She said she'd show me to my new room later."

"I don't think she will be able to do that any longer."

My head jerked up. "Why not?"

"Because more humans have come aboard today, as you can see, and a lot of them are greatly injured or have a severe illness. The three other healers aboard are now at max capacity of how many humans they can take in their charge. Surkah will need to heal many to aid them, and she will need plenty of rest before the day is over."

I didn't like it, but I nodded in understanding.

"I will have a strong male escort you," Kol continued.

I felt myself begin to sweat at the thought of being alone with a male whom I had never met before.

"What are you scared of?"

That stupid scent of fear was pissing me off.

"I'm fine."

"Do not lie to me, little one."

I rolled my eyes. "My name isn't little one; it's *Nova*."

"Okay," Kol said curtly. "What troubles you, *Nova*?"

When I hesitated to reply, Kol said, "Remember, no lying."

I blew out a breath of frustration, and absentmindedly placed my hand over the scissors in my pocket.

"I'm just nervous about this male you're assigning to escort me. I mean, has he met a human woman before? Does he even like my species?"

What if he doesn't and kills me the second he gets me alone?

"No, he has never met a human woman, but like the rest of the people, he is interested in learning about your species. Besides, even if he didn't like humans, it would not make a difference. He will be under orders to protect you, and even if he *wasn't* under orders, he'd still protect you as you're a female. Maji males would *never* harm a female of *any* species."

I didn't believe him. Everyone was capable of hurting someone else, humans and Maji alike.

"Can I not just wait around for Surkah?" I asked, looking down at my tray. "I feel safe with her."

I wasn't exactly lying. I did feel safe with Surkah—well, as safe as I could be in the company of a shady alien.

Kol sighed. "Surkah is on duty in the med bay for the rest of the day."

I frowned but didn't respond.

"Eat your food," he prompted after a few moments. "I'll escort you to your new quarters when you're finished ... unless you have a problem with *me*?"

I jerked my head upright and looked at him.

"No, I've no problem at all," I gushed. "Thank you *so* much."

Kol nodded then turned and resumed eating his food. I couldn't take another bite of my food, so I scanned the room instead, noticing how the males stared at the human females with obvious interest. A lot of the women were oblivious to the eyes focused on them, but a handful were aware of the attention. One woman with dark skin was coyly smiling at a grey-skinned male with blood-red hair that was styled like Kol's—short cut, tight on the sides, longish on top. I swallowed when he stood and crossed the short distance over to the woman who was focused on his every movement. When he reached her, he leaned down and said something into her ear to which she nodded happily, took his outstretched hand, and together they walked out of the room.

"It's not nice to stare."

I jumped when Kol's voice startled me.

"I wasn't ... I didn't ... um—"

"You lie a lot," Kol said, his voice surprisingly soft.

"I'm *not* lying, I just—"

"You were curious," he finished. "You watched a male approach a willing female and leave with her."

"Yeah, but he is ..."

"He is what?"

"A Maji and she is human," I said with a shake of my head. "You don't think that's a little ... gross?"

"What does grow-oss mean?" Kol quizzed.

"*Gross* is something that is disgusting."

I instinctively leaned back when Kol's features hardened, and a growl escaped him.

"There is *nothing* disgusting about a couple mating," he said, his eyes narrowing.

"Between a Maji couple, it's not, and between a human couple, it's not, but it *is* to do it with another species."

"Says who?"

I blinked. "Says me."

"And you speak for your entire species?"

"What? No, of course not, I'm just being—"

"Judgmental."

I pushed away from the table, my chair scraping loudly against the floor.

"Who the *hell* do you think you are?" I snapped at Kol, who placed his funny looking knife and fork down next to his tray. "You can't talk to me like that. I don't give a damn if you're a prince, a shipmaster, or the Almighty himself."

"Sit down, *Nova*," he said, his voice scarily deep. "You're making a scene."

"Sweetheart, you haven't seen *nothing* yet."

I spun away and stalked towards the exit of the mess hall very aware that all eyes were on me. I reached into my pocket, fisted my hand around my scissors, and sped up when I heard a lone chair scrape against the floor. My gut told me it was Kol and that he was coming after me. I got out into the hallway, and something inside me screamed at me to run, so I did.

"Nova!"

Oh, fuck.

CHAPTER FOUR

"**S**tay the *hell* away from me!" I shouted at Kol and picked up my pace to a sprint.

Two males who were walking down the hallway parted and allowed me to run between then. I could have sworn they were smirking, but I didn't pause to find out. I screamed when I was suddenly lifted into the air from behind.

"*Never* run from me," Kol growled into my hair. "My instinct is to chase after you."

Like a wolf.

I didn't think, I just reacted. I used my thumb to push the scissors into position in my hand, then I adjusted my grip, and slammed my hand down onto the arm wrapped around me. The point of the scissors broke the skin on Kol's arm, and when I released it, I noticed it was almost fully imbedded in his flesh. Kol released me with a roar, and as I landed on my feet, I instantly took off running once more. I heard another roar then the clink of metal hitting the ground. My freedom was short-lived because I quickly found myself picked up like a ragdoll once more. Only this time I had no weapon to defend myself.

"That *hurt*," Kol's menacing voice snarled into my ear.

I struggled against his hold. "I hope it did, you big grey bastard!"

He tightened his arms around me, and the action squeezed me enough to silently relay the warning for me to stop fighting, so I did.

"How do you move so fast?" I demanded.

I felt vibrations from Kol's chest rumble against my back, and I didn't know what it meant.

"My legs are longer than yours are, and I'm naturally superior to humans, so I do everything better."

His answer irked me.

"Can you fuck off better than a human?"

Kol hoisted me up against his chest.

"I can certainly *fuck* better than any human male. Would you like me to prove it?"

The gasp that erupted from me was real, but so was the spine-tingling shiver at his words.

"You're a pervert."

Kol laughed low in his throat.

When he showed no signs of releasing me, I lifted my hands to his arm. When I dug my nails into his flesh, I earned another vicious growl from him. I realised then that his mouth was dangerously close to my neck, and that he didn't need any more encouragement to rip my throat out.

"You attacked me," he said, his voice holding a hint of disbelief, and if my ears weren't betraying me, it also sounded like he was impressed.

I set my jaw. "I don't trust you!"

"Really?" He snorted. "I'd never guess that."

He was goading me.

"Put me down!" I demanded, hoping the fear I felt wasn't obvious from my tone or in my damn scent. "I'm going to be sick if you don't. I ate a lot of food."

Kol muttered something under his breath as he lowered me to the ground without protest. When I was sure I wasn't going to throw up, I turned to face him with lightning speed and pinned him in place with a well-earned glare.

"*Don't* put your hands on me again, asshole."

The corner of his lips quirked. "Is that an order, little one?"

"You're damn right it's an order, you son of a—Stop smiling at me like that. I'm being as serious as ... as a heart attack!"

"What's a heart attack?" he asked, an eyebrow raised.

I glared. "I hate you."

"I know." The infuriating idiot chuckled. "It is why I am so amused; this has never happened before."

"What?" I questioned. "No woman has ever attacked you and put you in your place?"

"No," he replied. "Never."

Because he is royalty.

"Yeah, well," I said, my nerves beginning to show. "You're not *my* prince, so I can say and do whatever I like to you."

I knew my behaviour was stupid, but I knew in my heart that I wasn't being irrational. I had a sick feeling in my gut about the Maji. Something about them didn't sit well with me. There was much more to what they were telling me, and it resulted in my frustration and violent outburst.

"I may not be your prince, little one, but as you're on my ship, I *am* your shipmaster, and you *will* do as I say."

His tone left no room for argument, but I argued anyway.

"And what if I don't?" I questioned. "What if I *refuse* to cooperate?"

"Then you will vacate this ship immediately and no longer be under Maji protection."

I didn't know what I was expecting Kol to say, but that certainly wasn't it.

"That sounds an awful lot like a threat, *Shipmaster*."

"It is a fact, not a threat."

"Fine," I said, lifting my chin. "I'll find Surkah, get my stuff that I was brought aboard with, and I'll leave."

"Your items were destroyed."

They were worthless anyway.

"Whatever. I'll just say goodbye to Surkah, and I'll be out of your hair."

"I don't understand that reference." Kol frowned.

I waved him off. "You don't need to."

If I had known that simply arguing with Kol would have gotten me kicked off the *Ebony*, I'd have done it a lot sooner!

I turned and walked away from Kol, grateful he didn't pick me up again. He did follow me, though, and the annoying ass gave me directions to the medical bay when I had no idea what turn to take in the enormous spacecraft. He laughed when my frustration began to show again, and it only caused me to want to pummel the idiot.

After what felt like an eternity, we came to the hallway I was familiar with. Mikoh was leaning against the wall adjacent to the medical room's entrance. I raised my brow, wondering how he got here, and then I wondered if he and Surkah were informed of the new humans needing medical attention by Kol with their mind comms when they went for second helpings. They must have left the mess hall when Kol sat with me. Now that I thought about it, I was sure he sat with me to appease Surkah because she knew I'd be scared to be left on my own.

"I smell blood," Mikoh said as we approached.

"She attacked me with a cutter," Kol said nonchalantly. "She hit the bone, too."

Mikoh burst into laughter, and it struck me as incredibly odd that he would find it funny that I stabbed Kol. What was weirder was that Kol had barely bled after I stabbed him. He wiped away the blood that was spilled, and nothing fresh had come from the wound since. I blinked when Kol manoeuvred around my body, briskly sliding by me and quickly entering the room that had housed me for the past two days

"I'm with him," I said to Mikoh, jerking my head towards the room where Kol disappeared into.

"He said for you to wait out here," Mikoh replied as he moved in front of me.

"He said no such thing," I argued. "I'd have heard him."

"Your ears don't pick up sounds as ours do. He said it so you wouldn't hear him."

"What an asshole."

Mikoh laughed. "You continue to surprise me, tiny one."

"Nova." I sighed. "My name is *Nova*; I wish you Maji would use it."

"You're pretty fierce for such a … tiny one." He laughed when I scrunched my face. "I am sorry, but you are tiny."

"To *you* maybe, but not to my people."

"How do you protect yourself?" he asked me curiously. "On Earth, how do you survive? Surely, you don't attack everyone with a cutter?"

I deadpanned. "You're just hilarious today."

Mikoh grinned. "Tell me how you survive."

"I run and hide."

He frowned. "You need to do that?"

You have no idea.

I humourlessly laughed. "The most threatening thing on Earth is *other* humans, Mikoh. Many of them have tried to kill me, maim me, or kidnap me to sell me into slavery or sex work—and that's just naming a few. I've been on my own since my father and cousin died when I was sixteen. Running is all I know, and I'm really good at it."

Mikoh looked furious.

"Are you okay?" I asked, wary of him.

"I wish to painfully kill the humans who have caused you pain and fear," he growled. "You're small and female. You're precious and should *always* be protected."

"Females don't have the same value on Earth, Mikoh. Our gender and size, for the most part, means we're an easy target. Our value is credits."

Mikoh gave his attention to the open door of the medical room and growled low and deep in his throat.

"You cannot allow it, Kol!" He suddenly snarled. "You heard what she just said. Her people will kill her or *worse*."

I knew exactly what the 'or worse' was as images of me working in a sex hole flooded my mind. I always swore that if I were ever caught by a gang, I'd take my own life before they could make a sex worker out of me. I was startled when Mikoh placed his large hands on my shoulders.

"Will you not stay with us?" he asked. "I will not … I will not tease you anymore."

I blinked. "Why do you care what happens to me? And don't say because I'm female."

He sighed. "My intended is fond of you."

"Uh-huh. What else?"

His lips twitched. "You're aggravating."

"So I've been told."

His laughter drew a small smile from me.

"If you were ever hurt, my intended would be hurt, and I must admit I would be furious, too."

"Aww, you care about me."

"Don't push it."

I laughed, and he smiled.

"Nova?" Kol's deep voice called.

Mikoh nodded for me to enter the room, so I did but halted my steps almost immediately when I found Kol and Surkah weren't alone.

"I'm sorry," I said when I saw a patient on the bed I'd slept on. "I didn't mean to—"

I cut myself off when I noticed the patient was a human female.

"It's fine," the light brown-haired woman assured me. "I'll just be one more minute. I have to get back to work anyway."

Work?

That couldn't be right. She couldn't work for them because Maji had only been on Earth a little over two days. They couldn't have established their own base of operations with human workers so quickly. It was ... impossible. I was about to ask the woman what work she was referring to when my eyes flicked down and landed on the wound on her leg that Surkah was examining. She wasn't touching her, which confused me because I knew that was how Surkah healed her patients. Instead, it was more like she was observing the wound as if waiting for something to happen.

I tilted my head to the side, and I too watched the wound on the woman's leg. My heart slammed into my chest, and my skin broke out in a sweat. The ripped open skin was knitting *itself* back together, and with each passing second, the wound became less and less. My breath got caught in my throat when the woman reached down with her left hand to adjust her pants. Her left *mechanical* hand that was previously hidden from my view.

Run.

Without a single word, I turned and fled the room.

"Nova!"

Kol shouted my name, and I guessed his footsteps pounded against the floor as he chased me down.

"No!" I cried out when I was suddenly lifted into the air.

"*Stop* running from me, little one."

"She's au-augmented," I stammered.

I struggled against Kol's hold, but he didn't release me.

"Let me go!" I shouted and clawed at his arm.

He growled, and it brought my movements to an abrupt halt.

"Be still," he said, his voice low.

"I can't," I argued. "Not around *it*!"

"I'm a woman just like you are, Nova," the filth's voice stated from behind us. "I won't harm you, I promise. My name is Sera."

Kol turned us around and placed me on the ground while keeping his arms around my body and his abdomen pressed against my back.

"Liar!" I bellowed. "You're a filthy aug! I've seen what your kind can do!"

"Kol, what in Thanas' name is going on?"

I looked around Kol and saw a male walking down the hallway towards us.

"An altercation of sorts, Nero," Kol replied with a sigh.

"Do you need assistance?" Nero asked, a snort laced around his words.

"No, but stand by," Kol said, and I heard the amusement in his voice. "She's human, but she's small, fast, and I wouldn't doubt her to attack."

Nero chuckled, and it annoyed me further.

I focused on Sera. "Get the *hell* away from me, abomination!"

"Nova." Surkah frowned as she stepped into the hallway. "Please, Sera is our friend."

I remember Surkah mentioned a human named Sera who taught them about humans and Earth.

"Friend?" I sputtered. "She is *augmented*!"

"Why is that such a problem to you?" Mikoh asked from behind Surkah.

He was standing close to her.

"Because," I spat angrily. "Augs are nothing but controlled murderers."

"What?" Surkah said with raised brows.

Sera sighed. "She means the war."

Surkah winced. "Oh."

"What war?" Kol questioned

"The Great World War that took place in 2104," Sera replied to him. "I've told some of you about it, but for those who haven't learned of it, listen closely. After the year 2080, any human that had augmentations fitted to replace limbs and organs were fitted with a collective chip that was fused into the brain. It was required for each augmentation to work with updates like it was supposed to. Each chip had a code, and unfortunately, an alpha code also controlled every collective chip. That code fell, or was sold, into the wrong hands. With the use of the alpha code, every collective chip was rewritten, and it turned people with augmentations into an unaware army. Hundreds of millions were slaughtered in mere weeks, reducing our already depleting population to almost extinction. Because of that, augmented people became the enemy." Sera gestured towards me with her hands. "As you can see, even eleven years after the Great World War, the dust between originals and augmented has still not settled."

I felt all eyes on me, but I refused to look away from Sera.

"I will *never* forget. I was twelve when the war started, and I helplessly watched an aug break my twelve-year-old cousin's neck when he tried to reach his dead father then two other augs gutted my other two cousins. I was *twelve*, a fucking baby, and I tried so damn hard to stop the bleeding, but I couldn't ... and they died in my arms." I said, a lump forming in my throat. "Augs will *never* be trusted. That collective chip is inside *all* your heads. It's only a matter of time before the alpha code is rewritten, and you will kill not only humans this time but Maji, too!"

Sera didn't reply to me; she only looked down and sighed. I turned in Kol's arms and looked up at him.

"How many augs are aboard this ship?" I demanded.

He held my gaze but didn't answer.

"How. Many?" I pressed.

"Surkah," Kol said, his eyes still on mine. "Answer her."

"Sixty-eight that I have examined so far."

My heart slammed hard into my chest. One aug could easily kill one hundred men, sixty-eight of them on board the *Ebony* would result in a massacre.

"I'm leaving," I stated.

"I don't think so," Kol said, his voice hard.

"Am I prisoner here?"

"No."

"Then I *demand* to leave."

"Nova." This came from Surkah behind me. "Your chances of survival—"

"I was doing just fine on *my* planet before you and your species showed up. I would rather take my chances in the wastelands than be anywhere *near* a filthy aug."

"Nova—"

"You cannot convince her, sir," Sera cut Mikoh off. "Originals ... they fear us, and *I* fear they always will."

Kol sighed. "Nothing I say will convince you, little one, will it?"

"On this?" I questioned him. "No."

He frowned down at me, displaying obvious distress. He gave me a light squeeze and used a hand to brush a stray hair from my face; the affectionate action surprised me, but what surprised me more was when he said, "Don't hate me, okay?"

An alarm went off in my head.

"What?" I blinked. "Why would I hate you?"

I felt a pinch on my neck, and then everything got fuzzy. My body felt heavy, my mind was a mess of colours, and then I was lost to darkness, but not before I heard one last conversation.

"She will awaken not only fearing augmented humans but Maji, too, when she learns we have lied to her," Kol said, his voice unusually deep. "Detain all humans and recall all rescue crafts for an emergency departure. The planet's core is cooling rapidly, and the surface is destabilising faster than we anticipated. I want to be on course to Ealra within twelve hours before the Earth becomes uninhabitable. I want a constant watch on her. And Surkah?"

"Yes, brother?"

"Alert me when she wakes," he rumbled. "I want to deal with her *personally*."

CHAPTER FIVE

Pain.

It flooded my senses and thumped away inside my head like sticks on a drum. I turned my head and pressed it farther into the cushioned pillow underneath me to escape it, but my actions proved futile. I was stuck with a headache that I prayed would disappear soon. I groaned and jerked my head to the side when I opened my eyes, and a bright beam of light attacked my pupils.

"What the hell?" I said, groggily.

I sat upright and placed my hands over my eyes until the spotting of light went away.

"Nova?"

"Yeah?" I rasped.

My throat felt like sandpaper.

"How are you feeling?"

I tried to swallow. "Like I've been kicked in the head."

Was I kicked in the head?

I groaned loudly and moved my hands to my pounding temples and rubbed in circular motions to ease the painful ache. I dropped my hands to my lap and exhaled a deep breath. Nothing but time would take away the pulsing pain.

"Nova, are you okay?"

The voice was familiar.

"Nova?"

I turned my head and smiled crookedly when I saw Surkah. "Hey."

"Hello," she said, a wariness to her tone. "Are you well?"

"No," I mumbled. "My head is killing me."

Surkah said, "Maybe the dose I gave her was too high?"

Huh?

"What are you talking ab—"

"I contacted Kol. He is on his way."

Mikoh cut me off. I squinted my eyes until his form became clear. He was standing behind Surkah with his arms folded across his broad chest. He was leaned back against the wall next to the doorway.

"How are you, tiny one?" he asked, tentatively.

"I don't know," I replied as I adjusted the gown I couldn't remember putting on. "My head hurts, and I can't remember falling asleep in here. Wait ... am I dreaming? Is this a dream?"

"Would that make me the male of your dreams then?" Mikoh asked, grinning.

"Stop it," Surkah growled. "You're not helping."

I smiled at him.

"I disagree," Mikoh replied and nodded his head at me.

Surkah saw I was smiling and rolled her eyes.

"It is the effects of the *konia*," she said with a wave of her hand. "She'd most likely spew her Earthly curse words at you if her mind wasn't ... What was the word Sera said? Cloudy?"

That was *exactly* what my head felt like. Cloudy.

"What is a *konia*?" I questioned.

"A medical agent we use to induce instant unconsciousness."

I stared at Surkah, trying to make sense of her words.

"And you used this *konia* on ... me?"

Surkah couldn't look me in the eye as she said, "My brother gave the order through his comm. We could not run the risk of you attempting to flee us because we feared you would be hurt in the process."

What. The. Hell?

"I don't understand any of this," I said as I placed my hands on either side my head. "Why would I flee? You're going to rebuild the Earth and fix everything. *Why* would I fight against that? Why would I fight my salvation?"

Surkah still couldn't look me in the eye. Hell, she couldn't even look in my direction. Dread swirled in my abdomen, and worry prickled my skin. I had a feeling something bad was about to happen.

"Are you my friend, Surkah?" I asked, my voice barely a whispered.

She jerked her head up and locked gazes with mine.

"Of course," she breathed. "You're my only true friend. I have bonded with you very quickly, Nova."

"Then *tell* me what I'm missing," I pleaded. "I can't remember anything after talking to your brother in the hallway."

That freaky Maji had picked me up off the ground like I weighed nothing when I ran from him.

"Everything will be okay," Surkah promised. "Nothing will happen to—"

Surkah was cut off when the door to the room opened, revealing Kol. I blinked as he entered the room. His stunning violet eyes were on mine, his thick dark brows were drawn together, and his lips were thinned to a line. He didn't look very happy, and after a few seconds, I knew why. My recollection of the events earlier suddenly hit me and caused me to draw in a deep, unsteady breath. My conversation with Kol, Mikoh, Surkah, and Sera flooded my mind and caused my already pounding headache to amplify.

They kidnapped me.

"Stay the *hell* away from me!" I bellowed as I scrambled off the bed and away from Surkah, who looked like she was about to cry.

She took a step forward, and I screamed, so she took five steps back. She did cry then, and Mikoh was there to comfort her. I had never seen them touch one another affectionately, but when he put an arm around her shoulder and hugged her body to his, she didn't fight him.

"Please," she blubbered. "Don't fear me. I am your *friend*."

Liar!

"No!" I shouted. "You pretended to be my friend so you could kidnap me! You're just like humans, Surkah. You lie, steal, and hurt people. You've hurt *me*!"

Surkah's whine was filled with pain and so were her whimpers that followed. Mikoh was glaring at me, no doubt furious that I had upset his intended, but I didn't care. I was hurting, too. I thought she was a good Maji, and that I could trust her with my safety, but she was like everyone else. She used me.

"Nova."

I narrowed my eyes to slits when Kol called my name, but I refused to look at him.

"Let me go."

He sighed. "We cannot."

"Why?" I demanded. "Why have you taken me?"

The many human women I saw in the mess hall filled my mind, and I knew in my heart that the Maji had taken them too. Was it under false pretences? Or were they aware of what had happened to them?

"It is complicated," Kol replied to me, his voice deep and husky.

His voice was so damn alluring. I felt like if I got my ear close enough to his mouth while he was speaking, my body would explode with bliss. I gritted my teeth, hating myself and my body for acting so foolish over an alien who *stole* me.

"*Un*complicate it then," I said through gritted teeth.

I looked at Surkah because she was still crying. Mikoh was still glaring at me, so I stuck my middle finger up at him, and he growled, "Sera told us what that action means."

I stuck my other middle finger up at him.

"Good."

"Enough," Kol snapped, causing me to flinch with fright and drop my hands. "Do *not* fear us. We're helping you."

I humourlessly laughed. "You're helping your-fucking-selves by taking me. I see no benefit in it for me."

"No benefit?" Kol repeated. "We're saving your life."

I made eye contact with him, and my anger was the only thing helping me keep that contact.

"How are you saving my life?"

"The sun is dying, and that means—"

"My planet is dying," I finished for Kol.

My heart pulsed with pain as the words left my lips.

"I *know* that," I continued. "We *all* know that. Do you think we humans are too dumb to realise that? We know the sun is becoming a red star, and that it will eventually vaporise the Earth, but what do you want us to do? Those who have credits live off the planet, and the rest of us are stuck here."

"That's where *we* come in," Kol said, stepping forward. "We aren't here to rebuild the Earth as Surkah told you. We're here to rescue as many human females as possible before your planet becomes uninhabitable. Being here right now is an incredible risk. No planet within a light year is allowing space travel in this district of the galaxy with the knowledge of the Earth's impending destruction."

I *knew* Surkah had lied to me! I fucking knew it!

"Why did you say females?" I demanded.

Kol blinked. "What?"

"Why did you say 'human females'?" I repeated. "Why not just use the term humans?"

"Because we're only allowing healthy human *females* aboard."

My gut tightened.

"Why?" I stressed. "I don't understand any—"

I cut myself off when my first meeting with Surkah replayed in my mind. She said her species was endangered like mine, and she also mentioned that human females were one hundred percent compatible with Maji ... Did that mean with the males?

Compatible.

"Almighty," I breathed when I knew why they wanted human women. "You want to *breed* with us."

"You're making it sound like we're—"

"Kidnapping us?" I angrily shouted. "Stealing us to ensure the survival of your own species?"

"And yours," Kol growled. "Have you forgotten humans are endangered?"

"No, but a human and Maji breeding won't create a human or a Maji; it'll create a new species."

"It will still be the continuation of both species, but our offspring would mostly likely be Maji as our genes are stronger than that of humans."

I felt sick.

"I can't believe this." I exhaled. "What if we don't *want* to breed with you?"

Kol didn't reply.

"Will you force us?" I asked, fear evident in my tone

"No," Kol replied, his hardened gaze telling me he took offence to my question. "We'd *never* force ourselves upon an unwilling female, and we don't have to."

"How do you know?" I demanded.

"So far, *you* are the only human female with a problem with humans and Maji breeding."

What?

"Explain that," I said as my body began to involuntarily shake.

"Your arrival on this craft was different than the other females of your kind. You were unconscious when you were rescued, but the other females were alert and healthy when they were informed of the terms for their rescue. They knew that their arrival aboard my craft was their acceptance of our terms."

"And *what* were the terms?" I asked, hearing pounding against my chest.

"Sanctuary on the *Ebony* and eventually on the Maji home world—Ealra—had only three requirements. A human female must be young, healthy, and willing to mate with a Maji male to ensure the survival of both species. In return, the females would be cared for, protected, loved, and cherished by their mate."

I stared at Kol, my mind trying to dissect his words and make sense of them.

"And they *all* agreed?"

"All aboard agreed. Those who did not were left on the surface."

I felt like I was sucker punched.

"You just *left* the women who didn't want to be part of your sick science experiment?"

"I do not understand your words," Kol growled, "but your anger is very clear. We have mission orders. We *only* take willing human females, and all those who opposed were left alone. If we brought them, *then* it would have been kidnapping."

"What a time to show you have morals!" I barked.

Kol growled at me, but I didn't back down. I advanced on him until I was an inch away and staring up at him with narrowed eyes.

"I'm *not* scared of you," I told him. "I *don't* agree to your terms, and I would like to be *left alone*."

"No, Nova!" Surkah yelled. "Do not ask us to leave you to your death. Please!"

"All my choices have been taken away from me, Surkah," I replied to her with my eyes still on her brother. "I was born on Earth, and I *will* die there."

"Your stubbornness will get you killed sooner than you think with this decision," Kol said to me. His voice was so low I knew only I could hear him.

"Why do you care if I live or die?" I asked, swallowing.

"That is a question I am asking myself right now too," Kol replied, his chest rising and falling fast.

"You have a craft full of women who are willing to breed with you; you don't need me for anything."

"Thanas damn me, but I *do* need you," he replied and took hold of my arms.

I didn't flinch because I was too concentrated on the glow that suddenly appeared around his irises, illuminating just how violet his eyes were. I blinked, worried I was seeing things, but I wasn't. Kol's eyes were glowing.

"What do you need me for?"

"Let me show you," he murmured, the indication to what he meant in his tone.

I shoved at his chest. "Don't touch me. I don't want you like … *that.*"

I don't want you at all.

"You don't?" Kol asked, suddenly grinning.

"No, I don't."

"You lie."

"I don't."

"I'll prove it."

Mikoh suddenly said, "Kol, you're not thinking clearly."

Kol's hold on me tightened as a menacing growl left his throat.

"Do you wish to challenge me for her?" Kol asked his friend, his voice gruff.

Surkah sucked in a huge breath while Mikoh cursed.

"You know I have no means for a challenge; your *sister* is my intended."

"Then back off," Kol growled, his voice changing to menacing.

Mikoh cursed again. "Friend, she does *not* want this."

I yelped when I was suddenly thrust backwards and pressed up against a wall with Kol's body covering mine.

"I can convince her," he murmured.

My eyes fluttered shut when I felt his head dip, and his luscious lips skimmed over the flesh on my neck. My skin broke out in goosebumps, and a shiver raced up and down my spine.

"Fight it, my friend. Do not let the need win."

The need?

Mikoh's words drew a growl from Kol, and the vibrations of said growl against my throat sent a jolt of heat straight to the centre of my thighs. I instantly squeezed my thighs together, but I knew it was too late when Kol inhaled and a different kind of growl left him. Surkah said everything had a scent, and I knew that the Maji in the room could smell my arousal.

My body was betraying me.

I placed my hands on Kol's large shoulders. "Kol, I said I'm *not* stayi—ohmyAlmighty."

He attached his lips to my neck at the same moment he spread my legs with his knee and pressed his thigh against my cunt. He moved his thigh ever so slightly, and the friction of his clothing and mine rubbing over my now swollen clit caused me to buck against him. He growled against my neck and placed his huge hands on my hips to hold me still. He flattened his body against mine, and I could feel his long, thick erection pressed snugly against my stomach. It sobered me and brought me back to reality.

How is this happening?

"Mikoh," I breathed. "Help me."

"Thanas curse it," Mikoh hissed. "Your body and its scent are telling a different story to your words, Nova."

"I know," I groaned when Kol's teeth nipped my neck. "I can't help my reaction to him, but he has to stop touching me or … or …"

"Or what?" Surkah asked.

"Or it'll end up in sex, and I *don't* want that."

Kol gently bit into my neck, and I winced in pain, but only for a moment because the sensation that replaced the pain was a greater pleasure than I had never felt in my entire life. I squeezed Kol's arms so tight my nails cut into his flesh. I felt myself clawing at him as if trying to get closer to him. I never wanted him to stop what he was doing, but in the back of my mind, I knew I would hate myself if I let this continue.

"Kol," I groaned. "You *must* stop this."

He didn't reply, but I felt him retract the tip of his teeth from my neck. His tongue flicked over the wounds he made, and each lick might as well have been on my clit because the orgasm I felt brewing was approaching fast and furious.

Kol moved his mouth to my ear and said, "Let go. I can *feel* how much your body wants to. Give yourself to me, *shiva*."

He moved his thigh against me, and the tiny movement threw me over the edge and into a pool of bliss. My breathing halted as wave after wave of delight slammed into me. I heard myself greedily suck air into my lungs when the pulsed slowed and I became oversensitive. Kol moved against me once more, and I choked on air, causing him to chuckle.

My eyes had closed during my orgasm, and they remained closed in the aftermath until Kol spoke.

"Leave us," he ordered.

I knew he was talking to Surkah and Mikoh.

"No," I said as I opened my eyes. "They're *not* leaving me alone with you."

I felt Kol's sly smile as he said, "Why not?"

Yeah, why not?

"B-because," I stammered.

"Because?" Kol repeated.

"Because I was making a *really* good argument as to why I'm getting off this spacecraft and away from you."

"You were making an argument," he agreed, "but I do not think it was a very good one."

"You're an asshole. Do you know that?"

He chuckled again. "I will allow your insults for now, but be warned, my little one, my patience *will* grow thin."

I leaned my head back against the wall.

"You forced me to do that," I said to him.

He knew I was talking about the orgasm I just had.

He growled. "I took what was owed to me."

"I *owed* you an orgasm?" I asked on a scoff.

"Yes," he replied, clearly annoyed. "I needed to relax you so you wouldn't try to harm me when I informed you that I was keeping you."

For a second or two, I did nothing, but as Kol's words sunk in, I felt an anger like never before.

He inhaled and said, "Should I make you come again? You're angrier than I would like."

"Come *on*, Kol," Mikoh hissed. "A Maji female would die trying to kick your ass over this, and a human female is clearly no different."

I placed my forehead against Kol's chest to hide when mortification stained my cheeks. Mikoh and Surkah were present when Kol brought me to orgasm. I would never be able to look either of them in the eye ever again.

"Get away from me right *now*, Kol."

"Make me," he challenged.

I gasped and thumped my fist on his hard chest. "You know good and well I can't physically make you do anything!"

I looked up at him when he laughed, and I noticed that his eyes were still glowing.

"My human," he murmured.

His?

"I don't understand what is happening here, but I know one

thing for certain, and that is I am *not* yours."

The glow in Kol's eyes shone brighter.

"Stop challenging me, Nova," he growled through gritted teeth. "You're making things *very* difficult for me right now."

"Yes," Surkah agreed. "*Please* stop challenging him. It is his instinct to counter it, and we do *not* want that happening."

"I'm not challenging *anybody*. I just want to be left alone!"

Kol suddenly roared, and I screeched with fright.

"Kol!" Mikoh shouted. "She is not Maji. She will *fear* you!"

Kol tensed, and his hold on me tightened for a moment before it relaxed. He dipped his head, placed his mouth on my ear, and said, "I will never hurt you, *shiva*. Do not be afraid."

Shiva?

"How can I not?" I asked. "You're scaring me. *All* this is scaring me."

"Surkah," Kol said, his voice gruff. "Move her to the corner of the room until I ... regain control."

"May I not bring her out of your space—"

"No!" Kol snapped, cutting her off.

I shoved at his chest. "Don't talk to her like that."

He growled and brought his face down to mine. I heard him sniff me, and I could do nothing but stand there and let him do it. Once or twice, he made a sound that was a cross between a growl and a purr. I didn't know if it was a good sound or not, so I remained deathly still when he made the noises. I licked my lower lip when he rubbed his nose against my cheek. He saw the action and snaked his own tongue across my skin. He hummed as if he were tasting something sweet, but I knew I was sweating so, if anything, he got a tongue full of salty twang.

"I could eat you," he whispered.

Like the horror stories!

"Oh, my Almighty." I whimpered. "You want to *eat* me?"

I think I heard Mikoh laugh then hiss as he muttered something to Surkah who was scolding him, but I wasn't sure because Kol's low laughter grabbed my attention.

"A different kind of eat, my human."

"What different kind of eat?" I demanded. "You're freaking me out."

Kol pulled back and stared down at me, his glowing eyes as radiant as ever.

"Are you a *vilo*?" he asked me.

"A what?"

"Have you ever shared sex with a male before? If you haven't, it means you're a *vilo* like Surkah."

A virgin. He was asking if I was a damn virgin. My words got clogged in my throat, so I had to clear it three times before I answered.

"What kind of question is that?" I angrily asked.

Kol smiled, his eyes glowing brightly. "You are."

I *was* a virgin, but I saw no reason for him to know that or even *want* to know that.

"We're not discussing this further."

He chuckled. "Okay."

He stepped away from me, and the glow in his eyes dimmed until it faded away completely. It was then that he glanced over his shoulder and nodded Surkah forward. Mikoh released her instantly, and she moved towards me. She kept her eyes on me as she approached, and she looked ... nervous.

"Nova—"

"I'm not your friend," I told her. "You lied to me."

"Under *my* orders," Kol cut in.

I looked at him. "I thought you were an asshole from the get-go so *that* doesn't surprise me, but I liked your sister. I knew she was keeping something from me, I just knew it, but it didn't stop me from liking her."

"I humbly beg your forgiveness, Nova."

Mikoh and Kol viciously growled the moment the words left Surkah's mouth.

"Why are you both growling?"

"A royal *never* begs," they replied in unison.

"Well, this one just did," Surkah said and stepped forward to me. "I am *very* sorry for hurting you. I didn't want to lie, but as Kol said, I was under orders."

I contemplated her words, but my head felt like it was a hotplate that was overheating.

"Let me think about it, okay?" I eventually said. "I'm trying to figure out how I feel about being kidnapped, being brought to a new planet, and used as a baby incubator."

"Thanas!" Mikoh suddenly hollered. "You're impossible. I thought Surkah was difficult, but you are ten times worse. I feel sorry for the male who winds up as your intended."

Kol growled and so did Surkah, but Mikoh paid them no attention.

I shrugged uncaringly. "I feel sorry for Surkah ending up with a dickhead like you, but you don't hear me hollering about it, do you?"

"What did you just call me?"

"A dickhead."

"Why is that an insult?"

"It means you're a stupid, irritating, ridiculous male with a dick on his head."

Mikoh narrowed his eyes at me but said nothing further. Steam might as well have poured from his ears to show his distaste for me at that moment.

"Don't give me crap if you can't take it being thrown back at you, asshat."

"I don't understand your Earth words, you imbecile human!"

"And I don't understand your way of thinking, you imbecile Maji!"

Mikoh growled at me, and even though it hurt my throat, I

growled back at him.

"I am going to find a male to spar with me," he said through gritted teeth before he turned and hightailed it out of the room.

"I hope you get knocked on your ass!" I shouted after him.

I angrily folded my arms across my chest and turned to Surkah. "Can you *believe* him?"

She was smiling at me, and a quick glance at Kol showed he was smiling at me too. It caught me off guard.

"You're a fierce female," Kol said as his chest puffed with what appeared to be pride.

"I agree with my brother; you would make a great party leader at our annual debates."

I raised my brows. "You have annual debates?"

"Of course," she said. "Maji citizens go to our Citizens Department and leave notes with formal complaints and requests for changes. For example, there are few Maji young, and we have no play sectors for them when they were not in their homes, at lessons, or during combat training. Mothers have complained about this and requested a play sector. We will discuss it at the monthly debate and then vote to decide on a decision in response."

"Who is 'we'?"

"The Council," Kol answered me.

"And who makes up the Council?"

"Twelve Maji. Four members of the Guard, four members of the royal family, and four citizens of Royal City who are voted by the people to represent them."

"I thought you said your father was the ruler? Why do you need a Council if he is in charge?"

"He *is* the ruler, and he is still in charge," Surkah replied. "He's been the Revered Father for over four hundred years now, and over the past hundred years, he has changed many of our laws. One of them is that the Council collectively makes decisions for the people. He deals with our warriors and all the hard stuff, but he lets the

Council deal with the lesser stuff."

He doles out the responsibility.

"He sounds like a good ruler," I commented.

"He is the best." Surkah smiled.

"Was he the one who gave the order to kidnap humans?" I questioned with a raised brow.

Kol stepped forward. "I believe the term you're looking for is *rescue*."

I didn't want to argue with him again, so I looked at Surkah and said, "I'm really tired, and my head hurts. I think you gave me too much of the *konia* stuff."

She pressed her hand against my forehead, and I felt a huge surge of relief, making my body sway.

"Surkah!" Kol scolded.

"She is fine, brother," Surkah said with a roll of her eyes. "I'm taking her pain away. She is not used to healing, so it just feels strange to her."

"A really *good* kind of strange." I sighed and smiled lazily when Surkah lowered her hand. "Your hands are magic."

She chuckled. "Yes, my *lissa* is a blessing from Thanas."

I nodded in agreement as she removed her hand from my head.

"Wait." I frowned. "What is this *lissa* thing you keep mentioning?"

Surkah looked at her brother. "How do I describe my *lissa*?"

Kol shrugged. "Look for the closest translation."

Surkah looked like she was racking her brain then she said, "It is a version of ... healing ability. You understand healing ability in your Earth words?"

Yes, I understand the words, but it left me with *more* questions.

"You have a healing ability?" I asked, wide-eyed. "I knew you somehow healed wounds with your hands, but you have a ... a *real* healing ability?"

Surkah nodded. "Well, yes, how do you think I heal the wounded and sick?"

I stared at her. "With medicine and machines?"

She raised her brows. "We only have machines to monitor, not heal. And our medicine is only a substitute until a healer reaches their charge. The kind of machines you mentioned, there is no point in having them when healers heal with our hands."

Well, shit.

"Enough talking," Kol said abruptly. "I'm being summoned to the bridge, so she needs to be escorted to human housing *now*."

Surkah nodded and then moved to the far side of the room where she placed her palm on the wall and took folded clothing from inside when it opened. She returned to my side and handed them to me. It was a t-shirt and pair of pants in a bright grey. Like before, there were no underwear, socks, or shoes.

I was about to take off my gown when I noticed Kol's eyes on me.

"Go away," I said, holding his gaze. "I don't want you here while I change."

"Nova." Surkah frowned.

I switched my questioning gaze her. "What?"

"You must learn respect for the shipmaster," she stressed. "You cannot be a bad influence on the other humans."

I hated that Kol was grinning at me like my being scolded by Surkah was amusing for him.

"Why're you looking at me like that?" I questioned him.

Surkah lifted her hands to her face and deeply sighed into them.

"Come with me, Nova."

I instantly stepped behind Surkah when Kol finished speaking.

"No," I said. "I want to stay with Surkah."

Don't ask me why because I shouldn't have felt safe with any of the kidnappers.

"And I said you're coming with me."

"But ... why?"

Kol stared at me, his violet eyes now filled with annoyance.

"You're healed, and as my sister fears, you would not do well being accompanied by another male, so I stepped up to bring you to our temporary human housing on board my ship. Do you not remember our conversation when we broke our fast?"

"Yes, but a *lot* has happened since then," I mumbled more to myself than to the Maji watching me.

Surkah was the closest thing I had to a friend among the Maji even though she lied to me, and now I was being taken away from her. Kol was placing me in 'human housing,' and I was worried sick about it. What if the other humans tried to hurt me when my back was turned or while I was sleeping? What if they feared me as I feared them, and they attacked out of instinct?

My thoughts plagued my mind as I changed back into my comfortable clothes, bid Surkah farewell, and followed Kol out of the medical bay.

"You're thinking so much that your skin is creasing."

I looked up at Kol as we walked and jumped a little when he gently tapped on the centre of my forehead. He chuckled to himself, seemingly amused.

"I'm just scared," I admitted.

He brought us to a stop, and all traces of amusement fled his sculpted face.

"Why?" he asked, and he sounded concerned.

I shrugged. "The other humans will try to kill me."

I knew they would; we were survivors and eliminating a threat meant survival. Everything was a threat to a human. Everything.

The shipmaster blinked. "Why would they try to kill you?"

"It's what my people have become," I said solemnly. "It is difficult to find someone civilised. Trust me, I've looked far and wide, and almost every person I've encountered has tried to harm me in some way or simply kill me. It is the way now."

I took a step away from Kol when he growled.

"Do not fear me," he said, "or your people."

I frowned. "It is hard when all I've known is to fear them."

Kol cursed, and then after a moment of tense silence, he said, "I will place you in private quarters until we have determined which humans are to be trusted and which are not. I am aware you're also fearful of Maji, and since I am the shipmaster, you will become my responsibility, and you will see that we're trying to help."

I raised my brows. "You don't have to—"

"It is decided," he cut me off.

I couldn't help but narrow my eyes at him.

"You can't just *make* decisions for me."

"Would you prefer I throw you to the mindless humans you fear instead?"

I flinched, and the tense look on Kol's face fell.

"Forgive me." He sighed. "I did not mean that. It is just … no one talks to me like you do."

"Because they know you," I countered. "I don't."

"We will have to change that."

I swallowed.

"Come," he said and began walking again. "You need your rest. The next few hours will be trying."

They will?

"Why will they be trying?"

Kol didn't speak until we got into an elevator that brought us to the highest level of the spacecraft. After walking down a few hallways, Kol stopped next to a black door that opened when he pressed his palm on the door. The area around his hand lit up green then the door opened.

"In mere hours, we will take off from Earth's surface, and I will activate the craft's warp so it will bring us closer to my home world—Ealra. I am aware you humans have never experienced warp, so get all the rest you can now as later it will be a little … unsettling for a few hours."

I was *not* looking forward to that. I was not looking forward to leaving Earth, no matter how terrible it was.

My worries faded when we stepped into a large, dimly lit room complete with a single bed and an entertainment unit of some kind that was fixated to the wall facing the bed. A fluffy white rug adorned the floor, and I resisted groaning out loud when my bare feet pressed down onto it.

It was so soft.

"I've never had this before," I whispered as I glanced around.

"Private quarters?" Kol asked.

"Quarters of any kind," I admitted. "I've never had a home. I slept where I could hide from sight. I've never had somewhere like this. I love it very much. Thank you."

Kol didn't reply to me, so I looked at him and found him staring at me with such intensity that I stepped back. For a moment, his eyes glowed like when he brought me to orgasm, but the light left his eyes almost instantly. I didn't bring it up in case I insulted him. It was probably a Maji thing like Surkah's ability to heal with touch, and I didn't want to say something about it and upset him because he'd probably take away my beautiful room if I did that.

"Well," he said, clearing his throat. "This room is now your quarters while you're aboard the *Ebony*, so you need not fear it being taken away from you. It is yours until we reach our destination."

"Truly?" I asked.

Kol nodded. "Truly."

Without thinking, I crossed the distance between us and wrapped my arms around his waist. I was considerably shorter than he was; my head just barely reaching his chest, and I couldn't get my arms to meet each other because he was so wide with muscle. But it didn't matter. When I felt Kol's large hands flatten against my back, I relaxed even more. He was hugging me back.

"Nova?" he murmured after a few moments.

"Hmmm?"

"Can you ... Can you release me?"

I opened my eyes and quickly stepped away from him.

"I'm sorry."

I had no idea what possessed me to hug him.

"Don't be." He cleared his throat. "I would gladly hold you all day, but I have duties to attend to."

I felt my cheeks burn with heat. "Of course, Kol. I apologise for keeping you from them."

"Do not apologise. Time spent with you is not time wasted."

I felt my cheeks heat even more, and I wanted to kick myself because of it. I was getting embarrassed, and my stomach fluttered with a sensation my father used to describe as 'butterflies.' I knew it wasn't right because Kol wasn't human—he was Maji—and I had *better* remember that.

"I am ashamed," he said after a long moment.

I raised a brow. "Why?"

"Because my earlier behaviour has made you fear me and fear that I will forcefully take you. You challenged me, and my reaction was to make you heel to me. And as you're an attractive female, my choice was an orgasm. I did not mean for it to happen, but my instincts can be hard to deny."

It was idiotic for his admittance that he didn't want to touch me willingly to sting. I couldn't help the emotion that stuck like a needle in my heart.

"I don't fear you," I said softly. "I just thought you wanted to touch me to see ... how I differed from you."

Big. Fat. Lie.

"Oh," Kol said, a light tint of purple staining his cheeks. "Well, yes, I wanted to see your differences, but I cannot find any other than size. You're very small, a lot smaller than Maji females. Weaker."

My embarrassment faded at the bristle of the insult. "I'm *not* weak."

Kol suddenly smiled. "I did not mean to wound your pride. I just was stating a fact that our females are naturally tall and strong. Not as tall or as strong as our males are, but compared to a human female, they are superior."

"Yeah, you're not helping your argument at all."

"Forgive me." He chuckled. "I meant no offence."

"Sure, you didn't."

Kol watched me for a moment then said, "Are you going to fight me on everything, Nova?"

I wanted to say no, but my pride and stubbornness wouldn't allow me to.

"Yes," I answered.

"Reconsider," he asked. "Accepting your new life will be a lot easier than fighting it."

I remained silent

"And Nova?" he said.

I looked up at him.

"My sister informed me I should apologise for … earlier."

I waited for the apology, but it never came.

"Aren't you going to say sorry?"

"Maji don't apologise when they're not sorry."

I gasped. "You *aren't* sorry?"

"Making you come, feeling you let go …" Kol paused and licked his lips. "I will *never* be sorry for that gift; I will only be thankful so … thank you."

"Are you serious right now?" I asked incredulously as he backed out into the hallway.

Just as the door closed, he winked and said, "As a heart attack."

I hated that he used my own words against me and that he made me smile. I also hated that he gave me butterflies when the only thing I should feel when it came to the Maji shipmaster was disgust and anger.

I shook my head clear and resisted the urge to punch the air as I glanced around my new room. Though I never voiced it to Kol or anyone else, I felt beside myself at the prospect of a new home, new law and order, a new life, and a new start. I hadn't felt safe since the night before my father died—so the feeling felt foreign to me. I wasn't stupid enough to believe everything the Maji told me after finding out they lied to me in the first place, but I didn't feel as nervous around them. I felt as though Kol was being honest when he said it would be a good change for me and my people.

I'd just have to cross the 'breeding with Maji' bridge when I came to it, or maybe I'd just go under the bridge when nobody was looking.

CHAPTER SIX

Voices woke me the following morning. Loud voices.

"Echo," an annoyed woman's voice clipped. "You're going to wake her up!"

"How the hell am I supposed to be quiet, Envi?" a second woman's voice quipped. "They just put our beds in here and told us to be nice to her and that it was 'the shipmaster's orders'. Whatever *that* means."

"It means they were the shipmaster's orders. *Duh.*" The first voice snickered.

I opened my eyes and instantly sat upright. I stared at the two *human* women who were busy putting clean linen on their beds. Single beds that were only a few feet or so away from mine. They weren't here when I fell asleep last night, so I had no idea how they were brought in without waking me up.

That pissed me off because my instincts were normally much better than that. It took a lot for something to get past me, but these women somehow managed to move into my room without disrupting me from my sleep at all. That disturbed me greatly.

I watched the two women with caution and decided if they attacked me that I could take them both on. They were skinnier than I was, which meant they were more malnourished. They were a bit taller than I was and had the advantage of backup, but if they backed me into a corner and left me no choice, I'd fight for my life. The last time that happened to me, I killed a person. The vision of my arrow piercing the watchman's eye socket replayed in my mind.

I shook my head clear and looked for something I could use as a weapon, but I saw nothing on my side of the room. Both women were silently struggling with their bed linens, so I quietly slipped from my bed and stood, facing them.

"Hello," I said, my voice gruff.

The woman with the waist-length black hair yelped and spun around to face me. The woman with shoulder-length dirty blond hair mimicked her actions but held up her hands in an awkward defensive stance. Both women had scars on their faces and some down the length of their arms. They both had sullen grey eyes, button noses, and round faces. They were related, that much was obvious. If I had to guess, I'd say they were sisters.

"You scared the shit out of us," the black-haired woman said and placed her hand on her chest.

"Sorry," I said, though I didn't exactly mean it.

Silence stretched between us until I said, "So, um, what're you both doing in here?"

The black-haired woman got defensive; I could tell by her change in demeanour and the narrowing of her eyes.

"What do you care?" she asked, her tone clipped.

I raised a brow. "Kol said this was *my* room."

"Which Maji is that?" Blondie asked, her tone much softer.

"The shipmaster," I said, keeping my eyes on Blackie.

She seemed to be the more threatening of the two.

"You met the *shipmaster*?" Blackie asked followed by Blondie saying, "And you're allowed call him Kol?"

I shrugged. "It's complicated."

"I'm sure it is." Blackie blinked.

I narrowed my eyes. "Are we going to have a problem?"

She stepped forward. "I don't know, are we?"

"Try me, and you'll see," I challenged.

Blondie moved to Blackie's side and grabbed her hand.

"We've gotten off on the wrong foot," she said, squeezing Blackie's hand. "I'm Envi, and this is my sister Echo. We're twins. Not identical ... obviously. We were brought here by a Maji fellow, and he told us this was our new quarters. We didn't ask to be moved here. I promise."

I believed her. She wore her emotions on her sleeve for all to see. Her dark-haired sister, on the other hand, didn't.

"I'm Nova," I said, nodding towards her. "I apologise for the lack of welcome, but if I'm honest, I don't trust anyone on this craft. Maji and humans ... both original and augmented."

Both women gasped.

"They've *augs* aboard?" Echo spat.

It seemed we had something in common as they clearly shared my distaste for the augmented.

"Unfortunately," I grumbled. "Last I heard, there were sixty-eight of them aboard. I tried to escape when I found out, but I was drugged and then brought here."

Both sisters widened their eyes.

"The Maji said they'd keep us safe," Envi said, her eyes welling up with tears. "It was in the terms of our rescue."

"I was assured that I was kept on board for my own safety," I said with a wave of my hand. "Something along the lines of the Earth imploding soon."

Envi began to cry.

Echo glared at me. "Don't say shit like that offhandedly; this is serious."

"I'm aware it's serious," I replied.

"You don't sound like you're taking it seriously," she snapped.

She pulled her crying sister towards the door that automatically opened.

"Where are you going?" I asked, curious.

"If there are augs aboard, we're getting as far away from this craft and the Maji as possible."

The doors closed, and they were gone.

"Good luck," I said to the empty room.

Not long after the sisters left my room, Kol appeared, but I made sure I kept my attention on my non-existent fingernails. I heard the door opening followed by heavy booted footsteps as I sat on my bed with my back pressed against the wall. I swallowed and cleared my throat to keep my 'tough girl' act intact.

"Ten minutes," his voice rumbled. "That's all it took for you to run not one but *two* females out of your quarters."

As expected, he was *pissed*.

"I wasn't informed that I would be sharing my quarters, so you can imagine my surprise when I wake up to two strangers in my presence. The last time I was around more than one human, I was almost killed. Sorry if my lack of social skills has caused problems for you, *prince*."

"Nova." He sighed. "You cannot remain hidden; you *need* interaction with other humans."

I jerked my gaze to his.

"You don't know what's best for me, so *stop* pretending you do."

Kol's eyes darkened. Literally. The almost neon violet turned to a dark shade of lavender, and it freaked me out.

"Keeping you alive is what's best for you, and I'm doing that, so give me a little credit, *human*."

I turned my back to him. "Leave me alone, *Maji*."

"No," he replied. "You're my charge while you're on my craft."

"So are however many other humans you roped into getting onto this *stupid* craft."

"My spacecraft is not stupid."

I laughed at his very male response and shook my head.

"You *and* your spacecraft are stupid."

Kol remained mute, and after twenty seconds of the stretched silence, I thought he had left the room. Until I felt fingertips brush over my neck. Goosebumps broke out over my skin, and I fought a groan that desperately wanted to break free. My reaction to him both embarrassed me and scared me to death.

"Why're you sad, Nova?"

He continued to slide his fingertips over my neck, and it distracted me. I moved my head, stretching my neck to give him better access, and I heard his soft chuckle.

"Stop touching me," I said, not really meaning my words.

Kol chuckled again, but he did as I asked.

"You'll be happy to know that the human females, Echo and Envi, will remain aboard the *Ebony*."

I snorted. "Did you have them drugged, too?"

"No," Kol replied curtly. "We explained away their worries, and they're happy to remain with us."

How did he explain away the worry humans had for the augmented?

"*I'm* not happy, so why aren't you letting me go?"

After a pregnant pause, he said, "Because you're an enigma to me, Nova."

"So that grants you permission to hold me captive?" I asked, hating that my voice was thick with emotion.

"I'm *protecting* you," he angrily replied. "Thanas only knows why because you're more trouble than you seem to be worth!"

I didn't respond.

"Look"—he exhaled—"why must you continue to fight me?"

"Because I can't just allow you to take me without a fight," I replied. "It's not who I am."

It's not who I was raised to be.

"I don't want you to be anyone other than yourself, but you must realise that had you stayed on Earth, you would have died within the next few days."

My palms got sticky with sweat.

"Do you want to die, Nova?"

I was a survivalist, and that meant I'd do just about anything to keep my life.

"No," I said quietly.

"Then stop fighting this. Fighting *me*."

I couldn't think of anything intelligent to say, so I remained quiet.

"Echo and Envi will be returning to share your quarters with you," Kol continued. "We have many females aboard, more than expected, and housing will be a problem if there is no sharing."

Again, I remained silent.

"The sisters will not harm you; though, they are worried *you* will harm *them*."

At that, I snorted.

"You won't hurt them, right?"

"I won't have anything to do with them."

Kol sighed but didn't press the subject further.

"I have someone whom I would like you to meet."

I heard the door opening, Kol saying something softly to another person, and then the sound of the door closing once more.

"Nova, this is Adus," he said from behind me. "She cannot understand you nor you her, so I will translate your meeting."

I turned to face Kol and this Adus person, and when I did, I nearly died.

Oh, my Almighty.

I stared at the alien female, and she stared right back at me. She was *not* Maji. Not even close. When she blinked her gigantic lone eye, I found myself widening both of mine. She really had *one* eye, and it was huge, and where there should be white there was pink, and it was just … "So weird looking."

"Nova," Kol grumbled.

I switched my gaze to him. "What?"

"You spoke your thoughts and were, as you humans like to say, rude."

I blinked and looked at the alien female who was still openly staring at me, her gaze rolling over me like a cool breeze. She whistled and kept on whistling, the tone of each whistle changing as the seconds ticked by. She didn't even take a break to inhale, and it freaked me out until Kol snickered and said, "She *is* kind of funny looking. I agree."

I frowned at him then changed my expression to an angry glare when I realised that the alien female had called *me* funny looking. Her whistling wasn't just a sound—it was her language. She spoke to Kol again; the whistling sound was higher pitched a second before she burst into laughter. Kol laughed too, and it bugged me.

"You're talking to her in English."

Kol shook his head. "Your translator is programmed to me, and as the shipmaster, you will hear whatever I say, in any language, in your own words."

I raised a brow. "Why?"

"Why what?"

"Why would you want humans to be able to understand you at all times?"

"To gain your trust." He shrugged. "If we spoke in front of your people in another language, it wouldn't be a sign of respect or trust from us to you, and we do not want that. We want—"

"Our wombs."

"Harmony," Kol finished as if I didn't speak.

"Well, what is she saying?" I asked, my annoyance evident.

"She said"—he chuckled—"that you remind her of a homely species on her home world. They have two eyes and are small with brown hair like you. All they do is eat, mate, and sleep. She asked if humans were a relation."

"You little bitch!" I bellowed at the alien.

She blinked her eye and looked at Kol. He placed a hand on her shoulder, and it seemed to relax her. He turned his attention to me and narrowed his eyes to slits.

"Easy," he said.

"Don't 'easy' me," I snapped at him. "She just called me ugly!"

He shook his head. "She said it in jest."

"Yeah, well, *she* is ugly to *me*!" I countered. "Her and her huge pink eye, which, by the way, is a sign of an infection on Earth!"

Kol laughed, and to the alien, he said, "She said you're very beautiful, and it angers her not to resemble a beauty such as yourself."

The alien's cheeks flushed a dark green colour. She then giggled as she said something to me before bowing her head to Kol and leaving the room with a spring in her step.

"You're an asshole," I growled to Kol. "Why did you tell her that lie?"

"Because," he said, "she is a princess."

I continued to glare at him, and he rolled his violet eyes.

"I mean that literally," he continued. "In the past one hundred years, *your* species has vacated the title of the largest populated species. You were a ten billion strong race, and Adus's species, Vaneer, was the second largest in the cosmos with six billion, but now they're the largest, and to insult the only heir to their throne is not a war my people are willing to fight. Besides, she *is* beautiful. Just because she isn't the beauty you're used to does not mean she is not beautiful. I told her the same thing about you, and she agreed."

I hated that he was right. I also hated that my heart pounded at the mention of him thinking I was beautiful.

"Yeah, I guess," I mumbled and looked down at my feet.

I practically felt Kol's smile, and it bugged me.

"Why're they here?" I asked. "On Earth?"

"They're passing through on a mission of their own and want to extract some resources from the Earth before it dies. They're leaving momentarily. Adus just wanted to meet a human in case you all die, and I figured you'd be perfect."

Perfect to annoy maybe.

"What'd she say?" I quizzed. "You know, before she left?"

"She said she likes humans and is going to talk to her father about keeping you even if you're ugly."

Horror slammed into me, and I'm sure my expression conveyed it perfectly. I felt like I would be sick until Kol suddenly burst into laughter. I forgot about my near panic attack and focused on him.

"You should have seen your face." He laughed and slapped his knee.

I felt my eye twitch in anger.

"What the hell are you talking about?"

"Adus said thank you for your compliment, and she wished you a happy life before she left. I was playing a game. I wanted to see what your reaction would be."

"You think that's funny?" I asked, my voice hollow. "You think it's funny to scare me like that when I've already been kidnapped?"

Kol dropped his smile, and for a moment, I thought I saw regret on his face.

"I didn't mean to upset you," he said.

"Well, you did."

"I apologise."

"I don't accept it."

"I don't care." He shrugged. "I mean my apology, and if you don't accept it, that's your issue. Not mine."

Anger swirled within me.

"Why humans?" I suddenly demanded to know. "Why us? It is because we're compatible, or was that a lie too?"

Kol's set his square jaw, and he stared me down.

"That was the truth," he said. "So far, we have managed to rescue two thousand seven hundred and ninety-three healthy human females—"

"What?" I gasped. "You *really* have only chosen to save women?"

"Maji males outnumber our females ten to one. We needed more females, not males."

My stomach churned as I digested the information.

"This displeases you," Kol commented. "Do you think us heartless?"

I nodded before I could help myself.

"I am sorry you feel that way, but we need females to ensure Maji survival, not males."

"What about *human* survival?" I demanded. "What about my people?"

Kol sighed and pinched the bridge of his nose like I was an annoyance.

"It ensures your survival, too. The offspring will be half Maji and half human."

That's not good enough.

"Bullshit. You said your genes would probably be more dominant, so the babies would have more Maji traits."

Kol shrugged, not bothering to reply.

"I can't believe this," I said more to myself. "I knew this would happen; I knew you Maji would be like everyone else. Just out for yourselves."

"Stop this, Nova," Kol angrily demanded. "Earth is going to *implode*. It's not a matter of if, it's a matter of *when*. We saved your human females, and—"

"You only 'saved' us because we serve a purpose." I cut Kol off, my rage matching his.

"You're impossible to converse with," he stated as he stood and began to pace back and forth like a caged animal. "We're bringing you to Ealra, a new healthy planet, and we chose females to ensure your species' survival, yet you're *still* unhappy? This is *definitely* a female trait. Maji females are terribly difficult and stubborn at times and seeing it in human females proves it is a flaw possibly in every race."

I threw my hands up in the air. "Almighty forbid I disagree with you."

"There is disagreeing, and then there is being difficult. You're the latter."

"Tough shit. I'm not going to change just because you don't like it."

"You will," Kol growled. "On Ealra, your sharp tongue will not be tolerated. I've allowed leeway with you and your fellow females because this is a traumatic event, knowing your world will soon die, but—"

"The traumatic event is being kidnapped by aliens."

Kol snarled at me, and it frightened me to death. I sucked in a breath and remained still.

"Change your attitude," he warned. "I will *not* be dealing with you any further if this is your behaviour. You will be rationed on food and confined to the group human holding for the rest of the journey to Ealra if you continue this ... defiance."

Panic surged inside me and so did a fresh wave of anger. He was using my fear of humans against me, and it both terrified me and pissed me off.

"You're horrible."

"I could be worse." Kol devilishly grinned. "Please, make me *show* you just how horrible I can be."

My pulse spiked, and my natural sassy response died on the tip of my tongue. This piece of shit knew exactly how to play me, and if I wanted the quarters he gave to me, then I had better keep my mouth shut and do what he said ... at least until I figured out an escape plan.

"That won't be necessary," I assured him. "I'll ... behave."

"I sincerely doubt that." Kol smirked

"You're infuriating! The second I give in, you throw your stupid quips back in my face. You're driving me barking mad!"

"*Me?*" he spluttered. "*I* am infuriating? *Me?*"

"Yes, *you!*"

"Thanas!" He laughed. "*You* are barking mad."

"Don't turn my words—"

"There is *no* pleasing you," Kol cut me off with an angry shake of his head. "Maji offer you a haven and a loophole to ensure your species survives longer than your home world, and you're not happy in the slightest. Humans ... you're ungrateful."

Before I could defend myself and my people, Kol left the room. The door shut behind him but quickly reopened and revealed Echo ... who was glaring at me.

"Hi," I said, surprised to see her so soon. "Where is your sister?"

"Envi is with the lady healer getting her leg healed. She hurt it when we tried to escape."

"Sorry to hear that."

"You can be a real bitch, you know that?"

I felt my jaw drop at Echo's declaration.

"What'd I do?" I asked, confused.

"You lumped us in the same boat as you."

I stared at her.

"I overheard your argument with the shipmaster," she continued, "and I'm pissed at you."

"Why?" I asked, shocked.

"Because you're sabotaging our women," Echo stated. "Where do you get off fighting against a species who wants to save their people and ours? Earth has been a lost cause for *years*. Even if it wasn't dying, it hasn't been considered safe since long before the war, especially for women. We were treated like slaves by our own people. *Humans* have attacked me and my sister, beat us, and treated us lesser than animals our entire lives. No other species has done that but our own, and you have the nerve to argue against the Maji for saving us from a hopeless fate? What the *hell* is wrong with you? I'm *very* grateful for them. Why they want us doesn't matter because their reasons ensure we *have* a future. You're bitching about someone saving your life and your species and giving us a future. You're fucking *stupid.*"

My heart thrummed inside my chest, my abdomen churned, and my palms were itchy with sweat. Echo angrily shook her head as she turned away from me. She climbed into her bed and pulled her blanket over her body.

"And if you scare my sister," she said as she adjusted her blanket, "like you did earlier, I'm going to beat the shit out of you."

I believed her, but I didn't fear her.

"I'm not scared of you, Echo."

"Upset my sister again, and you will be."

I said nothing further and neither did Echo, which suited me fine. I got back into my bed, and I kept my back to the wall so I would be facing Echo and Envi, when she returned, at all times. I didn't believe they would attack me, but I wasn't going to take any chances. An hour or so passed before Echo moved, showing she had awoken from her slumber. She turned in her bed to face me, and when she saw I was looking at her, she stared right back at me. Echo broke the silence after a few moments.

"You're going to have to be nicer to the Maji," she said, her voice husky with sleep. "They'll probably leave you here if you don't. They have hundreds of willing women aboard, if not thousands, and they'll dump you for one of them."

Fear gripped me.

"Kol wouldn't allow that," I said, hoping my doubt didn't reveal itself in my tone.

"From what I heard earlier, and how pissed he looked leaving this room, I wouldn't be so sure about that."

She got up from her bed, adjusted her clothing, and left the room without a backwards glance my way. Her words replayed in my mind, and the more I thought about it, the more worried I became. I hated how I came to be on the *Ebony,* and though I hadn't shown it, I felt lucky I was aboard the spacecraft, instead of just looking at it from an outsider's perspective. I thought of my conversations with Kol, Surkah, and even Mikoh, and I could only imagine the childish bitch they thought I was.

I didn't want them to think that because, despite my behaviour, I wasn't anything close to childish. The bitchy part was highly debatable, but I was a strong, mature—most of the time—adult female, and at that moment, I decided I had better start acting like it if I wanted not just a good future, but a future at all. I stood from my bed, adjusted my clothing, and left my room with the intention of mending my relationships with the Maji and doing what was expected of me. The first person on my list was the shipmaster.

I just hoped Kol hadn't already washed his hands of me.

CHAPTER SEVEN

"Are you lost, female?"

I spun around when a deep voice addressed me. When I saw two males walking towards me, I almost swallowed my tongue. Like every other Maji male I saw, they were suited up in the black armoured uniform that Mikoh and the shipmaster wore. They were big boys in both height and girth. I wondered if being muscular was a Maji gene trait because they were all in shape; even Surkah had a killer body.

"Hi." I awkwardly waved to the males who stopped a few feet away from me. "I am lost, actually. I'm looking for the bridge."

The male with the tight haircut raised a thick black eyebrow. "Why do you want to go to the bridge?"

"To speak to the shipmaster," I explained. "I kind of had a fight with him, and I need to apologise."

The males shared a look before returning their gazes to me.

"You fought the shipmaster?" the male on the right asked as his eyes scanned me. "I don't believe it. The shipmaster would never harm a female, not even if she attacked him."

At that, I laughed.

"I don't mean a physical fight. I mean a verbal one. We had an argument."

The male with silver toned hair and blue skin grinned. "That I believe. Females have a sharp tongue in every species."

"What are your names?" I asked, chuckling.

The black-haired male put his hand against his chest and said, "I am Dash." He jabbed his thumb at his silver-haired friend. "And this is Vorah."

Dash was clearly the older of the two. In human years, he looked around thirty years old while Vorah looked on the right side of eighteen.

"It's lovely to meet you both," I said and bowed my head a little. "I'm Nova."

"That is a strange name," Vorah commented.

Dash forcibly elbowed him in the ribs. "That is disheartening for a female to hear. How are you going to get an intended if you continue to insult every female we encounter?"

Vorah growled at Dash, but his cheeks did flare with a tinge of purple as he glanced at me through his silver eyelashes. His eyes were the lightest shade of blue I had ever seen, and when he was bashful, as he was now, they looked huge.

"Forgive me, Nova. I spoke out of turn."

I eyed him. "It's okay. I'm sure many human names are strange to Maji."

"Are Maji names strange to you?" Vorah asked, still blushing.

"Very much so. Your name is very unusual." Vorah frowned, so I quickly added, "But I like it a lot. It is a strong name."

His chest puffed out, and he said, "I am a strong male who will produce very strong offspring and bring my intended great pleasure. I will care for her, feed her, and put my family above all else."

Oooookay.

Dash seemed to be proud of Vorah's declaration and looked at me, along with Vorah, as they awaited my response.

"Um, I'm sure you will. You seem like a very strong and capable male."

Vorah stepped forward and said, "May we see if we're suitable?"

I froze because I instantly understood his meaning. He used different words, but the meaning was still the same. He wanted to see if we could have sex and, in turn, possibly become a mated couple. My instinct was to reject him, but my conversation with Echo stopped me from doing so. I once wanted to be off the *Ebony*, but remaining on the spacecraft was the only way I got to remain alive.

My escape plan had turned into a survival plan.

If I was to truly accept that being with the Maji was my life now, then I had to realise that eventually, I would have to take a husband. Kol himself said it was one of the conditions for rescue. The Maji seemed to be patient when it came to women, and Vorah was young. If I accepted his offer and did things in baby steps, he would surely not know any differently as he was probably a virgin like me. We could make a deal about getting to know one another before we made a full commitment.

He wanted an intended, and I could offer that to him.

"You need to clarify that for me, Vorah," I said, nervously. "Just to be sure, you want to see if we could be the other's ... intended, right?"

"*Yes*," Vorah answered so fast it prompted Dash to slap him across the back of the head.

"Relax," he murmured to his friend. "Females don't want such eagerness."

Vorah barely paid him any attention as his focus was entirely on me.

"Would you be willing to take things slow?" I asked Vorah, a wariness to my tone. "I can't believe I'm considering this, let alone saying this two minutes after meeting you, but I know that eventually, all my women must take a husband. I've been on my own for so long, though, that I don't want to rush anything. Is that okay?"

Please say yes.

Vorah was almost bouncing with excitement, and I knew I could use his eagerness to my advantage. His age was already proving useful, I just had to play his strings right, and I could possibly have a really good arrangement with him.

"Nova, I will wait until you're ready to seal our bond. I swear on my honour."

Dash's chest puffed out with pride, so I guess whatever Vorah just promised was respected amongst the Maji.

I licked my lips. "Then yes, we can see if we're suitable."

"Thanas blesses me," Vorah said and looked at Dash with so much happiness it warmed my heart. "I have possibly found my intended, Dash."

"I am glad for you, my friend. You're a deserving male."

Vorah smiled widely and looked back at me.

"It will take four days to reach Ealra, so we can meet daily to talk, walk, and get to know each other if that is okay with you?"

I felt a breath of relief rush from me.

"That sounds great, Vorah."

We were all smiling then, and it almost made me forget that I needed to apologise to Kol. At the reminder of him, my gut told me that my deal with Vorah wouldn't be well received, but I blinked the thought away. Surely, Kol would be delighted that I was accepting my situation and practically throwing myself into it ... so to speak.

I thought of the intimate moment Kol and I shared, but I reminded myself he only touched me because I challenged him. He said so himself. He wanted me to *heel* to him like a dog. I had to shake off the stupid butterflies and growing interest I had in him, and I reminded myself that I was reacting to him like a love-struck fool because he was the only single male I had encountered. Besides, he wasn't just the shipmaster, he was a prince to his people, and there was no way he would slum it with a common human girl like me.

Not that I want him to.

I refocused on the males before me and smiled because Vorah

seemed really pleased with my response. Dash appeared pleased as well because he kept patting his friend silently on the back.

"I *really* have to speak with the shipmaster before he throws me off the craft," I added with nervous laughter after a few moments.

"I will escort you to the bridge," Vorah offered.

I blushed. "Thank you." I looked at Dash and said, "It was great to meet you."

"And you, Nova."

When Vorah and I turned and began to walk away, I glanced back and found Dash watching us like he was a proud father or big brother or something. I shook my head clear and focused on Vorah as we walked.

"So is this your first time to Earth?" I asked him.

He smiled down at me, and I realised he had dimples. That shocked me. I never imagined aliens could look like humans, so seeing one of them with dimples almost floored me. Vorah was cute, and I couldn't believe I noticed that about him. I couldn't believe that his bluish coloured skin went unregistered in my mind until that very moment.

I think I'm getting used to the Maji.

"Yes," Vorah answered me, regaining my attention. "This is my first mission, and I'm thoroughly enjoying it."

"I bet you are," I teased. "All the females aboard must be strange to you."

"Very much so. There are so few of them on my home world, and fewer who are unmated."

"I've never thought of it, but I think it's like that on Earth, too. I come across more men than woman, and when I do, the woman is owned."

"*Owned?*" Vorah repeated.

I looked down and nodded.

"I am sorry for your people's suffering, Nova. I want to kill every human male that has brought harm to a female."

That sounded very violent, but I appreciated the kindness behind it.

I looked up at Vorah. "Thank you."

He nodded once, and from then on, we walked in a comfortable silence. I lost count of how many hallways we walked down and corners we had turned before we reached the bridge, but when he did, I gave Vorah a hearty laugh.

"Thank you. I'd have never made it here without your help."

He licked his lips. "You're welcome."

He stood waiting for something, and the only thing I could think of was the suitability thing.

"We can have dinner together this evening in the mess hall ... if you'd like?"

Vorah's eyes practically popped out of his head. "Yes, please."

"Great." I smiled. "You'll have to check with who oversees the housing because I'm not sure what number my room is."

I wasn't even sure how I'd get back to my room.

"I will find that information and seek you out when my shift ends."

"Great."

Vorah smiled widely then he turned and walked away with a spring in his step. I smiled too, knowing I could very well spend a lot of time with that male in the future. I forgot about Vorah when I turned to face the door before me. Without giving it too much thought, I lifted my hand and knocked on the door. Seconds ticked by before the large door slide opened and revealed ... Mikoh.

"You're everywhere," I said to him.

He grinned down at me. "Remember that."

I playfully rolled my eyes. "Can I speak to His Highness?"

"Who?"

"Kol."

"Why didn't you say so?"

"I did."

"No, you said His Highness."

"It was a joke."

"I didn't laugh."

"Because you're incapable of the action, you statue."

Mikoh's grin made me laugh.

"You're insufferable," I said with a shake of my head.

He winked. "So I've heard."

"Why aren't you with Surkah?" I asked him.

"She ordered me away." He shrugged. "She does that a lot, so my friend Nero is guarding her for me."

I nodded, so he turned to the side and gestured for me to enter the room. I did and came to a stop almost instantly. The room was ... huge. Maji males were everywhere, and they all looked like they had important jobs. There was high-tech equipment, chairs, flashing lights, and a huge ... window. It was overlooking the Earth.

I was no longer *on* Earth; I was looking at it.

"When did we leave?" I asked aloud as I stared at the dying planet that I called home.

"An hour or so ago," Mikoh replied to me. "After the Vaneer disembarked."

"I didn't feel a thing," I murmured.

"You wouldn't. The *Ebony* is virtually silent for takeoff, in flight, and landing. It is the perfect craft."

That was the perfect word to describe the *Ebony*: perfect. The entire spacecraft was truly something to behold. From an outsider's view, it was marvellously big, futuristic, and *definitely* not of Earth. The advancements within the ship were simply incredible. The cleanliness of it caught me off guard when I looked around, but when I looked past that, I saw the technological gems for what they were—simply mesmerising.

Nothing was plain on the bridge of the *Ebony*. From a few feet away, a white wall looked simply like a white wall, but when you got closer, you could see zips of light, the outline of digital handprint panels that were used to open doors and codes to lock and unlock them as well as a written language that I could not decipher. The more I looked, the more I saw; it was like the ship was alive, and it was—it was alive with technology.

I made a mental note to examine the walls of my quarters and those in the hallways to see if I missed the digital delight that was hidden in plain view all around me.

I returned my focus to the gigantic window and stared at my home world, noticing how defeated it looked. I had seen pictures of the Earth in its heyday on one of the many televised screens that littered the main cities. The oceans were once large, a deep blue, and they all connected. The land mass was just as big, and it was green and rich with life. The Earth that I gazed upon now was none of those things. Only small patches of water remained, but the blue hue was not as vibrant. The land mass was a sickly brown and choked out any green that tried to thrive.

I knew my planet was dying, but looking at it first-hand caused the realisation to slam into me with a force that pulled a strangled cry from my throat. I hadn't noticed the talking and movement around me until I cried out, and all that noise stopped. I covered my mouth with my hands and cried into them as I looked at the Earth. My entire life was on that planet. My father, mother, aunt, uncle, cousins ... they were all down on the surface. And I would be leaving them behind. That knowledge hurt just as much as the realisation that soon their bodies and the Earth itself would be no more.

"My home," I whimpered.

I didn't flinch when I felt hands on my shoulders, and I found a surprising amount of comfort in them. I turned to the male who rested his hands on me, and I hugged myself against his broad chest. For a moment, I thought the male was Mikoh, but when I inhaled and the scent of rain filled my nostrils, I was shocked to find that my subconscious had noted it belonged to one being.

Kol.

"I'm sorry, *shiva*," he murmured and folded his arms around me.

He held me for a few moments then released me when I turned in his arms and leaned my back against his chest as I stared at the Earth once more.

"I knew it was dying." I sniffled. "I knew it had gotten bad, but I never imagined it got to ... this."

Kol remained silent.

"My home is really dying, Kol." I hiccupped. "And there isn't a damn thing I can do about it."

He turned my body back to face him, placed his fingers under my chin, and tilted my head up so I was looking at him. His violet eyes were glowing once more, and his expression was softer than I had ever seen it before.

"You're with the people," he said. "You're ensuring the continuation of *your* people by being here."

At that moment, I understood why they were here. It was more than looking for mates to continue their species; it was a last attempt at survival. The Maji were survivalists too, and they were doing everything they could to save their species.

"Kol," I said, my lower lip wobbling. "I'm so sorry about everything. I've been beyond difficult for you to deal with and very childish and ... ungrateful. You were right. I apologise profusely. Please, forgive me."

I didn't know why, but I needed him to forgive me. Not to keep my place on the *Ebony* but to dull an ache rising in my chest that I was failing him. He stared at me for a long moment then nodded once.

"I accept your apology, and I forgive you."

My shoulders sagged with relief. "Thank you."

His vibrant eyes flicked over my face. "I admire you, Nova. I know it wasn't easy for you to apologise to me, nor for you to accept this change in your life."

I sniffled. "Echo pointed out how much of a bitch I have been and threatened a time or two to beat me up if I didn't change my attitude. Since I'm stuck with her and her sister until we get to your home world, I figured I'd better get real nice real fast."

Kol suddenly laughed, and I found myself smiling up at him, too.

"She will not harm you," he said, still chuckling. "Do not fear her."

"I don't, but she was right. I have been everything she accused me of, and I want to make it right."

"How?" Kol asked, his expression turning dark. "Do you wish to seek out a unit member to mate with?"

I felt my cheeks stain with heat, so I looked down at my bare feet

"Mating right away is not my intention, but Vorah did ask me out earlier."

"Vorah?" Kol repeated. "That young silver-haired tail chaser?"

Tail chaser?

"I guess," I replied, looking up at him once more.

Kol growled to himself then to me. "He is not a good match for you. He is too young to be searching for an intended. He is only forty years old! A single moon cycle older than Surkah."

"What's a moon cycle?" I asked. "I've heard it a lot, but I don't know what it is."

Kol blinked. "An Ealra year is divided into twelve moon cycles, a single moon cycle consists of eight terms, a single term consists of seven days. Do you understand? We use some terms that are like your Earth terms, but not all of them. Sera said you humans would adapt."

We had no choice *but* to adapt.

"A moon cycle is two Earth months, and a term is a week. Got it.

"You do realise that forty years is a lot to humans, right?" I quizzed. "I'm only twenty-three."

"Yes, but we have a longer lifespan than humans. Vorah is barely out of his minor years. He is *three* moon cycles shy of becoming a grown male."

"Well, he wants to see if we're suitable."

Sharp intakes of breaths were taken around the room, and I thought something was wrong with the *Ebony* until I looked around Kol and realised all eyes were on us ... or him. I looked at Mikoh when he slowly approached us. I hadn't realised Kol's arms went around me, but they did, and they were squeezing me tightly.

"I'll kill him," Kol growled, his voice sounding so unlike himself that I wouldn't have believed it came from his lips had I not been looking at him while he said it.

"Who?" I asked, unsure of what was happening.

"Vorah," Kol snarled and stretched out the 'rah' in Vorah's name.

"What did he do?" I asked, confused and a little frightened.

"He'd *dare* present himself to you as a mate when I—"

"Easy, my friend," Mikoh said softly, cutting Kol off. "Vorah is young, and he did not know Nova was ... unavailable."

I'm unavailable?

"Is it because I've been difficult?" I frowned. "Am I un ... mateable or something now?"

I didn't think I truly *wanted* to mate with a Maji, but being told I wasn't allowed didn't seem very fair. I behaved wrongly, like a real bitch, but my emotions fuelled my anger and the whole being kidnapped by aliens thing really freaked me out. Surely, I couldn't have been the only human woman to act out?

"Kol," Mikoh said firmly, ignoring me completely. "Remember what we said? Offspring steps for the human females so we don't *scare* them with their transition to the Maji way."

Kol growled at Mikoh, but then he looked down at me, and his features softened once more.

"Vorah wants to ... share sex with you to see if *you* desire *him* as a mate."

I was mortified for so many males to be listening to our conversation.

"Yes, I know. He told me so, but he also said he would take baby steps with me."

Kol's hold on me went extremely tight.

"You wish to ... mate with him?"

I didn't know whether he sounded mad, disgusted, or disheartened.

I cleared my throat. "*You* were the one who told me I'd have to take a husband."

"I never said you were to go out and seek a mate straight away!"

That was true.

"Look, I'm just as surprised as you are that this is going down," I expressed. "Vorah surprised me. I mean, who comes out and asks someone they just met if they want to have sex?"

"We shouldn't do that?" an unfamiliar male voice asked.

I looked around Kol to the orange-haired male who spoke to me, but before I answered him, Kol let out a vicious snarl.

"I beg your forgiveness, my prince," the male suddenly said and dropped to his knees with his head bowed.

I looked at Kol. "Stop that. He did nothing wrong."

"He spoke to you," Kol growled, his body shaking.

"I'm not Surkah," I informed him. "I'm not a princess. I'm just me. He can ask a question if he wants to. How will Maji and humans learn about one another if we don't ask questions?"

"He can ask another human, not you."

"Why?"

"Because I said so."

"Wow," I said with a shake of my head. "That's really mature."

"Being mature is not something a male remembers when his—"

"When his what?" I cut him off.

Kol looked like he was fighting an internal battle.

"Nothing," he eventually said.

I raised a brow. "For someone who wants me to accept that you're saving my people and that mating with your people is a good idea, you aren't very happy that one of your males wants to see if I could be his wife."

"We will discuss this later," Kol said, the muscle in his jaw rolling back and forth.

He turned to Mikoh and said something in his own language. I gasped when the translator didn't give it to me in English, and I knew straight away that Kol disconnected my translator with his comm again.

"Hey!" I said, frowning. "It's rude to talk in front of me using words I don't understand."

Kol ignored me as he continued to speak with Mikoh in a heated tone until Mikoh grunted and nodded once. Kol turned backed to me then, and he looked mad. No, scratch that, he looked pained.

"You're dismissed, Nova."

I blinked. "I'm dismissed?"

Kol nodded. "You sought out my forgiveness, and you now have it."

"Well, yeah, but—"

"But what?"

I swallowed. "You're one of three Maji who I'm comfortable with being around."

"Four, if you include Vorah, which you have," Kol responded.

I flinched. "Don't be mad at me, Kol. I'm trying to fall in line and do what's expected of me."

"I'm not mad," he replied. "I'm happy you agreed to Maji terms for sanctuary."

He didn't look like he was happy.

"It's not like that, though," I explained. "Vorah understands that I—"

"I don't want to speak of this anymore, Nova," he clipped. "Vorah is *not* going to be your intended."

I leaned back.

"Why the hell not?" I demanded.

"Because I have declared it!"

I jumped at the volume of Kol's voice, but instead of leaning into him for the comfort he provided before, I stepped away from him.

"You're to return to your quarters and meet with no males unless it is myself, Mikoh, or Nero."

I felt my lower lip wobble, but I refused to cry.

"What did I do wrong that Vorah—"

"Nova, enough!"

Kol was spitting mad. I could practically feel the anger radiate from him in waves. I took a hearty step backwards and swallowed. I didn't know him well enough—virtually at all—to reassure myself that he wouldn't attack me no matter how much I was told that Maji didn't harm women.

"Yes, sir," I said, trying my best to keep my voice even. "Thanks for your time. I won't bother you again."

I turned away from him and walked towards the exit of the bridge. I didn't dare look at Mikoh or anyone else, for that matter. I kept my eyes straight ahead until the doorway opened and gave me a view of the hallway. The empty hallway.

"Nova," Kol's said from behind me, his voice still thick with anger. "Mikoh will escort you back to your quarters … I will speak to you about this matter later."

He wasn't threatening me; he was promising me … and I'd be damned if it didn't have the same effect.

CHAPTER EIGHT

The Maji way.

I had been in the company of the Maji for three full days—though I was unconscious for nearly two of them—and all I had heard about was the Maji way this, the Maji way that, and it was driving me up the damn wall. Hearing about the Maji way from the Maji themselves was annoying after a while. Their customs were too bizarre to comprehend, but having to be subjected to it from humans as well was simply too much for me to deal with.

With my eyes closed, I gritted my teeth as Envi, my unwelcome roommate, chatted to her sister, Echo, my other unwelcome roommate, about the Maji way, and I could feel that I would break my word to Kol about not attacking the sisters if this continued to be the daily topic of conversation.

"Don't you ever *shut up*?" I hissed to Envi, keeping my eyes closed. "People are trying to *sleep*."

I wasn't trying to sleep. I was feigning sleep just so the sisters, mainly Envi, wouldn't be tempted to speak to me. I didn't trust them, and I knew they didn't trust me, so it was either pretend to be asleep or stare at them until they fell asleep. I was lying on my bed, my back tight against the oddly warm wall, and my body turned to the right so if I heard a noise, or felt a presence close to me, I could open my eyes and see everything I needed to.

"I'm sorry, Nova," Envi said softly. "I didn't mean to disturb you."

"Don't apologise to *her*. You weren't doing a damn thing wrong." Echo huffed. "This is *our* room, too!"

"Don't remind me," I grumbled to myself but knew that the sisters could hear me.

"If you've got something to say, Nova, then spit it out."

This was from Echo, and without opening my eyes, I knew she had stood, her challenge obvious in her tone. I kept my eyes closed just to show her how little of a threat I thought she was even though part of me was extremely wary of her. She had a sister, someone she loved and was willing do anything to protect, and that made her even more dangerous. People with something or someone to lose would do just about anything to ensure its safety.

"I've got nothing to say," I said, yawning for good measure. "I just wanna sleep."

"You're not sleeping, and you damn well know it," Echo quipped. "Your breathing isn't even, and your body is too tense for sleep. I'm not stupid enough not to see what's right in front of me."

Well, shit. The cranky twin is more perceptive than I gave her credit for.

I slowly opened my eyes and looked directly at Echo who was standing up next to her bed with her hands balled into fists at her side, showcasing how pissed she was. Envi was sitting on her bed, but she kept flicking her eyes back and forth between Echo and myself like we were going to come to blows at any second.

"Sit down, Echo," I said as firmly as I could. "I'm not interested in arguing."

"Are you sure?" she quizzed. "You seem like your fixing for a fight to me."

I rolled my eyes. "I'm sure."

"Well, tough. Get your ass up," she all but growled. "I *told* you not to scare my sister again."

"I'm not scared," Envi quickly shouted and jumped to her feet. "Lay off, Echo. I'm *not* scared."

"Bullshit," Echo snapped, still focused on me as I sat upright on my bed. "You've been walking on eggshells since that big Maji fellow brought her back here a few hours ago, and I'm not having you scared of the Maji and certainly not from this bitch."

Unwillingly, I stood from my bed, knowing exactly where this was heading. Envi and Echo were only a few years younger than I was, but it might as well have been decades. I was wise enough to know when to avoid a fight. Heck, I made running and hiding my entire life, but it seemed the twins didn't.

"Think about this," I said, flexing my fingers. "We don't have to fight."

"When you scare and disrespect my blood, we do."

I was surprised at how quickly Echo moved. She stood on Envi's bed and literally jumped at me with her arms extended. Envi was screaming hysterically before Echo even crashed into me, but as soon as her body hit mine and we flew backwards onto my bed, her volume increased.

"Help!" she screamed just as pain exploded across my face, and the metallic twang of blood filled my mouth. "Somebody help!"

All bets were off as I focused on Echo, who was straddling me with her arm raised and hand fisted as she threw another punch at my face. Venting my anger, confusion, and helplessness from the past three days, I unleashed it on Echo.

With a grunt, I rolled us over and pinned her under me before she could hit me again. I quickly slammed my fist into her face. I ignored the pain that shot up my arm and delivered two more quick punches, hitting Echo's jaw twice. I used my free hand to tangle in her hair, so I could keep her head still. I rasped in pain when her knee smashed into my side, knocking the air out of me. I applied all my weight on her to keep her from using her limbs as weapons, but the crazy bitch switched things up and head butted me. I saw stars for a few seconds before I turned to the side and rammed my elbow into her temple, dazing her.

Envi's panicked screams broke through my clouded mind, and I yelped when I felt my head being yanked back. The force of it pulled me clean off Echo and the bed and resulted in me hitting the floor with a mighty *thud*. I groaned in pain but opened my eyes to focus on the twins. Envi was the one who had grabbed my hair and pulled me off the bed, but it was only so she could get me off her sister. I knew that the second Envi went to Echo's aid instead of jumping on me.

I looked to my right when the door to the room opened and two male Maji hustled inside. I knew there would be no more fighting, so I closed my eyes and let my head fall back to the floor. I gripped my left side and silently cursed when pain pulsed with each breath I took. It didn't take a genius to figure out that Echo had cracked a couple of my ribs. The pain from it overwhelmed the throbbing on my face.

I heard rushed talking when Envi stopped screaming; she was still pretty hysterical as she shouted at the males, though. I opened my eyes and saw a familiar face was hovering over mine, and I tried my best to smile without wincing.

"Hey, Vorah."

He touched my face, and I hissed in pain which only caused *his* face to scrunch up in what appeared to be anger.

"You fought bravely, Nova," he said with a firm nod. "You fought with honour; your opponents did not."

How does he know how I fought?

"Thanks," I hissed as I moved. "I guess."

"You're a fierce female," Vorah continued.

He looked at me with so much admiration that I honestly felt gutted we couldn't go on a date to see if we liked one another. Kol, prince dick, made sure of that with his orders.

"I can't be your intended," I told him, gripping my side. "Kol forbid it."

Vorah's shoulders slumped. "I know. My prince requested an audience with me not long after our first meeting."

Worry surged through me, and it was only then that I noticed the discolouration to different parts of Vorah's face.

"He didn't hurt you, did he?" I asked, swallowing down the blood that filled my mouth.

Vorah didn't respond to me, but his expressive face answered for him. Kol had harmed Vorah for doing what the Maji were supposed to do—seek human females to be their wives.

"I'm going to kick his ass!" I swore.

Vorah smiled. "You truly are a mighty female."

"I don't feel very mighty right now," I admitted.

He frowned. "You were attacked without honour and could not defend yourself when the small female with yellow hair grabbed your hair from behind. Do not feel bad."

I blinked a couple of times. "How did you know Envi pulled my hair?"

Vorah pointed up at the blank ceiling. "Motion capture."

Motion capture.

I widened my eyes. "There's a *camera* in here?"

Vorah nodded. "Of course. How can we make sure human females are safe if we cannot see them?"

I didn't know how to answer that, so I remained mute.

"Are you angry?" Vorah asked me, his purple eyes scanning my face. "You look angry."

"I'm not angry," I assured him. "Just annoyed that I wasn't informed of the lack of privacy."

Vorah bobbed his head in understanding. "We don't track our females back home; it is only aboard the *Ebony* to protect human females until both Maji and humans are known to the other. And to make sure you humans play nice."

I understood the need for security, but it'd have been nice to be informed. Years of survival and the need to know every single little thing about my surroundings meant it was hard for me to hand over the reins to someone else where my safety was concerned, but I'd have to if I wanted to fit in with the Maji.

"It's okay, Vorah." I winced when my ribs screamed in protest of my breathing. "I just need to get to the medical bay. Is Surkah still working?"

"I'm unaware of my princess's schedule," he said, his face flushing pink.

I wanted to smile at how he reacted to my question about Surkah, but I couldn't because black dots began to spot my vision.

"Oh, shit," I murmured. "I'm gonna pass out."

Vorah's eyes widened, and aloud, he said, "My prince, she is losing consciousness. Permission to carry her to the med bay?"

I heard the door to the room slide open.

"Permission denied," Kol's voice almost growled.

I cried out when arms slid under my knees and neck and lifted me into the air. My ribs throbbed in protest, and I was pretty sure I was going to get sick.

"I have you, *shiva*," Kol's voice whispered seconds before I blacked out. "I have you."

I found more comfort in those words than I should have.

I awoke with a start.

Unlike the times before when I suddenly awoke from a dreamless sleep, I wasn't confused. I was aware of where I was, whose company I kept, and what had happened to me. I sprung into an upright position and instantly brought my hands to my ribs. I waited for the bone-crushing pain to consume me, but I felt nothing, not even a twinge of discomfort. I softly pressed on my ribs before rolling up my t-shirt and examining my bruise-free skin. No trace of my ribs ever being injured existed, and I knew who I had to thank for that. I lowered my t-shirt and exhaled a deep breath.

"Surkah."

"Yes?"

I screamed and instinctively covered my head with my arms to protect it.

"I'm sorry," Surkah's rushed out. "You said my name."

I lowered my hands and pressed them against my chest as Surkah stood a few feet away from me, mirroring my actions. It seemed I wasn't the only one who got a fright.

"It's okay," I said, trying to calm my rapid breathing. "I wasn't calling for you. I was thinking of you when I noticed my ribs were healed, and I guess I just said your name out loud without realising it."

Surkah lowered her hands to her side. "I healed you quickly. You had three nasty breaks and a couple of cracked ribs too."

I rubbed my healed ribs.

"Yeah." I snorted. "They felt pretty messed up."

"You harmed the human female greater if it helps your pride?" Surkah offered. "Her left eye socket was shattered, and her jaw was severely broken. It took longer to heal her."

That didn't make me feel better at all.

I winced. "I didn't mean to do that ... but she attacked me."

Surkah nodded. "Kol informed me of the incident. It is why we have separated you from the other humans. You don't have to share a quarters with them anymore."

Kol.

"Where *is* your brother?"

"The bridge." Surkah shrugged like that was an obvious place to find him.

"Can you call him for me?" I asked politely. "I need to speak to him."

I needed to find out why he attacked poor Vorah, and if he would kick me off his ship for attacking Echo when he gave me an order to leave her and her sister alone.

"I have already hailed him," Surkah said, blushing. "He ordered me to do so when you awoke."

I nodded but said nothing.

Surkah wrung her hands together, and after a minute of silence, she said, "Will you be my friend again?"

I wanted to correct her and tell her we weren't true friends in the first place, but I didn't.

"Why?" I asked with my shoulders slumped. "I'm not exactly good company."

I was miserable to be around if I was being honest with myself.

"I care for you greatly," Surkah said. "I have bonded with you very fast."

She said that to me the last time we spoke, too.

"Would you have lied to me if Kol hadn't ordered you to do so?"

"No," Surkah said instantly. "I would not have."

Surkah's face was too expressive for me not to see the truth in her words.

"I believe you," I said. "And I do want to be your friend, but I just don't know how to be a good one. I'm not very good with others … as you already know. I'll try my best, though, so yes, if you want me as your friend, you've got me as your friend."

Surkah let out a little cry as she quickly crossed the room and gathered me in her arms.

"I am so glad, Nova."

I was a little hesitant, but when I put my arms around Surkah, it felt right.

"I am too," I told her, and I meant the words. "I'm very sorry for upsetting you."

"It was I who upset you, so I deserved your anger."

We only separated when the door to the room opened. When my eyes landed on Kol, I narrowed them almost instantly.

"You're a huge bully; do you know that?"

Kol looked over his shoulder to—surprise—Mikoh and said, "What did I do now?"

"To annoy that female, your heart beating would surely do it." He grinned.

I scowled at Mikoh, and so did Surkah.

"Why are you upset with me?" Kol asked, regaining my attention.

I scoffed. "Do you want the list?"

He raised his brows. "There is a list?"

I rolled my eyes.

"You beat up Vorah, who is only a kid and was doing your bidding by searching for an intended, you shouted at me on the bridge and that both upset and scared me, and then you put me back in a room with Echo—who attacked *me* by the way. I wasn't exactly innocent in the build-up, but I didn't throw the first punch either."

"Why do you care what happens to Vorah?" Kol growled. "He is *not* your intended."

I gaped at him.

"Out of everything I just said, you focus on *that*?"

Kol growled at me once more, and I fought off the urge to throttle him.

"You're the most trying person ... being ... *Maji* I have ever met!"

"Do you care for Vorah?" Kol pressed.

I face palmed. "You're unbelievable, Kol."

"Answer me!" he demanded.

"I care for him as I would a new *friend*!" I angrily shouted. "I don't know him at all, but he seems very sweet, and he didn't do anything wrong, but you still hurt him. It's not right, Kol. You can't just hurt someone because their motives don't suit yours!"

Kol's stared at me, his expression hard.

"It is the Maji way to challenge a male for the intention of a female."

I sucked in a breath. "Excuse me?"

He was *not* saying what I thought he was saying!

"You gave your verbal consent to test a bond with Vorah, and I had to challenge him and beat him to break that consent and restore your status."

"My status?" I repeated. "My status as *what*?"

"A single female."

"Hold on a second," I said and held my hand in the air as I stood from the medical bay bed. "You beat up Vorah to break my consent to marry him? Is *that* what you're saying?"

"That's *exactly* what he's saying," Surkah murmured from my side.

"How can that be legal?" I shouted. "It's up to me who I pick as a husband, right?"

"Yes." Kol nodded. "But if another male challenges your intended male and wins, then the challenger wins your intention."

"That is barbaric!" I shouted.

Kol shrugged. "It is the Maji way."

"I can't believe this," I said with a shake of my head. "Are you telling me that you are my ... intended?"

Kol smiled. "Yes."

My heart slammed into my chest as I sat down.

"No!" I bellowed. "No, you will *not* take another choice from me. I picked Vorah!"

"And I beat him!" Kol snarled, the smile vanishing from his face. "I could have killed him to end the intention, but I didn't because I knew *he* didn't know that *I* had the intention of having you."

I had to sit back down on the bed by the time he finished speaking because I had a strong feeling I would have otherwise collapsed on the floor at his declaration.

"Since *when* did you have an intention for me?"

"Since the very moment I first laid eyes on you, and you fainted before me."

That was almost romantic, but I refused to admit that. I got up from the bed, spun away from Kol, and hugged myself with my arms.

"You're a *prince*," I reminded him. "Shouldn't you be married to a nice noble Maji female?"

"Nova—"

"Won't your parents, your society, expect the royals to keep their bloodlines pure?" I pressed.

"You let me handle my parents and the people."

That meant yes.

I swallowed. "I don't know if I can do this."

I noticed that Surkah had moved away from me, and when hands touched my shoulders, I knew they weren't hers.

"I will be a good mate," Kol said softly. "I will care for you, I will provide for you, and I will make you happy. Just ... just give me a chance, *shiva*."

My eyes welled with tears.

"I've been so horrible," I cried. "Why do you want an awful human like me?"

He turned me to face him and swiped his thumbs under my eyes.

"Because I have never known a female so fierce or one with so much pride. Because I have never seen true beauty until my eyes rested on you. Because you challenge me, fight me, and treat me like a regular male and not a prince of the people. Because your stubbornness matches mine, and because I have never wanted a female in my two hundred years the way I want you, *shiva*."

I brought my arms around his waist and pressed my forehead against the top of his stomach.

"I'm so scared, Kol."

I'm terrified that I have growing feelings for you.

He tipped my chin up until I was looking into his eyes.

"I will take your fear away. I promise, *shiva*."

I licked my lower lip. "What does that mean?"

"What does what mean?"

"*Shiva*," I said. "You've called me it a few times."

"I hadn't realised I have been calling you it"—Kol blinked—"but the closet words in your language are 'my treasure'."

I sucked in a breath. "That's so sweet."

Kol smiled down at me and brought both his hands to my face where he stroked his thumbs over my cheeks.

"Will you accept me as your intended?" he asked me, his voice soft.

I squeezed his waist. "I thought you won the right to be my intended?"

"I did." Kol grinned. "But I'm learning that you want to make some decisions instead of them being made for you."

Butterflies exploded in my stomach.

"I've never had a boyfriend," I whispered. "I've never … never known anything about being intimate with a man. I've never even *kissed* one."

"It will be my honour to teach you, *shiva*," Kol murmured as he lowered his head to mine.

His lips barely touched mine before Mikoh said, "We need to get to the bridge. If warp is not activated soon, we will lose time."

Kol growled so deep in his throat I felt it on my lips.

"Kiss your intended later, friend. We have work to do."

Kol turned to face his friend.

"I give the orders, Mikoh," Kol snarled. "Not you."

Without warning, Kol surged forward and smashed his fist into Mikoh's face, and before I had time to verbally react, Surkah was on her brother's back and was biting down on his shoulder. Kol's roar was deafening, but either he scented Surkah or knew with his mental comm thing that it was her, because other than letting out a roar, he didn't make a move to remove her from his body. He didn't make a move to touch her at all.

Surkah was growling, and I noticed it wasn't only her teeth sunk into Kol's flesh, but her nails were also all imbedded into Kol's skin. I winced for him, knowing how much it had to hurt. I moved towards Kol and Surkah, but a warning growl from him kept rooted me to the spot. Mikoh was already on his feet and moving towards Kol with his eyes on Surkah. I was suddenly so scared they would both team up and hurt Kol, and before I knew it, tears fell from my eyes and hiccups tore free from my throat.

"Come," Mikoh purred to Surkah. "Come to me, *faya*."

Surkah reacted like she was an android. She released Kol—who didn't even wince— and grabbed Mikoh's hand and pulled herself flush against his body. He stroked her back as she nudged his chest with her face and gripped his arms with her hands. Surkah didn't really look like Surkah; her eyes were charcoal black, and she looked like she was acting on instinct when she saw Kol hit Mikoh in a way that was not playful.

This must be the edge thing they mentioned.

"Leave," Kol ordered the pair. "We will be on the bridge in two minutes."

Without a word, Mikoh and Surkah left the med bay, and Kol turned to face me. I stopped a step away from him, not out of fear, but out of worry.

"Why did you do that?" I asked, wiping my tears away.

He rolled his neck onto his shoulders.

"Mikoh questioned me."

"So you punched him?"

"It is the—"

"Maji way," I finished. "Yeah, I know."

"Why do you cry?" he asked, frowning.

"I thought they were going to gang up on you, and it scared me."

"*Shiva.*" Kol rumbled with laughter. "Surkah attacks me at least three times a month when I hit Mikoh. Her instincts as his intended force it. Their bond is so close to being in place that they may as well have already mated. You have much to learn about the people."

I most definitely did.

Kol stepped towards me, and it was at that moment that I realised we were alone, and apprehension gripped me.

To drive the mood toward conversation, I asked. "Do you have cameras in all the humans' rooms?"

Kol blinked at my question but nodded. "Of course, we can't have a male assigned to every human, so monitoring you seems the best way to keep you safe."

I dropped my gaze to my hands.

"We want to give you freedom aboard the *Ebony*, and we don't want to scare humans any more than they already are, so motion capture was a good option."

"I never said they weren't," I mumbled.

"You never said they were, either," Kol countered.

I sighed and looked up at him. "I would have just appreciated it if you told me about them. I feel weird knowing Maji security were watching me."

Kol raised a brow. "Maji *Elite* weren't watching you. I was."

My pulse spiked. "Excuse me?"

"I had the feed from your quarters transferred to my comm so I could ... keep an eye on you."

My heart started to beat fast.

"Did you do that with other c-camera feeds?" I stammered.

"No," he said, his lips turned up in a half smile. "Just yours."

It was idiotic for pleasure to rush through me with that knowledge, but I couldn't help but like that Kol singled me out to watch over. Echo and Envi suddenly invaded my thoughts and ruined the joy I felt.

"Because you were afraid I'd hurt Echo and Envi?" I asked, not being able to stop myself from frowning.

"No." Kol chuckled, crossing the space between us to tip my chin up with his finger. "To make sure you were in no danger from them."

"They're skinny little kids," I scowled. "They weren't a threat to me."

Kol dropped his eyes to my ribs, and I gritted my teeth.

"My ribs were a minor setback," I stated. "I was handling Echo … It was Envi who caught me off guard."

Kol's lips quirked. "I know, I saw the fight through my comm, remember?"

That's right. He did see the fight.

"Did you send Vorah and the other male to help?"

Kol tensed. "They were the closest males to your room. I allowed them access to the feed, so they knew what they were rushing in on."

He really didn't like when I mentioned Vorah or something about him.

"Are you going to kick me off the ship for breaking your rule about not harming the twins?" I questioned. "Because if you are, I'd be much obliged if you touched back down on the Earth's surface *before* you do so."

Amusement flashed through Kol's eyes.

"I was thinking of changing your quarters, so you weren't around other humans at all."

Hope surged through me.

"Oh, yes, please," I practically burst. "I'll get better with having company in time, I promise."

Kol folded his thick arms over his broad chest.

"I'm sure you will."

I beamed at him. "I'm getting my own quarters?"

"Not exactly."

I furrowed my brows. "But you said I wouldn't be around other humans."

"And you won't be." Kol nodded.

"Who will I be around then?"

Kol leaned his head down to mine, stopping mere inches from his lips touching mine.

"I'll give you *one* guess," he whispered.

A shudder ran through me.

"Y-you?"

Kol winked. "Clever human."

I sucked in a deep breath.

"I ... I'm going to be staying wi-with ... with you?"

Kol laughed. "You looked terrified."

I am because I know exactly where this is headed.

"I'm not," I lied. "I just don't understand why you want me to stay with you."

"Yes, you do."

I felt heat stain my cheeks.

"Give me your answer," he said as his eyes started to glow.

I knew what answer he was referring to.

"I'm worried you'll regret asking me," I nervously admitted. "For your kind, marriage is for life, and I don't want you to regret me."

"I'll never regret you," Kol said, a hint of a growl in his tone. "*Never.*"

My mind was screaming at me to accept for two reasons. One, being with Kol, a royal prince of the Maji, would ensure my safety, and my safety was my number one priority. Two, I could no longer deny I was attracted to him, and if I had to mate a Maji, I wanted it to be with a male who I would willingly want to touch and have touch me in return. Even though it killed me to admit it, Kol was the only Maji I wanted that type of intimacy with. He was captivating to me.

With my heart slamming into my chest, I whispered, "Yes."

"Yes?" Kol repeated.

"Yes." I nodded. "I'll be your intended."

Kol suddenly picked me up off the ground and pressed my back against the wall. His lips covered mine as he gifted me my first kiss, a kiss that he claimed with assertiveness. It was a kiss of promise … a promise of so much more to come.

CHAPTER NINE

"You're going to be my sister-in-mate, Nova."

I looked at Surkah, and I couldn't help but beam at her. It had been only a few hours since she found out about me being Kol's intended, and she was happier than anyone about it.

"I hope I am up to your royal standards," I joked.

Surkah snorted. "Despite what the people believe, we don't set our standards *that* high."

I widened my eyes, and Surkah's face flushed purple.

"That came out sounding wrong," she blurted. "Oh, forgive me. I didn't mean *you* are a low standard; I only meant—"

I cut her off with joyous laughter, and after a few seconds, she shoved my shoulder but laughed, too.

"You tease too much!" She scowled, but her eyes gleamed with amusement.

I chuckled. "You don't have to worry about offending me so much; things are bound to get lost in translation between us from time to time."

Surkah nodded. "I know, but I fear I will speak out of turn, and Kol will ban us from speaking. He won't allow me to speak to you if I upset you."

I felt my jaw drop. "He'd really do that?"

Surkah bobbed her head.

"My father forbids my aunt-in-mate, his brother's mate, and my mother from speaking to each other because they always argue no matter what the topic of conversation is. They even once fought, and when my father separated them, he had to roughly pull on my aunt's arm to stop her from beating on my mother, and it sent my uncle straight to the edge at the sight of his brother not only handling his mate but also handling her roughly, so he attacked my father, and they fought viciously. Ten of my brothers were alive at that point, and it took seven of them to separate them. Since that day, my aunt and mother haven't spoken. It's been close to two hundred years, and they live in the same palace and see each other daily but act like the other doesn't exist."

I gasped. "Oh, my Almighty!"

Surkah smiled. "You seem shocked."

"I am." I nodded. "That is just unbelievable, and it's just *another* thing for me to worry about with Kol."

"Why is it a worry?"

I felt my own cheeks stain with heat.

"I don't know if you noticed," I murmured, "but I don't exactly follow orders all that well."

Surkah smirked. "I think everyone has noticed."

I playfully shoved her shoulder, making her giggle.

"I'm serious," I continued. "What if I mess up all the time? I don't know the Maji way, and now I'm promised to marry a *prince*. I don't think you all understand how low ranked I am in Earth's society. I just ... I don't want to be a disappointment to Kol *or* your people."

"*The* people," Surkah corrected. "The moment you agreed to be my brother's intended, you became one of the people. You're a Maji, Nova. The funniest looking one I have *ever* seen."

Surkah's teasing caused me to laugh loudly, and it drew the attention of the males on the bridge around us, though they never looked directly at us. I blushed deeper and tried to hide my face, but Surkah wouldn't let me.

"Don't be shy." She chuckled. "Males won't speak to you or look at you now that you have such a status. You're going to be a princess of the people, you know?"

I felt like the ground fell away beneath me.

"A princess?" I questioned incredulously. "*Me?*"

I tried to imagine myself in the best of clothes, in the best of accommodations, spending time with the noblest of people, smiling, being bowed to and fawned over … and I felt sick at the very thought of it. Surkah nodded happily, oblivious to my internal meltdown.

"Kol is a prince," she stated. "And as his intended, you will become a princess the moment your bond is sealed."

I lifted my hands to my face and groaned into them.

"This is *so* much to absorb," I grumbled. "It's actually starting to hurt my head a bit."

"The ache is just a side effect of the warp, and that will pass soon," Surkah assured me and patted my arm in a gesture of comfort. "You aren't used to space travel, and though I'm *not* saying you're weak, humans just aren't as resilient as us Maji are."

"You can say that again," I mumbled, rubbing my fingers in circular motions on my temples.

A few hours ago, after I had agreed to be his intended, Kol gathered all the human women aboard and directed them to the sector of the *Ebony* called the concourse. A section of that room opened into a massive viewing pane that overlooked the Earth. He and the other Maji paid their respects to our soon-to-be fallen planet and the people on the surface who were doomed with it. Kol allowed us humans to grieve our planet with the comfort of other women and gifted us one last look at our home because we all knew we would never see it again.

Not long after that, we set off on course to Ealra, the planet that would soon become our new home world. When the warp was activated, I got so lightheaded that I thought I would pass out for the hundredth time in a matter of days. Kol felt it was necessary for me to sit on his lap until I felt better enough to sit with Surkah. He overlooked the piloting from the shipmaster's chair on the bridge of the *Ebony*, and when he wasn't looking, *I* was overlooking *him*.

I felt like I was in a dream.

Days ago, I was wandering one of the many barren wastelands of Earth half-starved and dirty to the bone. I was just trying my best to survive, and now I was under the care of a royal alien who had claimed me as his future wife. I had a tummy full of great food, and there wasn't a speck of dirt in sight nor a hint of body odour. It was a dramatic upgrade, and despite my behaviour, I was indebted to the Maji for their care of my people and the future they offered us, but that didn't mean it wasn't hard to become accustomed to the many changes I was going through.

I suddenly had a family again; people who didn't even really know me cared for me and treated me like I was someone special. I went from being on my own twenty-four seven and never trusting anyone to giggling with my future sister-in-law, and stealing glances at my future husband when I knew he was distracted. I didn't know whether to feel incredibly lucky to be blessed with such a change in circumstances or like a complete idiot for considering fairy tales like this happened to a woman like me—a killer—and had a happy ending.

"You're thinking hard, *shiva*."

Goosebumps broke out over my skin the second his voice rolled over me.

"I do that a lot," I told him.

I shivered when his hand curled around the nape of my neck. Surkah said goodbye to me as she stood, placed her hand on her chest, and bowed her head to her brother before she left with Mikoh as her escort. Everyone, barring Kol, gave her the same respectful bow she showed her brother as she left the bridge.

"Anything you want to ask me?" Kol asked, putting my focus back on him.

To amuse him and his crew, I said, "Can I fly the craft?"

Everyone went silent around us.

Kol snorted. "No, you cannot *pilot* the craft."

"Why not?" I quizzed. "I'd probably be great at it."

"Or really bad at it."

I ignored his teasing and the chuckles from his crew.

"We'll never know until you let me fly it."

"Then we'll never know."

I huffed and folded my arms across my chest.

"I'll wear you down eventually."

Kol laughed, and I saw some of his crew members shake their heads with smiles on their faces as they got back to work. I liked that. I liked that they just accepted me as Kol's intended, and I liked that my teasing could amuse them. They were the people, and I really wanted them to like me.

"Are you ready to retire for the night?" he asked, his fingers softly brushing the sweet spot on my neck.

I gasped from both the action and his words.

"It's night-time already?"

I was exhausted and had fought for hours to remain awake, but knowing I would be *sleeping* with Kol kept me on the edge of consciousness. We were going to share a room, and I knew that meant we'd share a bed.

"It is," Kol replied, a hint of laughter in his tone.

"Oh." I flushed from head to toe. "I am *very* tired, and I *still* have a bit of a headache."

Kol raised a brow. "It sounds like you need a lot of rest, my little human."

"Rest." I repeatedly nodded my head. "So much rest."

Kol extended his hand to me and waited. I clenched my hands a couple of times before I lifted my shaking hand and placed it in Kol's steady one.

"Nova," he murmured as he tugged me to my feet.

"Yes?" I whispered, placing my free hand on his armoured sleeve.

He brushed lose strands of hair from my face. "I won't touch you intimately without consent. Please do not be afraid because we will share furs. I will be the perfect male. I won't even sneak a peek when you're undressing."

I choked on air, and it caused laughter to rumble from Kol.

"I swear on my honour not to touch you," he continued.

That's interesting.

Vorah also swore on his honour when I asked if we could go slow in our forbidden bonding. I was beginning to gather that was the Maji way of giving your word to someone. On Earth, amongst humans, your word was only as good as the person who spoke it, but to the Maji, it seemed to be a real badge of honour. As if their self-worth was on the line if they went back on their word. I liked it. I liked how much pride was in Kol's voice when he swore on his honour. I knew a Maji like him had plenty of honour, and to swear on it wasn't something to be taken lightly.

"Okay, Kol," I said, softly. "I ... I trust you."

I hadn't spoken those words to another being since my father was alive, and what was more shocking was that I meant them. In many ways, Kol was still a stranger to me. I knew next to nothing about him, but a part of me felt safer with him than I ever had in my entire life. My gut told me I could trust him, and I always trusted my gut. It hadn't steered me wrong yet.

"I value your trust, *shiva*."

I smiled up at him, and an expression of shock and ... longing crossed his face.

"What is it?" I asked, concerned.

He moved his hand from my neck to cup my cheek.

"You're beautiful when scowling," he murmured, rubbing his thumb over my skin. "But when you smile? Thanas. You take my breath away, *shiva*."

Never in my entire life had I had the urge to kiss another person, but the need to kiss Kol at that moment flowed like the blood through my veins.

"Kol," I rasped.

He closed his eyes and growled.

"Do not say my name in that needy voice," he said, his voice almost pleading. "I am only a male, *shiva*."

I surprised us both when I giggled.

Kol opened his eyes and stared down at me. "Shall we retire?"

I exhaled a deep breath. "Yes, Shipmaster."

Kol's lips twitched. "I think this is the first time you have complied with my request."

"The second," I teased. "The first time I complied was when I agreed to be your intended."

His smile was a thing of beauty.

"My intended," he murmured.

I heard a noise behind me, and I almost instantly remembered we were on the bridge of the *Ebony* with the bridge crew all around us. I felt my body flush with embarrassment from head to toe.

Kol laughed. "Come."

He spoke some last orders to his crew, and I jumped a little when, in unison, the males pressed their right arm to their chests and bowed their head in respect to their shipmaster and prince.

"I'll never get used to that," I whispered to myself.

"Trust me." Kol chuckled as we left the bridge. "You will. I barely notice it anymore."

I was very aware of him next to me as we walked and extremely aware of his arm around my shoulder. I was too short for Kol to walk comfortably with his arm around my waist, so he opted for slinging his arm around my shoulder, and it felt ... natural. As if he'd done it a million times before. That was another thing for me to freak out about. Everything with Kol was brand new, yet things with him felt old as time. It was like I knew him.

I didn't understand it.

"This is our quarters."

I blinked when Kol spoke, and I quickly realised we were no longer walking. I glanced around the hallway and saw males patrolling. I hadn't even noticed when we passed them as my thoughts were too consumed with a different male. I looked forward when the door to Kol's room opened, and I felt my mouth drop when I stepped inside.

"Holy moly." I whistled. "This is *nice*."

It was at least ten times the size of the room I had shared with Echo and Envi. There was a gigantic round bed in the centre of the room, and it was dressed in golden coloured linen and thick white ... furs. It had more pillows than what seemed necessary, and I knew I'd have a problem messing it up by sleeping on something that looked like it should remain untouched.

"The shipmaster's quarters are always more luxurious than the crew's quarters," Kol said from behind me. "I'm personally against it, and until now, I haven't stayed in here."

That surprised me.

"Why not?" I asked, stepping farther into the room.

"Why should I stay in luxury while my crew got basic accommodations? I'm no better than they are."

I turned to face him. "You're the *shipmaster*."

And a prince.

"More reason for me to stay in basic quarters. I already get more pay than my crew, and my job garners more respect, but without my crew, the *Ebony* does not fly."

"That's very noble of you, but surely, your life has always been luxury ... I mean, you're a royal."

Kol shrugged. "That's another reason I like being on the *Ebony*. Less Maji mean less of the people who treat me like I'm some sort of …"

"Prince?" I finished.

Kol's lips twitched. "Yes."

"You don't like being royalty?"

"I never said that," he mused. "It is a blessing from Thanas to be a part of the head family of the people. I just like a break sometimes, and my craft gives me that escape."

I nodded. "I can understand that."

Kol glanced around the room. "I will stay in the best of accommodations on the *Ebony* and off now that you're my intended. I assure you."

I raised my brow. "Kol, if you want to stay in basic quarters, we can stay there. I thought the medical bay was beautiful when I first saw it. Anything will be an upgrade from what I was used to on Earth."

"It is for that reason I want to show you all the beauty of Ealra and give you the best of everything. You will never know poverty by my side, Nova. I swear on my honour."

A ghost of a smile graced my lips.

"So … we're staying here then?"

"Yes." Kol nodded.

I turned and stared at the bed in the centre of the room, and I was delighted that it was so large. I had to lie next to Kol while we slept, but the chance that I could scoot away and have my own space slightly calmed my spiked nerves.

"You're scared?" Kol murmured from behind me. "Why?"

I closed my eyes. "I'm not exactly scared … just nervous."

"Because you will lay with me?"

I tensed.

"Yes," I whispered.

"You remember my oath?"

I do.

"Yes, you swore on your honour not to touch me."

Unless I give consent.

"And you still feel fear? Why? An honour oath is everything to the people."

I opened my eyes and turned to face Kol, not surprised to find him within arm's reach.

"I don't doubt your word," I said softly. "I said I trust you, and I do. I haven't trusted a person in a very long time. I know you have the best intentions for me, and I know you will keep your word, but I still can't help but be nervous. I've never slept with a man before. I mean ... you were my first kiss."

Kol lifted his hand to my face and cupped my flaming red cheek.

"I'm not a man, Nova. I am a male, a Maji warrior, an Elite, a prince ... but I am not human like you, and I never will be. Please separate Maji males from the bad human men you once knew. I will be the best mate to you. I will take away your nervousness, and in time, everything about me will feel natural to you, and you to me."

A breath of air left me.

"Thank you, Kol."

"If you want," he continued as he stroked his thumb over my cheek. "I will sleep on the floor while you take the bed. I do not want to share furs and make you uncomfortable."

I shivered but not with cold or nervousness.

"No," I said, touched by his offer. "We're to be married, and I want to get past this embarrassment before we reach your home world."

And meet your family.

"*Our* home world," he corrected.

It was nice of him to try to make us humans feel included, but personally, I couldn't call a planet I had no knowledge of days ago my home. I hoped in time that outlook would change.

"Where did you stay if tonight is your first night here?" I asked Kol, trying to focus on a normal conversation to set me more at ease.

Kol lowered his hand from my cheek, and I was surprised that the loss of his touch saddened me.

"I shared quarters with Mikoh, Nero, and Thane."

Thane?

"I don't think I've met Thane."

"You haven't," Kol said, his eyes roaming over me. "He is rarely out of the engine hall."

I gasped. "He is an engineer?"

Kol's eyes flicked back to mine.

"Yes," he said with a nod. "He is the chief engineer on the *Ebony*."

"Can I meet him?" I asked excitedly.

Kol's expression turned dark.

"No, you're *mine*."

Goosebumps spread across my body at his show of dominance.

"I'm interested in his job, not him."

I didn't know if it was my words that surprised me, or if it was the fact that I meant them.

"Why?" Kol pressed, not convinced. "Why would you be interested in a male's job?"

I rolled my eyes. "That is so damn sexist."

Kol furrowed his thick eyebrows. "I do not understand that word."

I snorted. "Of course, you don't. That's one word that won't be in Maji vocabulary."

Kol waited for me to continued speaking, so I did.

"Sexist means characterising a person based on their gender. This typically happens to women. You were sexist 'cause you implied being an engineer is not a job a woman can do... but you're wrong. Many women on Earth were engineers ... before the war."

"Were *you* an engineer?" Kol asked, and he looked as shocked as he sounded.

I would have been.

I snorted. "Not by trade, just by interest."

"But you wanted to be one by trade?"

I shrugged. "I was too young to be certified, but if the war hadn't happened, I'd have been well on my way to being one."

"Really?" Kol asked, not any less shocked.

"Yes. My father was an engineer, and he taught me many things … which is why I'm interested in meeting Thane. An engine hall is a place I am familiar with. A place where I am comfortable. Engines … put me at ease."

Kol growled, and I jumped with fright.

"Why're you growling?" I tentatively asked.

"Thane has a profession that impresses you … I will fight him if you smile at him or show interest in him."

My stomach lurched. "Are you serious?"

"As a heart attack," he all but snarled.

I blinked. "Kol, you can't just fight men—I mean males—I smile at."

"I can, and I will."

I didn't know why, but I laughed.

"This is *not* funny," Kol continued to growl. "Why are you laughing?"

"Because I am now part of a community of people who don't want to kill me, rape me, or sell me. I am one of the people, I am safe, and for the first time in my life, I have someone to keep me safe from all harm … and you're telling me I can't smile at anyone when smiling is all I want to do because I've never had any of this. Even when my father was alive, we lived day by day, but now … now I can imagine a future and not think myself a fool for doing so."

Kol's angry expression fled from his face, and compassion washed over him.

"I am sorry," he said. "I misunderstood."

I tilted my head to the side.

"I'm not angry with you," I assured him. "You aren't human, so you don't react to things the way I would. You have more animal instincts than not ... and I kind of like how possessive you are of me."

A rumble started at the back of Kol's throat, and it sounded like a rougher version of a purr.

"Does that sound mean you're happy, angry, or sad?"

He licked his lips, and the sight of it ignited a fire in my lower belly.

"It means I'm having lustful thoughts and would love nothing more than to act on them."

Oh.

"You're having lustful thoughts about me?"

"Since I met you, the only thoughts I have are of you, *shiva*."

My legs threatened to give way underneath me, and the fire in my belly seemed to be catching. Kol suddenly sniffed the air then his eyes fluttered closed when he inhaled deeply, and the rough purr rumbled louder this time.

"You're aroused," he rasped, his eyes opening and focusing on me. "The air is so thick with your scent I can almost taste you on my tongue."

I sucked in a startled breath and pressed my thighs together.

"I'm not ... You must be mistaken ... I ..."

"Nova," he purred. "I want to taste you."

If Kol hadn't surged forward and grabbed me when he did, I'd have probably dropped to the floor like dead weight.

"Give me permission, *shiva*," he whispered into my ear, licking the lobe. "Let me taste what is mine."

Almighty.

"You can't ... We're just supposed to sleep so you—"

"Will only have a small taste," Kol cut me off, his voice sounded deeper, huskier.

I suddenly felt lightheaded, and a fast-paced throbbing thrummed away between my thighs.

"Ealra," I squeaked, trying to regain my composure. "Tell me about Ealra, about your family, about *you*."

Hunger shone brightly in Kol's violet eyes but so did amusement.

"What would you like to know?" he asked, not releasing his tight hold on me.

"Everything," I blurted. "We're going to be married, so we should know everything about one another."

Kol's lips twitched.

"Okay, *shiva*," he rumbled. "Ask your questions, and I will reveal all there is to know about my home, my family, and me. Then I'll taste you."

I swallowed. "You'll answer all my questions?"

"Every. One."

I blinked and then asked a question that had been on my mind since I accepted Kol's offer to be his intended.

"I'm going to be your mate, and Surkah said that males are the lead Maji in each household … Does that mean you'll be the boss of me?"

At the teasing glint in Kol's eyes, I wasn't sure I wanted to know the answer to my question.

CHAPTER TEN

"You look scared, little one." Kol smirked.

His smirk might have been teasing, but the intensity in his eyes was anything but.

I swallowed. "I'm not scared of you, Kol."

I wasn't sure exactly when that happened, but my feelings towards Kol had changed. Fear was not something I felt towards him—not in the slightest—and like everything else, it freaked me out.

"Not scared of me?" he hummed, clearly amused. "Surely, a tiny female such as yourself knows an Elite warrior like myself can be *very* scary."

I lifted my chin. "I also know that you, a big, mighty warrior, will drop to your knees before me if I asked you to."

Kol's eyes locked on mine. "Is that so, *shiva*?"

"Yes," I replied, noting my voice wasn't as firm as I'd have liked it to be. "Surkah told me that a female mate is really the lead mate because her mate will do everything in his power to make her happy."

His lips twitched. "Surkah talks a lot."

I tensed. "So do I."

Sarcastically, he said, "I hadn't noticed."

At that, I laughed. Kol smiled too as he lifted an arm from around me so he could brush the tips of his fingers over my cheek. His eyes followed the trail his fingers made, and when he brushed them over my lips, he audibly swallowed. His face hardened, his body tensed, and his sharp teeth dug into his plump lower lip.

"You're supposed to be telling me about yourself," I reminded him, my voice barely a whisper.

Kol lowered his hand, removed his arm from around my body, and stepped back. He was still tense, still biting his lip, and he still gazed at me as if we wanted to eat me.

"Go to the bed so you can relax," he ordered, his hands flexing. "I will remain here and answer your questions."

I raised a brow. "Why don't you just come with me? It's a mighty big bed."

He growled in response.

"Okaaay." I exhaled.

I quickly turned, scurried across the room to the bed, and sat on the edge of it.

"Questions," Kol practically barked. "Ask them."

He is so bossy.

"Surkah said you come from a family of sixteen children," I began. "How many children did your parents have by the time you were born?"

"I am the twelfth born son," he answered. "I have eleven older brothers, three younger brothers, and one sister."

Wow.

"List everyone," I said, amazed that he had that many siblings. "In order of birth."

Amusement flashed in his violet eyes.

"Ryla, Silis, Kaiba, Aylee, Talin, Raze, Komi, Ezah, Killi, Arli, Arvi, me, Aza, Remi, Nesi, and Surkah." At my wide-eyed expression, he said, "Killi, Arli, and Arvi are from the same pregnancy, and Remi and Nesi are from the same pregnancy, too."

"*Triplets?*" I asked, amazed.

I had heard of such pregnancies happening in the past amongst humans, but I had never thought they were possible. I always thought my father and uncle were joking about multiple babies in a single pregnancy because they just didn't happen in the time I lived in. Echo and Envi were the first human twins I had ever met.

Kol blinked. "Yes, that is what my brothers are, but we don't have words for it like you do."

"What do you refer to them as then?" I wondered aloud.

"Three offspring and two offspring."

I giggled. "Maybe some human words should be adapted by the Maji."

"We will see," Kol mused.

I thought back to his siblings. "Are you close with them?"

Kol shrugged. "Some more than others but only because my five eldest brothers are in outer space."

I frowned. "When was the last time you saw the five of them?"

I watched Kol as he thought of an answer to my question.

"Twenty-two years ago," he eventually answered. "Ealra years, not Earth years."

I gasped with surprise. "That is an awfully long time."

"Yes, but they will be home soon enough," he said, and he looked happy with that statement. "They have been returning home from their mission for nearly two years, and they will reach Ealra within the next two years. They're on the final leg of their journey."

I whistled. "I hope they found whatever it was they were looking for."

That was a *hell* of a long time to be out in space.

"They didn't," Kol answered. "I did."

At my raised brow, he said, "Their mission was to find compatible females."

"Like humans?" I asked.

At Kol's nod, I frowned. "Earth is only a few days away from

Ealra, so with your warp speed, why have they been gone so long if Earth is so close by?"

Kol laughed. "Trust me, the rage my brothers and their crew feel at travelling for so long and going so far when we just had to search your galaxy is mind consuming for them."

I frowned. "I bet they're lonely."

"They have each other for company."

I flushed. "That's not what I meant."

At Kol's grin, I blushed harder.

"They have sexborgs aboard their vessel. Do not worry."

I felt my mouth drop open. "Aliens have sexbots, *too*?"

I thought it was just creepy humans who had those.

Kol laughed at my horrified expression. "It is required to have sexborgs aboard a vessel at all times. Maji males have very high sex drives, and if they did not share sex with a sexborg ... I don't even want to think about the fighting that would ensue between the males. We can get very ... edgy if we go for long periods of time without sex. Short haul journeys like this are terrible, but any longer and a wing would be created to house the sexborgs."

That was the most male thing I had ever heard in my entire life.

"Are your sexbots Maji-like?" I quizzed. "I've seen some broken sexbots on Earth, and they looked so lifelike at first, I thought they were dead bodies."

"Our sexborgs look and feel just like a real Maji female. They offer pleasant company, too. They were designed to trick a male's senses into feeling as though a real female is in his presence; it helps calm a space traveller, or a male in general, when a female is close."

I raised my brow. "Your species sounds obsessed with females."

"Very much so." Kol nodded, not in the least bit ashamed. "Females are everything, and we males know that. They make everything better."

I was doubtful.

"Does *every* male feel that way?"

"Yes," Kol replied.

"Even the gay ones?" I quizzed.

At Kol's puzzled expression, I said, "Males who are sexually attracted to other males."

He choked on air. "I've never heard of such a thing."

I didn't know if he was disgusted or genuinely shocked.

"Meaning it doesn't exist in your species, or you're just too pigheaded to believe it does?"

"It doesn't exist," Kol said firmly. "Maji are *definitely* not like humans, Nova. We are driven by instinct; the need to mate and breed with a female drives us. Males can't produce offspring together, and our bodies are only in tune with females, so no sexual arousal could occur between males."

"Oh," I said, wincing. "Sorry, I thought you were being homophobic."

"Being *what*?"

"Never mind," I said with a wave of my hand. "Being gay on Earth is punishable by death. My species is backwards in more ways than one."

"Where would a male even put his cock in another male?" Kol then asked, looking more confused than I had ever seen him. "They both have cocks so where—"

"I regret ever bringing this up," I said, speaking over him.

"Where do your human males put—"

"Kol," I cut him off, my face burning. "Forget it."

He shook his head. "I'm curious."

I covered my face and blurted, "The asshole."

Kol sounded like he would pass out. "That is a *waste* canal!"

"Seriously," I pleaded. "*Change* the fucking subject!"

Kol suddenly erupted with laughter.

"I can't wait to tell Mikoh of this." He chuckled.

I shook my head. "Let's get back to talking about your brothers. Why didn't they check my galaxy on their mission since it is close by?"

If six trillion miles is considered *close*.

"When they set off on their mission, nothing was known about your species," Kol explained as he leaned against a column in the room and folded his arms across his broad chest. "We Maji don't interact with many species unless on a mission. At a docking station on Vada, Vaneer's home world long away from here, my brothers searched different species, and an image of what a human looked like was incorrect. The creature they saw had no head, just a body and many arms and legs. It was not compatible with Maji, so my brothers blacklisted your galaxy as Earth is the only habitable planet then they continued their search which led them further into the cosmos."

"Okay," I began. "That's understandable, but how is it that *you* came across humans? And how did you get Sera to join you?"

I had wondered about the augmented woman since my encounter with her, and I couldn't figure out why she was with the Maji. I didn't understand the benefit for her. She wasn't defenceless on Earth. If anything, as augmented, she'd be pretty powerful. She was lethal, smart, and didn't have to do the things I had to do to survive.

"My father led a mission to an unnamed planet ten years ago. It was home to another species, but it held some humans that had been taken from Earth's trading posts over the years. My father went to the planet to trade for some samples of a new fuel the local scientists had created. It was dangerous, but fuel is vital to our space travel, and we're always looking for reserves in case our current source dries up, so my father made that mission a priority. My father met Sera, and he quickly realised that humans were very similar to Maji. He asked her what species she was, and they spoke a little. Sera was a slave to a docking master, so my father bought her for a small fee and offered her safety on Ealra. He wanted to help her and give her a chance at life, but he also wanted to have our healers examine her to see if we were compatible."

I processed that, and though Kol had answered a big question for me, it only left me wanting to know more.

"It has been ten years since your father's trade deal," I said, blinking. "Why did it take ten years for you to come to Earth to make an offer to Earth's government for us women?"

"We have tried," Kol stressed, his lip curling in annoyance. "We tried and failed six times within the first two years of our discovery of your species, but your leaders wanted an exchange we would not agree to."

I felt a little sick at the thought of what my people would want from the Maji.

"What did they want?" I asked, wrapping my arms around myself.

"They wanted to come to Ealra *with* us, but we refused. Maji are not the only species to inhabit Ealra, and we did not trust your leaders not to ruin our planet, considering they greatly aided in destroying yours."

The sorry image of the Earth I saw from the viewing pane of the bridge flashed in my mind.

"It was the right decision," I said with a firm nod. "Our human leaders are filled with greed, and they wouldn't have settled for living in harmony. Eventually, they'd have tried to take over Ealra as the dominant species, and Maji would have been slaughtered in the process."

Kol nodded solemnly. "That was our fear, so we declined their offer, and in return, they declined us any chance of having human females."

"Vindictive bastards," I scowled.

"It was why my brothers remained on their mission to find compatible females because we did not know if we could ever come to an agreement with your Earth government."

"I understand."

Kol licked his lips. "My father decided we would bide our time and come to your leaders when we knew our offer was one they couldn't refuse. My father ordered my brothers home two years ago because he knew the Earth government would yield to our wishes eventually."

I eyed him curiously. "Because the Earth is dying?"

Kol shamelessly nodded. "It is no secret that Earth is soon to be no more, so we used that to our advantage. We waited and waited, and when we went back to Earth days ago and made the offer for your females once more, your leaders jumped to accept our deal when we mentioned the unnamed planet was liveable for humans. They accepted our deal in exchange for credits and its coordinates."

I sat cross-legged and rested my elbows on my knees, completely invested in Kol's tales.

"I shouldn't be astonished that they opted to save their own hides but to turn tail and run without even informing the rest of us that our race had a chance on a new world is hard for me to believe. It just seems so ... evil."

Kol said nothing; he only watched me.

"I really *shouldn't* be surprised, though, right?" I said aloud. "The evillest acts I've seen and heard of were committed by humans ... Maybe it wouldn't have been such a tragedy for my species to become extinct. When you think about it, it's really a kindness."

I jumped at Kol's growl.

"Do not talk about dying," he snarled. "I cannot think of you not being in my life."

That surprised me more than my leaders' abandonment.

"A few days ago, you didn't even know I existed, Kol," I said softly.

"I am *not* human," he repeated for what seemed to be the hundredth time. "Maji form bonds very quickly to those we care for because it is my nature. I can't imagine you being dead. I *won't* imagine it because it won't happen for another thousand years or more. Thanas willing, I'll go before you, so I don't have to endure the pain of a mate loss."

I felt my mouth drop open.

"A *thousand* years," I stammered. "Have you lost your mind?"

Kol's brows furrowed. "No, it is still inside my head ... Why?"

I shouldn't have laughed at him, but when he took what I said literally, it was too funny.

"I mean, are you crazy?" I clarified. "My lifespan is very short, Kol."

He clicked his tongue. "Once we mate, you will receive my essence, and that will keep you alive for a very long time."

Hold up.

"Your essence?" I repeated. "Like your freaking *soul?*"

He barked a laugh before he nudged himself away from the column, crossed the room, and sat a couple of feet away from me on the bed. I turned to face him and waited.

"I've never had to explain this before, so *please* be understanding, okay?"

I gulped. "Okay."

Kol inhaled and exhaled. "When a couple mates, we males have instinctual needs that must be acted on for a mating bond to be sealed for life. If our instinct is denied, we do not mate the female, and no bond is formed."

"Okay," I said tentatively.

"When a couple shares sex, before or after an orgasm, the male will ... he will ... he has to ... Please, keep in mind that he doesn't *want* to do it, but his instincts are *telling* him—"

"Kol," I cut him off. "It's okay; you can tell me."

He watched me, and I got the impression he was scared I would run away from him.

"He bites the female."

I gasped. "He *bites* her?"

"On the neck."

"On the *neck?*" I repeated.

"And ... uh ... he doesn't release his hold on the female until his essence has entered her bloodstream and—"

"Wait, *what*?"

"When his body recognises the female as his mate, it has a strong urge to claim her. He bites her, and this releases his essence through the tips of his teeth." Kol winced when he looked at me. "It sounds a lot worse than it is, *shiva*, I swear it."

"Let me summarise," I said, holding my hand in the air so Kol wouldn't speak. "If we have sex—"

"*When* we have sex," Kol corrected.

I narrowed my eyes at him. "*When* we have sex, before or after we come, you'll bite me on my neck and won't let go until your essence is in my bloodstream. Do I have that correct so far?"

"Yes." Kol sighed. "But let me explain why."

"Please," I said with a wave of my hand. "Go ahead."

"On a Maji female, my essence would calm her *uva* contractions, which cause her pain and force her to seek a male to mate for sex to conceive a young one. It would not completely take the discomfort away, but it wouldn't be much more than small aches every month after she receives my essence. It is nature's way of telling her body that a healthy male is present in the female's life, and he will give her offspring, so there is no need to contract so much to remind a female to get pregnant. It also is a chemical bond between us; her scent is all a male would ever desire and yearn for, and his scent would be the same for her."

I scratched my head. "That's all fine and dandy for your females, but what will it do to a human? In this case, *me*!"

Kol hesitated, and I dangerously pointed my finger at him.

"No bullshit answers, either. Be straight with me."

"It is hard to say it in terms you will understand." He groaned and shook his head. "We have no way of knowing for sure, but Surkah is *positive* that my essence would enter your bloodstream, then your heart, and ... recode it. That is the best way I can explain it. My essence would be like ... a life potion to you. Once you have it, it will always flow through your veins, and keep you and your organs healthy for a very long time. It will dramatically slow down your aging."

This is too much.

I lifted my hands to my temples and rubbed.

"Stuff like this doesn't happen, Kol. It just *doesn't*."

"Yet here we are." He tentatively smiled. "Two different species intended to be the other's mate for life."

I lowered my hands and frowned at him. "I don't want your chance at a mate to be ruined if this doesn't go right."

Kol tensed. "I've never doubted my sister, and I won't start now. If Surkah says it's safe, then it's safe."

"I'm not talking shit about Surkah's ability, but this is a *big* risk."

He scooted closer to me and took my small hands in his large ones. "I would never hurt you, *shiva*."

Not intentionally.

"What if something backfires, though, and my blood makes *you* sick, and you *die*?"

The thought of Kol dying felt like a sucker punch.

"You cannot harm me, my human," he mused.

I glared at him, which only made him snort.

"Okay, if I *died* during our mating, which I *won't*, and my essence entered your bloodstream, then *it* will die, and then *you* will eventually die. My essence will only live in you and keep you alive as long as I live. Mates are nothing without the other, so it is a blessing when the female dies not long after her male does because it saves her pain. No one wants to experience a mate loss."

"A mate loss is a bad thing?" I questioned.

"The worst pain imaginable," Kol answered.

I sucked in a staggered breath. "Do males naturally die *first* out of a mated pair?"

"Always." Kol nodded. "It is cruel to us males, but if our female dies, we can survive. But if a male dies, the female never survives for much longer."

"But ... why?"

"Our essence becomes a part of them, and when the male dies, so does that essence. When it comes to death, even nature shows mercy to the females. We believe that Thanas does not want our females to suffer, so when her male dies, she will follow."

I frowned. "Aren't males important to Thanas?"

"Of course." Kol smiled softly. "But males need to protect the people, and Thanas gives them the strength to live on after a female's death. I think it is futile, though, because if a male lost his female, he would crumble from the inside out. His world, his life, his everything would die with his female."

A shiver shot up my spine

"Could a male not find another mate?" I asked, feeling sad for any male who had ever suffered a mate loss.

"Never," Kol instantly replied. "Even badly matched males and females still become the other's everything. My aunt and uncle once hated the other, and I mean *hated* each other, and though their mating started out unstable, their bond is one of the strongest I have ever seen. We mate for life, *shiva*. Even if one life ends, the mate bond never does. The need for the other is instant after a mating, and love follows eventually."

I was shocked at the knowledge, and my heart hurt knowing if I successfully mated with Kol, he would eventually die, and I'd exist on my own without him even if only for a short time. It didn't take long for tears to fill my eyes.

"*Shiva*," Kol hissed. "I have saddened you? I beg your forgiveness."

"I thought a royal never begs?" I whispered.

He pressed his forehead to mine. "You make everything possible, my Nova."

My tears fell and splashed onto my cheeks, and right away, Kol leaned in and kissed them away.

"Please," he rasped. "It causes me great pain to see you like this, Nova."

His words wrapped around my heart like a blanket.

"I'm sorry." I sniffled. "I'm sad at the thought of you dying and leaving me."

Kol placed his hands on my face, brushing his calloused thumbs under my eyes.

"We will have *many* centuries together, and when it is my time, your time will follow. We give our hearts to our mates, which is why a male's female joins him so quickly in death. She cannot live without her heart."

This is it.

At that moment, I *felt* I was beginning to lose my heart to this male.

"This is crazy," I said with a shake of my head. "How can I care for you so much in such a short amount of time?"

"We're destined mates," Kol answered. "I believe you were made for me, and me for you."

"Kol," I whispered as a fire ignited in my core and spread to between my thighs. "I *want* to be your mate."

He growled in response, and his hold on me tightened. "Can I have that taste of you now?"

Yes.

The need for him to taste me, to do *something* to relieve my body of the ache it was experiencing, became my prime focus.

"I'm yours," I told him.

The words were barely out of my mouth before Kol moved to his knees in front of me, and he did something I wasn't expecting him to do. He kissed me with so much hunger it sent a jolt straight to the aching spot between my thighs.

This is what he means by tasting.

The force of his kiss pushed my body flat on the shockingly comfortable mattress, and he held me in place with the added weight of his body as he moved over me. I was grateful he used his elbows to hold most of his weight, but what I could feel of him was enough. He was toned, muscular, and hard all over ... harder in one place more than others.

"Kol." I gasped against his mouth when he wiggled his hips and pushed my thighs apart.

He didn't answer; he only kissed me deeper as he pressed his pelvis against my throbbing core. I didn't know what to focus on—his kiss or the feeling of him rubbing against me. The kiss won when he suddenly sucked on my tongue before he lightly bit it. He tore his mouth from me and attached his lips to my neck. He left no patch of skin unkissed, and when I involuntarily moaned, he put all his weight on his left elbow and used his right hand to cup my breast. The friction of my clothing rubbing over my now hardened nipple caused me to shiver with delight.

"*Shiva*," Kol rasped.

I lifted my legs and wrapped them around his hips, squeezing him as an ache pulsed between my spread thighs. I arched my back when goosebumps broke out over my skin, and a tingling sensation covered the breast Kol held in his large calloused hand.

"Almighty," I panted. "I need to see you. Take off your clothes."

Kol growled, and before I realised what he was doing, he stood up and stripped out of his clothes at a rapid pace. I leaned up on my elbows so I could watch him. I wanted him to slow down so I could take his body in leisurely, but when he was naked as the day he was born before me, my pussy throbbed.

His cock was huge as it was thick and hard. The tip of it glistened, and a milky white substance seeped from the tip and slowly trailed down the length. The urge to lean forward and lick it away frightened me.

"You're perfect," I whispered and sat upright, moving my attention to his chest.

I reached over for him, and without my having to ask him to move, he came closer to me. My hand instantly went to his muscular chest and skimmed over the white *claw* marks slashed across it.

"What happened to you?" I whispered.

"A borak attacked me when I was forty years old," he rasped. "I was on my first hunt with my father and brothers; it marked my entrance into malehood."

The deep slashes made me wince.

"How come you didn't heal?" I quizzed, my hands now sliding over his stomach, feeling the curve of each abdominal muscle.

Kol kept his hands at his sides as I explored him with my touch.

"Boraks are nasty creatures," he said, tensing more with every passing moment. "Their talons hold a poison that prevents the body from clotting a wound. The purpose is to bleed out their prey. My older brother, Ezah, is a healer like Surkah, and he was on the hunt with us. His ability helped seal my wounds but did not prevent scarring."

"I'm sorry." I frowned.

"Why?" Kol chuckled, tipping my chin up with his fingers. "Scars are marks of honour to the people; it means I survived a great beast. It makes me even more desirable to females."

I playfully rolled my eyes. "You males are such idiots."

"Is that so?" he mused.

I squealed with laughter when he dove forward and pressed me back against the mattress. My legs automatically went around his waist. Without kissing me, he had shuffled his way down my body and gripped the hem of my pants, pulling them down to my knees in one fluid motion. I sucked in a startled breath and stared with wide eyes as Kol lifted my legs from around his body and pulled my pants the rest of the way off my legs. Kol's eyes locked on the centre of my thighs as he threw my pants over his shoulder without so much as a backward glance. It was when he bent forward and brought his face level with my pussy that my hips bucked involuntarily.

"What are you *doing*?" I cried out with embarrassment and tried to scramble up the bed away from him.

Kol's hands clamped down on my thighs and, not so gently, pinned me in place. He brought his mouth to just below my belly button and planted kisses on my skin.

"Tasting you," he growled against my abdomen.

He moved his mouth lower and lower, and I nearly lost my ability to breathe.

"You can't mean to taste me *there*!" I shouted in dismay and tried desperately to shut my legs.

Kol angled his hands and applied pressure to my thighs, forcing them apart as wide as they would go. I felt like I was frozen with shock, but it only lasted for a moment because the second I felt Kol's soft, hot, wet tongue slide over my aching pussy lips, my body nearly sprang up from the bed.

"You're hairless," he commented.

"I had it removed," I panted. "My father won some credits and paid for it. I couldn't bathe often, so having no hair made things easier."

He made a sound somewhere between an appreciative hum and a vicious growl. He unhooked an arm from around my right thigh and spread it over my stomach, using it to pin me down like an anchor. He kept the elbow of his other arm placed against my inner thigh and used it and his right shoulder to keep my legs apart. With his fingers, he spread my pussy lips apart, and after he had inhaled deeply once more, he brought his mouth down to the very spot that ached so badly and sucked the hardened throbbing bud into his mouth.

I screamed as a sensation I had never experienced shot up my spine.

It was pleasure, raw pleasure, but it was too much for my body to handle. I couldn't control my limbs. It was like they had a mind of their own and moved with every flick of Kol's hot, wet tongue. He did a good job at keeping my ass on the mattress, but he had no control over my hands that had buried themselves in his hair and tugged on the strands that were tangled around my fingers.

Kol growled, but he didn't slow the movement of his tongue or lessen the suction he applied to my clit; if anything, he increased them. My breathing was laboured, my heart was pounding erratically, and my screams were so loud I was sure the entire ship could hear me... but I didn't care. All I could care about was the pleasure I felt, and whether it would kill me.

"Oh, *oh!*" I cried out a moment later when the pleasure built up to a point where it almost felt like searing hot pain.

My body fell apart the second Kol's teeth scraped over my clit, which was the final nudge my body needed to be flung over the edge of sanity and into a pool of bliss. I held my breath as a new pulsing overtook my body. Instead of the pulse aching, it sent ripples of satisfaction through my body, soothing my tense joints and turning them into soft, relaxed pieces of flesh.

Almighty.

"Need you," Kol suddenly snarled, his voice breaking through my cloud of desire. "Now."

Even through my haze of pleasure, I knew what that meant.

"Oh, Kol." I trembled beneath him. "I'm so scared."

Kol surprised me when he said, "Me too."

"But you've had sex before."

He slowly nodded, his eyes now aglow with a ring of light as he said, "Yes, but I've never had sex with *you* before, and I desperately want to make it special for you."

His words touched me and wrapped their way around my pounding heart.

"I trust you," I told him in a shaky breath. "No matter what, I trust you."

"*Shiva*," he murmured as he reached between us. "I'm so sorry."

He didn't give me a moment longer to worry about our impending lovemaking as he gripped his shaft, rubbed it up and down my pussy lips, lined it up with my entrance, and with one more whispered apology, he thrust forward. I arched my back and screamed out when pinching hot pain cut through me. Above me, Kol went deathly still.

"I'm so sorry, s*hiva*," he rasped.

I looked at him, and it looked like he was in pain too. His face was twisted, his eyes were squeezed shut, and his body trembled.

"Are you hurting?" I asked, alarmed despite my own pain.

"Not like you," he growled. "A different kind of pain has me in its clutch, *shiva*."

A different kind of pain?

I couldn't focus on what he meant because sensation overcame me. I was acutely aware of his length inside me; it was thick, long, and to be honest, it hurt. I tried to focus on my breathing, but the foreign sensation of being filled and spread to within an inch of my life was I could think about, all I could feel.

"It hurts," I moaned when I involuntarily moved my hips. "I don't like it, Kol."

The sound he made in response sounded close to a whine.

"It will ease," he rasped.

I worried for him. He was struggling greatly with something, and I wondered if the pain he felt was worse than mine because it sure looked like it was.

"Breathe," I told him. "My papa used to always tell me to breathe through the pain."

Kol tried my method, and it didn't escape me that he looked so adorable whilst doing so. I focused on him and felt my body shiver when I adjusted my hips once more. It wasn't pain I felt. It wasn't exactly pleasure either, but it wasn't pain, and that was enough to calm my spiked nerves.

"You can move," I whispered to Kol. "*Slowly.*"

"Slowly," he repeated.

It took twenty whole seconds for him to withdraw from me, and before he withdrew completely, he moved his hips forward and stretched me once more. It still hurt, but the pain wasn't as consuming as before. I closed my eyes and wrapped my arms around Kol's trembling body. I lost count of how many times he thrust in and out of my body, but when I opened my eyes, I felt no more pain. Kol's cock sliding in and out of my body with ease began to feel … good.

"Oh." I gasped when my insides involuntarily clenched.

Kol's growl startled me, and I brought my attention to him once more. His eyes were still squeezed shut, and he was so tense that the veins in his arms and neck were bulged and sticking up from his skin.

"Are you okay?" I asked, acutely aware that my voice was husky.

"I'm going to die." He choked.

I tensed my insides once more, and it only caused him to growl, which drew a lazy smile from me.

"Faster," I told him, knowing it was what we both needed. "Go faster."

"Thank, Thanas," he almost roared as he began to thrust in and out of my body at a rapid pace.

I tightly wrapped my legs around his hips, and my arms around his neck. I adjusted my hands to his shoulders when each powerful thrust sent a spasm of ecstasy up my spine. I dug my nails into his flesh, and it drew a roar from him and only encouraged him to pound into my pussy harder, faster, deeper. *So* much deeper.

The buildup of bliss was different from the pleasure I felt with Kol's mouth on me; it didn't just consume the body, it also consumed the mind and soul too. It was like my very existence was on the line rather than a soul-shattering orgasm. I tried to pay attention to Kol, I desperately tried to, but my body had a mind of its own, and its only focus was getting to the bliss that was promised as soon as possible.

"Kol!"

Seconds after I gasped his name, my breathing halted, my mouth opened in a silent scream, and my back arched off the mattress. For a moment, I felt numbness before a bliss I had never experienced flowed through my veins and touched my every nerve ending. Molten heat fell over me like a blanket, and it covered me completely. It soothed away every ache, every pulse, and every worry I had ever had.

Heaven.

I was vaguely aware of a sharp sting pinching my neck, but that soon turned to pleasure. Though it was nothing like the wave to just wash over me, it was nice and caused my toes to curl in delight. I hummed for a long moment and wondered how long I would feel like this.

I feel so good.

I heard soft male laughter.

You do *feel good, shiva.*

Kol's comment would normally bring a blush to my cheeks, but now it only drew a lazy smile from me.

Do you feel like I do? I hummed. *I hope you do because it's so good, Kol.*

I gasped when the pleasure that started at my neck suddenly burned hot and drew a hiss from my lips.

Hush, shiva, only a few more seconds and our bond will be in place.

I didn't realise my eyes were closed, so when I opened them, and my surroundings came back to me, I was wondering why Kol was flush against me with his face buried against my neck. I had the intention of asking him, but the burning heat I felt at my neck suddenly attacked my core and spread outwards. It dragged a strangled cry from my lips.

"Kol," I whimpered and dug my nails into the skin of his firm back. "It hurts. Please, stop, it *hurts*."

Kol, who was still between my thighs and still *inside* me, didn't move a muscle. When I positioned my hands on his chest and began to push him away—to no avail—he growled, and it vibrated against my neck, and quickly after, a sting followed. Now that I wasn't swept away in pleasure, it didn't take me long to realise the sting I felt was from Kol's teeth ... They punctured my neck with a bite.

Please, shiva, let the bond take place. This is just my essence you're feeling.

His essence fucking hurt.

For a moment, I wanted to tell him to go and fuck *himself*, but then it dawned on me that not only was Kol biting me, but he spoke clearly to me, and I heard him when I shouldn't have because his mouth was a little preoccupied.

Calm, Kol suddenly ordered. *Do not panic; this is our bond. Our mental link is normal, shiva. I feared telling you we'd share a mental link because you were so worried about my essence. I didn't want to scare you further.*

The burning pain in my core continued to spread outward to my limbs, and like my mind-blowing orgasm, it touched every nerve and filled my body completely. I had heard my scream before I felt myself let it loose, and what was even more odd was that I felt how tore up Kol was that I was hurting so badly and he could not stop it.

I *felt* his emotion, and I *heard* his voice in my head.

Why are you doing this to me? I am your intended!

For a moment, I wasn't sure if I asked the question aloud or in my mind.

No, Kol growled as he slowly withdrew his teeth from my flesh. *You're my mate.*

One moment, I was hurting so badly that it caused all my joints to lock into place, and then the next, I was pain-free and more relaxed and physically satisfied than I had ever been in my entire life. I closed my eyes and fought off the urge to fall asleep, but it was extremely difficult.

I was vaguely aware when Kol withdrew his still rock-hard length from me only a few inches before he thrust back inside my body, causing the pleasure I felt earlier to leer at me with jealousy. The new sensation felt more heightened and more toe curling. My eyes flew open, my legs tightened around his hips, and my hands gripped Kol's muscular biceps.

"Our bond is in place, *shiva*," he said as he hovered over me. He was panting but had the biggest smile I had ever seen on his face. "You're mine. *Forever.*"

CHAPTER ELEVEN

*M*ate.

I kept thinking of the word and its meaning since Kol said it to me four days ago. Since the moment we officially became husband and wife, so to speak, it felt like I was on autopilot. The Maji way wasn't simple, and marriage to the Maji certainly wasn't as simple as saying 'I do'. It was something like a sacred ritual that tied individuals together for life. That terrified me because I didn't have time to wrap my head around the fact that I was beginning to fall in love with him before his saddle was hitched to mine.

We had a bond now—a chemical bond that allowed us to share a *mental* link. We could speak to one another through our minds. As if being claimed by an alpha male wasn't daunting enough, I had to have him inside my head, too. I didn't know where to begin to describe how I felt about the turn of events that had taken place in my life. On the one hand, I was extremely grateful for the new life being offered to me and my people, and on the other hand, I couldn't believe any of it was real.

The fact I was safe felt too good to be true, and the fact I was an alien prince's wife was something I couldn't even begin to comprehend. I'd had a few days to adjust since I became a mated female, and the only thing that I was used to was the Maji themselves. I barely noticed skin colour, height, or sharp teeth anymore or even acknowledged the company I kept was a different species. That all felt too trivial to focus on in light of my new status.

Not only was I married—mated—but I was also now a princess. Me. A skinny little runt from Earth who didn't know the first thing about being anything other than a peasant let alone a member of the Maji royal family. I felt like I was trapped in a dream. At times, it was the perfect dream, and at other times, when my worries became too much, it was like a never-ending nightmare I didn't know how to wake up from.

How did I find myself here?

I jumped when I felt a hand on my thigh.

In the mess hall? Kol asked.

I turned my head and glanced at him.

No, I told him. *In this situation. None of this feels real, and I'm beginning to wonder if it ever will.*

"Do not worry yourself, *shiva*." Kol winked. "You're the first female of your kind to mate with a Maji, and it's all happened so fast for you that it will surely feel strange for a while. Once we reach Ealra and settle into our life, that will change."

You don't know that.

"I do." Kol nodded.

"I wasn't saying that to *you*. I was just thinking it in general." I groaned and turned my attention to the food on my tray. "You have to teach me how to block my thoughts from you. I feel like I'm never alone … not even in my head. It's stressing me out, Kol. I've always been on my own, and I didn't realise how much I liked the peace and quiet until I heard your voice in my head."

I ignored the snickering from Mikoh, who sat across from me. Surkah, on the far side of the table next to him, glared at him.

Really? Kol asked, his tone amused. *You seemed to really like that I could hear your thoughts when you were too shy to voice how much you liked me licking you last night.*

I set my jaw and looked up from my breakfast tray and glared daggers at my grinning *mate*. We hadn't had sex since the night we mated. The first two days were because of sensitivity; not mainly because of the sex, but because of Kol's essence bonding in the bloodstream. It made me weak and a little uneasy on my feet. Not being at full strength didn't stop Kol from touching me when we were in bed. He never took it to the point of no return, but he did explore me with his fingers and mouth until I couldn't see straight. Everything about our intimacy was still new territory for me, so it meant I embarrassed easily. Kol wasn't allowed to discuss what we did in private, but he talked about it anyway,

"Get *out* of my head, Kol."

His lips twitched, but he nodded, which only caused me to eye him suspiciously.

"I want to learn the blocking thing you mentioned to me," I informed him. "You said it was possible for mates to screen our thoughts so we could have privacy, and I want that as soon as possible. And I *still* protest that you should have told me we would have a psychic link between us!"

"I *told* you." He frowned. "I didn't want to scare you."

"I just don't understand how any of this is possible. I know you've explained it, but I can't comprehend it," I said with a shake of my head. "I am human, and humans can't read one another's thought."

"I'm *not* human," Kol said.

You don't need to tell me that, big guy. I'm more than aware.

Kol grinned at me, and knowing he heard my thoughts, I scowled.

"How can we be so different but the same too?" I wondered aloud.

"Maji and humans," Mikoh began. "Our bodies are similar, yes?"

"Apart from skin colour and how freaking *huge* you all are ... yes."

Kol's lips twitched, but I ignored him because I knew he knew exactly what part of him I thought was huge, and it wasn't the head on his damn shoulders.

"Humans are the only other species we have found that resemble us with such detail. As you said, we're different, but we're the same, too. Species of the cosmos cross-breed all the time; it is how many species are born. Maybe Maji were once humans, or maybe humans were once Maji."

"Humans would have come from Maji, I think," Surkah thoughtfully interjected. "Our race is a lot older than theirs is."

Mikoh nodded as he leaned back in his chair.

"I think so too, but maybe another species has diluted their blood so much, and that's why they slightly differ from us, or perhaps they've evolved on their own ... but not entirely. Nova has bonded with Kol as any other Maji female would."

It was an irrational thing to do, but I slammed my teeth together and began to breathe heavily at the thought of another woman touching my husband. A frightening sensation of possession filled me from head to toe.

He's mine.

I jumped when I felt Kol's purr rather than heard it.

"Yes, *shiva*." He smiled and reached for me, pulling me onto his lap. "I am yours."

He nuzzled my neck and inhaled.

I could scent her forever ... my female.

"I'm going insane!" I said as I lifted my hands to my face. "I hear and feel you all the time, and now I'm getting possessive like you. Am I turning into a Maji? Is that what your essence is really doing? Is it taking the human out of me?"

Everyone's laughter only grated on my nerves, but instead of being angry, I felt emotional. It sounded funny to them, but I was so confused and scared about what was happening to my body, and I didn't know what to do about it ... so I began to cry.

"*Shiva.*"

No, don't shiva me, I sobbed. *You think this is funny, and it is to you, but it's not to me. This is all as natural as breathing to you, but it's one new thing on top of the other for me, and I'm just so scared, Kol. Nothing like this happens in my world.*

Kol tightened his arms around me.

"I did not think, *shiva*, and I am so sorry. Please, do not cry. It pains me when you cry."

He meant that literally. I could *feel* how upset my tears were making him.

"Do you want to pilot the *Ebony*? You keep asking me, and if you stop crying, I will allow it."

I heard male laughter. "Your father was right; our mates will have *us* under *their* thumb."

"Quiet, Mikoh!"

Mikoh only laughed louder.

I pulled back from Kol, sniffling and hiccupping.

"You'll ... you'll let me fly the c-craft?"

"If it makes you stop crying, *shiva*." He nodded frantically. "Yes."

I wiped away my tears. "Okay."

Mikoh's laughter aggravated Kol, and I could sense he was about to attack him.

Please don't, I pleaded. *I can't handle seeing you fighting with him right now.*

We must leave then, Kol almost growled in response. *His impatience to have Surkah is pushing him to challenge every male he sees.*

I don't want to go back to our quarters, though. We're always there.

Surkah had told me that newly mated males would go to great

lengths to hide their females from peering eyes. Everyone was a threat to a newly mated male, even a female. Their instinct was to keep their females hidden where nothing could harm them, and to Kol, that meant keeping us holed up in our quarters all day, every day.

We reach Ealra in less than one Earth hour, Kol hummed as his fingers stroked my thigh. *What do you want to do if not return to our quarters?*

I perked up. "I can fly the craft since we're getting off soon."

Kol glared at Mikoh when he laughed again, and without a word, he stood and brought us to our feet.

"We're going for a walk," Kol said, his tone clipped.

Surkah smacked Mikoh's chest with the back of her hand to stop him from saying whatever it was he was about to say, and the distraction worked wonders. She became his primary focus, and it enabled me and Kol to slip away from the table without Mikoh noticing our departure. When he was looking at Surkah, the world could have ended around him, and he wouldn't have noticed.

When Kol and I left the mess hall and walked side by side down the identical hallways, I slid my hand into his, and his expression of awe made me giggle like a little girl.

"I can't believe it was only a few days ago," I mused, "that I would have pushed you off the craft given the chance."

Kol's laughter caused my heart to leap as he squeezed my hand. "A mating changes everything, *shiva*."

It really had; the hard-headed Kol I had first met had been replaced with the most caring male I could have ever wished for. While he was still a typical male, he went about his alpha ways with a little more consideration for me. With every passing hour, I became more and more infatuated with him, and I knew it wouldn't be long until I had fallen head over heels in love with him.

He was perfect, and I didn't require the chemical bond of the Maji to become addicted to him. I was already knee-deep in my obsession with him, and like everything else, it scared me half to death. I was terrified that things would change when we landed on Ealra, and our time together would be cut in half. It was a fear I couldn't shake no matter how often Kol told me it would never come true. All I had ever known and loved had been taken away from me, so I couldn't see how the pattern would suddenly end just because Kol said so.

"Are you *really* letting me fly the *Ebony*?" I asked Kol when we stepped onto the bridge.

The crew on the bridge did their fist over the chest and bowing thing to Kol, and they did it to me too, but none of them looked at me. He nodded to me as he led me to a large control panel where someone was always stationed even if the ship was on auto pilot. The male moved away without a verbal order from Kol, though I knew he probably told him to move through their comms. Kol stationed me in front of the control panel, and he positioned himself behind me. He put his hands over mine and placed them flat on the control panel.

"You do not know how to physically pilot but just about anyone can do it mentally," Kol explained, his hands still pressed on the back of my hands. "I have given you clearance to fly. You don't have a comm of your own, but your translator has frequencies that my comm has just finished rewriting so you can think your commands to the ship."

I was suddenly terrified to fly the ship.

"This is a bad idea," I said, panicked. "I shouldn't have asked for this."

I noticed the males on the lowered section of the bridge suddenly grabbing the closest sturdy thing to them, and a few of them even laughed and said something that made Kol tense.

"Say a single word further," he growled to the males on the bridge, "and I will allow Surkah to do her annual assessment *early* this year."

Gazes quickly dropped, and bodies busied back to work. All except one.

"An early assessment is worth it."

"Nero—"

"That little human has you, as the humans say, by the balls."

I choked on air as I laughed. I looked to my right and found Nero, a male who I had met a few days earlier when I tried to escape the *Ebony*, and from his conversation with Kol, it was easy to tell he was another one of his close friends.

"Get back to work," Kol growled.

Nero winked but did as ordered. When my attention left him and returned to what I was about to do, I tensed all over again.

"You will do fine," Kol assured me and pressed a kiss to the crown of my head. "Now listen to me carefully, okay?"

I bobbed my head.

"We'll be reaching Ealra soon, so what we want to do is slow down, and to do that, you need to fire all forward-facing thrusters."

I knew that; my father had told me the functions of every part of every machine in an engine hall, but I still appreciated Kol's guidance because I suddenly forgot everything I had ever been taught about a spacecraft.

"Okay, and how do I issue that command?"

"You simply think it."

Uh.

"Okay ... is that all?"

"You have to start your command with 'Ebony', or she won't do what you tell her."

I gasped. "Is she self-aware?"

A lot of androids on Earth had become self-aware over the years.

"No." Kol laughed. "She is just programmed to react in conversation as if she were a living Maji female. She has a personality."

"Right," I said, relaxing. "Will I do it now?"

"Let me announce our heading to the passengers first."

I hesitated. "Okay."

He closed his eyes. "This is the shipmaster," he spoke, his voice stern. "Prepare for deceleration. Humans, you will feel odd for a few minutes, so I'd advise you to sit down and place your head between your knees now. All males assist any female in need ... Please note that my mate is heading the deceleration."

The crew on the bridge practically wrapped themselves around their consoles.

"Oh, that's reassuring!" I said sarcastically as I scowled at them.

"You can go ahead," Kol murmured to me.

I didn't know why I was so startled by his voice, but I was. I figured it was my nerves over flying the ship that was filled with not only Maji salvation but human too. I quickly looked down at my hands, and before I lost my nerve, I thought, *Ebony, can you fire all forward-facing thrusters to slow us down ... please?*

Yes, Princess Nova, a sultry female voice flowed through my mind.

I gasped when my body was suddenly, in slow motion, pulled forward. I felt so bizarre and almost instantly lightheaded. My hands slipped from the control panel, and before I knew it, I was sitting on my behind with my knees raised to my chest and my head resting on them. A large warm hand was stroking up and down my back.

You did well, shiva.

I was trembling.

I can't believe you let me do that. I'm never doing that ever again.

Kol laughed as he continued to stroke my back. It didn't take long until I was back on my feet and feeling normal again. I worried for the rest of the human women who were possibly weak, but Kol assured me there weren't many cases of humans fainting, and those who had were being cared for by males until Surkah or another healer could help them feel better.

"Do you want to see the engine hall?" Kol asked me. "You won't be back on board the *Ebony* in the future, so it's your last chance."

So he thought. I didn't tell Kol that I *eventually* wanted to start my trade as an engineer, but I figured I'd wait until we were settled on Ealra before I made that declaration.

"I'd love to see it," I beamed up at him.

We left the bridge hand in hand, and a few minutes later, we were on the lower decks of the *Ebony* and walking into the incredibly huge engine hall. I imagined the engines of the craft to be roaring with life, but they were eerily silent even though they were working from the look of them. I was a little unnerved that I couldn't tell which engine was the main one used for converting energy from the reactor core and which ones were the propulsion engines used to fire up the craft's thrusters. It all looked different from what I was used to.

"Thane?" Kol shouted, looking around for his friend.

I saw no males anywhere, and I found that extremely odd because an engine hall usually had a crew with specific skills who kept everything in check from the moment the rector flared to life until the moment it was shut off. I smiled when I suddenly heard the familiar growl of an engine, a hiss of pneumatics that flowed to the reactor core, as well as some reverberating. The *Ebony* was virtually silent, as Mikoh had once told me, but an engine was an engine, and all an engine wanted to do was to be heard.

"This is amazing," I said in awe.

I jumped when I heard a loud bang that was quickly followed by harsh curses.

"Is that you, Kol?"

The voice that spoke was deep and had a natural rasp to it.

"It's me," Kol confirmed. "And my mate."

I blinked when a male rounded from behind a black engine pump with a rag of some kind in his hand. His skin, or what I could see of it anyway, was a warm blue ... the patches that weren't covered in a thick black liquid anyway. Like every other Maji male, Thane was tall, muscular, and ridiculously attractive. His chestnut brown hair was tied into a knot on the back of his head, but wild strands escaped the tie and hung loosely around his chiselled face. His cat-like eyes were emerald green with white strikes throughout them, and a white scar stood out against his skin, curving up from his neck to his cheek in a jagged pattern. I didn't focus on it. Instead, I locked my eyes on the black patterns that decorated his neck, the top of his chest, and his bare arms.

He had spilled an oil of some kind on himself, and he was busy wiping it off, but I mistook some of his obvious tattoos for oil, too.

"I'm not presentable for the new princess," Thane angrily scowled at Kol.

My mate laughed. "I think you look just fine, like a young one with a skin rash after he got into an alder berries bath."

Thane's glare told me he'd love to beat the shit out of Kol.

"Stop teasing him." I clicked my tongue and nudged my mate.

He put his muscled arm around my shoulder.

"This is my female," Kol stated, his show of dominance not going amiss.

Thane rolled his eyes and focused on me.

"Princess," he said and placed his fist on his chest before he ... bowed.

I tensed. "You really don't need to bow. I'm not really a—"

"You're my mate, *shiva*," Kol cut me off. "You're a princess through our mating."

I was *never* going to be able to wrap my head around that.

"Yes, but still—hey, wait a second! How come you aren't freaking out at Thane for looking at me and talking to me?"

No male—except Mikoh and Nero—was allowed glance in my direction or mutter a word to me. And more than once, Kol had attacked them both when they made me laugh. Kol had been very firm about no one interacting with me since our bond snapped into place and I became his mate.

Kol raised a brow. "Because he is *Thane*."

He said that like I knew the meaning behind it.

"Explain," I demanded.

"He is my brother in arms." Kol shrugged. "I trust him, and my instincts do, too."

"In other words," Thane interjected, "he knows I pose no threat to take you away from him."

Oh.

"Well." I nodded. "Okay then."

Thane's lips twitched then he flickered his eyes to Kol.

"The deceleration wasn't very smooth. Are you well?" the male asked, worry laced in his tone.

"Did you not hear my announcement?" Kol asked.

As if on cue, one of the engines roared.

Thane raised a brow. "I never hear you in here unless you contact me through our comms."

"I forgot." Kol waved him off. "It was nothing anyway."

"Nothing?" the male blinked. "It stalled engine one."

I winced and looked up at Kol. "You said I did well."

"You did," he assured me. "Gravity pockets are all over space. Anyone could fly into their path when deceleration is issued, even you."

"Excuse me?" Thane cut in. "Did I hear that correctly? You let a *female* pilot the *Ebony*?"

I could hear the amusement in his tone.

Kol set his jaw. "For *one* minute, yes."

"Why?" Thane asked, astonished.

"She ... she was crying ... and I wanted her to stop."

Thane stared at Kol, and he waited about two seconds before he burst into a fit of uncontrollable laughter.

"You've ... gone ... insane."

My lips twitched as Thane bent forward and whacked his hand against his knee as he laughed. I didn't mind that I was the source of his laughter. I quickly realised that women—females—have a very long way to go before the males of the Maji race will see them as equals. To be honest, I didn't think the males would ever see the females as something other than gems to protect. And I wasn't sure that was a bad thing.

"I am still in my right mind," Kol growled.

"You're not," Thane insisted, still laughing. "You're letting a *female* pilot the *Ebony* because you wanted her to stop *crying*."

Kol scowled. "She is my mate; it pains me when she cries."

"That is why I won't *ever* take a mate," Thane said with an amused chuckle. "The only female I will let rule me is the *Ebony*."

Kol tensed. "Nova does not rule me."

Thane deadpanned, and it only caused Kol to scowl at him harder, and that made *me* laugh. Thane switched his gaze to me, and he beamed a huge smile. It was a gorgeous smile even if he did have sharper gold-capped teeth than what I was used to.

Kol suddenly growled, and almost instantly, Thane dropped his gaze from me, but he was still smiling.

"You have tamed him, princess."

Kol grumbled something under his breath that made Thane snicker.

I sighed. "I don't believe this one will ever be tamed; he is prepared to attack every male I glance at."

"He won't be like this forever." Thane winked. "Your mating is fresh. After a few decades, his instincts will calm, and he won't be bothered if other males look at you and speak to you … within reason, of course."

"A few *decades*?" I spluttered.

Thane laughed. "At least five."

Normally, that kind of talk would prompt me to say 'I'll be dead in five decades', but Surkah had assured me many times since Kol and I became mates four days ago that the chemical essence of my bond with him *would* slow my aging dramatically. She had no proof other than a reading her *lissa* thing projected to her. For Kol and every other Maji, Surkah's word was as much proof as they needed, as she was a healer, but for me, it didn't hold much promise or make a lot of sense. It made as much sense as being able to hear Kol's thoughts and feel his emotions. I was either going to be young for very long time or get old and wrinkly sooner than the Maji thought.

Only time would tell.

"It'll take him *that* long to calm his ass down? Are you *kidding* me?"

Kol belly laughed along with Thane.

"I'm not human, *shiva*."

"Yeah, you've said that a million times, but how different you are *still* baffles me. I honestly don't think I'll ever get used to it. You're a complete weirdo, *mate*."

Kol stared down at me then lifted his hands to my face, rubbing his thumbs over my cheeks before he lowered his mouth to mine. Almost instantly, I leaned up on my tiptoes and returned his kiss. My arms went around his waist, and my lips moved with his. I hummed when I parted my lips, and his tongue snaked inside. When he pulled back from our kiss, he was making that rough purring sound I loved so much.

Kol chuckled softly. Placing the tip of his nose against the tip of mine, he dragged the tip up the bridge of my nose before he stopped at the point between my eyes. He pulled back slightly and replaced the tip of his nose with his lips as he planted a gentle kiss to the spot. My stomach instantly burst into butterflies. Kol had done that very action the morning after our mating. I had woken up, and he did the exact thing with his nose on mine, and when I asked him what he was doing, he told me it was a mate kiss, a sacred gesture between mates and cherished family members. He explained it as an action of deep love between mates.

I was greatly touched by the action, and the meaning and emotion behind it, but I quickly turned the conversation to our being able to hear each other's thoughts and began to learn all about *that* part of being a Maji's mate. I didn't want to discuss love with Kol because I wasn't anywhere near that point with him to be able to say it. He hadn't told me he loved me, but I knew he was very close to doing so. I knew our mating was different for him; it had a completely different effect on him. He didn't just feel possessive of my body; he felt possessive of my heart, too. Our mating not only ensured he was mine and I was his, but it also gave me his heart without asking if I wanted it. I knew I had to be *very* careful, or I'd break it.

He regained my attention when he kissed me once more, and it caused me to hum with delight.

His kisses are awesome.

"I'll be sure to give you plenty of them, my mate."

I smiled up at him. "I'm going to hold you to that."

"You're lucky I have not had lunch; it would be all over your feet right about now if I had."

I blushed wildly when Thane spoke, reminding me of his presence.

I turned my head towards him. "I'm *so* sorry; that was incredibly rude of us."

"Don't apologise." Kol snorted. "He has done a lot more than kiss a female in my presence—and Mikoh's and Nero's, for that matter. I think he even once brought a female to her knees when my father was close by."

Thane devilishly grinned. "Guilty."

I snorted, and just as I was about to speak, Kol closed his eyes, and a slow grin spread across his lips.

"Why're you smiling?" I asked, appreciating how handsome he was.

"I'm being hailed to the bridge." He looked down and pinned me in place with his violet eyes. "Ealra is within sight."

CHAPTER TWELVE

After Kol had been hailed to oversee the descent and landing of the *Ebony* on Ealra, we made it to the bridge within minutes. Along the way, Kol kept projecting his lustful thoughts my way. I not only heard words in my head, but I could also *see* whatever he projected to me. And right now, I saw a slideshow of being fucked by Kol through his eyes.

Having his desired effect on me had him grinning from ear to ear as I gnawed on my lower lip and tried to keep my breathing even. I was *very* aware of my scent, and that my arousal would sting the nostrils of the Maji on the bridge. Kol assured me that every male within sniffing distance wouldn't breathe if they could help it just to avoid his wrath. He promised they would treat me as if I wasn't there, but even being ignored by them wouldn't change the fact they could smell that I was turned on.

I was mortified.

I made it a point to sit on Kol's lap and keep my thighs plastered together to mask my scent with his. I wished that I could avail of our cleansing unit, but until we landed on the new home world, I just had to deal with everyone being able to smell that I was horny.

This is so embarrassing.

Laughter vibrated in Kol's chest, but he said and thought nothing. Instead, he issued an order to open the viewing panes for the humans in the concourse of the ship so they could see Ealra. Seconds later, the viewing pane on the bridge opened, and instead of staring at a wall, I was staring at a *huge* planet. I sucked in a startled breath, jumped from Kol's lap, and rushed around the consoles and males until I was all but pressed against the viewing pane with my hands and forehead flattened on the glass. I stared wide-eyed at the monster of a planet we were nearing.

"It's so big," I gushed. "And it's so colourful!"

It must be at least three times bigger than Earth is, and through the different shades of green that covered the surface, there were streaks of brown, blue, and red too, and *huge* portions of vibrant *purple*. Freaking purple! The size of the planet and the stunning colours of it aside, the main thing that stood out was the obvious life on the planet. One look and you could see it was thriving. It was a true thing of beauty and something to behold.

"Ealra," I whispered.

I didn't jump when I felt hands on my shoulders because I knew only Kol would touch me … unless someone had a death wish. His hands gave me a gentle squeeze, and I felt his delight at seeing his planet. He was happy to be home.

"Isn't she beautiful?" he murmured.

"Yes." I nodded. "Stunningly beautiful doesn't cover it. I've never seen something thrive with so much colour and life."

Kol hummed in agreement.

"How far away from Earth are we?" I asked him.

"Just three light years," he answered.

Just three light years?

I gasped. "We're eighteen trillion miles away from Earth?"

I felt the large hands on my shoulders squeeze me once more.

"You know one light year is six trillion lengths?"

I managed a snort. "I'm not stupid, Kol."

"I know that, but education isn't available on Earth."

I shrugged. "It used to be."

"When you were a child?" he asked, surprised.

"No, not in my time, but it was in my father's, and he taught me what he knew. He taught me how to read, write, and count. And since he was *obsessed* with space, he taught me useful things like how many miles were in a light year."

"He sounds like he was a great male."

I smiled, my eyes scanning Ealra.

"He was the best," I agreed.

"He taught you well," Kol said proudly. "We *are* eighteen trillion lengths away from Earth."

"How fast are we travelling?" I asked, amazed. "Shouldn't my insides be liquidised or my blood boiling from moving so fast?"

Kol chuckled. "No, your anatomy is like ours, so you can space travel easily. All spacecrafts are designed to protect our bodies during warp."

I figured as much being as I was still alive.

"You never answered my first question," I said, my eyes flicking to the *double* moons that were to the far right of Ealra.

"Maji have intergalactic space travel, *shiva* ... The technology of Earth has always been far less advanced than other species that exist in our cluster. Planets within a light year distance of the Milky Way have already activated their solar shields to protect their planets from the debris of *your* planet when it implodes. Debris won't reach them for a long time, but precautions are a must when dealing with a dying planet in close proximity. While humans have barely passed two hundred thousand years in existence, many races have seen this before because they're billions of years old. Your planet was old, but your species was not. We read the signs you could not, and we have saved you."

I focused backed on Ealra. "It looks like Earth, just more colourful."

"Ealra is three times bigger than Earth is. Out of every planet we have visited, Earth is the closest in detail to my original home world. We have all the same elements and many more that your world does not. We have water, but it's all fresh, not salted like on Earth. The main reason we took humans, aside from being reproductively compatible, was because you inhale and exhale the same gases to keep you alive as Maji do on Ealra. Once we knew you could survive here, everything else would be figured out in time."

A bright beam from my left caught my attention, and I couldn't look directly at it. I knew it was the sun, but not the sun I was used to. For starters, it was enormous, bigger than Ealra … and *blue*.

"Is that your sun?" I questioned.

"Yes, but we call a blue star. It functions the same way your sun did in the Milky Way."

"It's beautiful is what it is … but seriously, it's fucking *blue*!"

Kol laughed, and we both turned our heads when the door to the bridge opened.

"Surkah," I beamed when I saw my sister-in-mate.

She perked up when she saw me and walked towards me with a spring in her step. It shocked me how much I had come to care for Surkah in such a short amount of time, but I was so grateful for her. She was my dearest friend.

If I do the mate kiss thing to her, I said to Kol, *will she be okay with it?*

The admiration I felt from Kol for me warmed my heart.

She will never forget it, shiva.

I continued to smile at Surkah as she approached us. She did her arm on chest bow thing to her brother, and when she focused on me, I stepped forward and gestured for her to bend down. She furrowed her brows in confusion but leaned down to me. I placed my hands on her shoulders and watched said eyes widen when I placed the tip of my nose to hers, ran it up the bridge and stopped between her eyes. I replaced my nose with my lips and pressed a gentle kiss to the spot. With a smile, I pulled back, but that smile was instantly wiped away when I saw tears now *streaked* Surkah's face.

"Almighty." I choked. "I'm terribly sorry. Please, don't cry!"

I wrapped my arms around a bawling Surkah and practically screamed at Kol in my mind.

She's sobbing, Kol!

With joy, shiva. You only share a mate kiss with Maji whom you truly love and care for. It is sacred.

That relaxed me, and unlike when I thought of love with Kol, I wasn't scared because it was different with Surkah. She was my sister-in-mate and had quickly taken up the long-vacant role of cherished best friend. I had only known her for six days, but I felt like we went way back.

"Surkah." I frowned as I hugged her. "Please, I'll cry too if you don't stop and none of us would like that."

"No, we would not," Kol agreed, "because we know I'll do anything to stop the tears, and that means Thane will reach the edge if another engine stalls."

That made me and Surkah laugh.

Kol and Mikoh both moved over to a couple of crew members to discuss the plan to disembark the humans from the *Ebony*. I hadn't heard much of the conversation, but I knew Kol would fill me in later when I asked him.

"What do you think?" Surkah asked as she wiped her face free of tears. "Isn't Ealra something to behold?"

I turned back to the viewing pane.

"It most certainly is," I agreed. "I can't believe there are so many different colours."

"Everything that is not purple is land," Surkah offered.

I gasped. "The purple is ... water?"

"Yes." Surkah nodded. "Why is that a surprise?"

"It's ... purple."

"Yes, was water on Earth not purple?"

"No," I replied. "It's clear."

"How do you see it then?" she asked with a brow raised.

I laughed because I didn't know how to answer the question.

"It's complicated," I eventually said.

Surkah's lips quirked. "I imagine it is."

"From space, our water sources appear blue, but in person, it's clear."

"Very strange," Surkah commented.

I chuckled and glanced at Kol when I felt tension pour from him in waves. It looked like he was having a heated discussion with a few members of his crew, Nero, and Mikoh.

"What are they saying?" I asked Surkah.

"Mikoh is relaying a report to Kol about the Earth's Officials."

Say what?

I turned my full attention to Surkah.

"What about them?" I quizzed.

She looked at her brother then back at me and said, "Maybe you should ask Kol about that."

I did exactly that.

"Okay," I said to her then focused on her brother.

Why is Mikoh talking to you about Earth's Officials?

I heard his growl from across the room.

"Surkah!" he snapped, spinning to face us. "This conversation is not for Nova's ears *or* yours!"

Surkah didn't even flinch.

"I *told* you I wasn't going to be dishonest to my *sister-in-mate* when she asks me a question," she said firmly. "If you don't like that, then that is your problem. Not mine."

I looked at Surkah. "You go, female."

"Go where?" she asked.

I burst into laughter.

"Nowhere." I cackled. "It's just a bit of praise for standing up to Kol."

"Oh." She smiled. "Thank you."

Kol scowled at her, but when he switched his gaze to mine, it softened.

In private, I will discuss it.

I raised a brow. *Do you need to be here to land the craft?*

No, he hesitated, *my crew can do it if I give the order.*

Give the order then because we're going to discuss this. Now.

I turned to Surkah. "I'm going to discuss this with him in private."

I hugged her and walked towards the exit of the bridge, noting Kol angrily gave out the orders I asked him to. I made it about twenty feet down the hallway outside the bridge before I felt him behind me.

"You're *not* to walk alone without myself, Mikoh, or Nero to escort you, Nova."

I rolled my eyes, glad he couldn't see the action.

"*Nova,*" Kol growled. "Are you listening to me?"

"Yes. I just don't want to talk to you until we're in our room."

"Fine," he clipped.

The tension between us was thick, so by the time we reached our room, I felt like I could breathe again, and I was glad of it.

"We're in private," I said, crossing my arms over my chest as the door to our quarters closed. "Start talking."

Kol scowled and began to pace from left to right in front of me.

"Kol," I prompted.

He growled. "I am trying to think of a way to word it, so you don't get angry."

I raised a brow. "Is there a reason for me to *be* angry?"

"No, but you'll still manage to find a way to be angry."

I narrowed my eyes. "You aren't helping your case to keep me calm when you say shit like that."

"I apologise," he said and continued to pace from left to right.

I had to look away from him after a few moments because he was making me dizzy.

"Okay," he finally said, coming to a stop before me. "Two days ago, spacecrafts belonging to Earth's Officials were in range of us, and Mikoh was just confirming the course they took with coordinates brought them away from Ealra."

"Earth's Officials?" I repeated. "They were in range?"

"Before they changed course, yes."

I frowned. "How did you know they were Earth's Officials, though?"

"We tagged their vessels when they took off from Earth."

A flashback of the night I snuck close to the WBO surged through my mind. When the compound lit up next to the WBO before I focused on the *Ebony*, I had noticed a bunch of smaller crafts take off from the surface.

"The crafts," I murmured. "The smaller crafts I saw take off from the surface before the watchmen found me. The ones you gave the coordinates to for the unnamed planet. Those were the WBO's officials? They truly abandoned us?"

"Yes." Kol nodded. "We told them why we were there, and they said they would fully surrender Earth's females to us if we gave them credits—they're a source of currency everywhere—and coordinates."

I didn't know why I felt hurt, but I did.

"The cowardly bastards," I spat.

Kol nodded slowly, his eyes watching me carefully.

"Did you tell them that the Earth would implode quicker than we thought?" I questioned.

Kol nodded again. "It's why they wanted credits to get to—"

I narrowed my eyes at him when he cut himself off.

"To get to where?" I questioned. "The unnamed planet?"

"Before I tell you, remember how humans have treated you all your life, okay?"

As if I could forget.

"Okay," I said, my teeth grinding together.

"You mentioned once that your human royals lived off the planet, but you didn't know which planet or galaxy they fled to."

I nodded.

"Well, we know where they went." Kol dropped his gaze. "I hid this information from you before our mating. The name of the planet they fled to is called Terra, and it is the planet I referred to as the unnamed planet."

Kol's father traded with the species on the unnamed planet. I processed this for a moment then gasped.

"The species your father trades with are ... *human*?"

Kol nodded, his eyes watching me carefully.

"The *royal* humans?" I asked, gobsmacked.

"Yes," Kol said. "As leader of our people, he met with your human King, and they devised a trading agreement and a truce between our species."

I couldn't speak.

"We have known for a long time of the existence of humans on Terra, but part of the trade agreement between the Kings was that it be kept a secret until humans could grow and defend themselves and their new planet. Otherwise, they would be vulnerable to attacks. Maji and Vaneer are the only species to know that humans have relocated from Earth to Terra."

Still, I could not speak.

"We keep track of planets within our galaxy and in the bordering galaxies, and Terra is inside our galaxy, only seven hundred million miles away from Ealra. Your humans don't have the space travel we have, so it takes them considerably longer to get to where they are going, but they're close to us, considering how quick we can reach them, so we keep an eye on them."

"I can't believe this," I eventually whispered.

Kol tensed. "I am being truthful."

I looked at him. "I don't mean you're lying. I just mean it's hard to believe that they're on a new planet and left us on Earth to die."

Kol relaxed.

"Terra is the name of their new planet?"

Kol nodded. "Yes, it is twice the size of Earth, but virtually identical with its elements and natural gases. Terra and Ealra are two planets in many light years where humans can survive. You can breathe the air on either just as you once did on Earth. Before humans, no intelligent life lived there."

"Almighty," I rasped. "They have a new home, and no one ever knew."

"Your royal humans," Kol began, "have been on Terra at least eleven of your Earth years. Their numbers are greater than that of Maji but fewer than the humans on Earth ... but they are rebuilding your race. You breed far quicker than Maji."

I stared at Kol, my mouth agape.

"Why didn't you tell me any this?" I whispered, wrapping my arms around my midsection.

Thoughts were running through my mind a mile a minute.

"I ... I wasn't sure you would stay with us," he admitted, his shoulders slumping. "You were so sure you were being kidnapped and used, and when you met Sera, you demanded to leave. I feared you would refuse to mate with me if you knew, and that you would jump at the opportunity to go and be with your own people if you knew about their plans to rebuild your race. We had not bonded. I didn't want you to leave me. I ... I was scared you would."

My heart slammed against my chest, and my ears felt like they were burning. This was the break I had been looking for since I woke up on the *Ebony*. Things had certainly changed since I plotted ways to escape the craft, but in a way, they hadn't. The Maji were still withholding vital information from me.

"You lied to me," I said, my voice husky. "Again."

"Forgive me," Kol pleaded.

I didn't answer him.

"My people really have a new planet?" I asked, my voice sounding distant to my ears.

"Yes," Kol said tentatively. "Only humans with enough credits were able to gain admittance. They have a toll in operation around the planet. The humans who did not pay the toll were taken as workers to join the workforce for building their new world. Your human royals have done away with slavery; they're trying to establish a peaceful equality between all humans."

I didn't believe that shit for a second. Humans could never be equal. There would always be people who looked down on others.

"We Maji have done many missions over the decades and obtained a lot of credits. We gave your officials many of these credits in exchange for approaching and taking willing humans females with us back to Ealra. They didn't stick around once they got the credits and the coordinates ... That's when you saw them taking off. They set course for Terra. It will take them at *least* three months to reach the planet. Their crafts don't have the warp power that the *Ebony* does."

I felt the blood rush to my head as a pounding took up residence in my temples.

"The other w-women aboard," I stammered. "Were they aware of this?"

Kol was silent for a moment then he said, "Yes, it was part of the briefing we gave them, but they either didn't *want* to go to Terra or had no credits to *get* there. All aboard took their chances with us because they didn't believe humans could ever be equal. They still feared other humans ... like you did."

Did.

He assumed because I had talked to a few human women during breakfast in the mess hall over the past few days that I wasn't terrified of them. For someone who stared at me all the time, he didn't exactly see me.

Every time I was in a human presence, I was observing them, waiting for them to attack me, to do something to me. I knew Kol thought it was foolish, but I couldn't just change my way of thinking because he wanted me to.

"You need us humans a lot more than we need you ... don't you?"

Kol chewed on his inner cheek then he nodded in response.

"I feel sick," I told him. "I want to lie down for a while."

Panic flashed in his violet eyes.

"Let me carry you to the be—"

"No," I cut him off. "I can walk to the bed just fine on my own, thank you."

He didn't speak.

"I want to be on my own, if you don't mind."

"I *do* mind," he instantly replied.

His response didn't surprise me, but I also wasn't going to deal with it. I shook my head, turned, and walked over to the huge bed we shared.

"Go oversee the landing of the *Ebony*," I told him as I climbed onto the bed, lay on my back, and closed my eyes. "I just want to think about everything you've said. I need this alone time. Give me a moment to have my thoughts to myself. Please."

I felt his worry and indecisiveness, but when I heard the door open and close, I knew he'd granted my wish.

He lied to me.

Kol knew my people had a new planet, a new plan of order, new hope that we could be a whole race again ... and he kept that from me. Part of me was angry because of that, but another part of me understood. Kol had wanted me to be his mate at that point, and he feared that if he told me, I'd want to leave him. I knew with *certainty* that if I knew about Terra and our royal humans' intentions of rebuilding our race on a new world when I encountered Sera, then I *would* have demanded to go to Terra where I'd take any chances at survival. I had no bond with Kol when I'd met the augmented woman, and I'd have hightailed it towards Terra without a backwards glance just to get away from her.

And I knew that Kol knew that.

I hated that he kept Terra and the lost human faction from me, and I was already going through what I wanted to say to him in my head to make it clear to him that lying was *not* going to work for me in our relationship. If he wasn't going to level with me one hundred percent, then things weren't going to work between us. Period. Since we were already mated, I knew the threat to leave him would prompt him into heeding my warning.

It seemed cruel to me to mess with Kol's emotions and use my bond with him as a bargaining chip, but I couldn't be a part of something wrapped in layers of lies. I just couldn't do it. He needed to understand how serious lying was, *especially* when it involved something as huge as my race *not* going extinct.

I wasn't sure how long I had been lost in thought, but Kol's voice suddenly sounded in our room, and it took my focus.

"Crew, human females," he began, his deep and shiver-inducing voice surrounded the room. "Welcome to *Ealra*."

CHAPTER THIRTEEN

"Nova?"

I lowered my hand from brushing my hair and smiled at Surkah as she entered my room ... alone.

"Hey ... where is Mikoh?" I asked, shocked that he wasn't three steps behind her like he always was.

Surkah grinned. "Nero is outside; he escorted me. Mikoh has disembarked the *Ebony* to meet with his unit on the ground. He's overseeing the females leaving the craft to make sure they disembark safely."

I hummed. "Kol is with him?"

"Of course," Surkah replied. "His mission does not end until all the females are handed over to the Guard on the ground."

I nodded in understanding then allowed my gaze to drop to Surkah's body. She wasn't wearing the med bay uniform I had been so used to seeing her in. Instead, she was wearing a sparkling golden wrap of some kind. I squinted my eyes, and the more I looked at it, the more I realised it wasn't a wrap but two separate pieces of clothing.

The top of the outfit was a shell garment and was cut to fit the top half of Surkah's body perfectly—the layered fabric hugged her breasts tightly. It had low-cut sleeves and a low V-neck. Surkah's midriff was exposed, and a large, thin white sparkling chain wrapped around it, resting above her belly button. It reminded me of necklaces I had seen wealthy women wear around their necks back on Earth, but this was designed as an accessory for the waist. The bottom half of Surkah's outfit was a long skirt that almost touched the ground; it was pleated and had a slit on either side that exposed Surkah's legs right up to her bare hips.

"Holy shit," I exclaimed, gaping at her. "You look incredible."

Surkah looked down at herself and flushed. The action brought my attention to her white hair. It hung loosely and fell in waves down to her waist. On top of her head were three braids in a row next to the other, keeping the hair from falling into her face while aiding in adding a touch of elegance to her appearance. She had clips snagged between the braids that glistened like diamonds when they caught the light.

"Thank you," she said, her eyes lifting to meet mine. "This is my typical day-to-day clothing. I wear much fancier ensembles when I have to attend Court."

She looked pretty fancy to me.

"Court?" I questioned.

Surely, it wasn't like the Court that used to exist on Earth.

"Court is a monthly event my mother holds in the palace ballroom. It is a time for mothers to present their unmated sons to the unmated females of Royal City."

Maji matchmakers?

I blinked. "That sounds ... interesting."

Surkah snorted. "It is boring for me because I can only sit and observe. I am not allowed to mingle. I am already promised to Mikoh, and being a princess means no one can look at or speak to me."

I frowned. "Well, you'll have me to look at you and talk to you at the next Court thing ... if I'm invited?"

Surkah clapped her hands together merrily. "I'm positive *Kol* will give you permission to attend. It is an event that females enjoy, so he will want you to fit in."

I wasn't going to lie. This Court thing sounded like it would have my anxiety levels rising, but logically, I knew I was in safe hands with the Maji, so I reminded myself of that and thought of something more miscellaneous ... more female. I looked at Surkah's stunning outfit and frowned down at my own.

I can't wear this to Court.

"I'm grateful for these new clothes," I said, hoping the sincerity I felt showed in my tone. "I promise I truly am. I don't care that they're all the same, but I will look silly next to you when you look like *that*."

Surkah furrowed her brows. "What do you mean? You cannot wear *Ebony* attire on Ealra. I'm here to fit you for an ensemble of your own."

I widened my eyes. "You *are*?"

Surkah nodded, closed her eyes for a few seconds, and then opened her eyes when the door to my quarters open. Nero walked in with a bundle of blue fabric and some black jewellery in his arms.

"Hi, Nero." I awkwardly waved.

He winked at me. "I'll be right outside. Just call me if either of you need my help ... but please, *don't* need my help."

Surkah laughed when he fled the second she took the fabric from him.

"Males hate aiding females in a fitting."

I chuckled. "Because it's boring?"

Surkah grinned, a devilish glint in her eyes. "Because the female must be naked and the males can't touch her even though they're only a few steps away. It is torture for them, especially when a female is in heat."

"Holy shit." I choked. "Kol would *kill* him if he saw me naked, friend or not."

One thing I knew about Kol was that he was extremely possessive of me. *Extremely.*

"Which is why he pleaded for us not to need his help." She cackled.

I shook my head. "What's the 'in heat' thing you mentioned?"

Surkah looked thoughtful a moment then, with a snap of her fingers, she said, "Ovulation. In heat means ovulation. I remember Sera told me that was the human term for it. It means when a female's body is ready to become pregnant, a female in heat gives off a scent to males that is almost irresistible. Usually, unmated females are required to stay inside their homestead when they're in heat because too many fights have started in our villages between unmated males who wish to claim them. Some females enjoy the attention, though, and do it anyway."

"What bitches," I said.

Surkah laughed. "I do not know what that means, but it sounds funny."

I smiled. "Do you think human women go into heat?"

My friend nodded. "They have to; they can't get pregnant otherwise."

I flushed. "Sorry, I should know this kind of stuff. I mean, it happens to my body."

"Don't be embarrassed," Surkah said and patted my arm. "How could you know about this unless you were taught about it?"

I shrugged in response.

"Do you bleed every month?" I then asked.

"Not yet," she said. "I will once my *uva* activates."

The reminder that Surkah still hadn't hit her version of puberty amazed me once more. She was close to forty years of age, but she looked like an eighteen-year-old girl. It amazed me how youthful the Maji remained throughout time.

"My father told me it was normal for girls to bleed when they reached puberty," I said with a snort. "I remember the first time. I had just turned eleven when I got my period for the first time, and I thought I was dying. I cried for days ... I still sometimes cry when the bleeding occurs. I don't know why, though; the tears just start and are hard to stop. It's a messy time. Literally."

Surkah giggled. "That is adorable."

"It is now because I expect it," I mused. "At the time, it was terrifying and so embarrassing because I was the only girl in my family."

"Even though my mother is present in my life, I am always surrounded by males, so I understand what you mean."

I smiled. "That's why we get along so well, you ... you just get me."

"We're sisters-in-mate," Surkah said with pride. "We get each other."

I smiled.

"So," I said with a gestured towards the fabric. "How are we going to do this?"

"You are going to remove your clothing, and I will show you how to correctly wrap your ensemble."

I was hesitant.

"I'm a bit embarrassed," I admitted.

"Why?" Surkah asked, her eyebrows raised.

Heat creeped up my neck.

"Your brother is the only other being who has seen me naked, and I'm still embarrassed about *that*."

"I saw you naked when I bathed and changed your clothing when you arrived aboard the *Ebony*."

I rolled my eyes. "I was unconscious then. That's different."

Surkah giggled. "You Earthers are funny. A few of your females who I have examined had the same fear of being seen without clothing."

I glanced at her exposed skin. "I'm guessing Maji females don't have a problem with nudity?"

"Not at all." Surkah grinned.

I snorted. "I figured as much."

"I can turn around if you wish?"

I sighed. "It's okay. I have to start getting used to your customs sooner rather than later."

Though *much* later would help my sudden anxiety.

"I'm proud of you for taking this step," Surkah praised.

My lips twitched. "Thanks."

With flushed cheeks, I stripped out of my clothes as fast as I could to get it over and done with.

"This is mortifying," I said as I stood naked as the day I was born.

Surkah chuckled as she gathered my *Ebony* clothing and moved it aside.

"Your body is like mine, just smaller and not grey. You're hairless like our females, too."

I resisted the urge to cover myself. "My father won credits from gambling when I was sixteen, and he got me laser hair removal. At that point in time, we were sleeping outdoors and couldn't bathe very often. Not having to deal with excess body hair helped me."

"The more you speak of your father, the more I adore him."

I beamed. "He'd have loved you and the rest of the Maji. He was *such* a space freak."

Surkah giggled. "Are you ready to get started?"

I looked down at my naked body. "This is so embarrassing."

"You'll move past it in time. Trust me."

"I believe you," I said as I left my hands hanging awkwardly at my sides. "So ... what now?"

"Now I dress you since I'm *confident* you would tie the fabric in knots."

I snorted. "Go ahead."

I tried to watch what piece of fabric went where, and how many times a certain section was wrapped around a limb, but I got confused and gave up early on. It took Surkah ten minutes until I was ready. She had to measure, cut away a lot of fabric, and sew new hems until it fit me perfectly.

"Where did you learn to sew like that, Surkah?" I asked in amazement. "You measured the fabric, cut it, and sewed it before I even knew what you were doing."

Surkah blushed. "My mother taught me and so did my aunt-in-mate. We spend a lot of time together, and sewing is an activity females enjoy. You get pretty good at something when you've been doing it for so long."

I had no doubt.

"Could you maybe, if you wanted to, teach me?" I asked, shyly. "I'd love to learn how to make my own clothing. I could barely sew on a patch while mending my clothing back on Earth. If I'm being honest, it was a real pain in the ass."

Surkah smiled so wide, her eyes lit up with joy.

"I would *love* to teach you. It would be my pleasure."

"Great." I smiled back. "I'm looking forward to it."

I watched as Surkah picked up the black sparkled body jewellery and held still as she adjusted it over my neck and around my waist and hips. When she was done, she moved behind me and got to work on my hair. She liked the colour of my hair and wanted to leave most of it down, so she braided the top section of my hair back and used a small black device that automatically tangled itself around my hair when placed on my head.

"What the fuck is that on my head?" I asked in a panic.

Surkah blinked. "There is no direct translation, but it is a small device that wraps around your hair, gets hot, and then, after few seconds, it untangles, and your hair falls in nice big waves. The longer you leave it on, the curlier your hair gets."

"What in God's name can do such a thing?" I demanded, terrified of the object on my head.

Surkah was amused. "You didn't have devices on Earth for your hair?"

"None that I could afford," I said as Surkah reached for the device and lifted it from my head.

I waited for pain, but none came.

"It didn't hurt," I said, surprised.

"Of course, it doesn't hurt. Why would we use something that would hurt?"

I shrugged. Surkah snorted.

"Sera says your Earthly haircare products are not as advanced as ours are."

I shrugged again. "I can't say if she is right or not. I've never had anything put on my hair other than cheap scissors to control the length. I lived in poverty on a war-ridden world, remember?"

Surkah frowned. "I didn't forget. I just can't imagine how awful things were for you."

I didn't mean for the happy atmosphere to turn sour, so I gestured to my body with a smile.

"Am I ready?"

Surkah instantly perked up. "Yes, and you're even more beautiful."

Before I could reply, she called for Nero, who entered the room with his hands over his eyes not a second later.

"My Princess," he began. "Kol will cut my eyes from my head if I see his mate naked."

I smiled. Surkah giggled.

"All is well, Nero," she assured him.

He didn't move a muscle. "Is this a test, Princess? I am not very good with tests."

At that, I laughed. "I'm fully clothed, Nero. I promise."

He slowly lowered his hands and opened one eye to a slit. When he saw I was clothed, he lowered his hands fully and opened his eyes. Then he surprised me by placing his fist over his chest and bowing.

"You're a sight to behold, Princess Nova."

When he stood right and smiled at me, I couldn't help but blush.

"That is very sweet of you, Nero. Thank you."

He nodded once. "Are you both ready to be escorted from the *Ebony*? The humans have nearly fully disembarked, and festivities are already underway."

"Festivities?" I questioned. "What *kind* of festivities?"

"A grand welcoming feast followed by song and dance, of course," Surkah answered me. "Tables will line the streets with mountains of food for Maji and our new human citizens. The people are very excited about our new additions. The feast will not be until dusk, but the people are all very excited."

That seemed a little too much too soon to me, but I didn't want to sound ungrateful. Instead, I smiled and brought the attention back to my outfit.

"Do you think Kol will like the clothing?"

Nero snorted. "You could be covered in tree leaves, and he would still find you the most attractive being in the cosmos. You're his mate, so he will only every see beauty in you, Princess."

I placed my hand on my chest. "Nero, that's so sweet of you to say."

He shrugged, but his lips twitched.

"Nero's future mate will be lucky to have a male who has a way with words," Surkah commented.

"I agree." I nodded. "You're quite the catch, Nero."

He scuffed his boot against the floor. "Princesses, I have no interest in a mate. My duty is to the Guard."

Surkah rolled her eyes. "You can be mated and still have a duty to the Guard."

Nero scowled at her, and it made me laugh.

I watched the exchange. "You're the only male, besides Mikoh and Kol, who backtalks Surkah."

Nero smiled wide. "I am her kinsperson, so I can get away with annoying her."

Kinsperson?

I looked at Surkah. "He is your *what*?"

She was silent for a moment as she thought then she said, "It is another way to say blood relative. Nero is my cousin. Like the cousins you once had."

I nodded in understanding. "Whose son is he?"

"My uncle and aunt-in-mate," she answered. "Nero is a very special member of our family. He is the *only* son born to my uncle and aunt-in-mate."

I blinked. "The only one? But I thought a female's *uva*—"

"My aunt-in-mate became very sick not long after she birthed Nero." Surkah cut me off. "It is a miracle she did not die, Father says. She recovered, thank Thanas, but the mysterious sickness affected her body... her reproductive system, to be exact. Her *uva* never contracted after the sickness; she never had another monthly bleed, and she never bore another young one. Nero is greatly spoiled because of this. His mother and father love him very much."

"By love me very much, she means they suffocate me with emotion and question me at every turn to see when I will take a mate and make them grand-offspring," Nero said with a teasing grin.

I raised a brow. "What kind of son are you to keep them waiting?"

"Ha!" Surkah giggled. "Nova agrees with the family. You should take a mate and produce little ones!"

Nero groaned. "You females always stick together."

I snickered and bumped my fist with Surkah, but she looked down at her hand then to mine with furrowed brows.

"Why did you hit me?" she asked, baffled.

I laughed. "I didn't hit you; I bumped you."

She stared at me blankly, and so did Nero. I laughed harder.

"I can't believe I'm going to have to explain what a fist bump is." I smiled as I shook my head. "It's kind of like a high five."

I was met with more blank stares.

"Oh, my Almighty." I giggled.

Surkah looked at Nero. "She is amused at us not knowing what she is talking about."

Nero smirked. "I can tell."

"A fist bump like what I did to you, Surkah," I said, regaining her attention, "is just a gesture of greeting or affirmation."

Surkah nodded slowly. "And the highest of fives that you mentioned?"

I cackled. "Just 'high five' not highest of fives."

"Okay," Surkah said, her lips twitching. "What is a high five?"

I lifted my hand in the air with my palm facing Surkah.

"Mirror my action," I asked. "Then clap your hand against mine."

After our hands had clapped together, I said, "That's a high five. I used to do them with my father, uncle, and cousins whenever one of us brought down a nicely sized buck or caught some juicy fish. It kind of a celebratory gesture."

"Is my hand supposed to sting?" Surkah questioned, staring at her palm.

"Sometimes." I grinned.

"And this is a custom with all humans?" Nero asked.

I shrugged. "I've never thought about it, but yeah, I guess so."

Nero looked like he made a mental note of that information, and I made a note myself to talk to him about it just so he didn't scare a human woman half to death by shoving his big hand in her face as he waited for a high five.

"Are you both ready to go?" he asked. "Kol is requesting our presence."

"Tell him a few more minutes. Nova has to see herself first in the viewing glass."

"Females," Nero said with a playful shake of his head. "I will wait outside. *Please*, do not take long."

Surkah waved Nero on, earning another scowl from him before

he left the room. I laughed when Surkah took my arm and tugged me across the room until we stood in front of a blank section of the wall. I blinked and looked at my sister-in-mate.

"It's a wall," I commented.

"Everything is not what it seems to be, Nova," Surkah said before she leaned forward and placed her hand against the wall. When she removed her hand, the wall slid upwards, and it revealed a huge floor-to-ceiling mirror.

"Wow!" I gasped. "That is gigantic."

Surkah smiled wide as my shock became evident when my eyes landed on myself.

"Holy fuck," I exhaled as I stared at the woman in the mirror. "Surkah, how is that *me*?"

I had on the same wrap or dress thingy that Surkah had on, only mine was blue, and my body jewellery was black. My neck, arms, lower back, waist, and hips were exposed, but it looked … good. My skin was a beautiful porcelain white and clear with not a speck of dirt in sight. It almost looked as if it gleamed. I used to think I had a shapeless, average body but not in the ensemble I was wearing. It showcased just how feminine I was. There was a curve to my hips, a narrowing at my waist, and then slight fullness to my chest. My legs looked very long with the slits in the skirt going right above my exposed hips.

"You're a beauty," Surkah beamed.

I smiled back at her. "You're very sweet."

Surkah's brows shot up to her hairline. "Sweet? You know what I taste like?"

I burst into surprised laughter.

"*No!*" I choked. "I mean, your words are kind. Saying you're sweet is just another way of saying you're being kind."

Surkah sighed. "Your human words do confuse me at times."

"I can see," I said with a playful shake of my head. "I hope the Maji off the *Ebony* don't have as hard a time with language barriers as you seem to have."

Surkah snorted. "Our smartest Maji will shadow a lot of your females to learn your way and words, and they will document that information and make it available to the rest of our society to help us understand humans more."

"Wow, who came up with that idea?"

"The Elders, of course."

I raised a brow. "Who are the Elders?"

"The oldest and wisest of the people," Surkah explained. "They're my father's Council and hugely respected amongst the people. Four of them were alive when we had to flee our original home world. They were only youngsters, barely twenty years of age, but they had to quickly become grown males and help the people find a new planet and establish a home there. They helped find Ealra and aided in the people starting our life here."

"Wow," I said, dumbstruck. "That is incredible. How old are they?"

"Very old," Surkah replied. "Five centuries."

"*Five centuries?*"

"It still shocks you that our lifespan is so long?"

"Uh, *yeah*."

Surkah giggled. "You'll adjust. Eventually."

"How many Maji were saved when your planet died?" I quizzed.

Surkah frowned. "Only 1900. It happened so suddenly; there was no warning when our planet began to break apart, so getting off the planet was a scrambled effort. Many of those rescued were females. Our males caring for females so greatly is what led to our race being endangered."

"I don't understand."

Surkah sighed. "Many of the females who were rescued were mated, and their mates died back on our original home world. That means a few days after…"

"The females died," I finished. "Their mates died, so their essence did, too."

"Yes." Surkah nodded, glumly. "My father and uncle, whom are from the same pregnancy and were just a few days old at the time, were saved. Their remaining brothers were not, as they were on a hunt and too far away to make it to the crafts to flee. My father was not the firstborn, but he was older than my uncle, so when all his brothers died, he became the oldest living son and the new Revered Father. My grandmother was saved also, but my grandfather was not, so she died six days after they escaped. She stayed awake the entire time and extracted milk from her breasts for her sons to drink after she died. She produced a lot of milk that would last weeks once stored in freezers on the craft they escaped on. Females can overproduce when they choose to."

I was wide-eyed.

"How did your father and uncle survive?" I asked, astonished. "Surely, the milk would have run out before Ealra was found."

Surkah nodded. "It did run out, but as I said, a breastfeeding mother can overproduce milk if she chooses to do so. Many females who were saved with their mates had infants and overproduced to help feed the Revered Father and prince."

I nodded in understanding.

"Did it take long to find Ealra?"

Surkah nodded. "Our race took refuge on Vaneer, Vada's home world, and along with the Vaneer, they searched for a suitable planet we could survive on. Ealra was discovered three years later, and a few months after its discovery, our entire race moved there."

"Kol said Maji weren't the only inhabitants on Ealra. What other species live there?"

"Many creatures live there, but only one other intelligent species like us call Ealra home, the Eedam. They're tribespeople. Very primal and not advanced like Maji at all. We don't bother them, and they don't bother us."

I nodded.

"What else did Kol tell you?" Surkah asked, an eyebrow raised.

"A lot." I sighed, my shoulders slumping. "He told me about Terra, about the humans there, and about the deal your people made with Earth's Officials."

Surkah swallowed. "I urged him to inform you of Terra and its rulers, but he was scared you'd want to go to the new human planet."

"He told me as much," I said with a shrug. "He got what he wanted, though. We're mated, and I'm by his side instead of on my way to Terra."

"You ... you feel betrayed, though?" Surkah pressed. "By Kol?"

I did. I felt like my options were once again taken away from me. I wouldn't have chosen Terra over Kol, or the Maji in general, but he never gave me the choice. He made it for me, and that was what bothered me.

"I do," I admitted. "I hate lies, Surkah, and he has lied to me. Something he has done more than once."

"It pains him, Nova," Surkah assured me. "He would never lie to you unless he was in fear of something."

To me, that still wasn't a good enough reason to lie about something that involved my very way of life.

I inhaled and exhaled, trying to force him from my mind.

"Let's just go with Nero so we can get the introductions to your planet underway," I said, locking eyes with Surkah's through the mirror. "My argument with Kol is the least of my worries right now."

"You need not worry about Ealra and the people, dear sister. Your arrival is a celebration ... You'll see."

CHAPTER FOURTEEN

"Nova—"

"What am I doing wrong now?" I cut Surkah off as we stepped onto a huge ramp that was lowered to the ground of Ealra.

I was anxious and felt highly out of place, and with every step I took, I seemed to do something wrong. First, I walked ahead of Nero when I was supposed to walk behind him then I smiled and said hello to a male who was also escorting us—he was so caught off guard he looked at Nero with panicked eyes. Apparently, no male is allowed talk to me without Kol's permission.

"You have to wait for the Guard," Nero answered.

I looked at Surkah. "The Guard?" I related.

She nodded. "They'll be here in mere minutes."

I looked at Nero. "Can I talk to any members of the Guard?"

Nero gnawed on his lower lip. "By law, you shouldn't, and they shouldn't reply if you do speak to them, but the Guard members coming to escort us are you brothers-in-mate, so no matter what Kol says, they'll talk to you. They're his older brothers, and they give him a hard time whenever possible."

I sucked in a strangled breath. "What if they don't like me?"

That was such a trivial thing to be concerned about, but it was what worried me at the current moment.

"They'll adore you," Surkah said with a loving smile. "They'll be shocked that Kol has mated, but then they'll be joyful for you both."

"How can you be so sure?"

"Because"—Surkah winked—"I know my brothers."

Surkah was trying to reassure me, but my nerves were still spiked.

"Change the topic. Discuss something else to distract me until they get here."

Nero drew a blank, so I focused on Surkah who was deep in thought.

"Housing," she suddenly announced. "All the human women should be excited with their housing."

"Housing?" I repeated incredulously. "You have *housing* on Ealra?"

Surkah muffled a giggle with her hand. "Of course. Where did you think we lived if not inside a residence?"

I paused. "I ... I guess I never thought of it."

I never thought about what life would be like on Ealra, which was stupid considering I had a one-way ticket to the planet. Thinking about my life there should have been on my mind, but it seemed Kol had taken up all my focus over the past six days.

Surkah vibrated with laughter. "We have modernised homesteads for our citizens. Each family builds their own on their land. The Revered Father gifts every new family a plot of land as a mating gift."

That's nice of him.

"But I'm the only human female who has mated so far." I frowned. "There are no other new families."

"That is a technicality," Surkah said with a wave of her hand. "Each female will eventually take a mate, so my father thought ahead and had large family-size homesteads built for them in advance. Each homestead has five floors. It consists of a large kitchen, a living area, a washroom for clothing, fifteen sleep rooms, and six cleansing rooms—each has a relief pod."

It sounded like they built mansions and not just simple houses.

I raised a brow. "How far in advance were these homesteads built?"

"Construction of the human housing started five years ago," my sister-in-mate replied.

I whistled. "Your father was certain Earth would give its women up, huh?"

Surkah grinned. "Pretty certain."

"So each human woman will have a home of their own?"

She nodded. "Two thousand homesteads were built in a new brand-new section of Royal City. We weren't sure how many would be needed. We *hoped* for two thousand females, but we're overjoyed to have many more. Royal City is the name of our main city, in case you were wondering. It was named by the people. The human housing section is very large itself, so it has been given its own name as it's now an official district of Royal City."

"What is the new district's name?" I prompted.

Surkah devilishly grinned. "Human Burrow."

I almost instantly burst into laughter. "Is it really called that?"

"*No*," Surkah tittered. "It's called Harmony."

I shook my head, amused. "I'll live in Harmony with the other humans?"

Surkah shook her head. "No, you'll live in the palace with the rest of us royals."

Oh.

"Right," I exhaled. "I'm a princess now."

Surkah's eyes gleamed. "You don't like being a princess, do you?"

I swallowed. "I'm just scared. I really don't want to mess anything up."

"You won't," she assured me. "You can't beat anything I have ever done to bring dishonour to my family."

That intrigued me.

"What have you done to bring dishonour?"

"As of late?" she asked, her lips quirked.

I nodded.

"I snuck aboard the *Ebony* for this mission *without* permission."

I felt like the floor fell away from beneath my feet.

I screeched. "You did *not*!"

"Oh, she did," Nero mumbled to himself, earning a muffled chuckle from the male beside him.

"I did." Surkah giggled. "My brothers, Killi, Arli, and Arvi were chosen by Mikoh to watch over me while he was away on the mission to retrieve our new females, and as usual, I was not asked what I wanted, so after Mikoh bid me farewell, my brothers escorted me back to our palace where I pretended I was tired and went to my quarters. While I was there, I changed clothing, left a note for my brothers so they wouldn't think I was abducted, covered my face and body, and snuck out. The *Ebony* was still boarding goods into the cargo hold, so I slipped in there and just sat down behind a large crate and waited."

I was fascinated.

"How did no male see or scent you?"

Surkah grinned. "I sprayed *fotha* essence on my coverings."

"What is *fotha*?" I asked, perplexed.

"It is a repellent for tiny creatures that like to eat flowers in my mother's garden. It stinks when freshly sprayed. The tail end of the *Ebony* was situated right next to a flower field that was recently sprayed with the repellent, so to the males stocking the cargo, the air would have just smelled like the *fotha*, not a female."

I blinked. "You're like an evil genius."

Surkah devilishly grinned.

"Was no alert sounded when your brothers realised you were

missing?"

"My brothers know *never* to interrupt my sleep cycle because I can be *really* cranky. I knew I had at least five to six hours before they would worry and enter my quarters to check on me. I also knew, according to Kol's flight plan, that he planned to active warp on the fifth hour after takeoff. Once warp is activated, they wouldn't have been able to return me to Ealra. It would have cost too much fuel and caused problems with Kol's schedule since we already knew Earth was dangerously close to imploding."

I smiled widely.

"I'm really impressed," I exclaimed happily. "This is seriously great."

"I'm glad you think so." She chuckled.

"How did Kol and Mikoh find out you were on board?"

She giggled. "A crew member was retrieving some goods from the cargo hold, and he happened to need the goods from a crate that was behind me. I had already removed my coverings at this point and stuck them inside an empty crate, so I couldn't scent them. The male who found me is the youngest male aboard the *Ebony*. He is only thirty-five years old, and he froze with fear when he realised who I was. He stared at me then said 'Princess' before he dropped to his knees, pressed his head against the cold floor, and begged my forgiveness for making eye contact and speaking to me directly."

I pouted. "The poor kid."

The irony that I was calling someone who was twelve years older than me (even *older* in Ealra years!) a kid was not lost on me.

"I know." Surkah grinned as she rocked back and forth on the heels of her feet. "I pardoned him so he'd stand, and then I ordered him to the bridge so he could have Mikoh come and fetch me."

"Surkah!" I said, giggling.

"I know," she beamed, pleased with herself. "He was in disbelief when he entered the cargo hold with my brother and Nero right behind him."

I lifted my hand to my mouth and lightly chewed on my nails.

"What happened next?" I asked.

She blushed, and it only caused me to squeal with delight.

"*Tell* me!" I demanded.

"Mikoh spanked me," she whispered, her cheeks aflame with purple.

I sucked in a breath. "No!"

She bobbed her head, "As my intended, he has the right to inflict simple physical punishment when I endanger myself, and the cargo hold is *very* dangerous. I took the spanking even though it made me cry. Of course, my tears caused all three males to lose their anger and gain a whole lot of sympathy for me. They quickly began to fret over me like a child. Mikoh insisted I strike him to take my revenge for the spanking he gave me, but I didn't, and it distraught him even further until he apologised over and over."

I shook my head. "You have everyone wrapped around your little finger."

Surkah only smiled, and it made me snort with amusement.

"Will you be in trouble when you disembark the craft?" I questioned.

I hoped not.

She nodded with a reluctant sigh. "Yes, but it's not like I can *really* be punished. I already can't leave the palace without an escort. My father will refuse me food for a few days as punishment, but the second I say I am hungry and cry, plates of food will be shoved under my nose. Being female on Ealra has its advantages."

I cackled. "As I said, you're an evil genius."

Surkah beamed as she stared down the ramp before looking back at me.

"You bathed?" she asked, sniffing the air.

I grinned. "I have used the cleansing unit three times a day since that first day in the medical bay."

"Why so many times?" Surkah asked, shocked.

I shrugged. "I'm making up for lost time, I guess."

Surkah processed this then said, "Well, you smell wonderful."

I laughed. "Thanks."

"Are you ready to meet some of my family?" she asked as I moved closer to her.

"Are you serious?" I grumbled. "I could wait another ten years if I was given the chance."

"It will not be bad, I promise. They will be overjoyed that Kol has mated."

"Even though I'm a human?" I questioned.

"It will be a shock, so expect wide eyes, but Mother and Father will not oppose the mating. They'll celebrate it."

My stomach churned. "I'm scared they won't like me."

"They'll adore you," Surkah assured me. "We're already best friends, so they'll see how wonderful you are ... Just give them the chance to get to know you."

"The princes approach," Nero murmured from behind us.

"Surkah!" a booming voice bellowed. "You're a deceiving little terror!"

Surkah groaned. "Go away, Killi ... and take Arli and Arvi with you."

I instantly moved behind Surkah as three huge figures appeared at the end of the ramp and began to trek up it.

"Oh, I think not, *darling sister*," another voice stated. "We have means for a quarrel with you."

"I'll tell Father if you even *think* of circling me, Arvi."

That made her brothers, and Nero laugh.

"What does she mean?" I whispered to Nero.

"When males circle a female," he whispered back, "it is usually because she has played games that each male was unaware of. When a female is circled by a male or more than one male, her instincts are to automatically bow to show submission. Surkah is a fierce female, but her instincts would force her to bow to her brothers if they circled her, and that would wound her pride. It a harmless revenge antic that males have for females."

"I think you deserve to be circled."

"Arli, as my favourite brother, you should not say such things!"

All the males snickered.

"I am your favourite now?" Arli asked jokingly. "It was Ezah last moon cycle, Killi the moon cycle before that, Kol the moon cycle before *that*, and Aza that mo—"

"Oh, close your lips," Surkah hissed, earning her more chuckles.

"You should not have stowed away aboard the *Ebony*," Killi spoked firmly when the chuckles ceased. "The worry and fear you caused were cruel, Surkah."

I knew Killi, Arli, and Arvi where now stood in front of Surkah, but I couldn't bring myself to step out from behind her and face them.

"I did not mean to cause any of those emotions," Surkah replied, her voice cracking like she was about to cry. "I just wanted to help Kol, and our new females, and—"

"You defied direct orders from your intended," Killi cut her off.

"I know." Surkah sniffled. "He already punished me for it."

"Not nearly as much as he should have." Killi growled, the sound just enough to show he was displeased and not truly angered. "You have lost my trust and will not win it back so easily, do you understand?"

"Yes, Killi," Surkah whimpered. "I am sorry."

"Your tears do not sway me, sister. Your actions do."

Killi was a fucking hardass.

"Before you continue, brother, can someone address why a small alien female is hiding behind our sister? And why she scents of Kol?"

Oh shit, that's me.

Nero cleared his throat. "I believe Kol should formally be the one to answer that, but as he is not here, Surkah … you can do it."

Surkah looked over her shoulder and glared at Nero, her eyes red and swollen from crying. She turned back to face her brothers and said, "She is our sister-in-mate."

Silence.

Long fucking silence.

"Almighty," I whispered.

"I don't believe it," Killi stated, the shock evident in his tone. "Kol has mated? One of the alien females is *his*?"

"Yes, he has," Nero answered. "He is behaving worse than any newly mated male I have ever seen, too. He has contacted me seventy-three times since I began our escort for an update. He's attacked Mikoh over her more times than I could count, growled at me and Thane, and even Surkah. If I ever think about taking a mate, I will think of Kol's behaviour, and it will quickly kill that urge."

Kol's brothers burst into gleeful laughter.

I peeked out from behind Surkah and gasped when I took in the three males. They were each massively tall, and their bodies were thick with muscle, but their grey skin looked a lot more vibrant than any of the other Maji I have encountered. Their attire distracted me for a moment because they didn't have on matching navy top and pants with armour plates on them. They had different coloured loose fitted pants ... and that was it. No shoes, no socks, and no t-shirts.

They looked like they belonged between the pages of a thin, worn paper book I had found years ago on Earth where attractive men and women were spread out in the pictures. It was easy to see the family resemblance between the brothers, Kol, and Surkah. They were, to be honest, very beautiful.

The male to my far left had shoulder-length silver hair, silver eyes, and a splash of white dots over his nose and under his eyes. His cheekbones were high, his jawline sharp, and his mouth was shaped exactly like Kol's. A quick glance at the other two males confirmed similar features, only they both had black hair like Kol. None of them could ever deny that they were relatives because it was plain as day to anyone who looked at them.

The male with silver eyes locked them on mine, and before he could say a word, I got spooked. I sucked in a harsh breath, turned, and ran like the devil himself was on my heels. I ignored Surkah and Nero's calls for me and somehow navigated my way back to my and Kol's quarters. I ran into the cleansing room and hid inside the cleansing unit, hoping and praying for my heart beat to return to normal.

I felt like a coward. One look at Kol's brothers had me fleeing. I had always prided myself on how tough I was, how I could take care of myself and deal with any situation, but the second an alien male locked eyes with mine, I bolted.

Almighty, I thought. *What I would give to be back on Earth.*

CHAPTER FIFTEEN

Nova?

I hugged my legs tighter to my chest. I didn't have to lift my head to see that Kol had entered the cleansing room because I felt him the second he showed up outside our quarters. The closer he came, the more it made my body tingle as it became hyper aware of his presence. It was another reminder of his essence in my blood, binding us together for the remainder of our lives.

"*Shiva,*" he murmured.

He kneeled before me and placed his large hands on my forearms.

I'm fine, I answered him mentally, not trusting my voice. *I don't know what happened. I just got scared when I met your brothers, and before I knew it, I was in here.*

Kol sighed. "It is my fault. I should have been by your side to take away your unease."

I didn't look at him. "You don't exactly make me feel good right now, Kol."

When I lifted my head and saw that he was frowning at me, it warmed my heart… and that bugged me.

"No," I told him firmly. "Don't look at me like that. I have a very good reason to be angry with you, Kol."

"You do," he agreed, his thumbs stroking my bare skin.

"Then wipe that sad puppy dog expression off your face," I warned.

He raised a brow. "The what?"

My shoulders slumped. "Never mind."

"My Nova"—he continued to frown—"I am sorry."

"That I got scared and ran from your brothers?"

"No," he said, his lips twitching slightly. "I am sorry that I lied to you and caused you pain. If ... if I could undo it, I would."

"I hate the lying part, I *really* hate that, but I also hate you making decisions for me. I know you're the lead Maji in our house and whatever, but Kol ... on some things, I need to have some independence. I risked my life every day on Earth, running and hiding to avoid being owned by someone, and I'll be damned if our mating makes me feel that way."

"I do not and will never own you, *shiva*," he assured me. "When I say you're mine, it is an act of dominance to other males, and when we're alone, it's just me confirming you're the only female I crave. My ways aren't what you're used to, and I sincerely apologise for the confusion. Before, even though I felt guilt, I kept information from you because that is what male mates do. They make the big decisions, but I am learning that you want to do that together."

My heart thrummed against my chest.

"Yes, we're a unit. I want us to be a team in everything. I don't want to be the only one who is clueless."

"Nova, I am just as clueless as you are," Kol revealed, sitting back on his heels. "I have never had a mate before, so I am only going off my instincts when it comes to you, and I pray to Thanas that I am a respectable male and caring mate."

I stared at him, slack jawed.

"You weren't part of the mission, *shiva*, but here you are," he continued. "You're my female ... my *mate*. I am learning what that means right along with you, so please, don't ever feel like you're the only one who is unsure. There is no written text for mates and how to be a good one. We have to figure that part out by ourselves ... but I promise, though we will have verbal exchanges and may get angry with one another, it will be worth it. Our mating ... it's everything. *You* are everything to me."

I gasped when that stunning glow appeared in Kol's eyes as he gazed at me, and this time, I couldn't help staring at them and passing comment.

"Your eyes," I murmured.

Kol's brows furrowed with confusion.

"My eyes?" he repeated in confusion. "What about them?"

"They're captivating," I responded, feeling as if I was in a trance.

A small smile tugged at the corner of Kol's mouth. "Are you doing the sweet word talking?"

"Just sweet talking," I corrected. "And yes, I am because your eyes take my breath away."

I desperately wanted to remark on the glowing, but since neither Kol nor Surkah had ever mentioned anything about a male's eyes glowing when he was mated, I assumed it wasn't the norm, and I didn't want to comment on something that might be considered a flaw to the Maji. I might have been at odds with Kol, but I didn't want to go out of my way to make him feel bad about himself.

"I love your eyes too, *shiva*," Kol replied with a smile. "They are my new favourite shade of blue."

I snorted. "You may be confused about what sweet talking means, but you sure don't have a problem demonstrating it."

His smile deepened. "My female."

I closed my eyes when he leaned in and pressed his forehead against mine.

I licked my lips. "My male."

A rumbling sound started at the back of Kol's throat, and it made me grin as I reopened my eyes.

"No sex, big guy. I don't want to meet your family smelling like I just took a tumble with you."

Kol leaned back, chuckling.

"My scent is now your scent to others. They can't smell your natural scent, only mine. When we mated and shared sex, my essence made sure of that."

I widened my eyes. "So to everyone, I smell like you?"

Kol nodded. "It's just another natural defensive mechanism of my essence to tell other males that you're claimed."

I raised a brow. "Claimed, huh?"

His lips twitched. "Not the slavery kind of claimed. Just the Maji kind of claimed."

I lifted my hands and placed them on his face, strumming my thumbs over his cheeks.

"You're mine just as much as I am yours."

"Yes, *shiva*. Always."

With a confident smile, I said, "I'm ready to get off the *Ebony* and see my new home... and meet my new family."

The smile that overtook Kol's face caused my heart to skip a beat.

"They're itching to meet you too. Killi, Arli, and Arvi are saddened they scared you. They did not mean to."

I shook my head. "They did nothing wrong. It was all me. I was so anxious about meeting them, hoping they'd like me, and I just ... I just freaked out and ran away. Running when I'm scared is what I do."

Running was all I knew.

Kol placed his hands on top of mine and stared deep into my eyes.

"Before, you were all alone in a dangerous world, but now, I'm by your side, and I will do everything possible to take your fear away."

My lower lip trembled.

"You're going to make me cry."

"I've saddened you?" Kol frowned.

I shook my head. "No, you've made me feel safe, protected ... loved."

Kol eyes glowed brightly. "I *do* love you, *shiva*."

My mouth fell open, and I was confident my heart stopped beating, but before I could even think of a response, my mate chuckled.

"Do not feel like you must say it back. Sera told me humans feel love at a different pace to us Maji, and that is okay. We have a lot of time together for you to love me."

I inhaled and exhaled a deep breath.

"If you told me a week ago that I'd be mated to an alien prince and he would be declaring his love for me as we touched down on his home world, I'd have called you crazy."

"And now?" Kol pressed.

My lips curved upward into a smile. "Now, I say it's my reality."

Kol smiled wide, and I noticed he had gold caps on his back teeth.

"Why do you have gold caps on your teeth? Mikoh and Thane have them, too, and your brothers."

"Are you changing the topic?" he asked, grinning.

"Maybe."

Kol continued to grin as he brushed a few strands of hair out of my face. "It's just fashion."

"Fashion?" I repeated, baffled. "Maji have *fashion*?"

"Yes." Kol chuckled. "We have many customs that I'm sure will be bizarre to you, but do not worry. I will teach them to you."

My heart fluttered, and my stomach burst into butterflies.

"Come on," I said, taking his hand in mine. "I've waited days to see my new home."

That brought a smile to Kol's face, but his smile grew wider when his eyes trailed down my body.

"By the stars," he hissed, sucking in a strangled breath. "You look like moonlight, *shiva*. Perfect."

I smiled. "Thank you."

Kol licked his lips. Twice. "Maybe we should —"

"Disembark the *Ebony*," I cut him off. "I agree."

I began to walk and pull Kol along behind me.

"Wait, let me look at you," he rasped.

"No," I protested, "because you'll want to touch me if you stare at me too long in this getup."

"I don't know what a getup is, but I want to stare at you in it."

I laughed as Kol's eyes dropped to my body once more, but this time, that sexy rumbling growl started at the back of his throat. I halted, and I looked down at my ensemble and looked back up at Kol.

"Do you think I'll fit in?"

"No," he rasped. "And I don't want you to because you were made to stand out."

A blush rose to my cheeks.

"My Nova, I have never seen such beauty."

I ducked my head in embarrassment.

"You see Surkah all the time," I commented.

"My sister's beauty is *very* different to me, I assure you."

I raised my head, my cheeks still aflame, and said, "Let's just go before I turn any redder."

Kol's twitched lips, but he didn't argue. Instead, he held out his arm and waited for me to take it.

"I cannot wait to unwrap you from that fabric later," he rumbled.

He projected very explicit images of what he wanted to do to my body once the fabric was gone, and it made me shiver with anticipation.

My pulse spiked. "Easy, boy."

This earned me a grin. Kol's teasing set me at ease as we left our quarters and journeyed back to the exit of the *Ebony* where I had fled from not long ago. I removed my hand from Kol's arm, instinctively reaching for his hand. When I made contact with it, I threaded my fingers through his and gripped his hand firmly.

"Calm, *shiva*," he murmured. "I can hear your heart beat increasing. You have nothing to fear."

I knew that—I did—but man, I was nervous.

"They probably think I'm an idiot for getting spooked and running away."

"They think no such thing," Kol assured me. "They're concerned for you. They wanted to make a good first impression, but they know they scared you, and they feel regret at that."

That made me feel worse.

"It wasn't them. It was just the anticipation of meeting them. I got worked up, and when it came down to it, I ran. It's my instinct to run when I'm unsure of something."

"I've made them aware of that," Kol continued. "But this time, I will be by your side, and with me there, running is the last thing you will want to do. I swear on my honour, *shiva*."

I smiled up at him and squeezed his hand.

We didn't slow down as we approached the large exit from the *Ebony*, and when I turned the corner, I saw Kol's three brothers, his sister, and his cousin all standing in the same place I had left them when I ran away. For a moment, they reminded me of statues, and that mildly amused me.

"Brothers," Kol said, his voice suddenly deeper as a vicious growl wrapped around his words at the same time his arms came around me. "This is Nova, *my* mate."

A throat was cleared. Twice.

"Thanas," one of his brothers grunted. "He is declaring her to us as if we're just any males!"

"Calm," another brother murmured, the silver-haired one. "It's just instinct; he is newly mated."

All three brothers sort of lowered their heads and never once looked my way or attempted to make eye contact with me. They remained that way, and as the seconds passed, Kol's growling lessened until it faded completely. I stood there awkwardly in his embrace and resisted the urge to rock back and forth on my heels.

Am I allowed to say hello to them?

No, Kol instantly replied, his hold on me tightening. *Mine.*

I tilted my head and looked up at him, my brows raised.

"I know I'm yours, bossy. No need to be grouchy about it. I just asked you a question."

I heard a snicker, but it stopped almost as instantly as it started.

"I cannot help it," Kol replied, his voice still shockingly deep as a growl climbed up his throat.

"I'm your mate, big guy. I know it, and so does everyone else."

Kol hummed in approval and dipped his head to kiss me. I smiled when his lips pressed against mine, and before he could deepen the kiss, I pulled away.

"I'm human, remember? I don't have the same views on PDA as Maji."

Kol furrowed his brows. "PDA?"

"Public displays of affection," I explained. "I like our kissing and touching to happen in private."

Kol's eyes burned with passion, but he nodded once before he lifted his head and refocused on his brothers.

"I missed you," he said.

I practically melted into a puddle at his sudden declaration.

"And us you," the brother farthest right said with a smile. "I am shocked you have mated, brother, but I am overjoyed for you."

"I thank you." Kol smiled.

"The male who just spoke is Arli," he then said to me. "In the middle is Arvi, and next to him is Killi. These are three of my many older brothers, the ones from the same pregnancy."

"Triplets," I murmured. "They're triplets."

"Tripe-lets?" Arvi blinked. "What does that mean?"

"Triplet," Kol corrected. "It is a word humans use for three infants born in the same pregnancy. They use the term 'twins' for two infant pregnancies."

"Huh," Arli said with a tilt of his head. "We should adapt these terms. It is much shorter than saying three offspring from the same pregnancy."

"Why have we not thought of a word like that before?" Arvi asked Arli. "I like the human words; they are clever."

That made me giggle, and I knew Kol was smiling without having to look up at him.

You can speak directly with them, he said to me. *I am calm.*

I swallowed down my nerves and exhaled a deep breath.

"Hello." I smiled. "I am Nova, and I am very happy to meet you."

I froze when the three princes placed their hands over their chests and bowed their heads to me.

They are giving you the most formal and most rare greeting a royal can give to another. This does not happen very often, shiva. Apart from Surkah, no royal has ever bowed to me.

I gulped.

"Sister-in-mate," Killi said as he rose back to his full height. "Welcome to Ealra and to our family."

"Yes, Princess," Arvi chimed in. "You're a most welcome addition to our homestead."

Arli cleared his throat, and after a long moment of silence, he said, "Hello."

Killi and Arvi snapped their attention to him and growled. Arli didn't seem bothered by the scary noises. He simply shrugged his shoulders.

"You both took the good greetings, so hello was all I could think of."

Nero snorted, and that made Kol chuckle. I smiled, too.

"It is a fine greeting, Prince Arli," I said.

He beamed at me after giving his brothers a told-you-so grin.

"Just Arli, Princess. Royals never use our titles with one another, only when addressing our sister ... when she is behaving."

Surkah scoffed, and to Kol, she said, "Killi made me cry."

A growl tore free of Kol's throat as he focused on his older brother who rolled his eyes. "I was addressing her stowing away aboard the *Ebony*. It was her guilt that forced her tears, not my words."

Kol relaxed and looked at his sister with a brow raised in question.

She shrugged. "I wasn't crying until he made me feel bad."

Kol grunted. "What you did was wrong, so if you feel bad because of your actions, then it is rightly deserved."

Surkah tucked her chin against her neck, and she looked down at the ground.

"Kol!" I scowled. "She has been punished for stowing away and has apologised. Do *not* upset her by making her feel guilty."

"She has to be—"

"Kol," I cut him off, glaring up at him. "Leave her alone."

Kol held eye contact with me before he sighed and let the argument go with a brief shake of his head.

"Thank you," I said before looking at Surkah and winking.

She smiled, though she tried to hide it.

"I cannot believe my eyes," Arli murmured. "He was just bested by a female."

"I was not!" Kol all but snarled; the vibrations started in his chest then continued to rattle outwards.

"You were," Arvi agreed, wide-eyed. "I saw and heard it. You backed down from a female because she *ordered* you to do so. Wait till I tell Ezah!"

Kol snarled again.

"When he attacks you, do not blame anyone but yourselves," Killi commented, looking bored with the situation unravelling before him. "You *know* males pick their battles with their females. Father has submitted to Mother for less. He says that sometimes, it's just not worth a female's wrath ... They can say no to sex just to punish their mate."

Arli had considered this before he laughed. "I would *never* submit, no matter what, because we can seduce females easily enough. Kol was bested by a female, and that is that."

Killi facepalmed himself while I barely registered the moment Kol let go of me and lunged for Arli. I wasn't certain, but it looked like Arli grinned a second before Kol punched him in the face, and that led me to believe something was seriously wrong with him.

He enjoyed the fighting. The sick freak.

Arli, though he had moments ago been laughing, was now in offensive mode and was growling and snarling. Both he and Kol punched, kicked, and headbutted the crap out of one another.

"Kol!" I screamed. "Stop!"

I moved without thinking and gasped when I was suddenly grabbed from behind and hoisted up into the air.

"No, Princess," Nero's voice said firmly. "You will get hurt."

Please, I reached out to Kol. *Please, stop. I'm begging you.*

"Enough!" Kol snarled. "This is upsetting my mate!"

He punched Arli one more time before he stood, turned to me, and then snarled at Nero, revealing his sharp gold-capped fangs. Nero quickly released me and stood back away from me like I was on fire. A glance over my shoulder told me he had his hands in the air in front of his chest in surrender.

"She was going to intervene in the brawl," he explained cautiously. "I didn't want her to get hurt."

Kol quit snarling and jerked his head in a nod. He closed the space between us and had the audacity to looked surprised when I slapped his hands away when he reached for me.

"Don't touch me!" I snapped, sniffling. "You *know* the fighting scares me."

Kol frowned. "Sometimes, it cannot be helped, *shiva*. I'd never fight my brothers in anything other than jest or annoyance. Arli annoyed me, and my instinct was to hit him … We do this a lot when he gets bored."

"It's true, Princess," Arli added. "I goad him into fights to entertain myself. I apologise for causing you fear. I did not realise humans were scared of brawls."

"More like terrified," I corrected.

"I'm sorry," Arli repeated.

I nodded at him in acknowledgment of his apology then focused on Kol.

"Are you okay?" I murmured as I noted his right eye was swelling a little.

Kol winked. "In an hour, any marks will be healed."

I frowned. "I don't know if I can get used to the fighting thing. The thought of you being hurt makes me sick."

Kol embraced me, pulling my body flush against his. "I will … work on it. Okay?"

"Okay." I nodded and put my arms around him, hugging him tightly.

"My *shiva*," he murmured.

I smiled against his chest. "Can we go and see my new home now? I'm ready to be off the *Ebony*."

"Can I lead her, Kol?" Surkah asked excitedly. "Oh, please? Can I, brother?"

Kol chuckled at Surkah but nodded his head to her request. Surkah squealed, bounced over to my side, grabbed my hand, and tugged me down the huge ramp of the *Ebony* alongside her.

"I am *so* excited to see your face when you see Ealra for the first time. I have been thinking about it since I awoke."

I went with Surkah happily, though she did cast me a worried looked when I inhaled deeply as a gust of fresh air rolled up the ramp and slammed into me.

"I can almost taste how clean the air is," I said, taking deep breaths. "No pollution."

"There is none. The *Ebony*, other spacecrafts, and ground vehicles are fuelled by natural resources. Pollution has never been a problem on Ealra."

It was nothing but a problem on Earth.

When we neared the end of the ramp, I had to lift my hand to shield my eyes from the glare of the sun. Instead of the painful burning I felt back on Earth during the daytime, I felt the delicious heat on my skin. I squinted my eyes almost shut as we disembarked the craft, and when my eyes adjusted to the lighting, I lowered my hand and sucked in a startled breath.

"Almighty!"

"It's beautiful, isn't it?"

Beautiful didn't begin to cover it.

Colour and life were everywhere. I had no idea what kind of landscape to expect from Ealra, but the backdrop was of green and bright *red* enriched forests, lakes of vibrant *purple* water, and vibrant green and brown mountains so high in the distance they disappeared in *blue* clouds and into the *white* sky. My mouth hung open, and my eyes widened to the point of stinging pain.

"This is too good to be true," I whispered to no one.

Far away, on the left side, I could see tall buildings that I assumed to be Royal City. They weren't like the destroyed ones on Earth. They were, well, perfectly erect and untouched by war ... Everywhere I looked was untouched by war. To the far left of the city was a gigantic building that looked almost gold from where I was standing.

I wondered what it was, and I was about to ask Kol until I glanced down and froze when I spotted something a couple of metres away. I stared at the green blanket that coated the ground, and I felt my heart begin to pound.

I heard Kol saying my name, but it sounded like he was far away, and I didn't have any intention of answering him or giving him any attention because my focus was solely on the view before me. I took a few tentative steps forward, and when my bare feet stepped onto the light green *grass*, I laughed as the soft blades tickled my toes. I dropped to my knees, and I spread my fingers apart and pressed them to the surface, running my hands along the bed of grass with a huge smile on my face.

"Brother," Arli murmured. "Your female is smiling at the grass."

Shiva, are you okay?

Tears filled my eyes as I nodded my head. "Everywhere was dead back home. If you had no money, you were living in poverty. I saw grass once in my life behind a huge security fence of a wealthy man, but I never got to smell it, to see it up close … to touch it. I've *never* touched grass before. I've never felt it on my skin. It's wonderful."

I heard many voices, female voices, human female voices, but my normal reaction of being cautious was placed on the back burner. Instead, I sat back on my heels as a few males led a large group of human women towards a section of road that had large ground vehicles of some kind. Nearly all the women hustled after the males, too scared to stop and stare, but two women broke away from the group and made a beeline straight for the grass that had captured my attention. I felt Kol tense, even though he wasn't that close to me, but I relaxed even more and pushed that relaxation towards him to show him that the two women, Echo and Envi, didn't worry me.

"It's grass!" Envi squealed as she dropped to her knees a few metres from me. "Real freakin' grass!"

"It feels so soft!" Echo stated.

The sisters laughed, and before I knew it, I was smiling again, too. When I caught their attention, though, they tensed, and the smiles fled from their faces. Echo moved closer to her sister and put herself slightly in front of her. The stance was defensive, and I didn't blame her for it, since the last time we encountered one another, it ended badly.

"Isn't it beautiful?" I said, running my hand over the soft blades of grass.

Echo nodded, and Envi licked her lips.

"I was just telling the Maji behind me that I had never touched grass before. They thought it was weird it has excited me so much."

Envi giggled, and even Echo cracked a smile.

"I guess we do look pretty weird, gushing over something that they have everywhere."

I continued to smile.

"You look ... different," Envi commented before a blush rose to her cheeks. "Not a bad different or anything, a pretty kind of different. I like your outfit is what I mean, and your hair is really cool and pretty and, um, okay, I'll shut up now."

I smiled at Envi's word vomit, and how easily embarrassed she was ... It was sweet.

Echo flicked her eyes from me to the Maji behind me a couple of times before she cleared her throat and said, "I'm sorry about our fight, and I'm not just saying that because you married the shipmaster—congrats, by the way. My sister brought to my attention that while we were scared of you, we posed a greater threat because there are two of us and one of you, and you had the right to put distance between us."

"Thank you for your congratulations, and I appreciate that, Echo, but to be honest, everything that happened was my fault."

The twins frowned.

"What do you mean?" Envi asked, her forehead creased with confusion.

"I'm stubborn," I said with a teasing grin. "Very stubborn. I was fighting my rescue and the Maji for the simple reason I did not trust them. Trust is an issue for me, and when I met you both, I didn't trust you. I expected the worse from you because I've always experienced the worst back home with other people. I pushed you guys, knowing what it would lead to, so for that, I am sorry."

The twins shared a look then looked back at me, and in unison, they said, "Apology accepted."

"Thank you," I said, feeling a sense of relief. "I know the three of us have our own issues, but we have a new start in a new world, so I hope that means we can start over, too?"

Envi beamed. "We'd love that, Nova."

"Yeah." Echo nodded. "We would."

Well done, my little human.

I smiled widely at the praise from Kol.

"Crap." Envi suddenly gasped as she jumped to her feet. "Our group ... They're *gone!*"

"Oh, hell." Echo winced as she got to her feet and looked around frantically.

I stood too and turned to my mate and his family.

"Can you make sure they get to their housing without trouble?" I asked Kol.

He nodded, but before he could speak, Arli and Arvi practically jumped forward and offered to take the twins to their homestead. Kol shared a look with Killi, who shrugged his shoulders while behind them, Surkah grinned, and Nero rolled his eyes, muttering, "Here we go again."

"It would be our honour to escort you *lovely* females to your homestead," Arli said, his eyes trained on Envi, who was trying and failing to hide behind Echo.

I looked at Echo and found she was staring at me. I walked towards her when she nodded for me to do so.

"Um," she whispered. "Do you know those guys?"

I grinned. "They're Kol's older brothers. The three of them are triplets, not identical as you can see. Arli and Arvi are the males who have offered to escort you to your new homestead. They are royal princes, and members of the Guard, a company of the fiercest Maji warriors on all of Ealra. You won't be in safer hands."

"I adore your female, brother," Arvi whispered, earning a growl from Kol and a chuckle from Surkah and Nero.

Echo turned to her sister. "What do you think?" she asked in a low tone.

"Nova trusts them, and she is married to their brother," Envi whispered back. "They're part of that Guard thing we've heard about as well, and from what I can tell, only the bravest and most honourable guys are a part of that, so I say yes. After all ... it's only them escorting us."

Echo nodded then turned back to the brothers who hadn't moved an inch *or* taken their eyes off the sisters.

"You'll ... you'll just escort us, right? You won't expect ... payment or anything?"

When the brothers blinked when confusion, Kol murmured something to them that hardened their features.

"No, female, you will not have to do a single thing to receive our escort," Arli said with a firmness in his tone. "We just wish to see you safely to your homestead. If you wish for different males to escort you, that can be arranged with no problem."

Envi, who was still behind Echo, smiled softly, and it caused Arli to gulp, and that made me smile wide.

Arli likes Envi.

And Arvi likes Echo, but could the sisters return that interest?

I glanced at the twins before looking back at my mate.

I think so; I don't think it'll be a whirlwind mating like ours was, though. We're on Ealra now, and even though all my women have to take husbands, your males will have to prove themselves to the women and build a relationship before any claiming takes place. We're the exception to that rule.

Kol was silent for a moment then he said, *I have relayed your instructions to my brothers.*

How do you know they're interested in mating the twins?

They feel a pull towards them, a pull they've never felt towards a female. It feels like more than a simple attraction to them.

I hummed. *That will be interesting.*

Indeed.

I looked at Echo when she turned to me. "How can we contact you? You're the only woman who we're somewhat close to."

I looked at Kol. "How do you guys contact each other?"

"Our comms," he replied.

I frowned. "Humans don't have them, though, so how are we supposed to contact one another?"

Surkah stepped forward. "Humans will receive comms of their own once they are finished being designed. It won't take very long; our technicians are working on it."

I nodded and turned back to the sisters. "Until we all receive comms of our own, I can come by your homestead—"

"*Shiva*, you're a princess." Kol cut me off. "Remember, there are rules for princesses."

Oh yeah, how could I forget?

I frowned. "Can they come see me in the palace then?"

"Of course."

"Perfect," I chirped. "Someone will escort you to the palace tomorrow once you've had the day to settle in and gotten a good night's rest."

"You will see them this evening," Surkah commented. "It is morning time, not yet midday, and we have a welcoming feast for all humans before dusk. All human females are being brought to their homesteads, so they become familiar with their new homesteads and get some rest before being brought back to the city for the great feast in seven or so hours."

I looked at the twins. "Are you okay with all that?"

They nodded, and this prompted Arli and Arvi to step forward.

"If you join us, we will bring you to your homestead. A ground vehicle is being brought for our use."

Though they were nervous, Envi took Arli's offered arm with a timid smile while Echo was content to simply walk by Arvi's side. We all watched them leave in silence, but I jumped when Surkah squealed.

"They will mate those females. I would bet all my rubies on it."

Rubies?

Nero shook his head, and to Kol, he said, "You have started a mating effect, cousin."

Kol grinned. "Shall we find you a nice female to—"

"No," Nero cut Kol off hastily. "No, thank you. I am enjoying being a single male."

Kol snickered, and absentmindedly put an arm around me when I came to his side. Though I was enjoying the playful family bickering, my attention drifted back to the grass. It was so shiny, so green, and so freaking pretty.

"If you like the grass so much, you will enjoy flowers even more," Surkah said. "They come in all shapes, sizes, and colours."

I hummed. "I can't wait to see them all."

"Would you like a garden?" Kol asked me, his thumb brushing over my shoulder. "That way you can plant and grow whatever you wish."

My breath caught. "I can have my own garden?"

"You can have whatever you want, my princess," Kol said, stroking his hand over my shoulder.

"Yes, please," I beamed.

"It is settled." Kol nodded. "We can pick a spot once you're settled into our wing of the palace."

That surprised me.

"We have a whole wing?" I asked.

Kol snorted. "We all have our own wing. It is made for our future families."

"Wow," I murmured. "How big is the palace?"

"Three times bigger than the *Ebony*."

I gasped. "Holy shit."

Everyone laughed, and before we could speak further, another group of women got our attention. Only this time, it was a Maji female who got my attention as she stalked towards another *Ebony* ramp to the right where some humans were still exiting. I watched with wide eyes as the tall female with jet black waist-length hair picked up what appeared to be a blue rock, and she lobbed it at a male Maji who was laughing with a redheaded human and helping her down the steps at the end of the ramp. The blue rock hit the male in the back of the head, and he spun around almost instantly. I gasped when I saw the male's face. It was Dash, Vorah's friend, and he looked pissed until he saw the Maji who threw the rock at him.

"My Isa—"

"Don't you *dare* call me 'your' Isa," the female bellowed, her growl loud and menacing. "I saw you with … with … *it*."

Dash continued to carefully approach her with his hands raised in surrender, and I could have sworn he wasn't even blinking as he kept his eyes trained on her.

"I was only talking with the human female, that is all—"

"Liar!" Isa shouted.

I felt sorry for her when I saw she was now crying. Many of the female Maji came to her side, and nearly all of them hissed at Dash who looked distraught himself. He stopped when it was obvious the other females weren't going to let him get close to her. If I had to put credits on it, I'd say he knew they'd attack him if he moved any closer.

"What is going on?"

I didn't have to look to know it was Mikoh who spoke. He rounded Nero and stepped in front of Surkah in a defensive stance.

"Brother," Isa cried and reached for him, her arms fully extended.

Mikoh was lightning quick as he rushed to Isa's side.

"What has happened?" Mikoh asked Isa, placing his hands on her shoulders and scanning her from head to toe for signs of injury.

"It's Dash," Isa cried, latching onto Mikoh's arms. "He was with a human female. Laughing and smiling, he had his hand in hers. I saw it."

I heard a terrifying growl come from Mikoh, and it sent the nearby female Maji scattering.

"I was helping her off the craft, Commander," Dash explained with his hands still raised in front of his chest. "The shipmaster ordered us to be kind to the humans. I was just following orders. I would never dishonour your sister. I swear on my honour."

I looked at Mikoh's *sister* who was behind her brother with her face pressed between his shoulder blades as if she was hiding from Dash's view while finding comfort from her brother.

"Did you tell her so?" Mikoh asked Dash as he used one arm to reach behind him and pat Isa's back.

Dash lowered his hands when he realised Mikoh was no longer a threat.

"She didn't give me the chance." He sighed, his shoulders slumping. "She threw a rock piece at my head."

My lips twitched when Mikoh laughed.

"Act first, ask questions later. I fear I taught her that."

"I am not surprised." Dash grinned.

Mikoh turned and placed his hands on his sister's shoulders once more. Isa wasn't as tall as Surkah was, so the top of her head only came to Mikoh's shoulders.

"I believe him," he said softly.

Isa sniffled. "Of course, you do. He is in your unit."

Mikoh clicked his tongue. "You're my darling sister, Isa, and there is next to nothing I would not do for you, but harming your intended for following orders from our prince will not happen."

Dash is Isa's intended?

"I have *never* touched another male out of respect for Dash," Isa shouted at Mikoh and shoved his chest with both of her hands. "And I never would, not even if it was a direct order from the Revered Father!"

Gasps were heard, though I had no idea what was so shocking about her exclamation.

"I know that, my Isa," Dash said as he moved closer with tentative steps. "I was only being friendly to the human female."

"He was," the redhead said from behind Dash with a shaky breath. "He was just helping me down the steps, ma'am."

Isa peeked around her brother and growled viciously at the woman, and it caused the woman to gasp with fright and stumble backwards until she was within the safety of her group.

"Isa," Mikoh and Dash said in unison while I said, "Hey!"

All eyes landed on me, and I could have sworn Mikoh rolled his.

"Don't scare her, you big bully!" I said to Isa, marching over to her and ignoring Kol's groan from behind me. "Your intended said he was helping her, and the woman backed him up on it. Don't get pissy with her because you're insecure about your relationship with Dash."

"Nova," Dash groaned. "You're *not* helping."

"I don't care," I stated. "Your female had better learn that us human women are on a new planet with another species and we are very scared. Having her and any other scare us further is not cool! We're making the best of a very shitty situation, so give us a damn break!"

I wondered why the human women looked past me and every Maji in sight bowed ... until I heard a familiar growl.

"I thought I told you to be nice, *shiva*."

Without turning around, I pointed at Isa. "*She* started it by throwing a rock at Dash and growling at my fellow human. You heard it just as well as I did."

Isa gasped and looked at Mikoh, who shook his head as if to say, *It's not worth going there.*

I turned to face Kol, who was staring down at me. I smiled up at him, but his face remained stone like. I raised a brow and smiled wider until my cheeks started to hurt, and when his lips twitched, I relaxed my face.

"You smiled so you can't be mad at me," I stated.

His eyes gleamed with amusement. "Is that so?"

I nodded. "It is."

"I shall remember that."

I snorted and turned when I heard murmurs. Some of the human women were muttering amongst themselves while nearly all the Maji females were whispering and staring at me like I was on display. I turned back to Kol.

"Do I have something on my face?" I asked him.

His eyes scanned my face.

"No," he replied.

"They why are your people looking at me and whispering?"

He snorted. "*The* people are looking at you because you're talking to me."

"I don't understand."

"Nova." He chuckled. "I am a prince, and to speak to me, you need *permission* from me."

I stared at him blankly, and he laughed loudly.

"I know you'd talk to me with or without permission, but my people will not. It is a sign of respect, just like the bowing."

I scratched my neck. "I bet you think I'm pretty disrespectful, huh?"

"No," he said. "I think you're human and do not know the Maji way, but you and the other humans will learn in time."

"Yeah, I'll bet you'll *love* whipping us into shape."

Kol raised his brows.

I waved my hand. "Never mind."

"Your words hurt my head sometimes," he said and rubbed his right temple.

I snorted. "That's nothing I haven't heard before."

"I'm sure."

I stuck my tongue out at Kol and laughed when he made a play to grab me. I jumped away from him, but he caught me around the waist and pulled me back against him, moulding the front of his body to my back. I was about to pinch him to let me go when I felt the burn of eyes on us.

"They're still watching us," I murmured, knowing Kol could hear.

He cleared his throat and shouted, "Back to work."

Everyone got moving almost instantly, and I smiled and patted the back of his hand that was resting on my stomach.

"Nice job."

He grinned. "Thank you."

I looked at the group of women to my right. "What do they do now?"

"When they reach their homestead, they will bathe and possibly sleep before the feast this evening. Tomorrow, they can choose their form of work and then explore the city with their assigned guide."

I licked my lips. "This sounds like camp."

"What is camp?"

"Just a place my father's father used to attend when he was smaller. It sounds just like you described it."

"We want to make this transition as easy as possible, Nova."

I nodded. "I know, and I'm not going to fight anymore."

Kol looked down at me with suspicion, and it made me laugh. He leaned down and kissed my cheek before he straightened. We then returned our attention to Isa and Dash, who were still at odds with one another. Mikoh backed up and took his place by Surkah's side, next to me. I hid a grin when Surkah stepped closer to Mikoh; he glanced down at her and stared at her face as her eyes were trained on his sister and her intended. Even though he annoyed me to murder sometimes, I loved the way he looked at her. His emotion for her was pure, and it played out on his face.

It was cute, and I wanted to tell him so, but commotion brought my attention back to his sister. I looked forward and widened my eyes when Isa slapped Dash's hands away and bared her teeth at him when he reached for her.

"She's *definitely* your sister," I told Mikoh. "Your tempers match."

Mikoh's lips twitched. "Isa can be a lot meaner; I have the scars to prove it."

"Why do you say that like it's a good thing?"

"She is female," he said as if that was the answer to life.

"So?" I pressed.

"So," he continued, "she is spoiled. Not only mates spoil females, but brothers, fathers, uncles, and cousins do, too. Maji care deeply about our relations, and as females are so few, they're greatly favoured. I'd do just about anything for my sister. She is a piece of my heart."

Aww.

"That's adorable."

Mikoh grunted but suddenly groaned when a group of males and a lone female approached.

"Father!" Isa suddenly screeched when she noticed the group. "Send Dash away."

Isa's father, the male who led the group that approached Isa and Dash, laughed like she'd just said the funniest thing in the world. I wouldn't believe he was her father or Mikoh's either, but he looked just like Mikoh, just ten or so years older!

"He's not going to help her, is he?" I asked Mikoh.

He snorted. "No. We don't come between an intended couple unless there is concern a male cannot care for his female."

"Mother," Isa then shouted, her tone desperate. "He *touched* another female!"

Isa's mother roared in outrage.

"I'll have your head!" She swore and charged for Dash who, to be honest, looked like he was about to shit himself.

Mikoh had to scramble so he could run forward and grab his mother midair after she *leaped* for Dash when his brothers and father failed to restrain her in time. I watched the scene with wide eyes and made a note that a snack would only make it better. I was witnessing family drama … amongst aliens.

"This is fucking awesome."

Kol, Surkah, Killi and Nero snickered, but none of them disagreed with me.

"No!" Isa cried when Dash approached her. "Stay away!

Dash took another step forward, and he growled. Isa whined in response, and I wondered if she was actually scared of Dash, or if she was just angry she was losing this argument so epically. From the uncaring reaction of her family, I figured it was the latter.

"Mikoh, I *need* you," Isa whimpered, but Mikoh turned his back on his sister as he returned to Surkah's side, and it caused her to wail. "Brother!"

She called for her other brothers, but they gave her the same reaction. I looked at Mikoh's face, and the poor male was cut in two. He was respecting the right of Dash as Isa's intended, but his obvious need to help his sister was proving difficult for him to fight. The longer she cried, the tenser he became. I jumped when Isa suddenly screamed, and when I looked back, it was because Dash now had a hold of her.

"Do not be afraid," Mikoh said, his eyes on me, and his back still to Isa. "She is not in pain or truly scared. She feels like Dash has disrespected her, and that is why she cries. She is trying to gain my brothers' and my favour by calling our names because she knows how deeply we care for her. She knows she can convince us to hurt him; she wants him to feel pain for hurting her."

"She sounds mighty scared to me," I said to Mikoh as Isa's cries got louder.

"This is how our females express themselves," Mikoh explained. "Do humans not behave this way?"

Like hyped-up drama queens?

"Not that I have seen," I admitted.

"That's odd," Mikoh said, making me chuckle.

I looked back at Isa when I realised her cries had suddenly turned to snarls and growls, and I gasped when she suddenly struck out and hit Dash across the face. The impact of it sent a sickening noise through the air. I flung my hand over my mouth when I saw blood on his face.

"She's injured him," I said, stepping back into Kol's embrace, my back pressing against his stomach.

Mikoh smirked and turned to watch the couple.

"Told you she wasn't scared," he said.

"Well"—I swallowed—"she's a damn good actress because she looked and sounded terrified."

"We can read females very well. We knew she was not truly worried, just angry and upset. Her scent reeked of anger, not fear, so her sounds did not have the desired effect."

Isa lashed out at Dash once more, and he did nothing to stop it.

"Do you *all* allow females to abuse you?" I questioned.

Mikoh laughed. "Abuse? Nova, this is the Maji way. Females will strike *any* male or female who upsets them."

"That's physical assault, Mikoh."

"Not with Maji," he said, shaking his head. "Look at Dash. Does he look scared of Isa?"

"No, he looks like he wants to calm her," I said, noting how the male looked at the female.

There was nothing but worry in his eyes.

"Which is why he allows her to strike him," Mikoh explained. "Males will allow a female to express her anger when it's deserved through striking, but when he has had enough, he will end it. Dash knows Isa is upset with him for touching the human female, so he allows her strikes to relieve herself of anger. It does not hurt him; our males are very tough. The scratch she inflicted is already healing."

Isa wasn't striking out anymore, so Dash let her go and took a step back. Both of their breathing was laboured.

"My female," Dash rasped. "My reason for life is you."

Isa looked up at him, and without warning, she jumped on him. She wrapped her arms around his neck, her legs around his hips, and she placed her throat in front of his mouth.

"Uh, what's she doing?" I asked.

Mikoh yawned. "Apologising."

I blinked. "How?"

"By exposing her throat to Dash," he said like it was obvious. "It is symbolism. She greatly regrets her actions, and the scene she has caused, knowing it could reflect badly on Dash's reputation since I, his commander, and Kol and Killi, his princes, are present. She offers him her throat, giving him the option to kill her. It shows how much she trusts him, and how badly she feels for what she has done."

I stared in horror. "She could have just said sorry."

"She is," Mikoh explained. "This is how our females do that."

"Seems a bit drastic to me," I said with a shake of my head.

"Everything seems drastic to you," Mikoh joked.

That was true.

We all watched as Dash kissed Isa's exposed neck, and it made me smile.

"He forgives her," I said.

"You're learning," Mikoh teased.

I waited for Isa to let go of Dash, but she would not remove her body from his, and it made him and the males close by laugh.

"What's funny?" I asked Mikoh.

"My sister will not let go because she fears he seeks the company of a willing female."

"Why the hell would she think that?" I asked, my shock not going amiss. "He just let her hit him and cause a big scene, and he forgave her for it."

"She made him angry with her behaviour, and when a male is angry, he either relieves his tension with his fists or between a female's thighs."

I felt heat stain my cheeks.

"*Will* he seek a female?" I asked, willing my face to return to its normal colour.

Mikoh shook his head, seemingly unaware that I was so embarrassed at the turn in the conversation.

"Not while he has an intended. Isa is just young and cannot help her fear."

"I'd help her and your mama kick his ass if he *did* seek another woman, though. Respectable human women don't play that cheating game; we hunt for blood if a man does us wrong."

Mikoh blinked down at me. "That's nice to know."

I grinned and looked back at the couple.

"Is she gonna cling to him much longer?"

"Just until she feels the tension leave Dash. He may be smiling and stroking her back affectionately, but Isa can sense, scent, and feel the tension in his body from their fight. She will remain as close to him as she can until he is calm and her fear of him seeking a female is gone."

"It's sad that she feels the need to do that, though. Does she not trust him?"

"She does, but this reaction is her instinct, and we cannot help instinct. In her mind, she is aware that Dash is a respectable male, but her instinct is telling her to keep her intended close until his rage passes so he cannot impregnate another female. They have not mated and sealed their bond yet, so the possibility that Dash could stray lingers in Isa's subconscious. This is nature."

"This is so weird is what it is!"

Mikoh laughed loudly, and it drew the attention of his family, who beamed and headed his and Surkah's way. I moved back with Kol and Nero to give them some privacy while they greeted one another.

"Are you ready to meet *my* parents?" Kol murmured in my ear.

I looked from Mikoh's family up at Kol and simply nodded. I was ready ... I thought I was, at least. As long as nothing as dramatic as what just happened with Mikoh's family happened when I met the king and queen, I'd be *happier*.

Shit, I thought. *I'd better start praying.*

CHAPTER SIXTEEN

"Don't ask me why, but I thought Ealra would be *very* different."

"What kind of different?" Surkah quizzed.

"Like caveman kind of different."

My sister-in-mate frowned. "What does that mean?"

I swallowed and gripped the arms that were around my waist a little tighter. I was sitting on Kol's lap as he, myself, Mikoh, Nero, Killi, and Surkah travelled to the palace. I had never been in a car, truck, or any kind of vehicle back on Earth, but I had seen more than a few battered military vehicles and old, burned out cars in my time, and none of them resembled the vehicle I was currently in. It had the build of a truck but was shaped like an advanced car … just a fucking huge one. Seat belts were also not a thing on Ealra. Instead, when you sat in a seat, it closed in around you and fit perfectly to your shape, locking you in place.

Yeah, the car seats fucking *moved*.

I refused to sit in one even though everyone explained to me that the seats weren't alive, but the design was for passenger and driver safety during a possible collision. They 'released' you when the vehicle engine switched off or when you pressed and held a button on the side of the seat. I explained what a seat belt was, but no one paid me any attention because their system worked perfectly fine for them. They didn't see a need to change it ... so I decided to sit on Kol's lap as we drove to the palace.

Nero drove the car, and he nearly gave me a heart attack at least four times, which is a reflection on his driving skills.

"Nova," Surkah said, recapturing my attention.

"Huh?"

"What does caveman mean?"

"Caveman?" I repeated, confused.

"You said you thought Ealra would be 'caveman type of different.'"

"Oh, right," I said, remembering our conversation before I spaced out about the vehicle. "Caveman is just something primitive ... I never expected Ealra to be so technologically advanced, which is dumb considering you picked me up on a craft like the *Ebony*, and you have comm things in your heads and can do all these other cool things, but yeah, I didn't think your home would be so wonderful. Ealra is very different to what I thought it would be."

"Is that a good thing?" Surkah asked.

An awesome thing.

I nodded. "Yes, it is ... I'm just going to have so much to learn."

Kol kissed the back of my head. "I will show and teach you everything you need to know. Do not fret, *shiva*. All will be well."

I sucked in a breath and squeezed Kol's arms to what I knew would be the point of pain when Nero suddenly lurched to the left then centre, and the vehicle went just as quickly.

"A pest ridden *makiv* was in the roadway!" he announced, cursing up a storm in the driver's seat.

I didn't know what a *makiv* was, and I didn't want to know either.

"How long left?" I asked, hoping to get out of the vehicle soon.

"A few more minutes, *shiva*," Kol cooed.

Everyone suddenly began speaking about grass and flowers and outfits, and in the back of my head, I knew Kol had told them through their comms to discuss those things. I guessed he was trying to take my mind off the drive. I appreciated what everyone was trying to do, but the more they spoke, the worse I felt. I felt like the space we were in was getting smaller by the minute, and my stomach began to churn. This continued for a few more minutes until the vehicle came to a sudden stop.

"I need to get out," I croaked.

Killi, who was closest to the sliding door on my side, pushed it open for me. He even held out his hand to aid me in stepping out of the vehicle, but I ignored his hand as I surged forward, just wanting to get out into the open air. I tripped over my own two feet and fell to the hard ground and hit it shoulder first with a resounding thud. I heard Kol roar, but I ignored him, and the pain in my shoulder as I flipped myself over, got to my hands and knees, and without warning, puked up my stomach contents.

Hands were all over me then, and I heard a lot of growling and even a whine or two. I focused on nothing other than calming myself enough to control my stomach. For a minute or so, I continued to heave, but when nothing came up, I sat back on my heels, and without meaning to, I whimpered out loud.

"I h-hate being s-sick." I sniffled and turned to Kol, who was on his knees next to me.

He gathered me in his arms, got to his feet, and moved away from my puke puddle. He whispered sweet words in my ear as he lifted me and set me on the bonnet of the death vehicle I would *never* be getting inside again.

He brushed my hair back from my face and growled when he examined my shoulder. I winced when he grazed it with his finger. I looked down and saw I had scraped off a layer or two of skin, and blood dotted the minor wound.

"Don't touch it." I winced. "It hurts."

Kol looked so distraught as if my arm was hanging off instead of just being grazed.

"Surkah, heal her."

Before I could open my mouth, Surkah was in front of me with her hands on my shoulder, and her eyes closed. I felt the most awesome sensation of relaxation come over me and noticed an arm suddenly hooked around my back, keeping me upright. I opened my eyes when Surkah removed her hands, and I looked down at my now untouched shoulder.

"That is so amazing!" I exclaimed. "Seriously, that is never going to *not* be the best thing ever!"

Surkah snorted, and so did Mikoh while Nero and Killi chuckled. Kol, who was to my left with his arm around me, moved back in front of me, and without releasing me, he visually examined my arm and nodded in approval.

"Thank you, sister."

"My pleasure," she replied.

Now that I wasn't freaking out or hurt, I groaned loudly and allowed my head to fall forward onto Kol's thick shoulder.

"I am so freaking mortified!" I stated. "I just got sick in front of all of you."

"Do not feel embarrassment for being sick," Kol scowled. "It could not be helped."

I felt the heat on my face as I lifted my head and stared into Kol's eyes.

"I could handle being aboard the *Ebony*, warping trillions of light years through space, but one journey in a car on steroids and I'm sick? That *is* embarrassing."

"It is not!" he argued.

"If it was Surkah, you would say it was, and you'd laugh, too," I pointed out.

He rolled his eyes. "She is my sister; it's my job to tease her."

I huffed. "I'm still embarrassed."

"No one will mention anything about it. Will you?" Kol asked the group, his not-so-subtle warning growl not going amiss by anyone.

"Mention anything about what?" Nero asked Killi.

He shrugged. "No idea what you're talking about, cousin. Surkah, any idea?"

"No, not an inkling, brother ... Mikoh?"

I locked eyes with Mikoh, and the second I saw his grin, I knew he would be his sassy self.

"I think Kol doesn't want us to mention that we witnessed his mate vomiting up her stomach contents like a pregnant female with a weak stomach ... but maybe I'm wrong. Who knows?"

Kol growled at his best friend, but I laughed.

"You're such an idiot," I teased.

Mikoh shrugged. "You say idiot; I said reserved genius."

I laughed louder but stopped when I looked to my right and gasped when the mother of all ... palaces came into view.

"Almighty!" I said, struggling for words. "It's gigantic."

And gold ... everything was freaking gold.

"Is this ... this ...?"

"This," Kol hummed, "is home."

Home. I had a freaking home made of gold.

"Not bad for an Earthly peasant girl," I murmured to myself, but of course, Kol heard it and chuckled.

"You could give me endless tours of this place, and I don't think I'd ever see it all."

I glanced around and found that the palace was high upon a hill overlooking the Royal City, its many pointed towers giving it the look of an eccentric crown. The walls looked like solid gold glistening in the dancing sunlight, and the roof seemed to be made of gemstone slate. It was easily three times the size of the *Ebony*, which I could see docked not far off in the distance and being serviced. I let my gaze roam and found that I was inside an elegantly decorated courtyard, and the ground was lined with shiny pebbles of some sort.

Surrounding the courtyard and palace itself was a glistening white cobblestone wall that wasn't built that high, just four or five feet off the earth. I knew why it wasn't that high when I saw Maji after Maji walking along the wall. Patrolling. Protecting.

"This is incredibly beautiful," I said to Kol, who was watching me take everything in.

He smiled when I locked eyes with him. "You have seen nothing yet."

I believed him.

Kol lifted me down from the bonnet of the death vehicle, and as I opened my mouth to speak, a sound from my right got my and everyone else's attention. I watched as huge golden doors were opened, and a female in a deep purple ensemble similar to Surkah's rushed from inside the palace and shot down the staircase leading to the courtyard like it was no one's business. Two males followed closely behind her, but it was obvious they were just moving fast to remain at the female's side.

"Surkah!" the female cried as she rushed towards my friend. "Surkah!"

Literally, tears streaked her cheeks, and it only caused Killi and Kol to glare at their little sister.

"Mother." Surkah sighed as she put her arms around her mother as she crashed into her. "I am well. Do not cry, please?"

The poor female cried harder and gripped Surkah even tighter.

"I'd strike your behind for making Mother cry if Mikoh was not in biting distance of me," Kol hissed at his sister.

Mikoh all but snarled at Kol, not liking that he was threatening his intended. I paled when the largest of the two males who accompanied Surkah's *mother* suddenly shot forward, got in Mikoh's space, and viciously snarled at him. Mikoh instantly dropped to one knee and dropped his gaze to the ground.

"I do not wish to fight, my prince," Mikoh said to the male who was glaring down at him.

I widened my eyes when I realised this scary motherfucker was one of Kol's brothers. And I felt stupid for not figuring it out sooner because the resemblance was there. He had Kol's skin tone, and Surkah's white hair and pink eyes.

"You forget your place," the male snarled down at Mikoh. "He is royal, *never* forget that."

Mikoh nodded once and kept his gaze downcast.

"Ezah," Surkah angrily hissed. "If you hit him, Thanas will not stop me from inflicting you harm."

Ezah switched his gaze to her and growled at her, so she stalked over to him, placed her hands on his huge chest, and pushed. I didn't think Surkah had the power to move the male, but he stepped back a couple of spaces to appease her. She stood in front of Mikoh, who was still on one knee with his head bowed.

"Rise, Mikoh," Surkah demanded.

He did so in an instant.

She pointed her finger at Ezah. "Leave him be. He is *mine*."

Surkah stepped back into Mikoh, and he made a grunting sound. It looked like she visibly relaxed when he placed his hands on her waist and stroked his thumbs against her bare skin.

Surkah's mother gleefully clapped her hands together, and to the remaining male, she gushed, "Their bond has strengthened! She defends him when he is threatened now, not just when he fights."

"I see." The male chuckled

The Hailed Mother turned back to Mikoh and Surkah and said, "Daughter, you can speed up your mating if you wish to do so."

Surkah sighed dramatically. "Mikoh insists we wait until my fortieth natal day."

Surkah's mother raised a brow as she switched her gaze to Mikoh, who didn't make eye contact with her.

"What do you fear, Mikoh?" she asked him.

Mikoh looked at the male at the Hailed Mother's side, and when he nodded, Mikoh, with his eyes still lowered, replied, "I feel she is too young for our mating, Hailed Mother. However, I do not wish her to feel the pain of her *uva*, so I agreed to our mating, but only *after* her fortieth natal day. I will not mate her in her minor years."

The Hailed Mother smiled. "You're a good male, Mikoh. I am happy you will sire the future Revered Father."

Mikoh's cheeks slightly flushed as he bowed his head and said, "Hailed Mother."

This is so weird.

I jumped when Kol chuckled from behind me but remained silent. I felt myself flush with heat when the three new pairs of eyes fixated on me and caused me to gulp as I stood unmoving under their watchful gazes.

"A human!" the Hailed Mother suddenly beamed. "And a *pretty* human. I feared you would all be ugly after Sera said you all wouldn't look or sound exactly like her."

I choked on air, and it made Surkah laugh as she bounced to my side.

"Mother, this is Nova, and she is a *very* special human to our family."

Oh, shit.

"And why is that?" Surkah's mother asked, smiling.

Shiva, do not flinch when I approach you from behind and press my lips to your neck. This is a trivial act of dominance a male makes to show the others that you are his female. This action will show my family that you are my mate. I am the first son to mate, so please welcome my parents' and brothers' embrace when they offer it.

If they offer it.

I felt my cheeks flush with heat once more as Surkah stepped away from me. I closed my eyes when Kol's body pressed flush against my back, his large hand coming around my waist and holding me firm. He nudged my head with his, so I tilted it and gave him access to my neck. When he leaned down, he brushed the tip of his nose against my skin, causing me to shiver before he gently pressed his lips to my flesh.

I opened my eyes when war cries and crying sounded. I felt Kol's mouth curve into a smile as he pulled his mouth away from my neck. I looked from Kol's parents to his brother, and I was shocked that they looked ... elated. Except for the big guy who threatened Mikoh, he looked angered and ... pained.

"My son!" the Hailed Mother wailed. "Thanas blessed my son with a mate!"

She shot forward, got in my space, and embraced me and Kol since he was still pressed against me.

"Oh," she squealed excitedly. "I have not been this happy since Thanas blessed us with Surkah."

When she released us, Kol beamed at her, "Thank you, Mother."

"Son," a deep voice spoke.

I wasn't sure why, but I was surprised when the male who accompanied Kol's mother spoke and turned out to be his father because it looked like ten to fifteen years separated them in age. Kol's mother would easily pass for Surkah's older sister because everything about her was similar. It was quite freaky to see how much this family resembled one another, and I had no doubt when I met the rest of Kol's brothers that I would see him in them, too.

"Father," Kol said, dipping his head respectfully.

"My heart is full for you," his father continued. "For both of you."

Kol's chest swelled as he moved around me and embraced his father with a big hug that involved heavy patting on one another's back. When they separated, both of their eyes fell on me, and I wished the ground would open up and swallow me whole because I hated being the centre of attention.

Hated. It.

"Princess Nova." The Revered Father smiled, revealing a small indent of a scar curved around the right side of his mouth. "Welcome to our family."

I did the arm over chest thing everyone did when they encountered Kol and Surkah, and with my head bowed, I said, "Thank you very much, Revered Father. I am honoured."

"So respectful," the Hailed Mother beamed. "I adore her already."

When I stood upright, the Hailed Mother surprised me by hugging me once more, which made everyone chuckle. When we separated, she came to my side, and to her son, Ezah, she said, "Greet you sister-in-mate."

Ezah didn't move a muscle.

Kol's smile slowly slipped from his face, and a frown replaced it.

"Brother," he murmured. "What is wrong?"

"You mated outside our species," Ezah replied. "That is what's wrong, *brother*."

Kol blinked. "You ... you have a problem with my mating?"

"Yes," Ezah quipped. "I do."

I expected Kol to growl, shout, or at the very least agree with his brother, but he looked so shocked, all he could do was stare at him, unblinking.

"What problem do you have?" Surkah demanded.

"He is royal," Ezah snarled, looking at me as he answered his sister. "He cannot taint his bloodline with ... with ... *it*."

Fuck you too, buddy.

"Ezah!" the Revered Father suddenly barked. "Cruel words harm females!"

Ezah dropped his head and said, "My apologies, Father."

I felt Kol's anger spike, and I just knew he would attack Ezah, so I shot forward, and wrapped my arms around him, hoping to contain him before he exploded with rage.

"Don't!" I screeched.

He viciously growled, but I didn't release him.

"Nova," he snarled. "Move aside."

I squeezed his waist tighter. "I hate it when you fight. *Please!*"

"Ezah! Look what you have done!" the Hailed Mother bellowed. "You have ruined our first meeting with our daughter-in-mate. I am very disappointed in you, my son."

Ezah didn't reply to his mother, and a peek at him told me he didn't really care what she had to say, which I knew was a big deal because everyone heeded the Hailed Mother and Revered Father's words, even their children.

"Apologise!" Kol demanded of his brother. "You have hurt her feelings. I *feel* her pain as if it were my own!"

Still, Ezah remained mute.

Killi suddenly rounded on me and Kol, coming face to face with Ezah, and growled. I heard them conversing in hushed tones with snarling mixed in-between. Killi grunted when Ezah suddenly shoved him back out of his space. Without a word, the big guy turned and stormed up the steps of the palace entryway, taking the steps three at a time. We all watched him go, and after he had disappeared through the palace doors, all eyes fell on Kol.

"*Shiva,*" he said to me as he glared up at the palace doors. "Get acquainted with my parents. I must go and speak to my brother."

I didn't want him to leave me, but I understood that he wanted to resolve things with his brother as soon as possible. For my sake and for his.

"You go," I said, giving his arm a squeeze. "I'll be fine."

Without another word, Kol took off up the steps, taking them three at a time like Ezah. When he was no longer in sight, I turned to his parents and smiled nervously.

"Well ... your home is beautiful."

"It is your home now too, Nova," the Hailed Mother exclaimed happily. "Come, we will give you a mini tour while Kol and Ezah converse."

I smiled when she hooked her arm around mine and led me towards the staircase with a spring in her step. A glance around and the visual of smiles on everyone's face, even Mikoh's, told me the bust up like what just happened with Ezah and Kol was a normal occurrence ... but in the back of my mind, something told me a quick chat with Ezah wouldn't change anything.

The male seemed to hate me, and I doubt even Kol could talk him around.

So much for a big happy family.

CHAPTER SEVENTEEN

Fourteen living rooms, sixteen cleansing rooms, six kitchens, six servant quarters, nineteen stairways that led to the second floor, ten stairways that led underground, twelve relaxation rooms, eight sun rooms, six libraries—each were *full* of textbooks!—and four rooms that were made for pets, but the pets, I did not see. Thank Almighty. What I also didn't see was the rest of the first floor because my feet began to ache so badly that the 'mini tour' had to be halted so my little legs could take a break.

Surkah commented that we had barely made a dent in exploring the palace, and that blew me away.

I didn't think the palace would ever do anything other than wow me. It was huge. Like fucking *huge*. If I ventured off on my own without food and water, I could easily die before I ever found my way to the outside. It seemed to be massively big just for the sake of it. Nearly all the rooms we entered were empty, except for servants who were dusting and cleaning with smiles on their face.

The servants were dressed better than any of the wealthiest people I had ever encountered on Earth, so that told me the Maji looked after their own, and I liked that. I liked that a whole lot. I didn't get why the palace needed to be so big, but I wasn't going to question it. I would roll with it and pray to Almighty that I never found myself wandering the hallways alone.

"Nova?"

I flinched and jerked my gaze to the Hailed Mother when she spoke my name.

"Yes, Hailed Mother?"

She smiled, dimples creasing her cheeks. "You may call me Mother."

I knew better than to politely reject her because I would most likely end up offending her without meaning to, so I simply smiled in response.

"You are very beautiful," she continued. "My son is very lucky."

I felt the blood rush to my cheeks. "Thank you ... Mother."

The Hailed Mother, who had my hands in hers and was playing with my fingers, asked, "Do you think you're pregnant yet?"

I felt my jaw drop at her question, and for once, I was at a loss for words.

"Mother," Surkah quietly chided. "You cannot ask her questions like that. Humans are not as bold as we are when it comes to such topics."

The Hailed Mother clicked her tongue. "There is no need to shy away from such topics. What is more natural to converse about than pregnancy?"

Surkah shot me a look that said *Sorry, I tried* then she shrugged her shoulders at her mother's question.

"I, um ..." I cleared my throat. Twice. "I do not think I am pregnant ... Mother. Kol and I ... well, we, um ... we just had sex one time when we mated."

"But you mated *days* ago!" the Hailed Mother exclaimed. "I mated with my mate over one hundred times by our fifth mated day. Why have you not mated my son more? Is the sex bad? Does he not bring you pleasure? I can have my mate talk with him if he needs tips to pleasure a female."

Almighty.

"Mother!" Surkah scowled. "Look at how red her face is. She is embarrassed."

The Hailed Mother rolled her orange and silver eyes heavenward. I had found myself staring at them more than a few times since I noticed them. The colour combination was so unlike anything I had ever seen. It was unusual but also absolutely gorgeous. A thick ring of shimmery silver wrapped around the blackened pupil and an ombré effect began as the silver blended into vibrant orange. They were captivating.

I shook myself out of my trance and focused on the Hailed Mother's words.

"She will adjust and get used to our openness."

I *really* doubted that.

"Kol needs no lessons on pleasuring me," I choked out, the words difficult to speak. "He is very ... skilled."

I couldn't believe I was telling Kol's mother that he was a skilled lover. He would be *so* embarrassed if he ever found out. I never planned on telling him, and neither would Surkah if I had any say in the matter.

"Then why have you not shared sex more?" she asked me, a brow raised.

Even though I was extremely uncomfortable with the topic of choice, I could see that the Hailed Mother was not asking such personal questions because she was teasing me. It was, in fact, quite the opposite. She was genuinely interested in what she was asking. I didn't know how to feel about that. I mean, it *was* her son's sex life she was prying into.

"Well"—I gulped—"after the first time, I was very ... tender. I was a virgin, a *vilo*, before Kol, and he has given me space because of that, but also to adjust to being mated. I have experienced things I never thought possible through our mating, and my body is sometimes overwhelmed since I am not used to the changes. I guess ... I guess he is taking it easy on me."

The Hailed Mother bunched her hands together and leaned them under her chin, smiling wide.

"He is such a caring male."

"He truly is," I agreed bashfully. "I am ... I am blessed he picked me. I never ever dreamed of having a romantic relationship, but the one I have with your son, though it's brand new and we have a *lot* to learn about one another, I wouldn't trade it for anything in the cosmos. I'm coming to love it."

I'm falling in love with it.

With *him*.

"I am overjoyed for you both," the Hailed Mother beamed. "I thought Surkah would be my first child to mate, since none of my sons paid me much attention when I spoke of mates, especially Kol, but his mating to you has given me hope."

"Hope?" I questioned. "Hope for what?"

"Hope for grand-offspring!" She squealed and clapped her hands too excitedly.

Was this lady already thinking about grandchildren?

I swallowed. "I, uh, I don't it will happen right away ... We haven't discussed it yet."

Surkah raised a brow at me. "Humans discuss when they want to have offspring?"

Doesn't everyone?

I nodded. "Yes."

"If they don't want to have offspring, do they avoid sex?" she then asked.

I shook my head. "On Earth, if you have enough credits, you can buy birth control. There are different kinds, but basically, it is a medicine that prevents pregnancy from happening."

Both Surkah and the Hailed Mother sucked in a dramatically sharp breath. They even went as far as placing their hands on their chest and leaning back in their chairs with their eyes widened in shock. A glance around the room showed me the four servants cleaning inside the living room had also stopped what they were doing to turn and look at me like I had ten heads.

I cringed. "I take it that there is no such thing as birth control on Ealra?"

"Absolutely *not*!" the Hailed Mother stated. "Our population is under threat, so we would never provide medicine to stop pregnancies when what we need is *more* pregnancies."

I shifted uncomfortably.

"What about Maji who engage in casual sex? Surely, they wouldn't want to have a baby with someone who isn't their mate?"

"Of course not," Surkah agreed. "But those who engage in casual sexual activities have methods they practice which prevents pregnancy."

That stumped me.

"Like what?" I quizzed.

It was Surkah's turn to blush.

"I do not know," she admitted. "My brothers will not tell me. They told me to ask Mikoh, and when I did, it just made him flustered and demand I discuss something other than sex."

The Hailed Mother chuckled. "Before a male orgasms, he would most likely pull his cock out of the female he is sharing sex with and release his seed *on* her body instead of *inside* it. The seed is where life comes from, and it needs a female's womb to take root. Nowhere else will work."

That made sense.

"But," the Hailed Mother continued, "accidents can happen. A male could misjudge his release and not remove his cock in time. I know a few females who have become pregnant that way."

I gasped. "Are they single mothers now?"

The Hailed Mother reached over and patted my hand. "No, my daughter. The males who fathered the offspring mated the females. It would bring dishonour to a female to birth a child without being mated, so the males, being that they were involved in the offspring making process, did right by the females and mated them."

I frowned. "Are they loveless matings?"

The Hailed Mother frowned. "No Maji mating is a loveless one."

I blinked. "But you said they mated just because the females got pregnant."

"Yes," she agreed, "but once a male and female mate, they become the other's world and fall deeply in love. No matter how you feel about a Maji male or female, once a mating takes place, love will follow."

"So matings can happen on their own but can also be decided?"

"Yes." The Hailed Mother nodded. "During sex, a male can decide whether he wants to bite a female and give her his essence. In some matings, the urge is so strong that a male cannot help but bite and mate a female. *Those* are the matings we call fated."

I blushed. "Kol said he believes we were fated for one another."

The Hailed Mother clapped her hands together. "This pleases me so."

"What pleases you so, stardust?"

I looked at the entryway of the room and saw the Revered Father fill the space in the doorway. His very presence made me feel like I should get on my knees and bow to this powerful male, but instead, I did what the servants did. I stood, placed my fist on my chest, and then I bowed my head.

"She is so respectful. It makes me very happy," the Hailed Mother gushed.

I didn't look up until the Revered Father called my name. I saw he had crossed the room and stood behind the chair his mate was sat on, and he was smiling at me while he reached out and placed a hand on the Hailed Mother's shoulder.

"You need not bow to me, daughter," he said, his voice warm and inviting. "You're my family, and I request that my family not bow to me."

I swallowed but managed to nod my head in acknowledgment.

"So," he said with a grin as he rounded the chair and sat down, tugging his mate onto his lap, "what pleases you so?"

He was speaking to the Hailed Mother, so I remained mute.

"Kol said he believes that he and Nova are fated mates."

The Revered Father widened his eyes as he looked from his mate to me.

"That is wonderful," he said happily. "You have my congratulations."

I had no idea why he was congratulating me, but I smiled and thanked him nonetheless.

"Father." Surkah spoke. "Where is Mikoh?"

The Hailed Mother squealed, and it caused Surkah to roll her eyes.

"I'm only curious," she informed her mother who was still giddy with delight.

"He is with Kol ... calming him."

I looked at the Revered Father and swallowed.

"Is he okay?" I asked, my voice low.

"He is." He nodded. "He is just frustrated with Ezah. Their conversation did not go well, and they fought."

I gasped and jumped to my feet.

"Is he hurt?" I asked, panicked.

Everyone smiled at me.

"She is *so* caring," the Hailed Mother praised me to her mate.

"I see that, moonlight," he murmured and kissed her cheek as she rested her back against his chest. "And to answer your question, Nova, he is fine. Fighting is normal amongst the people ... Kol mentioned it scared you, though."

I slowly retook my seat.

"It scares me." I nodded in confirmation. "I guess I'd prefer every other option before fighting becomes a possibility."

Running away and hiding to be exact.

"That is worrisome." The Hailed Mother frowned. "Brawling is very common amongst our males."

"I know." I sighed. "I guess I just have to get used to it."

Along with everything else.

"All will be well," the Revered Father hummed before he nuzzled his mate's neck.

The Hailed Mother grinned and made a rumbling sound that sounded similar to the one Kol made when he wanted to have sex.

Oh, shit.

"Nova," Surkah suddenly said. "Let me escort you to your wing of the palace so you can rest up before the feast this eve."

Surkah to the rescue!

I practically jumped to my feet. "I'd like that very much. Thank you."

My parents-in ... mate turned their attention back to me, and they smiled.

"We're overjoyed to have you as a part of our family," the Revered Father said. "We will take great pleasure in getting to know you."

I bowed my head slightly. "And I you. I am very happy to be here."

Surkah took that as our cue to leave, but her father calling her name halted our steps when we reached the doorway of the living room that the servants were now exiting, no doubt to leave the king and queen to their privacy.

"Yes, Father?" Surkah said, without turning around.

"I will discuss your punishment with Mikoh before the feast."

I resisted the urge to laugh when Surkah stomped her foot on the ground and spun to face her parents.

"But Father!" she complained. "Mikoh already punished me. He swatted me *five* times ... it hurt, and I cried. A lot."

"Surkah," her father said, his voice dropping an octave. "I have decided you will be punished for your actions. You put yourself in incredible danger, and I will not stand for it, nor will I stand for your disobedience."

"But Father—"

"Surkah," he cut her off, growling now.

I widened my eyes and dropped my gaze, feeling uneasy.

"Mother, please, aid me!" Surkah implored.

The Hailed Mother clicked her tongue, but other than that, she didn't respond.

"Do not speak to me *ever* again, Father!" Surkah exclaimed before she grabbed my arm and all but dragged me from the living room.

I heard her father's deep chuckle follow us into the hall, and just before the servants closed the double doors, a growl mixed with a moan sounded, and it left no doubt as to what the king and queen were up to.

"The servants left there in a hurry," I joked.

"They have to," Surkah grumbled. "Ealra is not the planet for such behaviour."

I raised a brow. "For sex?"

"For *public* sex," she explained. "You aren't allowed to engage in such activities here without penalty. My parents rule our people, but they still abide by our laws. They have sex where they like, but they have the dignity to clear the room first."

I nodded. "Understandable."

"Females wouldn't care if someone saw her share sex, but the males would. A male would fight *any* male who so much as looked at a female he was sharing sex with. Even if she wasn't his mate, he would be as possessive as if she was during sex ... dominance can be very annoying."

I snorted. "A race where all males are alphas ... What can possibly go wrong?"

"What does alpha mean?" Surkah questioned.

"The male in control, the boss."

Surkah chuckled. "All our males are dominant to their females, but not all are, as you say, alpha by nature. The trade workers and farm goers are harmless, and they rarely fight but can be vicious when pushed. It's the warriors, like Mikoh and Kol, who are the true alphas. They fight *all* the time just because they can."

"Sounds dreamy," I replied sarcastically.

Surkah grunted but didn't speak further. I followed her up two flights of stairs and down four hallways to two large white double doors.

"This is Kol's wing and now your wing, too. It has two living quarters, twenty sleeping quarters, six cleansing rooms, multiple storage units, and one very large high-tech kitchen."

I felt like I swallowed my tongue.

"Why so many rooms?" I quizzed.

"For your family," Surkah replied, her tone relaying a hint of 'duh' to it.

"I really doubt I'll be able to fill up all those bedrooms with children. Human women can't pop out that many kids without physical problems."

"These wings were built when all my brothers were infants, and they were expected to take Maji female as mates. You don't have to fill all the rooms with offspring, but a few would be nice."

"That's a relief," I muttered.

"Go," Surkah said, nudging me forward. "Go freshen up and get fed. The kitchen is stocked with food for your use, but until you learn how to cook our meals, a servant will come to prepare any meal you desire when you call for them. The call system on the wall—there is one in every room—takes care of it. You hold your palm on it, and someone will come to aid you."

I nodded. "I'm sure I can handle that."

Surkah smiled weakly. "I see will you this eve at the feast."

"Hey," I said, stopping her before she turned away. "What's

wrong?"

"I am fine," she said, forcing a smile that I could see through.

"Surkah," I said, giving her a knowing look. "Talk to me."

She sighed. "I dread my punishment from my father because he consults Mikoh on it, and I know that male will advise my father with a punishment that will displease me."

I wickedly grinned. "Go talk to Mikoh before your father does. Sweeten him up a little, and maybe he will go easy on you with the punishment."

Surkah's brows raised. "That's ... a good idea."

"I'm not just a pretty face," I teased.

Surkah laughed and hugged me before she turned away to go in search of Mikoh with a spring in her step. I pulled open one of the large doors to Kol's and my wing with a surprisingly amount of ease. It was wooden and heavy but easy to open and close, which I liked. When I closed it behind me and found myself in a new hallway, I couldn't help but smile. The décor was plain and simple but beautiful. Plants and flowers filled stunning pots arranged in all the rooms around the wing, and there were lots of them, which excited me greatly.

The different colours made everything just pop.

I navigated around the wing, found out what was behind each door, and when I found what was obviously Kol's and my room, I smiled. The last time he was in here, before he left on his mission on the *Ebony*, he was a single male and had no idea I was about to barrel into his life. It reminded me that it only took something small to make a huge impact on your life. With a spring in my step, I found the high-tech kitchen last, and just as I was about to call someone to come and show me how to prepare a simple meal, a growl from behind me brought me to an immediate halt.

I slowly, *very fucking slowly*, turned around, and when I saw nothing at my head height, I looked down and nearly shit myself as fear gripped me in its clutch.

"Nice li-little mo-monster," I stammered, holding my hands in front of me.

On the floor before me was a little blue creature with its head tilted to the side as it watched me. When it blinked, I took in just how big its golden eyes were. They were huge, and the longer I stared, the longer they remained unblinking.

"You ... you just stay away from me," I whispered. "Okay?"

I began to back out of the kitchen carefully, but the little monster followed me with its feet pattering against the floor. I sucked in a breath when it opened its mouth and sharp, pointy teeth were revealed. Teeth that would shred my flesh to pieces with one bite. That was just about all I could take. I turned and fled from the kitchen, bolted down the hallway of our wing, flung open the double doors, and sprinted out while screaming fucking murder.

I looked over my shoulders and saw the little monster was chasing me, and it was *fast*.

"Get away!" I screeched.

I flew past servants who were waving at me and shouting for me to stop, but I couldn't. I wouldn't. Not while the little blue monster of death was hot on my heels. I barely slowed down enough to turn a corner, and I unintentionally skidded into a wall, smacking my shoulder against it. I yelped with pain but didn't stop to assess my arm because I could hear the laboured breathing and growling coming closer.

The little blue bastard was still coming after me.

"Kol!" I hollered. "Kol!"

Kol! I screamed for him in my mind. *Help me!*

Nova?! His voice sounded in my head. *What is it? Where are you?*

It was odd, but I assumed the reason his voice didn't sound very clear was because I wasn't close to him. The mental thing only worked when we were close to one another, and right now, Kol was farther away from me than I would have liked.

Hallway. Near our wing. It's after me!

I'm coming, his voice shouted in my head, and he sounded louder now. *What's after you?*

A monster!

I'm coming, shiva. I'm coming.

I kept running and screaming until I came to a huge set of double doors. I flung myself at them, and they burst open and slammed against the walls with a resounding boom. I skidded into a hallway I had never seen before and cried with relief when I saw door fling open at the other end of the hallway, and Kol was sprinting through them towards me.

"Kol!" I roared. "Help me!"

He was already running towards me, but my roar made him run even faster. When he realised I wasn't slowing down, *he* slowed down, opened his arms, and caught me with a grunt when I jumped on him.

"It's going to eat me!"

"What is?" he panted, and I heard the worry in his tone.

"A monster!" I cried. "It was in the kitchen, and it chased me!"

Kol tried to calm me down, but when I looked over my shoulder and saw the very monster pattering up the hallway towards us, I nearly had a heart attack.

"There it is!" I screeched and clung to Kol for dear life.

His entire body tensed, and he turned in the direction of the monster. A whole five seconds passed by before I realised he wasn't tense anymore but was vibrating instead. I pulled back from my death hold on him and found he was … laughing. I frowned at him when his laughter became audible. I noticed what I didn't notice before. Other Maji were in the huge hallway/gigantic room, and they were laughing too, though they had the decency to try to conceal it. I struggled against Kol, who set me down on the ground when I realised *I* was the source of amusement.

I shoved his broad chest with both hands.

"You want to tell me what the hell you find so damn funny?"

"You're ... scared ... of ... Tosha."

Kol was laughing so hard he could barely speak.

I glared at him. "What the hell is a Tosha?"

"*This* is Tosha."

I turned in the direction of Surkah when she spoke, but when I saw she was *holding* the vicious monster in her arms like it was a baby, I screeched once more and sprung back onto Kol, who was laughing so hard I thought he would cease breathing altogether. I clung to him like a spider monkey, an extinct species on Earth, and squeezed my eyes shut. I held my breath and waited to feel some sort of agonising pain, but instead, I felt my bare shoulder being ... licked.

"It's tasting me first!" I cried into Kol's chest.

The licking stopped after a moment, but the laughter filling the room did not. I swallowed when it dawned on me that if the monster was really a flesh eater, no one would be laughing their heads off.

"It's not a flesh-eating monster, is it?" I whispered to Kol, keeping my face securely tucked under his chin.

He gave me a tight hug.

"No, *shiva*, she isn't a flesh-eating monster."

She.

I didn't speak; thick embarrassment clogged up my throat and prevented me from doing so. Without a word, I turned and quickly began to walk away from Surkah, Kol, the still chuckling Maji, and the not really flesh-eating monster. I picked up my pace to a soft jog to get away from the laughter, but I was scooped up into the air instead.

"Did not be embarrassed, *shiva*." Kol softly chuckled against my ear. "You were not aware that Tosha was harmless. I should have informed you that she is my pet."

"Yes, you should have." I wiggled in his arms.

He continued to chortle as he lowered me back to the ground.

"You're upset."

"I'm mortified," I corrected. "And I was scared. Everything is new to me, and I really thought it would kill me or at least bite a chunk out of me."

"She won't bite you; Tosha is a *kit*."

"What the hell is a *kit*?"

"A species of small tamed animal. They are just little pets who sleep a lot, eat a lot, and can be a bit mean from time to time if you don't scratch their underbelly."

I eyed Tosha when Surkah steps closer with the pet still in her arms.

"I've never seen an animal like Tosha, but you just described a cat. That's a feline pet on Earth."

"Think of Tosha as one of your cats then," Kol suggested.

I scoffed. "I can't do that."

"Why? Because of her teeth?"

Yes.

"Because she looks nothing like a cat," I clarified. "She looks like an extremely tiny version of a fully grown bear."

"She's harmless."

"Her teeth are off putting," I said as I watched Tosha stare at me with her purple tongue hanging out. "Why are they so sharp? And why in Almighty's name does she have so many of them?"

"I do not know." Kol shrugged, the corners of his lips twitching. "Why do you look the way you do? Why do Maji look the way we do? Why do we exist at all? It is just another thing we cannot explain."

I accepted that.

"I'm so embarrassed," I whispered. "Everyone will laugh at me over this."

Kol growled. "Trust me when I say *no* Maji will mention this to you."

I glanced around the room and noticed that all the Maji who

were laughing at me were back to tending to their chores and not paying me a lick of attention.

"I may mention it," Surkah interjected.

Kol growled at her, and it made her laugh.

"Does it bother you that you can't intimidate her?" I asked him.

"Yes," he snarled, glaring at his sister who smiled sweetly at him.

The sibling quarrel brought a smile to my face.

I focused on Surkah. "You could have given me a heads-up to Tosha's existence."

She winced. "My mind was elsewhere. I am sorry."

I eyed her. "Did you speak to Mikoh?"

"Yes," she said, her smile fleeing her face. "He was his typical ornery self and refused to be on my side when my father requests his presence to discuss my punishment."

I cringed. "How did you take it?"

Surkah lowered her gaze. "Not particularly well. I shouted and hit Mikoh, but he still refused to change his mind. I refused to ever have sex with him, even when we mate."

"That is a lie." Kol snorted. "You will not be able to resist once your uva comes into season."

Surkah scowled at her older brother but didn't correct him.

"Hey, if your mother holds out on your father for three weeks, Surkah can do it for *longer* when it comes to Mikoh."

"Thank you, Nova," Surkah said and raised her fist.

I laughed and bumped it with mine. "You're welcome."

"Did I do the bumping correctly?" she asked, lowering her hand to Tosha's head so she could scratch it.

"Yeah." I grinned. "You did."

"What are you both talking about?" Kol asked, looking back and forth between us with a raised brow.

"Nothing," Surkah and I said in unison then grinned.

"Thanas save me from females," Kol murmured.

I hip checked him and said, "Come to our wing with me. I'm tired and want to nap before the feast later."

A heated look passed over Kol's face, and before I realised what was happening, I found myself flung over his shoulder while he took Tosha from Surkah then proceeded to jog out of the room with me flailing left, right, and centre.

"Have fun!" Surkah had shouted with a chuckle and a wave before she disappeared out of sight.

Kol had something planned for us, and somehow, I didn't think it would be napping.

CHAPTER EIGHTEEN

"You smell of sweet berries and cream," Kol rumbled as he stalked into our bedroom and dropped me onto the most comfortable mattress I had *ever* laid upon. "I *love* berries and cream."

I had no idea where Tosha had disappeared to, but I hoped it was far away until I had the courage to *consider* getting acquainted with the creature.

"Thanas," Kol growled. "I ache for you."

My breathing was laboured from being over Kol's shoulder, but I continued to pant in anticipation when I realised we were about to have sex. I noted that unlike our first time together, I wasn't nervous. I was excited, ready ... and so unbelievably turned on.

I smiled coyly. "Maybe I should leave before you eat me up. I've seen what you do with cream-coated berries when they touch your lips."

Kol's eyes glowed brightly, and the image was captivating.

"Would that be so bad?" he asked, his voice thick with desire as he kneeled on the bed.

I pressed my body back against the mattress as far as it would go. "Would what be so bad?"

"Eating you," he replied, leaning over me and placing his hands on either side of my shoulders.

I shuddered. "Kol."

"Say it again," he growled. "I *love* when you say my name."

"You're being so naughty."

His tongue slid over his lower lip. "Will you punish me?"

My eyebrows jumped, and a pulse thrummed straight to my clit. "Maybe."

Kol inhaled and growled deeper in his throat.

"Your cunt truly smells good enough to eat," he said gruffly. "I need a taste."

Need, not want.

"Just a little taste?" I whispered.

"Yes, my Nova," he purred. "Just a little taste."

When Kol shifted down the bed, I found myself squeezing my hands into fists to avoid tangling them in his hair.

I hope he kisses the inside of my thighs first.

Kol's soft growl caused my clit to pulse with need.

"I'll kiss you anywhere you want, *shiva*."

If I wasn't already flushed, Kol's words would have turned me crimson.

I gnawed on my inner cheek. "Pay no attention to what I think when we're doing this."

"Definitely not," Kol hummed as he placed his large calloused hands on my bare shins and slid his hands up my legs, pushing the fabric of my outfit upwards, too. "You think what you're too shy to say to me when I have you like this. This way, I learn what you like and what you wish for me to do to you."

"It's so invasive, though," I rasped as the fabric of my skirt was pushed up to my waist.

"And sliding my cock into your warm, tight cunt isn't invasive?" he asked, his voice deep and husky.

"Holy shit," I practically panted. "That was *so* hot."

You like when I talk to you like that?

I sucked my lower lip into my mouth and bit down on it.

I love it.

Kol growled as he lowered his head to my thighs, and I cried out when his tongue snaked out and slid over the flesh of my inner thigh. He was so close to my pussy. The anticipation of him sucking my clit was teasing me in the most delicious of ways. He tongued and kissed one thigh before switching to the other and giving it the same attention. By the time he brought his mouth to my pussy, I was trembling with need.

"Thanas save me," Kol groaned. "Your cunt is so pink, *so* soft, and so fucking swollen."

I gasped when his tongue slid over my clit. The hardened bumps of his taste buds acted as ridges, and I'd be damned if they didn't heighten my already immense pleasure.

"Tell me what you want me to do," Kol snarled, his hot breath spreading over my cunt. "Out loud, not in your mind."

Kol, please.

"Out. Loud," he hissed. "If you want me to suck on this pretty pussy, then tell me what you want. *Now!*"

It took all I had not to fist the hair on his head and force his mouth onto my clit after he finished speaking. His dirty words and the forcible way he spoke them sent a thrill shivering up my spine.

I fisted the furs under me. "Tongue my clit then suck on it."

"That's my female." Kol hummed in approval.

I inhaled a deep breath but released it in a scream of delight as Kol's hot, wet tongue parted my pussy lips, glided up my hot slit, and then ran over my throbbing clit. I found myself growling at Kol and projecting how I wanted him to fuck me with his mouth. I knew he liked what I projected when his arms hooked around my thighs and his entwined hands flattened on my stomach. He applied pressure with his hands, and that acted as an anchor and pinned the lower half of my body to the bed.

"Kol!" I screamed as he sucked my clit into his mouth and

flicked his tongue over the swollen flesh, causing pleasure to flood my senses.

"Yes!" I shouted. "Yes, yes, *yes!*"

My lower body bucked involuntarily, but Kol maintained pressure on my hips so my movements wouldn't disrupt his meal. My mouth dropped open, and my eyes closed of their own accord as mind-numbing pleasure built in my clit, turning into a raging fire that seared hotter with every lick and suck. I knew I was moaning, screaming, and shouting Kol's name over and over, but it all sounded like background noise to me.

Sensation became me.

For a moment, numbness consumed me, but then sharp pulsations of bliss spread outward over my pussy and straight up to the base of my stomach. Within me, the walls of my pussy clenched with each pulse of my orgasm, and the longing to be filled to the brim took over when the pulsations slowed.

I gasped when Kol released my clit and placed a gentle kiss on it before he kissed his way up my body, only to pause at the fabric bunched around my waist. He didn't look at me, nor did he utter a word; he simply fisted the material in his hands and ripped it apart. I sucked in a shocked breath as the stitches Surkah had sewn earlier gave way, and my outfit was no longer an outfit, just torn fabric.

"Surkah is going to *kill* you," I panted, my chest rising and falling rapidly.

"She'll understand my need," Kol snarled before he lowered his face to mine and captured my mouth in a kiss.

Kol had gone down on me every night since we mated, but this was the first time he ever kissed me after doing so, and I was momentarily stunned at how erotic the act was before my shock gave way to passion. I lifted my arms, pushed my hands into Kol hair, and tangled my fingers around the strands. Kol growled into my mouth and kissed me harder. I returned his kiss hungrily and lifted my legs, wrapping them around his clothed hips.

Naked. I pleaded. *Get naked; I need to feel every part of your skin against me. Please.*

Kol tore his mouth from mine with a snarl. He didn't bother removing his t-shirt over his head. Instead, he ripped the fabric from his body and threw the discarded material over his shoulder without a backward glance. He jumped to his feet on the bed, shoved his pants down his legs, and kicked them free from his ankles. I licked my lips at the sight of his fully erect and throbbing cock. Kol dropped back to his knees between my parted thighs, causing my body to bounce and my tits to jiggle, which became Kol's focus.

I didn't have to ask him to do a single thing because with a groan, he dipped his head and latched onto my right nipple, sucking it into his mouth. I went cross-eyed and arched my back off the bed as he swirled his tongue around the hardened point before he released it with a loud pop. He showed the same attention to my left nipple and threw me back into a state of being achy and desperate with the need for release. But as much as I wanted Kol to fuck me, I wanted to suck his cock even more.

My state of need allowed me to be brazen enough to act on what I wanted to do.

"Roll over," I panted, placing my hands on Kol's rock-hard chest.

My mate tried to knock my hands aside, but I wouldn't let him, and this caused him to growl and get in my face. My instant reaction to duck my head and bow to him surprised me. I was aware that Kol was driven by instinct, and his instinct to my challenge was to counter it and make me heel to him, but that wasn't going to happen. Another time, maybe, but not today.

My mate, I purred to him. *I want to suck you.*

Kol growled and brought his mouth to mine.

"Need you," he rasped, his voice sounding as if he was in pain.

"Let me suck you," I repeated, but this time, I said it aloud.

Kol groaned loudly. "Females do not ... suck."

What?

Females, he repeated. *They do not put their mouths on a male's cock.*

That shocked me. *Human women do it a lot. I've seen them do it.*

Public sex on Earth was not a big deal to most people.

I cannot move. The urge to mate with you right now is too strong.

"I want to. Please," I pleaded, "let me."

With a roar, Kol flipped onto his back, reached up, and gripped the top of the mattress. He was gloriously naked and spread out for my viewing pleasure. His body was incredibly tense, and his breathing was laboured. His eyes seemed to burn as they glowed.

"Hurry," he growled. "I cannot resist fucking you for much longer."

I quickly climbed between his spread legs, placed my hands on his thick muscled thighs, and looked at him, my teeth grazing my lower lip. I lifted one hand and gripped his thick, rock-hard length, and it caused Kol to hiss and groan at the same time.

"I don't know what I'm doing, so just … just tell me if you like it or not, okay?"

Kol looked like he was about to weep as he said, "Okay."

He sucked in a breath as I lowered my head and positioned my mouth over the head of his cock just millimetres away. A milky liquid glistened from the tip, and before it could slide down Kol's cock, I flicked my tongue out and lapped it up. Kol both groaned and whimpered while I hummed as the sweet but slightly salty taste of him slid down my throat. I smacked my lips together and smiled before I parted my lips and wrapped them around his throbbing head.

When I sucked on it, Kol's hips bucked, and the action caused his cock to push its way into my mouth and down my throat. I gagged and pulled back until his cock fell from my mouth, and I placed my hand on my chest as I coughed.

"I'm sorry," he panted. "So sorry. I tried not moving, but I didn't expect ... Your mouth is so hot and wet ... and when you sucked ... Thanas, I need to fuck you. Please, *shiva. Please.*"

I'd been told that royals never begged anyone for anything, but Kol was most definitely an exception to that rule.

"You don't want me to suck you?" I asked him, licking my lips.

He sat up and cupped my cheeks with his palms.

"Another time," he whispered. "I am wild with need for you. I need your pussy. Now."

My pussy throbbed.

"It's yours."

"Mine!" he growled.

He flipped us over and pushed my legs apart with his hips.

"I crave you," Kol rasped as he placed kisses over my face. "Your touch, your scent, your voice, your beauty, your very presence is intoxicating. An intoxication that I *never* want to recover from. I am entranced by you and want nothing more than our bodies to be intertwined until only the two of us exist."

The world seemed to fall away from around us whilst Kol spoke. I could hear my heart beat and feel every single pound against my chest as if it was beating for him and him alone.

"If I don't mate with you right now," he panted. "I will die."

Without another word, he thrust his hips forward. As he drove into me in one fluid stroke, the scream that tore from me was one of immense bliss. I felt every ridge on his cock and every inch of his length and thickness as he filled me up. I wrapped my arms and legs around him, moulding myself to his body. He leaned over me and rested his weight on his elbows so he could kiss me while he made love to me.

IloveyouIloveyouIloveyouIloveyouIloveyouIloveyou.

Kol repeated the life-changing words over and over, and it filled me with raw emotion. He was perfect. This male who cherished me, cared for me, and *loved* me was *mine* until the day I died, and I couldn't be happier about it. At that moment, we were more than a mated couple having sex; we were two souls so completely taken with the other, and together, we were everything.

Tears coated my lashes as my emotions overflowed. I squeezed my eyes shut as I kissed Kol, only pausing every few seconds to gasp and groan when the sensation of bliss he provided me with reached a new level and then kept on climbing. I tried my best to move with him, but his weight on me prevented that. Luckily, he didn't need the help.

"Kol," I panted against his lips. "Don't stop. I'm so close."

"Never," he swore.

He pounded into me harder, faster, deeper, and each thrust pushed me towards an orgasm so intense, I could already feel the pulsing pleasure before it even started. I tore my mouth from Kol's and screamed at the same time I dug my nails into his back. A powerful wave of raw ecstasy slammed into me and quite literally took my breath away. Through my haze of heaven, I felt Kol tense as his hot semen spilled inside my body as he came. I opened my eyes and focused on him. The look of sheer bliss that transformed his face was one I would never forget. He was the most beautiful male—the most beautiful being—I had ever laid my eyes upon.

He collapsed on top of me but positioned himself on his elbows and held his body up off of mine enough so he wasn't crushing me. With my body still wrapped around his, and him still inside me, I panted for breath but pressed feather kisses to the sections of his face I could reach. I let my head fall back against the mattress and groaned in toe-curling, satisfying delight. My earlier exhaustion hit me like a plasma blaster, and all my energy gave way to sleep, but before I fell into darkness, I smiled.

"Kol," I whispered as his face rested against the side of mine while he caught his breath. "I love you, too."

CHAPTER NINETEEN

"Nova?"

I dug my head further into my pillow, and a low rumbling chuckle sounded.

"My *shiiiiiva?*"

The hum of a voice singing low was so relaxing, it did nothing but make me want to remain asleep for a little longer. I tried to push away from the hard, warm mass next to me, but when it vibrated and deep laughter sounded, I became aware as I began to awaken.

"Kol?" I murmured. "Please, sleep."

His arms tightened around me slightly.

"I cannot, little one," he replied. "You have napped for five long hours, and me for four. The feast will begin soon, and we must be in attendance."

I groaned loudly.

"I just warped eighteen trillion miles through space to get here for this damn feast," I grumbled. "Let me sleep some more, or you'll be carrying me to it."

Kol laughed merrily, and it only made me groan louder because I knew any chance of going back to sleep was well and truly off the table. I sighed as I rolled onto my back, shivering when my body touched a cold section of the mattress.

"Are you tired?" he asked softly.

"Uh-huh." I rolled back over, coming face to face with him. "But so incredibly relaxed at the same time."

Kol's lips twitched as he reached up and pushed strands of hair from my face. His eyes scanned my face, and a soft glow formed around his irises. I sighed in appreciation but made sure I kept my gaze adverted so he wouldn't see the reflection of the glow in my eyes.

"Nova," he hummed.

I looked at his plump lips. "Yes?"

"You told me you loved me," he whispered.

I blushed as I smiled. "I remember."

He swallowed, his Adam's apple bobbing. "Did you say it because of the amazing sex?"

"No." I laughed. "I didn't say it because of the *uber*-amazing sex."

Kol smiled wide. "You said it because you truly love me?"

"Yes," I said, reaching up to cup his cheek with my hand. "I said it because I love you, sweetheart."

His chest swelled, and I swear he was about to burst with how happy he felt, and that made me happy.

"You aren't scared that you think it's too fast?" he asked, worry laced in his tone. "I know you humans do things at a slower pace."

I shrugged. "It's not like I can control loving you. Every human person is different. No rules or time limit exist about falling in love with someone. I used to think time was a huge factor, but you have proven me wrong. I've known you seven days, and I am in love with you. Would some people find it insane, impossible, or completely stupid? Sure, but they aren't a part of this relationship, so the opinions of sheep don't matter."

Kol pushed himself up, placed his right palm against the side of his face, and then rested his hand on it as his elbow pressed into the mattress to support him. He stared down at me with confusion.

"What are sheeps?"

"A *sheep* is an animal back on Earth. It can be used for food, and its fur can be used to make fabric. It is a sweet animal, very placid," I said then grinned. "And it's never sheeps, just sheep, even if you're referring to more than one."

"Oh," Kol chirped. "Like Maji."

"Huh?"

"Maji is used as a plural and singular when referring to the people."

I nodded in understanding. "Yup, that's exactly it. Sheep means one of the animal and many."

"Then I agree with you; the opinions of sheep do not matter. I love you, and you love me, and that is all that matters."

"You bet your ass it is."

Deep laughter rumbled up Kol's throat. "I want nothing more than to lie in our furs with you all day and night, but we must ready ourselves for the feast. It starts soon."

I suddenly shot upright. "I don't have anything to wear."

"What?"

I looked down at my naked torso now that the furs had fallen away, and I groaned, loudly.

"You ripped my outfit from my body. Surkah made that to fit me especially, and you ripped it. Shit."

"Do not fret," Kol said as he sat upright and placed a kiss on my bare shoulder. "I contacted Surkah when I awoke and told her about your ruined clothing, so she made you a new one."

"A *new* one?" I questioned, turning to look as he got out from under the fur blankets and stood from the bed, naked as the day he was born. "But she didn't fit me for this new one."

Kol snorted as he walked over to a large door and entered it. "Surkah has the memory of an Elder; she forgets nothing. And I mean it. She memorised your measurements and made you another ensemble based on that memory."

Well, colour me impressed.

"Surkah is awesome."

"What does aw-som mean?" Kol called from the room he entered.

I wondered what he was doing.

"Awesome means something really impressive."

He snorted then. "Surkah will *love* that you think she is awesome then."

He still didn't say awesome correctly, but I didn't correct him.

I grinned. "I'm sure she will."

Kol re-entered the room, and to my disappointment, he was no longer naked. He had thick, gold, fitted bracelets around both of his wrists. Loose fitted bright blue pants hung shockingly low on his hips but were cuffed tight around the ankles. He was in the middle of clipping small shiny objects between the freshly braided pieces of hair on his head. They looked similar to the jewellery Surkah had in her hair when I first saw her without her *Ebony* attire on. I also noticed that his skin had more of a glow to it, too.

"Why does your skin look like that?" I questioned. "It didn't have a radiance to it on the *Ebony*."

"It's Ealra." Kol shrugged. "When we're away from our planet, our appearance becomes a little dull. Spacecraft air is Maji-made, and our skin is a living, breathing organ, so it suffers a little out in space, but when we return home, it can breathe easier. Does that make sense?"

"Yes," I said. "Human skin is the same, I guess."

"My brothers who have been out in space the longest will look very sickly when they return, but once they are reintroduced to Ealra's atmosphere, they will regain their healthy appearance."

I focused on the claw mark scars on his chest and swallowed.

"I shouldn't find those scars as attractive as I do," I muttered.

I flicked my eyes up to Kol and found him grinning. "Females of all species are impressed by strength, and that is what scars represent. They mean you survived whatever greatly hurt you at one point. They're badges of honour, and I carry them with pride."

I hummed. "You carry them *very* well."

Kol shook his head, grinning. "Come. I have sent for servants to aid you in dressing."

I froze. "I'm naked."

"They're *female* servants," he said, an eyebrow raised. "No male would *ever* lay eyes upon your naked form; they know the penalty is death."

I remained unmoving. "Kol, I was mortified when *Surkah* was dressing me ... I'm not comfortable with being naked. Even right now, I'm embarrassed because we're aren't having sex."

"Shall we have sex to take your embarrassment away?" he teased, but the flash of hunger in his eyes told me if I said yes, he would be on me in seconds.

"Nice try, buddy." I rolled my eyes. "But you're the one you said we had to leave soon... Isn't that why you woke me?"

"Yes." He nodded. "The feast begins in"—he closed his eyes for a moment then reopened them—"fifteen minutes."

"Shit!" I panicked. "Where are the females who are going to help—"

A loud rap sounded on the door and cut me off midsentence.

"They're here," Kol said as he moved towards our bedroom door and opened it.

"Kol!" a female voice bellowed. "You're going to be late to the feast for humans. Why did you not call me earlier?"

I widened my eyes when a tall female with blue skin entered the room, her hands on her hips and her eyes narrowed at Kol. She looked like she was in her late thirties, but I knew that meant she was a hell of a lot older in Maji years. She also wore a basic ensemble—not flashy like the one I previously wore—and she had no jewellery on, yet she still looked stunningly beautiful. Her fiery red hair only hung to her shoulders, but it was a thick mass of curls that made a statement all on their own.

"It is good to see you, Eena."

Kol leaned in and kissed the female on the cheek, but she gasped and quickly leaped backwards away from him.

"You're mated!" She spat at Kol. "And you kiss me in front of your female? Kol!"

She turned to me and bowed her head. "I beg your forgiveness, my Princess. I will accept any punishment you offer without resistance."

Excuse me?

I looked at Kol with wide eyes and saw that he had rolled his.

"Eena, she is not Maji. She does not attack over simple things like a Maji female would. She doesn't have those kind of instincts."

"It does not matter!" the female quipped at him, her head still bowed to me. "You do not disrespect your mate like that. Have I taught you nothing?"

Who the heck is this lady?

Kol sighed. "I apologise."

"Not to *me*," she snarled. "To your *female*."

With another sigh, he said, "I'm sorry, Nova."

I shrugged. "It's all good."

Eena rose back to her full height then and regarded me with a warm smile.

"I am overjoyed to meet you, Princess. I am still in shock that our Kol has mated!"

Our Kol? I asked my mate.

Kol stepped up alongside Eena. "Eena was my nursemaid during my minor years. She cared for me when my parents could not, so she is very much like a mother to me."

Eena waved him off. "I am a servant of the Royal Family, nothing more, nothing less."

"A servant wouldn't talk to me the way you do," he teased her.

She growled at him, and it made him laugh. "I'm going to feed

Tosha while you aid Nova in dressing. She does not know how the ensembles work yet."

He left the room without another word, leaving me alone with Eena.

"I appreciate you coming to help me," I said, softly. "But I must warn you ... I'm very shy about my body."

Eena nodded. "Kol informed me that humans are more reserved about nakedness."

I remained unmoving on the bed.

"Come. Do not worry about your body. I barely notice anything other than the fabric when I aid a female in dressing."

I plucked up the courage to do as she asked. I got out of the bed, completely naked, and it was only then that I realised I hadn't cleaned up after Kol and I had sex because I went right to sleep instead.

"I need to relieve myself first. Is that okay?"

"Of course," Eena replied. "There is connecting cleansing room next to Kol's clothing quarters. I'll have your ensemble and body chains laid out and ready for you by the time you return."

I nodded and quickly crossed the room, my arms crossed over my chest to cover my breasts. I entered the cleansing room and availed of the relief pod first. I entered the cleansing unit and activated it with my hand on the wall. I let the water fall over my body and washed my hair and body at a rapid speed with the wash gel. I quickly exited the unit when I finished and stood still as a blow dryer started up automatically. When I was bone dry, less than a minute later, I quickly brushed my teeth with Kol's toothbrush—I couldn't find a new one—then re-entered the bedroom.

Eena had everything laid out on the now made bed and gestured me to her side. I saw the fabric of my outfit was jet black and had a reflective shine. There was blue body jewellery this time and hair clips and pins with what looked like gems attached to the top of them. I followed Eena's every instruction during the dressing; I didn't even make a sound when she styled my hair even though sometimes she hurt my head while she braided my hair back into a thick, chunky, long braid hung down the middle of my back.

"Beautiful," Eena beamed in her assessment after I was dressed. "You will steal Kol's breath."

I blushed. "Thank you, Eena."

"It is my pleasure and honour to serve you. If you do not need my aid any further, I will see if Princess Surkah needs any last-minute assistance."

I shook my head. "I think you've taken care of everything."

She bowed as she backed towards the exit of the room. "Until our next meeting, my Princess."

And like the snap of my fingers, she was gone.

Kol, I said reaching out to him. *I'm ready.*

He entered the room a couple of minutes later with Tosha in his arms. He stilled when he saw me, and I froze when I saw the *kit*. God, it was so adorably tiny and terrifying at the same time. I kept my eyes on it as Kol released her and set her on the ground. She sniffed around the floor for a few moments then trotted out of the room and away from me.

I exhaled a deep breath. "She scares me still."

When Kol didn't respond, I looked up and found his eyes were glowing so beautiful, I gasped.

"What?" he asked, closing the distance between us. "What is it?"

"Your eyes," I murmured, seemingly caught in a trance. "They are so stunning; that glow makes my heart stop."

"Thank you, *shi*—what?"

I blinked. "Hmm?"

I flinched when Kol gripped my upper arms and pulled us both to our feet. "What did you just say?"

Oh, hell. I knew I should have never mentioned the glow.

"I'm so-sorry," I stammered. "Is that a sensitive subject for

Maji? I didn't know—"

"When have you seen my eyes glow?" Kol asked, cutting me off.

"When you first made me orgasm back on the *Ebony*." I spoke fast. "And a bunch of other times since then. The ring of black that usually lines your irises glows brightly, and it enhances how violet your eyes actually are."

Kol moved us over to the far side of the room and stared at himself in the full-length mirror that appeared from the wall. He stared at himself for a long time, and I had no idea what to say or do, so I just stood next to him and waited for him.

"It is not common for a Maji's eyes to glow," he eventually rasped. "It only occurs when a Maji has found his or her fated mate."

Fated mate?

"I don't understand," I said. "A fated mate? What is that?"

I recalled the Hailed Mother mentioning the term, but I couldn't recall exactly what she said.

"I am foolish," Kol said with a shake of his head before a huge smile stretched across his face. "I should have known I had found my fated mate. That is w*hy* the first moment I saw you, I got a pain in my chest. It's why I crave to see you, to hear your voice, to scent you, to touch you … to claim you. The glowing of my eyes when I'm in your presence is alerting you and me that you are mine, and I am yours. We're truly fated mates, Nova. We say males who claim females when the urge is strong are fated mates, but true fated mates … Their eyes glow when in the presence of their fated mate."

"But I'm not a Maji." I frowned. "How can we be fated mates if we're a different species, and I don't have the same internal structure as you?"

"I am unsure. I never thought it possible have a fated mate outside our species, but it changes nothing. *You* are my fated mate, Nova."

"I'm still unsure as to what that means, exactly," I replied.

"Does it change anything about our mating?"

"What?" Kol shook his head. "No, it just means we are the others' fated mate."

"Again," I said, scratching my neck awkwardly. "Still not understanding why that has you smiling so wide, and why it makes your eyes glow."

"How do I explain?' he said more to himself than to me. "Okay, imagine us as two halves that make one whole thing ... That is what fated mates are to the other."

I choked on air.

"Soul mates," I stated. "You just described soul mates."

"Are soul mates destined to be with one another?" Kol asked.

I nodded. "Yes."

"Then I say fated mates means the same as soul mates."

I didn't know what to say, so I just stared up at Kol in disbelief.

"Do you know how rare this is?" he asked, his eyes glowing brightly.

I shook my head.

"*None* of the people has mated their fated mate on Ealra," he explained. "My parents are not even fated mates."

I frowned. "What if your father met a female who *was* his fated mate?"

"As he is already mated to my mother, he would mostly likely befriend her with my mother's blessing. He would feel connected to her but not romantically because of his bond with my mother. It would be the same if my mother met her fated mate. It has happened a few times before we came to Ealra; the Elders told tales of such matings."

"So fated mates don't always end up together?"

"No," Kol said. "And that it why our mating is even more special ... We are meant for each other and have bonded together, *shiva*."

Holy shit.

"How has it only been seven days since we met? Two of which I was unconscious for."

Kol laughed as he lifted his hands to my face, cupping my cheeks. "I keep asking myself the same thing. I can't remember what my life was before you entered it."

"Me too," I whispered before a small smile spread across my face.

"I should have known the pull to you was too great," he continued. "I should have trusted my body's need for you."

My smile faded, and I leaned back.

"Your body's need for me?" I questioned.

Kol lost his smile, too. "What's wrong?"

"Why did you word it like that?" I asked, stepping out of his embrace and putting some space between us.

"*Shiva.*" He frowned and reached for me.

"No," I said after a moment of silence. "Don't touch me. Just answer my question."

"You deny me?" he asked, and I felt the pain in his words as if they were a thousand physical blows.

"I'm just saying I need a little space right now to—"

"No," Kol cut me off.

"Kol," I stressed. "Be reasonable."

"You hesitated when I asked if you're denying me," he growled.

"Because I don't understand it," I explained. "You have to give me a moment to absorb and understand what you're saying."

"I don't understand, Nova. Why are you upset?"

"You said your body knew I was yours."

"My body *does* know you're mine."

"Your *body* knows?"

Kol bobbed his head, and it made the sudden pain in my chest intensify.

"Do ... do you think you would have mated me if we weren't fated mates?" I asked, my heart pounding against my chest. "If your body didn't hurt for you to have me like you said it did?"

Kol blinked. "I don't know."

I stepped away from him, but he quickly followed.

"What is it?" he demanded. "Why are you hurting so badly?"

He could feel the pain of my heart breaking.

"You only mated me because a chemical in your body told you so?"

Kol frowned down at me. "Well, yes, that is how a mating works, *shiva*."

I pushed his hands away when he reached for me.

"*Don't* call me *shiva*."

He froze. "What?"

My heart was pounding against my chest, and hundreds of questions were zig-zagging through my head at a mile a minute. From the moment I woke up on the *Ebony*, I had been confused about the Maji, but I thought I was somewhat beginning to understand Kol. Now I was back to square one; only this time, I was mated to him.

"You don't understand why I'm upset, do you?" I asked him.

He shook his head. "I have no idea."

"I thought from the beginning that everything with your people moved at a rapid rate, so while I was surprised at your declaration of your intention for me, I wasn't surprised that you wanted to mate right away. I understand things work differently with your people, and you don't do the dating thing, but that made me blind to—"

"To what?" Kol cut me off, his body tensed.

"To the fact that you've mated me just because your dick got hard for me."

Kol's mouth dropped opened. "It's more than that, Nova."

I wasn't so sure about that, and what was worse was I couldn't even distance myself from Kol to clear my head because we were mated. That meant a mental link and a growing bond that I had no understanding of. Adding a new planet, a royal title, and a large new family to the mix caused a throbbing to take up residence in my head.

"What would you have done if I wasn't at the WBO last week and needed rescuing?" I asked. "What would you have done if you never met me?"

Kol blinked. "I would … I would have continued on with my life and my mission as normal."

"Hmm," I said, folding my arms across my chest. "You'd have eventually taken a mate, right?"

He placed his hands on his hips. "Eventually, yes."

I stared at him.

"I don't understand the point of this conversation," he said, throwing his hands up in the air. "We're mated, so it doesn't matter what *could* have happened because it *didn't* happen."

"Your eyes are still glowing," I commented.

Kol's features softened. "They'll do that when I'm in your presence being as *you* are my *fated mate*."

That meant something to Kol and his people, but to me, it just meant his bodily instinct made it difficult for him not to claim me when he first met me. There was nothing even close to it being about having an interest in something other than my body. To me, it sounded like everything was strictly physical and that hurt. Kol had said how much he cared for me and loved me and so forth, but it wasn't real; it was his instinct, his genes, telling him he felt that way.

He couldn't have come to care for me so quickly because he didn't even know me. Not really. We'd been in the other's life for *seven days*—even less before we became a mated couple. During that time, we weren't even civil towards one another. I was painfully aware that I didn't know him either, so I had no excuse for my stupidity at falling in love with him. I had no instinct telling me I needed him, so I just had my heart to guide me, and I could foresee that my final destination would end in heartache.

"Nova," Kol said, gaining my attention. "Talk to me."

I stared up at him. "Can we just go to the feast? I really need some fresh air."

Kol's stare was unwavering, but after a moment, he nodded. I turned and made a move to leave the room, but Kol grabbed my arm and tugged my body flush against his.

"Mate," he began. "Tell me what I can do to fix this?"

"You don't even know what you're asking to fix, Kol," I said with a sad smile.

That was the point. He didn't understand why I'd be upset over him just claiming me because some chemical ... some *instinct* told him to. I had nothing other than my foolish heart telling me to accept his intention. I didn't think Kol's heart even had the freedom to decide if it wanted to fall in love with me, and that made me sad. I wanted Kol to come to love me like I had come to love him ... on his own. I didn't want it to be because his body was telling his heart to love me. I wanted it to come to that conclusion all on its own, but I didn't think that was possible, and talking about it wouldn't change that.

He didn't understand. Even with an explanation ... he just didn't understand.

CHAPTER TWENTY

I felt dejected.

Kol, who was sitting sit next to me at a massive head table during the welcoming feast, knew I was upset, but he didn't understand why, so he finally decided to stop asking me what was wrong both out loud and in my mind. My chair was so close to his that my thigh mashed against his, and though I wanted space, I knew I couldn't have it out in public. His arm was protectively around my shoulder, resting there while he conversed and laughed with Killi, who sat on his right.

On my left was one of Kol's younger brothers, Aza. He was twenty years younger than Kol was, putting him at one hundred and eighty years of age. Of course, to me, he was ancient, but he looked in his early twenties, which blew my mind. He greeted me formally and didn't utter another word throughout the entire feast.

I paid attention to bits of the festivities, like when the Revered Father made a huge speech into a device that carried his voice all over the town as he welcomed the human females to Ealra. His announcement of my mating with Kol was met with war cries, cheers, and deafening clapping. Kol and I didn't have to speak, which I silently thanked Almighty for.

I ate food because I was hungry, but even while eating, I felt a little sick. I kept replaying my conversation with Kol over and over in my mind. The more I thought about it, the worse I felt. I wished I could have been seated next to Surkah, but she was in the centre of the head table to the right of her father with Mikoh by her side while I was on the far end of the table. All Kol's brothers, the ones on Ealra, each greeted me and welcomed me to the family. Apart from the triplets, Ezah, and Aza, I couldn't remember who was who, and when I tried to figure it out, my head hurt.

I want to go to sleep.

I jumped when Kol squeezed my shoulder. "A little while longer then we can retire."

"I wasn't speaking to you," I mumbled. "I was just thinking in general."

I leaned back in my chair, not interested in consuming the odd-looking dessert in front of me. I glanced at my now empty glass container that housed a juice of some kind. It was delicious, and my glass was refilled four times. Drinking so much of the liquid was a dumb move because the sudden urge to relieve myself was painful.

"Kol," I said, gaining his attention. "I have to go to the cleansing room."

He excused us from the table, took my hand, and led me towards a huge building to the right of the street we were on. The layout for the feast was incredible. Marble tables lined both sides of the streets, starting a few metres away from the head table, and continued all the way down the street to the point where I couldn't even see the end. Maji and humans were everywhere, but it was a very coordinated event for such a large gathering. The Maji worked well together, and my women followed orders easy enough, causing no problems.

"Nova!"

I jumped when my name was called, and when I glanced over my shoulder, I saw Envi heading towards me with a bright smile on her face. She had on a long pleated hot pink skirt and a tightly fitted black sleeveless top that showed not only her midriff but also her cleavage and the side of her breasts. It was a beautiful outfit—bold but beautiful.

I smiled at Envi but quickly lost my smile when two huge males suddenly blocked her path. They both had daggers strapped to their muscular thighs, and one of them even had a small sword in the centre of his back. There was some sort of device on his skin that the sword stuck to.

"Make way," Kol suddenly spoke. "She is allowed to speak to my female."

The two males parted instantly, placed their fisted hand over their chests, and bowed to Kol ... and me. Envi swallowed, looking back and forth between the two males before she quickly darted between them to reach my side.

"That was weird," she whispered.

I snorted. "Tell me about it."

"I was just going to a cleansing room when I spotted you."

"I'm heading there right now. Walk with us."

Envi flushed scarlet as her eyes flicked to Kol, who was glancing around, his eyes flying to every being close by as if waiting for them to step out of line.

"Envi," I began. "This is ... Prince Kol. My husband, or as the Maji say, my mate."

At the mention of his name, Kol turned his focus to Envi, and he grinned at her attempt to curtsy to him.

"It is wonderful to meet you, Your Majesty."

Kol looked down at me. *What does that mean?*

"It's just a title used when addressing human royalty," I explained quietly to him.

He nodded and looked back at Envi. "Hello, Envi. Welcome to Ealra, and welcome to Maji society."

"Thank you very much, Majesty."

The poor girl was crimson. I smiled, and after a moment's hesitation, I held out my hand and was glad when Envi quickly grabbed it and moved close to my side. Kol placed a hand on my lower back and guided us both into the large building that turned out to be the Sorting Centre, a place where Maji enlisted for jobs they wished to do. The Maji didn't work for a wage; they worked to provide for one another. Each job the males and females worked at provided or contributed to the Maji society, and I fucking *loved* that.

On Earth, credits were the only thing that could keep you fed, healthy, and safe, so without credits, you were on your own. Just like I was before the Maji came into my life and saved me from a helpless fate.

When we reached a vacant cleansing room, Kol checked every corner of it before he let me enter. It took a five-minute conversation for him to relent and wait outside while Envi and I relieved ourselves. When he assured me he'd be right outside if I needed him for the tenth time, he finally closed the door. I exhaled a deep breath and shook my head.

"He is very ... protective of you."

I turned to Envi. "That's putting it lightly."

She giggled then went into a vacant relief pod stall, so I entered the one next to her. When I finished, I left the stall and walked over to the large sinks to wash my hands. I coated my skin in water, pumped some gel from a tiny dispenser, and rubbed my hands together as I waited for Envi.

"Wise men say," I softly sang as I washed the lather from my hands. "Only fools rush in, but I can't help falling in love with you."

I exhaled a deep breath, wiping away the water droplets from my hands with a hand towel to my right, all the while feeling sorry for myself.

"I have never heard that song you were just singing." Envi frowned as she exited her stall, the sound of the relief pod still flushing. "Who sings it?"

I glanced at her through the mirror before us. "Elvis Presley."

"Who is Elvis Presley?" she asked.

I stared at her, certain she was playing a joke on me.

"You've nearly heard of *Elvis*?"

Envi shook her head. "Is he from before our time?"

Long before.

I nodded. "He is a singer from the 1940's. I know that's a very long time ago, but he was an icon while he lived and a legend after his death. My father played his songs all the time when I was little then when music was no more, he would sing them to me."

"How old was your father to know about a singer from the 1940's?"

"My father was born in 2049, and he died seven years ago. He knew of Elvis because back then, the world was not in *that* much chaos. Papa said they had something called the internet, and that contained lots of information about pretty much everything in history."

"I've heard of that too; I wish *we* were born long before aliens were discovered by humankind."

I leaned my hip against the sink. "You and me both, Envi. I can't imagine Earth as anything but a wasteland in chaos. It must have been nice to walk by people and not fear they would attack. I can't imagine a time when you could just say hello to a stranger and not expect them to attempt to take your life or goods. A world without murders, imagine that?"

Envi became silent.

"Hey." I nudged her leg with mine. "Are you okay?"

Envi looked down as she whispered, "I'm a murderer. I ... I killed a man."

I widened my eyes at her shocking admission. "You did?"

She nodded, her head still downcast.

"He ... he tried to rape Echo ... seven years ago when we were eleven," she choked out, making sure to keep her voice low. "It was our birthday, and my mother left our shelter to get us some chicken.

She saved up all her credits and wanted us to have something nice to eat to celebrate. Our four brothers, older sister, and my father died in the Great Illness the year before, and we were the only ones to survive it. She ... adored us. We were all she had left, and she put us first over herself. She thought no one saw her leave the morning, but *he* did."

I instinctively reached out and took Envi's hand in mine. I didn't speak; I just held her hand as she told me of her ordeal. She didn't look up or flinch. Instead, she gripped my hand and held on tightly.

"He was a mutant," Envi said, her voice thick with emotion. "He didn't look very human anymore. He had been exposed to a lot of radiation, and it made him look like a monster. He entered our hut and tore it apart until he found me and Echo in our makeshift basement. We hid down there when we were left alone so no one could find us. He knew we were in the hut somewhere. He told us he saw our mother leave on her own and that he'd find us. He did. He grabbed Echo when she put her body over mine to protect me."

I gave her hand another squeeze as her voice grew tight with emotion.

"He stripped her of her clothing, tore it from her body, and forced her legs open. I screamed so much that he punched me when I smacked his back to let her go. The force knocked me to the floor and caused me to pass out for few seconds. When I opened my eyes, I found my face was throbbing, but that the man was undoing his pants. He was over Echo one second then on the floor beside me the next. I heard my mother's voice then."

Envi sniffled. "It was a blur of activity when she returned home. She was screaming, and I remember hearing her hands smack against the man's flesh as she punched and slapped at him. She tried ... so damn hard, but he was just so much stronger than she was."

Oh, no.

"He broke her neck," Envi choked. "He didn't even have to try.

He just broke her neck and let her body slump on the floor. I looked at her face, and her eyes were still open. It was like she was looking right at me … right through me."

My heart broke for Envi and Echo and what they had been through.

"I can't remember how, but one second, I was on the floor next to my mom, and the next, I was beside the man with a knife in my hand. He was just about to hurt Echo in a way she would never truly heal from, so I used every ounce of strength I had to ram the blade into his face. It went through his right eye and got stuck in his head. We started running then, and we haven't stopped since."

Tears fell from both of our eyes.

"Envi," I said, clutching her hand tightly. "You're the bravest person I have ever met."

For the first time since she started speaking, she looked up at me, tears streaking her cheeks.

"What you did was fight for your life and your sister's life. What your mother did was fight for your sister's innocence and both of your lives. She died a hero, and you ended the life of a waste of space. You're *so* brave."

Without another word, I stepped forward and hugged Envi tightly.

"I'll *always* have your back," I told her firmly, and I meant it with every fibre of my being. "Things will be different here on Ealra; it will be *nothing* like Earth."

She whimpered. "Me and Echo, we've only ever had one another. We've never had a real friend."

"Me either," I admitted, "but we'll figure it out together. All I know is you are my friend. Echo too. I haven't done a lot to show that, but that's going to change. I'll earn your friendship, I promise."

We remained in each other's embrace, and that is the visual Kol walked in on when he opened the door. Two human women hugging and crying in the middle of a cleansing room. We separated as he literally leaped towards us, startling us both.

"What is wrong?" he asked, panicked.

He seemed to forget Envi was in the room as he focused solely on me.

"Nothing," I replied, wiping my face clear of tears. "We just had a really personal talk and had a cry. It's a normal thing for women to do, Kol. At least my father said it was."

He looked like he didn't believe but didn't want to voice his doubt.

"We're fine," I assured him. "Truly."

He nodded slowly, watching me carefully as if I would burst back into tears at any given moment.

"Do we have to stay at the feast much longer?" I asked Kol. "I'm so tired."

He scratched his neck. "The feast ended moments ago, but my father wants all his family to gather in his main living area in the palace so we can formally welcome you to our family."

Shit.

"Does that take very long?" I questioned, hoping I didn't sound like a brat.

Kol shook his head. "Not long. They will understand you need plenty of rest. You *did* just travel through space to get here."

"Okay then," I said, relieved. "Let's get to that."

I turned to Envi. "Do you think you and Echo would want to come to the palace tomorrow, or do you guys want to rest?"

She gnawed on her lower lip. "I'm going to guess we'll be resting; I'm exhausted from the journey here. The next day we'll come by for sure, though."

Kol hooked an arm around my waist. "I will arrange it."

He looked over his shoulder, whistled, and a second later, a muscular, tall, bald male with white scars all over his green face entered the cleansing room. The male didn't make a sound, and I was certain he didn't so much as blink.

"This is Evra," Kol said, his voice firm. "He will escort you back to your sister, Envi, and then guide you both back to your homestead."

Envi's face was red as she bid me and Kol farewell before leaving the cleansing room with the silent but watchful Evra. Kol wasted no time in guiding me out of the cleansing room then out of the Sorting Centre. Like the journey to get to the feast, Kol talked me into getting back into the death vehicle with the promise that Nero was not going to be driving. I didn't sit in one of the grabby seats; I remained on Kol's lap. While my stomach still got queasy, the journey to and from the feast was a breeze compared to travelling with Nero at the wheel.

When we exited the vehicle, night-time had fallen, and for the first time in my entire life, I could see stars when I looked up at the sky. I sucked in a deep breath, gripped Kol's arm tightly, and simply stared up at the wonder of space. Kol looked from me to the sky and then back at me. I thought I caught him smiling out of the corner of my eye, but I wasn't sure.

"You're beautiful," he murmured to me.

"What's beautiful," I began, "is this spectacular view. I have never seen anything like this."

"Nova." Kol chortled. "You just had to look up on Earth for the same view ... with one less moon, of course."

"No," I said with a shake of my head. "Air pollution is so bad on Earth that a permanent smog exists in the sky and only the rays of the sun can break through. It has been like that for as long as I can remember."

There was a pregnant pause.

"You've never seen stars before now?" he asked, shocked.

"I saw some through the viewing pane on the *Ebony* but not a backdrop like this," I replied, staring up into the unknown. "I want to stare at it always."

"When you're fully rested in a few days," Kol spoke softly, his thumb strumming my forearm. "I'm going to take you stargazing ... just the two of us."

That sounded like absolute heaven.

I looked at him, and I hated that I felt hurt when I found that his eyes were glowing.

"*Shiva*," he murmured, brushing strands of loose hair from my face, "what saddens you so?"

That you didn't come to love me on your own.

"It's nothing," I said, brushing it off with a dismissive wave. "I'm just tired. After I get some rest, I will be okay."

"Come," he beckoned, moving towards the palace entrance. "The welcoming gathering will not take long; everyone is waiting for our arrival."

I followed Kol, and I noticed male after male guard as we passed by. There were *so* many of them, but I guess I shouldn't have been so surprised. There were a lot of royals to protect, not to mention the ridiculously large palace that needed constant guarding. Guarding against who, I wasn't sure. All the Maji were obedient and followed orders without hesitation ... but Mikoh did mention, back on the *Ebony*, that disloyal Maji were amongst the people.

Maybe that was who they were protecting the royal family and their residence from.

I wanted to ask Kol if that was the case, but I was simply too tired to hold a steady conversation with him. I felt exhausted, even more so now that I had a tummy full of delicious food. If Kol had allowed me to do so, I would have curled up like a *kit* on the floor and slept the night away.

"Ah," Kol murmured. "Here we are."

I knew we were still on the first floor of the palace, but I just wasn't sure exactly which part of the building we were in. I wasn't paying attention. I simply allowed Kol to lead me and followed him without question. I didn't have a chance to prepare myself for a gathering of Kol's whole family because my impatient mate pushed open the door to the Revered Father's living area and tugged me into the room after him.

"Kol," Surkah chirped when she noticed us enter. "Nova, welcome."

I gripped Kol's left arm with both of mine when the gravity of whose presence I was in dawned on me. The Revered Father and Hailed Mother stood, along with Kol's nine brothers, sister, cousin Nero, and a male and female whom I had yet to glimpse before that very moment. After some thought, I figured them to be Nero's parents, Kol's uncle and aunt-in-mate, and after Kol introduced everyone to me, it confirmed who they were.

"I am delighted to meet you all, and those of you who I have already met, I am glad to see you again." I smiled. "Forgive me if I seem out of sorts, I'm afraid the weight of the journey from Earth to Ealra has suddenly registered with my body and pushed me towards exhaustion."

"Kol." The Hailed Mother frowned. "Bring your female to your wing and allow her rest. This gathering need not continue any longer. She has met our family and will have plenty of time to get to know us all."

The Hailed Mother was awesome.

"If I may, brother," Ezah's deep voice suddenly spoke. "I wish to escort your female back to your wing of the palace. I regret my behaviour and hurtful words towards her. I seek your permission to make amends with her as soon as possible."

Kol was silent for a long moment, and just when I thought he was about to deny Ezah's request, he said, "Granted."

I wanted to thump Kol for not consulting me before he answered.

"Son," the Revered Father then spoke to Kol. "Come and give me your statement of the day Surkah was discovered aboard the *Ebony* before I decide her punishment."

I had to be escorted by Ezah *alone*? Fuck!

Kol kissed my temple. "I will join you very soon."

I could only nod as he crossed the room to his father. I tried to catch Surkah's attention, but she was stood next to her father with her gaze down as he spoke to Kol and Mikoh. I swallowed when Ezah approached me and offered me his arm. I took it with a forced smile, bid everyone a good night, and left the living area with my brother-in-mate. For a whole minute, we walked in silence as we climbed up stairs to the second floor.

I had a really bad feeling, so I had to address it.

"You didn't offer to escort me so you could apologise," I said warily. "Did you?"

"You're more attentive than I gave you credit for, human."

I came to an abrupt stop and dropped my hand from his arm.

"If you do anything to me, I'll call for Kol through our mental link, and he will hurt you. You *know* he will."

Ezah chuckled gruffly. "You need not fear me, Nova, or call for my brother. I just want to talk to you."

I looked up at him. "About what?"

"Kol, of course."

I nervously wrung my hands together. "What about him?"

"You have dishonoured a prince of the people by agreeing to be his mate."

Hurt pierced my heart.

"It was *his* decision to mate me, not *yours*."

Ezah's chuckle was unnerving. "You have no inkling about what has happened because of your mating."

I swallowed. "What are you talking about?"

"Kol mated you," he acknowledged with a jerk of his head. "But do you *know* at what cost?"

A veil of wariness wrapped around me.

"No," I spoke softly. "What did it cost for Kol to mate me?"

"His intention to another," Ezah practically spat.

I stumbled back as if he struck me.

"You're lying," I whispered. "He wasn't intended to another. He would have told me so; he—"

"He said what you *wanted* to hear," Ezah cut me off with a growl. "You're smaller than our females, no doubt ... tighter, too. He wouldn't need much more persuading than that to claim you."

My stomach churned.

"You're disgusting!" I managed to say with firmness.

Ezah's face hardened, but he had a sadistic grin on his face that told me he enjoyed the emotional pain he was inflicting on me more than he was letting on. At least, I thought so; there were moments where he looked unsure, but of what, I did not know.

"The knowledge that my brother was to mate another burns you?" he asked, his brows raised. "It must hurt more to hear that Kol never wanted a noble mating and once told me he'd mate *any* commoner to get out of it."

Pain and self-doubt laced around my cracking heart.

"You're lying, Ezah," I whispered. "I can feel how *he* feels for me when I'm with him."

Ezah's booming laughter startled me.

"We can seal off our minds to our mates if we choose, and we can project to them any thought that we choose ... so what makes you think we cannot project feelings, too?"

I froze and looked up at Ezah, whose brow was raised in question as he awaited my answer.

"I ... I ..."

"You were available, little one," he rumbled. "You were convenient, and something new to play with. That is all."

My breathing became laboured even though I was standing still.

"Maji mate for life," I said, my body beginning to involuntarily shake. "Why would he choose me if he would have to keep me for life?"

"Isn't it obvious?" Ezah snorted. "Sex, dumb human. *Exotic sex.*"

It took every ounce of strength I had not to burst into tears there and then.

"Do not fret, my *sister-in-mate*," he sneered. "Kol will make you a fine mate. He is a strong male, and I'm *sure* he will really develop love for you after spending a few decades with you."

My lower lip was wobbling, so I locked it between my teeth.

"That's not enough for you, is it?" Ezah asked as he began to circle me. "You cannot move beyond Kol's lies and deceit ... can you?"

No.

I squeezed my eyes. "You're lying!"

"If you really believe that, little one, go back to your welcoming gathering and have a wonderful time with my siblings. I'll not keep you a moment longer."

I looked up at Ezah, hoping I'd see some truth on his handsome face, but all I saw was ugliness spilling over from his blackened heart.

"You asked—"

"I didn't ask for *any* of this!" I stated, my voice finally breaking. "All I wanted was to be left alone! When I woke up on the *Ebony*, I just wanted to be *left alone*."

Ezah came to a stop and towered over me. "If you want to leave Ealra, I will help you."

Sickness swirled in my abdomen.

"Wh-what?"

"I can get you to the human planet Terra," he said with assertiveness.

"But Kol—"

"Go and ask him if what I have said is truth or lies." Ezah gestured me away with his hand. "Go and seek the knowledge of my words, and when you find them, I will still be here with my offer standing."

I backed away from him slowly.

"Go, Nova." He laughed, the sound echoing through the halls. "Do not be afraid; you already know what I say is the truth."

I turned and ran down the staircase and back in the direction we came from with one thing on my mind.

Confronting Kol.

CHAPTER TWENTY-ONE

I had no idea how I managed to do it, but I found my way back to the Revered Father's living area. Then with strength I didn't know my tired body possessed, I pushed the doors of the room open, and my entrance snagged everyone's immediate attention.

"Nova," Kol said, crossing the room to me instantly when his eyes landed on my form. "What is—"

"Did you have an intended Maji?" I cut him off, my chest rising and falling as I caught my breath.

My heart slammed into my chest, and my stomach was tight with apprehension.

Kol's eyes widened. "What brought this conversation—"

"Kol!" I angrily cut him off again. "Were you intended to mate a Maji before you met me?"

His eyes, which were glowing, couldn't hold contact with mine, and I felt my stomach drop.

"Almighty," I whispered.

Kol reached for me but dropped his hand when I tensed.

"Answer my question," I demanded of him, though I had an awful feeling I already knew what the answer was. "Answer it *out loud*."

He remained silent.

"Answer me!" I screamed.

"Nova—"

"Don't *touch* me!" I cried, stumbling back from him when he reached for me once more. "Ezah said you were supposed to mate a female. Is that true, Kol? Don't you *dare* fucking lie to me!"

His eyes were wild.

"Yes," he choked out after what felt like an entirety of silence. "I gave my verbal intention to another, but you must allow me to explain why."

Kol was intended to another female, but he had mated me instead because his body liked me better. That was all that ran through my mind. His *body* liked me, and that was the only reason I was by his side.

"I feel sick," I said, my hands clutching my stomach.

"Forgive me," he pleaded desperately. "I feel your pain, and I wish to take it away. Let me explain."

"How can you explain away that you were promised to someone else?" I bellowed, my eyes filling with tears. "You fucking lied to me. Again. All you *do* is lie to me. Over and over and over. I am a fool. You are in my life seven days, and look how many times you have lied to me. Look how many times you have lied over life-changing things!"

"My Nova—"

"Never," I growled. "Never call me yours *ever* again."

"You *are* mine," he replied, his voice firm but his expression lost.

"Am I yours like when you said I was your only one?" I questioned with a humourless laugh.

My laughter quickly dried up, and my lower lip wobbled as gut-wrenching pain began to stab at my chest.

"You told me I was your one!" I stated as I shot forward into his space and smacked my fists against his chest. "You told me I was your heart! You told me I was your *fated mate*!"

Sharp intakes of breath sounded around the room.

"You *are* my heart, *shiva*," Kol stressed, emotion filling his voice. "You *are* my fated mate. Just look at my eyes. They glow for *you!*"

"They are *true* fated mates?" I heard a female voice gasp with surprise, but I ignored whoever it was.

I shook my head. "I don't believe a word you say or have *ever* said to me!"

A wave of helpless expressions crossed over Kol's face, but anger was the one to settle when I made a move to turn and walk away from him. He shot forward, grabbed my arms, and held me tightly. He was shaking, I could feel his body tremble against mine, but I didn't allow myself to be concerned for him. I wanted to get away from him. Far away as Ezah could get me.

To Terra.

"Let me *go*!" I demanded. "I need to be away from you right now; I need to think without looking at you, without feeling you, or fucking hearing you."

"No," Kol growled, his hold tightening.

I struggled harder. "I'm *not* Maji. You can't just dominate me and expect me to heel to you."

"*Shiva—*"

"Just stop!" I screamed at the top of my lungs. "If you don't let me go, I *swear* I'll hate you for as long as I live!"

More sharp intakes of breath filled the room.

Kol instantly released me, and when I moved towards the doorway, I said, "Do *not* come near me. Give me the space I deserve."

I turned and fled the room before he could speak or do anything about it. I heard him roar, and then there was loud commotion and a hell of a lot of growling and snarling, but I blocked it all out and ran. I ran all the way back to Ezah and found him leaning against the wall next to the staircase, right where I left him.

"You were right," I blurted, my hands wrapped around myself.

"About everything."

I expected to see a satisfied grin on Ezah's face, but I didn't. What I saw looked an awful lot like ... pity.

"Maybe you should—"

"You said you could get me to Terra," I cut him off, panicked he changed his mind.

He licked his lower lip. "I can."

"Then I want to go," I said, hugging myself tighter. "I want to go right now."

"Nova—"

"Please, Ezah," I pleaded, helplessness consuming me. "Please, take me away from here."

He regarded me with a look that was *definitely* one of pity, but when he jerked his head in a nod, I knew he was agreeing to do what he offered and what I pleaded for. He would take me away from Kol, the people, Ealra ... and he would bring me to Terra and back to my people. For once in my entire life, the knowledge that I was purposely going somewhere to be surrounded by humans didn't scare me. I felt nothing other than the pain that Kol's lies and deceit had inflicted.

Seven days ... That was all it took for him to break me.

CHAPTER TWENTY-TWO

Once Ezah agreed to help me escape to Terra, he turned into a fierce male on a mission. He decided right then and there that we would leave while his family was distracted with Kol in his father's living area. He didn't allow me to bring a single thing with me, and all this suited me fine. I didn't need anything. I wanted to be gone from Ealra, and I wanted it immediately.

We exited the palace a hell of a lot quicker than I thought possible, but as Ezah had grown up within the solid gold walls, he knew every shortcut imaginable, and he used that to our advantage.

"We have minutes," he muttered lowly as we briskly walked by two guards who were bowing to either Ezah or both of us. "Once Kol realises you're gone, and I am nowhere to be found, an alarm will sound and every patrolling warrior will be on high alert and searching for us. He will try to reach you mentally, so you'll have to block him out."

I gaped at him. "He never taught me how."

"My father said he imagines a wall, and that puts a blockage from my mother hearing his thoughts or projecting hers to him."

I felt sick to my stomach with worry in case I failed with the blocking thing, but I imagined a large wall in my mind and tried to focus on it. I felt even sicker as we neared a death vehicle. I didn't hesitate like I thought I would have. Instead, I jumped into the front passenger seat and remained still as Ezah climbed into the driver's seat and started the engine. I held my breath as the seat closed in around me, but when I realised it wasn't going to crush me, I relaxed.

Ezah pulled out of the vehicle's parking space, and within seconds, we were driving so fast, it made my stomach lurch in what felt like slow motion. We left the palace and everyone in it behind in a matter of seconds. I flung my hand over my eyes and wished for the journey to get wherever we were going to end.

Three or so minutes after entering the vehicle, it returned to sitting idle, and I was stumbling out of it, clutching my stomach before I vomited up its contents. Ezah didn't give me a moment to gather my bearings; he came to my side, gripped my arm, and pulled me towards a ... spacecraft. A small spacecraft but *definitely* one that could do the job and get me to Terra.

"Move quicker," he scowled.

I threw a glance over my shoulder and saw the lit-up palace off in the distance.

"I *have* been moving quicker," I snapped at him, wiping my mouth with the back of my hand. "I'm lightheaded and feel like I'm going to be sick again. You drove too fast, and my body cannot handle it."

"Because you're weak!" he growled.

I surprised us both when I smacked him as hard as I could across his chest with my free hand, and for a moment, he paused mid stride, looked down at his chest then at me, and he did something that astonished me. He smiled and followed it up with a gruff laugh. Two things I would *never* have thought him capable of.

"I cannot *believe* you just struck me," he said, shaking his head in clear amusement.

I didn't get a chance to reply before he had us both moving towards the spacecraft once again. I came to a stop when he released me and jogged over to a closed control panel at the base of the craft's hull. He placed his palm on the panel cover, and I wasn't surprised to see that it opened. Ezah was a prince; he probably has clearance for everything. I stared at the craft when a hissing noise sounded just before a ramp lowered.

"Get aboard," Ezah ordered. "I can hear the guards approaching on their patrol."

I hustled forward.

"This is so unreal," I said as I shot up the ramp and came to a stop in the middle of the craft's small bridge. "This is seriously crazy, Ezah. Are you sure you can fly this thing?"

I knew engines, not pilot controls, so if anything went wrong, I would be absolutely no use to Ezah. He grunted as he jogged up the ramp and cleared it just before it closed behind him. It clicked shut with a bang, and it made me feel like what was happening was very final.

"Who do you think taught Kol how to pilot?" Ezah asked me, distracting me from the doubt that slithered into my mind. "He is not the only prince who holds the rank of shipmaster. He just won father's favour to lead the mission to Earth on the *Ebony* to retrieve your females."

I stood idle as Ezah moved about the narrow bridge—flipping switches, pressing buttons, and turning dials—before he sat on one of two large seats in front of a huge control panel. He nodded at the spare seat, so I moved forward and took it without hesitation. As soon as I sat down, the seat moulded to my body shape and locked me in place. The same thing happened to Ezah; only his chair moved with him as he tapped on a clear screen next to him. I gasped when writing I had never seen before filled the screen, along with diagrams showing different levels of what I assumed could be fuel for the craft.

I had no idea; I was just guessing what Ezah was doing because if I didn't think about what he was doing, I'd think about what I was doing, and I couldn't allow myself to give in to doubt. Kol lied to me one too many times, and this final lie, about him being promised to another, was my tipping point. I wasn't meant to be loved or to love in return. I was meant to be on my own … Nothing could truly hurt me when I had no one to care about.

"Hold on," Ezah suddenly said as the craft roared to life. "Ascent is green."

I frantically looked to my left and right for handles, but there was nothing for me to grab.

"Hold fucking *what*?" I screeched.

Ezah laughed. "The rest of your stomach contents."

I was sucked backward against my seat as the craft suddenly lurched forward and flew down what looked like a wasteland through the viewing pane, but Ezah quickly pulled on a control handle that lifted the nose of the craft and took us up into the air. It was only then, as we ascended towards the heavens, that I realised I wasn't breathing. I greedily sucked air into my lungs and groaned when a dizzy spell struck that caused my eyes to roll back.

"Nearly there," I heard Ezah say, his voice rough. "One more minute until we leave atmo."

Ezah's voice fell away, and I felt like my body was swaying from left to right, but when I lazily blinked open my eyes, I saw that while my chair was perfectly still, it was the craft that was moving left to right. I gasped when the view through the viewing pane changed, and I was not looking up at space; I was now entering it.

I jerked my gaze to Ezah.

"Did I pass out?" I asked him, my breathing laboured as I took slow, deep breaths.

"Yes," he griped. "You missed a transmission from Kol."

I froze. "He knows?"

"He knows." Ezah confirmed. "He is also coming after us."

I felt like I would be sick.

"Ezah, I don't want to go back."

"I know," he growled. "I told him that, but he was not rational enough to do much more than tell me, in detail, how he would kill me."

I stayed mute, my throat suddenly unable to form words.

"He has reached the edge," Ezah continued. "My father informed me I was to be withheld for severe judgment when we are apprehended."

When we were apprehended.

"What do we do?" I asked him, my eyes wide. "Did you lie when you said you could get me to Terra?"

The muscle in Ezah's jaw rolled back and forth as he tensed.

"I can get you there … I just can't outrun my brother and the *Ebony*. This craft is just a maintenance shuttle used to bring our miners to and from nearby planets when they go to harvest minerals."

I was at a loss for words.

"I … I did not think this through, Nova."

I looked at him. "Yeah, Ezah. That makes two of us."

I was *so* fucked.

Kol would catch us and then take me back to the palace and probably put me under house arrest. I would probably face charges of some sort with the Revered Father and Hailed Mother. I technically aided Ezah in stealing a shuttle craft and left their planet without their permission … not to mention bailing on their son and leaving him to reach the edge over my decision.

"This is so fucked," I said, and not a second later, I burst into tears.

"Nova," he mumbled. "Do not cry."

"Why not?" I asked, sniffling. "I have *no* idea what the hell I'm doing, Ezah. I know leaving Kol is wrong; it's cruel to abandon him when we're mated for life … but I felt so hurt, so *angry* over his decisions. When I feel those emotions, I run. Running is all I know."

It's the only fucking thing I'm good at.

"He lied to me so easily," I continued with a shake of my head. "How can he truly expect me to believe I'm his fated mate when all he does is lie?"

The craft suddenly lurched.

"Ezah!" I gasped. "Are you sure that you can fly this thing?"

"This is *very* important," Ezah almost growled as he tapped on the control panel, stood from his chair, moved over to me, and placed his huge hands on my shoulders. "When Kol is intimate with you or just standing close by looking at you, does something happen to his face?"

I raised a brow. "His eyes glow."

Ezah sucked in a startled breath then stumbled back away from me like I had the plague, and during his stumble, he lost his balance and plonked right down onto his behind, drawing a wince from me.

"Are you okay?" I asked, unsure why I was concerned for him.

"What have I done?" he said, aloud.

I blinked. "You tripped and fell. It's not that big of a deal. You'll be okay."

"We must return to Ealra right this—"

"What?" I cut him off as I tried and failed to jump to my feet because of the damn grabby chair. "No! You said you'd bring me to Terra."

Ezah got to his feet and stood to his full height of hu-fucking-mongous, towering over me with ease.

"That was before I learned you were my brother's fated mate."

I slapped my palm to my forehead. "I thought we agreed that Kol is a liar?"

"He cannot lie about being your fated mate when the glow in his eyes shines bright, Nova," Ezah said and surprised me by kneeling before me and taking my tiny hands in his large ones. "Please, forgive me. I have committed a crime."

I had no idea what was happening, but I was confident that Ezah was starting to lose it.

"What crime?" I demanded. "*What* are you talking about?"

"Taking a Maji's mate away is punishable by imprisonment but taking a Maji's fated mate? I will receive death for such an act, and it is no more than I deserve."

My heart sunk to the pit my stomach.

"No," I said, squeezing his hands. "No, you won't be killed. You're a prince."

"And I stole *another* prince's fated mate away from him," Ezah replied, the words sounding choked as he spoke. "I thought I was helping him. I thought I was saving my brother the pain of a mate loss. You're human ... tiny, weak, and vulnerable. It is only matter of time before you die on Ealra, and I do not want my brother to feel the pain that I do."

I shoved down my instant reaction to defend my species because there was a much bigger problem at stake ... Ezah had a mate who died?

"Ezah, I'm not Kol's—"

"You *are* his fated mate," he growled in annoyance. "Our eyes only glow when we find our fated mate."

I froze, and not because he scared the shit out of me, but because I could see in his eyes that he was telling the truth. It was the same look Kol had in his eyes when he told me I was his fated mate.

"Almighty," I whispered, feeling like I had been sucker punched. "What have I done?"

"Not you," Ezah said firmly. "Me. I have done this."

"Only because *I* begged you to," I countered.

Ezah set his jaw. "You begged me because I instilled doubt in your mind about Kol."

"Not everything you said was a lie, Ezah," I almost shouted, furious with him for taking the blame entirely on himself.

"What was truth?" he demanded.

"Kol *was* intended to another and never told me!" I snapped.

"Ah!" Ezah growled with a wave of his hand as he pressed

something under the seat of the chair so it released me. "He was never going to mate Keeva, and we all knew it. She did too. She just agreed to be his future intended to get our mother to stop bothering Kol about finding a mate."

"Wh-what?" I stammered.

"That intention was make-believe, and it was never binding because both Maji did not want it."

I stared at Ezah for all of two seconds before I flew at him, my arms swinging in rage.

"You made me believe he had a true intention to this female. You made me—"

"I made you doubt your mate, your bond, and your place by his side," Ezah finished for me as he grabbed my hands, halting them from connecting with his face. "I made you do this, Nova. I was as horrible to you as I could possibly be to a female on purpose. I am truly sorry."

"But why?" I asked, now crying. "Why did you do this?"

"A mate loss," he rasped. "I couldn't bear for Kol to suffer it. I believed because your bond is so new, I could make you leave, and in time, Kol would ... move past you. I do not know why I thought of this. I *know* how matings work and how unbreakable a bond is, but my worry for my brother made me think irrationally."

"You've suffered a mate loss?" I asked, my throat hurting from crying.

"Not a true one, but something very close," he replied, releasing my hands from his grip. "My intended female, she was ... she was killed by a stealth beast on an outing with me not long after my sister was born, and the pain I feel is as strong today as it was the day I watched her die."

I lifted my hands to my mouth.

"I am so sorry, Ezah. I cannot imagine what you have gone through," I wept. "I have lost all my family, and I know that pain will never go away, but it does gets easier to bear. But I cannot fathom the thought of losing Kol. I know I'm not Maji, but I love your brother with all my heart. It is why this whole thing hurts so much. I want him to love me like I love him, and not just because this fated mate business means he has to."

"Nova." Ezah frowned deeply. "A male's body does not decide a mating, a male's heart does. If a male decides to bite a female and give her his essence, it's because his heart decided it before his head did. The body reacts to what it finds attractive, and the heart reacts to what it can grow to love … You have much to learn about the people, little one."

Tears streaked my face, and before I knew it, I was hugging Ezah tightly.

"Take me back to him," I pleaded. "Please. I've messed this up terribly, and I need to make it right."

Ezah gently patted my back. "I will."

When we separated, Ezah got to his knees and closed his eyes.

"Thanas, forgive me," he rasped, his head bowed. "I have purposely caused my brother and his female great pain. Pain I had no right inflicting."

I froze to the spot the second I realised Ezah was praying to Thanas out loud.

"Please," he whispered. "Please end my life. I only cause turmoil and pain; the people would be better without me. Please, I … I am not a strong male. I cannot live without Kovu… Is she okay? Is she with you? Does she know how broken I am that I could not save her?"

No one answered Ezah. Instead, more tears freely flowed down my cheeks in response to his words as I watched the fiercest Maji I had ever met break in front of me.

"Why are you sp-speaking aloud?" I stammered.

Ezah kept his head bowed.

"I hoped if I spoke aloud, He would hear my prayer clearer."

My heart broke in two.

"Ezah," I whispered. "I forgive you."

He sucked in a breath and looked up at me with misted eyes.

"No," he rasped. "I do not deserve your forgiveness."

"Tough shit." I sniffled. "You have it anyway."

"But why?"

"Because I relate to you," I told him.

He widened his eyes. "How?"

"I could not save my family." I swallowed. "My two cousins were attacked by augmented humans and bled out in my arms, and my other cousin, as well as my father, died of sickness in my arms. Nothing I did saved them, and I believe that Almighty blames me for it. It is why I walked alone for so long in heartache."

"But you did not cause your cousins' injuries or make your father and cousin sick." Ezah frowned.

I blinked down at him. "And you did cause the injury that killed Kovu."

He shook his head. "I'm a male, Nova. I should have saved her or died trying."

"Listen to yourself," I pleaded, dropping to my knees, too. "If you knew of the beast's presence, you would have acted and saved her. It was an animal that took her, not you, Ezah."

He squeezed his eyes shut for just a moment before he opened them and focused on me.

"You should not forgive me or be so understanding ... I do not deserve any of this. I have not been kind to you."

"It doesn't matter. You are my brother-in-mate, and I *will* love you like a brother," I said with assertiveness. "Let Kol and anyone else try to break through that, and they will quickly find out that I protect my own."

Ezah's eyes glazed over with unshed tears. "You would truly claim me as your family after what I have done?"

"I would ... I *have*. You're my brother-in-mate, Ezah. You're my family."

A single tear fell from his right eye and splashed onto his cheek. He widened his eyes as he lifted his hand to his face and rubbed at the tear streak with his fingertips. He stared down at the wetness on his skin in shock, and it made me laugh.

"I take it you're not used to crying?" I joked and wiped my tear-streaked face.

He frantically rubbed at his eyes as he shook his head.

"I have never," he said with assertiveness. "Not in my entire life. I don't even think I wept at birth."

I was surprised by the laugh that erupted from me.

"Never tell that I cried," Ezah pleaded. "I will never have my honour restored."

His dramatics tickled my funny bone.

"I promise, I'll never say a word."

Ezah raised a brow. "Not even to your mate."

My mate.

I winked. "Not even to him."

"You're a kind female, Nova."

I flung my hands over my ears when a soul-crushing wail filled the craft. Ezah jumped to his feet, pressed on the control panel, and then returned to me, lifted me up, and placed me back in the grabby chair. He retook his seat and hollered, "Hold on."

"*Stop* saying that!" I shouted. "There is *nothing* for me to hold!"

Ezah laughed as he turned the ship around and surged us back towards Ealra. We didn't make it very far away from the planet. If anything, it looked like we were just grazing the atmosphere.

"Planet fall in five, four, three, two ... one."

I screamed as heavy pressure sat on my chest, and thanks be to Almighty that it only lasted for a few seconds before it disappeared.

"Sorry," Ezah shouted moments later. "I needed to enter the atmosphere quickly before the *Ebony* broke through it. I've relayed to the *Ebony* that we're returning."

I didn't have time to think of facing Kol because my heart was in the pit of my stomach until the shuttle touched back down on Ealra close to ten minutes later. I looked at Ezah when he came to my side and released me from my seat before helping me to my feet. I was a little shaky on my legs, but after a few deep breaths, I could stand on my own.

"This will happen fast," Ezah said to me as the ramp of the shuttle began to lower. "Do not mourn me if he kills me. I deserve his wrath."

What the hell?

"Stay back and do not interfere," he then said to me, his tone leaving no room for bullshit.

I looked at him as he walked a few feet in front of me and frowned. "What do you mea—"

"Ezah!"

I almost jumped a foot in the air when an uproarious bellow echoed throughout the craft when the ramp finally lowered. I sucked in a breath when a male barrelled up the ramp and clashed with Ezah, spearing him up against the wall of the shuttle. And that male was my mate.

"Kol," I screamed as he bared his teeth and went for Ezah's throat. "*No!*"

Ezah managed to avoid Kol's teeth, and it allowed me get in front of Kol. I pushed him with both of my hands, and when he didn't move, I kept them on his chest.

"He is your brother!" I shouted, hoping to break through the madness that had hold of him. "Your *brother!*"

His eyes weren't his own. They weren't violet anymore. They weren't glowing, and they were jet black. At that very moment, he was no longer the Kol I knew and loved.

"Nova!" I heard a roar.

I recognised the voice as Mikoh's.

"Help me, Mikoh," I screamed, still trying to push Kol backwards. "Help restrain him until he calms."

I saw Mikoh come up behind Kol, but the second he reached for *me*, Kol turned on him like an animal. He roared, turned, and speared Mikoh to the ground. Ezah instantly went to Mikoh's aid and speared Kol off Mikoh and to the ground. I was screaming the entire time, and when Killi, Aza, and Arvi sprinted up the ramp, I had never been so relieved in my life.

I nearly collapsed when Killi helped Mikoh to his feet, and Arvi moved me behind him but then they didn't move or make a move to stop Ezah and Kol from fighting. They just stood and watched them like Kol wasn't trying his best to kill their brother.

"Stop him!" I screamed, smacking my hands on Arvi's back.

Killi jerked his gaze to mine, and the pain I saw in them made me gasp.

"Ezah's life is in Kol's hands," he said, and the emotion in his voice shocked me. "Ezah's crime is punishable by death, so if Kol kills him, it is his right."

"No, *no*!" I cried. "He has reached the edge; he would not want this if he was in his right mind."

Killi looked back at his brothers, and he clenched his hands into fists, but he didn't move. I looked from brother to brother then at Mikoh. They wanted to stop Kol; I could see it on their faces. Their loyalty to their laws prevented them, but it didn't prevent me.

I rushed around Arvi before he had a chance to stop me, making a beeline towards Kol and Ezah.

"Stop!" I begged.

Kol didn't stop. He punched Ezah over and over and over. I had no choice but to jump on Kol's back to try to stop him. My action worked instantly, and Kol stilled over Ezah, not moving a muscle, but I could feel that his entire body was tensed. He stood very slowly, but didn't move away from standing over his battered older brother.

"If you kill him," I said into Kol's ear, "you'll have to kill me too because I asked him to take me away from you."

My mate growled, and I could hear the pain that was wrapped up in it.

"You don't want this," I sobbed as I kissed his neck. "You don't want to kill your brother over a mistake. This was a mistake, and I'm *so* sorry. Please, come back to me."

Ezah, who was dazed and injured so badly I feared he would never recover, tried to stand, but Kol snarled, placed his foot on his chest, and pinned him to the ground. Ezah slumped on the ground as blood poured from his mouth, nose, and forehead. His face was already swollen beyond believe.

"Kol," I said firmly into his ear. "Look at me."

I slowly slid down his back until my feet touched the ground. I kept my hands on him and applied pressure to his arms, turning him to face me. He was breathing heavily, and his eyes were still jet back. His teeth were bared, and he looked absolutely vicious.

"Come on, big guy," I hummed. "Come back to me."

I lifted my hands to my breasts, and Kol's eyes instantly locked on my movements. I pulled the material down, exposing my bare breasts to him. I hoped that sex with me would become his primary focus, and that I could pull him back from the edge with my touch.

Kol snarled, reached forward, and pulled my body against his. I could feel his hardened length against my stomach, and when he suddenly hiked me up his body, I wrapped my legs around his waist and gasped when he latched his mouth onto my exposed nipple.

"Get Ezah"—I hissed when Kol's teeth grazed me—"out of here while I calm him. *Now!*"

I heard movement, and when Ezah groaned in pain, it made Kol snarl. He released my nipple and made a move to turn his head in Ezah's direction, but before he could, I leaned in and latched my lips onto his neck, and I bit down. Kol's focus quickly returned to me, and when I heard the ripping of fabric as he adjusted me against his body, I knew his instinct was driving him crazy with need to claim me.

I looked over his shoulder and saw Killi had Ezah over his shoulder and was descending the ramp with Aza, Arvi, and Mikoh following behind quickly. I breathed a sigh of release but gasped when Kol reached between our bodies and plunged his fingers into my body. I wasn't wet, so the action made me wince. Kol paused, growled, and removed his fingers and brought them to my clit instead.

"Oh!" I gasped and arched my back as pleasure gripped me.

Kol purred in response and returned his mouth to my nipple. He licked and sucked one before showering the other with same attention. It didn't take long for my clit to pulse to life, and my pussy to clench as it wept with need.

Sh-shiva.

"I'm here," I whimpered to him as his voice broke into my thoughts, his fingers on my clit sweet torture. "I'm here, Kol."

Need. You.

"You have me, sweetheart. You have me."

His fingers moved down to my entrance and dipped a finger in. It slid in and out easily, to which Kol growled in approval. I lifted my head and stared at his face as he fumbled with his pants and freed his cock with a groan. I focused on his eyes, and while they were still dark, they were no longer black as darkness.

Come back to me.

He growled as he gripped his cock, lined it up against me, and thrust forward. I cried out as he filled me in one fluid motion, and he roared in response. My back was suddenly pressed up against the wall of the shuttle as Kol's adjusted his grip on my hips, spread his legs, and fucked me so hard, it quite literally took my breath away.

It felt good, it felt *really* good, but the pressure building in my core didn't feel as good as it previously had, and I knew it was because my mind and heart wasn't in it. This sex was not about my pleasure; it was about letting Kol's instincts completely overtake him so he could come back from the edge and think rationally.

I cried out as an unexpected orgasm slammed into me, and I gripped Kol tightly when he tensed seconds later before he tipped his head back and roared. His hips jerked in violent motions as he came, and came hard. I pressed my forehead to his, making sure I kept myself as close to him as I possibly could so all his senses were filled with me. My eyes were open, and I was staring at his closed ones with worry.

It took a couple of moments, but when Kol blinked his eyes open, I whimpered when I found them to be back to their beautiful, glowing violet self. I cried, buried my face in Kol's neck, and held him as tightly as I could. We remained that way for a few minutes, holding each other and not speaking. I pulled back to look at him when his softening cock slid from my body.

"I am so sorry," I said, trembling. "So, so, *so* sorry."

"Nova," he rasped. "Did I hurt you?"

I shook my head. "No, sweetheart, you made love to me. You did not hurt me."

He looked terrified.

"Ezah?" he choked. "Did I—"

"He is well," Mikoh's voice shouted from outside. "Surkah is here with him. Welcome back, my friend."

I felt the tension flee from Kol's body but not entirely.

"You left me."

My breath caught in my throat.

"Yes," I whispered. "I did."

"You're my mate," he said, firmly. "You do not leave me, not ever."

"I won't," I swore. "Never again."

"Why?" he asked, his voice tight.

I wept.

"Ezah didn't want you to suffer a mate loss. He feared, because I'm human, that I will die and leave you. He thought he was helping you, so he instilled doubt in my mind about you with your fake intention, but it all just got *way* out of hand, and before we both knew it, we were flying away from Ealra. We quickly realised what we were doing, and we talked and set each other straight. We were wrong, we know. I'm so sorry."

Kol stared at me as I spoke, and when he slowly lowered me to the ground without speaking, I feared he would go after Ezah again, so I wrapped my arms around his waist. He put his arms around my shoulder, and when I felt him kiss the crown of my head, I relaxed and let him go. I stood still while he tucked himself back into his pants, and then readjusted my clothes to cover me as best as he could with the rips he made.

"I lied to you repeatedly, so I played a big part in making you run. I know that's what you do when you're scared."

Slowly, I nodded.

"You explained what a fated mate was horribly to me, Kol. You made me think you only wanted me because of my body."

"I told you it was more than that!" he countered angrily. "You just didn't listen."

"I know," I whispered. "I'm sorry. I wish I could take it back."

"We're mated, Nova," he said firmly. "For the rest of our lives, you are mine and I am yours."

"Yes," I gushed. "I want that more than my next breath."

"I'm glad to hear that, but I am going to give you what you previously asked for."

I froze. "Which is what?"

"Space," he answered, and it sounded like it was difficult for him to say it. "You requested to have space from me, and I'm going to give it to you. What I did was wrong. I kept another thing from you when I promised I would not. I know I hurt you, I felt your pain, and if what you need is space to … clear your mind and return to me with no more anger and worry, then that is what I am going to give you."

My heart stopped.

"I don't want that," I choked. "I don't want you to leave me."

"I'm not leaving you," Kol replied. "I never will, but right now, things are bad for us. You do not trust me to tell you truths, and I do not trust you not to run from me again."

My heart beat a mile a minute.

"What will space do for us?" I questioned.

"Time for thought," Kol answered. "We need this. I know he played a bad role, but my rage and fear at finding you gone sent me to the edge, and I nearly killed my brother this night because of that, Nova. My *brother*."

I gnawed on my inner cheek.

"You're right," I said. "You're totally right."

"When you know you are ready to be together," Kol said, his voice rough, "you come to me."

"I won't see you at all until then?" I asked, already hating this set-up.

"If you request to see me, then you will see me, but I hope you take the time you need to trust me once again. Now that I am thinking without fear of losing you, I know your trust will not return overnight like mine will not return overnight for you. For both of us, this will be a good thing." He exhaled and shook his head. "I *hope* it will be because I'm going against every single instinct in my entire body, against everything I've ever known, to make this possible."

I pressed my forehead against his chest. "Okay, I'll ... I'll come to you when I'm ready."

Kol hugged me to his body. "I love you, *shiva*."

I swallowed down a whimper.

"I love you, too."

I was surprised when Kol released me and walked away from me. He headed down the ramp of the shuttle and out of sight without so much as glancing back at me. He was serious. We were taking time away from one another and giving each other space. When I felt like I was ready to put this shitstorm behind us, I would go to Kol ...

The only thing that now plagued me was what if it took a while for that to happen?

How long was too long for Kol to wait for me?

CHAPTER TWENTY-THREE

Eight weeks later...

For years, I roamed Earth by myself without nothing other than a handmade bow and some arrows for company. I was content with my solitude, I accepted that it was vital for my safety, and thus, I accepted that I would never have any kind of relationship because of it. Then the Maji happened, and within the space of a week, my entire existence was turned upside down as I was whisked away to a new planet, a new life ... a new beginning.

During those seven days, I fell in love.

I now know that people do the *dumbest shit* when they are in love. Like when you find out your husband was engaged to another woman, and rather than let him explain, you completely overreact and enlist his older brother to help you not only escape him, but also escape the new planet he brought you to.

I still can't believe I did that shit.

When I thought of how far I'd gone to get away from Kol, I couldn't help but feel embarrassed. I had to train myself not to just up and run at the first sign of trouble, and it proved to be rather difficult. For a long time, my entire life was running. If I didn't run, I died, so I'd made running my main priority, and Kol got that. He got that before he entered my life I was alone and had no one, so from time to time, he knew I needed the space and time to myself that I was used to having before I became his mate. It was why he suggested we take a break from one another.

Not a break from our mating—that was impossible, we were mated for life—just a time out to put our ducks in a row, and time for me to mentally prepare myself for the change in my life that the first seven days of knowing Kol didn't give me.

So taking some time to myself was exactly what I had done, and what I had learned from it was that I really, really, really … fucking *really* missed Kol. I missed him all of two seconds after we decided to take a break. After the first week of not seeing him at all, I was constantly emotional, but it gave me time to grow, to think, to reflect. After week four, I requested to see him because I just need to lock my eyes on his, to simply touch him. I was more than a little relieved when I saw he needed to see and touch me just as much as I needed to see and touch him. When week seven rolled around, I wondered why I asked for space from him, but when I thought about what he'd done and still felt some emotion over it, I knew I needed to stay strong.

When I woke up that morning and realised it had been *eight* whole weeks since I came to Ealra and tried to leave Ealra, my heart decided that enough was enough. I didn't need any more space. What I needed was my mate, and if either of us still had any hang-ups about what happened, we would *talk* it out and *listen* to one another and get through it together because we were stronger when united.

We were made for each other. Literally.

I planned on finding Kol and telling him in person rather than reaching out to him in my mind, but after multiple mornings of being sick and feeling tired and sore, I went in search of my sister-in-mate to find out if I had an illness I should be worried about. I found Sur-kah in her wing of the palace, sewing on her own. Sewing was kind of my thing now, too. I had done a lot of it over the past eight weeks, and it turned out that once I got the hang of it, I could make some pretty cute outfits. I wasn't as skilled as Surkah, her mother, or even her aunt were, but I was getting there.

"Nova." Surkah smiled when I entered the living area. "I didn't know you were coming by to see me."

"Yeah, sorry for just dropping in unannounced. I just wanted to ask you something before I find Kol."

My sister-in-mate widened her eyes. "You seek Kol?"

I smiled. "Yeah, I think we've had more than enough space from one another, don't you think?"

Surkah abandoned her sewing, jumped up, rushed to me, and enveloped me into a heartfelt hug that made me boom with laughter.

"I am so happy," she gushed.

"Me too," I said. "I'm ready to put all the bad behind me and focus on my future with Kol. I love him."

Surkah beamed with delight. "Why come see me? What was so important that you had to ask?"

"I have a problem."

"Do explain."

I huffed. "I don't know where to start. I think I'm sick, but I'm not sure."

"Sick?" Surkah frowned.

I nodded. "The past few days I've been getting sick in the mornings, and sometimes at night if I smell something bad. My breasts are tender, and I'm always hungry. I don't know what to think other than I'm sick."

Surkah stared at me, and I mean really stared at me.

"Do not play your human tricks, Nova," she said, firmly.

"Huh?"

"What tricks?" I frowned. "You're a healer. I've come to you for your help."

Surkah didn't respond to me. Instead, she reached forward,

gripped the hem of my loose fitted torso wrap, and pushed it up until the material was bunched under my breasts. When she gasped, I felt my cheeks burn with heat.

"I was not used to eating before I came to Ealra," I said in a rushed breath. "I eat every day now, and sometimes I eat a lot. I just gained a little weight. It's not a big deal."

It really wasn't a big deal; my stomach was the only place I had gained any weight, and it wasn't like it was a huge amount or anything. My stomach just wasn't flat anymore.

"Thanas," Surkah whispered. "It looks like an *ikon* stung you."

I had no idea what an *ikon* was, but I knew nothing had stung me.

"Do your *lissa* thing and see if I'm sick."

Surkah placed both of her hands on my stomach, and her eyes misted with tears.

"I don't need to use my *lissa* to know why you've been poorly."

I raised a brow. "Then why am I feeling so shitty?"

"Because," she spoke softly, "you're with offspring."

I stared at Surkah, and she stared right back at me.

"I'm sorry," I said, shaking my head. "Can you repeat that?"

She laughed. "You're with offspring."

I shook my head again.

"You're wrong; I am sick."

"No," she pressed, snickering now. "You're with offspring."

"Surkah," I deadpanned. "I'm going to smack you if you say that again."

She cackled. "Why? It's true."

"It *can't* be."

"Why not?" Surkah asked, staring down at my stomach like it was a beacon of hope. "This is a gift from Thanas."

"I had sex with Kol three times, Surkah. Three times," I stated but was even embarrassed to admit that.

"Three times is enough." She shrugged. "It only takes one

time."

For a moment, we were silent; then I felt overwhelmed, so I laid down on the sofa and stared up at the landscape painted ceiling.

"Are you sure?" I questioned. "I mean, are you *really* sure?"

Surkah kneeled next to me, pushed the material of my top back up to my breasts, and placed both of her hands on my stomach once more. She didn't speak; she just closed her eyes and did her *lissa* thing. I learned over the past few weeks that Surkah's healing ability could also scan the body to track illness, locate pain points, and track pregnancy.

"Oh, Nova," she suddenly cried. "You're truly with offspring and not just the one."

I screeched. "What?"

"There are two little ones," Surkah sobbed.

I sucked in a breath. "I'm pregnant with *twins*?"

"Yes!" Surkah screamed and pulled me up into a hug.

I didn't hug her back; I didn't think I even drew in a breath.

"I'm pregnant," I repeated when our hug ended. "Holy fuck, Surkah."

"Two offspring," Surkah breathed. "Kol has sired *two offspring*."

I felt like I was going to be sick.

"Surkah," I whispered. "You can't tell him yet."

She looked at me like I'd grown an extra head.

"I *must* inform him," she stressed. "He is my brother *and* the father to your young."

"I know"—I nodded—"but *I* want to be the one to tell him."

Surkah eyed me. "You will give me your word that you will tell him today?"

"Yes," I said. "I was going to find him and reconcile with him anyway. I would never keep this from him."

She smiled then she was silent for a moment.

"You seem shocked at this result."

Is she serious?

"Of *course*, I'm shocked."

"Why?" Surkah quizzed, a white brow raised. "You shared sex with Kol. What else did you expect to happen?"

"I didn't think I'd get pregnant." I scowled. "He is Maji, and I am human."

"I informed you on your first day with us that Maji are one hundred percent compatible with humans—"

"You really aren't helping," I cut Surkah off. "I know what you said, and I know sex leads to pregnancy, but we had sex only twice before the mishap with Ezah, and once more when I brought him back from the edge ... I just ... I guess I didn't think it would happen so fast."

Surkah's chest puffed with pride as she said, "Maji have strong sperm; your womb never stood a chance."

I placed my face in my hand and sighed.

"Yay for Maji," I grumbled.

"Nova," Surkah said softly. "Please do not be sad. Do you know what this means for our species? Maji and humans, we're endangered, but now that we know reproducing between us is a fact, we will *save* one another. This is ... it's wonderful."

I looked at Surkah, and when I saw her eyes welled up with tears, I gently smiled at her. "Do you think your *lissa* can tell the gender?"

She perked up.

"I can try. It tracks Maji pregnancy extremely well. I will try for you."

She did her *lissa* thing for a few more minutes before she opened her eyes and looked at me.

"A male *and* a female," she said, beaming with pride. "You carry both. We're truly saved."

I began to cry, and when I realised it was with joy, I cried harder.

"These young are already fully formed. Tiny but formed," Surkah said with awe. "At this point in Maji pregnancy, they're only cells, but your offspring have all their limbs and organs. They're just *very* small. I think it will be an eighteen-moon cycle pregnancy, not twenty-four."

Eighteen months.

"Wait." I paused. "Maji females are pregnant for two fucking years when they're pregnant? Ealra years?"

"Yes," Surkah chirped. "It is why our species is taking a long time to repopulate. Long pregnancies and many males being born."

I inhaled and exhaled. "Eighteen Earth months or eighteen Ealra months?"

Surkah devilishly grinned. "Ealra."

"That's about *two* Earth years then." I groaned. "That's seriously more than *double* a regular human pregnancy; it's nearly *triple*."

Surkah shrugged. "It is almost half a Maji pregnancy, so it kind of meets in the middle."

I snorted but said nothing further.

"I have dreamed of this for many moons," Surkah said, "but to have you before me and pregnant by not only a Maji, but by my brother is better than any dream."

"I'm shocked. I'm happy, don't get me wrong, but I'm shocked."

"How did you not pick up on the pregnancy signs?" she questioned. "The sickness, the tenderness, the increase of appetite, the swell of your stomach?"

I felt heat creep up my neck.

"I was the only girl in my family, and no one ever talked about babies or pregnancy."

Surkah patted my hand. "I understand; you were not educated on the subject."

"No," I acknowledged, "but you can bet your ass that I'm going to learn everything I can *now*."

"You speak so oddly sometimes that it makes my head feel fuzzy."

I laughed. "Welcome to my world."

Surkah was about to speak when the door to the living area open and in walked the Revered Father and Hailed Mother. They were laughing and snuggling one another as they walked, but when their eyes landed on me lying down on the sofa, and Surkah's hands on my stomach, the room went silent. The Hailed Mother broke away first and rushed over to my side, kneeling next to Surkah.

"No!" she cried, and to me, she said. "Truly?"

I bobbed my head. "Surkah confirmed it."

She gasped and looked at her daughter, a lingering question in her violet eyes.

"Scent her, Mother," my sister-in-mate encouraged. "If you do not believe your eyes or Nova's words, believe your nose."

Not a second after the words left Surkah's mouth, the Hailed Mother nudged Surkah's hands off my stomach then pressed her face against the base of my exposed stomach. If she had been anyone else, I'd have smacked the daylights out of her for putting her nose so close to my nether region, but being that she was the Hailed Mother, of the people, I could do nothing but lay deathly still and allow her to do whatever it was that she wanted to.

"Thanas," she stated after she inhaled and exhaled deeply a few times. "I can scent offspring. It is a mixed scent, but that must be because she is human."

"Actually," I piped in, "it might also be because I'm carrying twins. A male and a female."

The Revered Father tipped his head back and let out a roar—of what I now knew was delight thanks to Surkah's explanation on Maji roars—and he was quickly mimicked by the Hailed Mother who put her arms around me and hugged my stomach to her face as she spoke her thanks to Thanas. It was such a bizarre moment to be sharing with two people, but I put myself in their shoes and looked at it from their point of view. They had just recently found out their son had found his fated mate when the last Maji to do so died on the old Maji home world. Not only was I pregnant from their son and would make them grandparents for the first time, but I was also carrying twins, a male and female. Proof that humans really *were* compatible with Maji. They had just been informed that the Maji's gamble to save us humans to save their species was a gigantic success.

There would be future generations of Maji, and my two babies would be a huge part of that.

"Send for Kol!" the Hailed Mother demanded as she jumped to her feet. "Right now."

"Already done, moonlight." The Revered Father smiled before he looked at me and aided me in getting to my feet from the sofa. "Do you still require your space from Kol?"

I managed to laugh as I readjusted my clothing. "No, I think we have had more than enough."

He grinned. "My mate is not my fated mate, but she is my sun, my moons, and my sky. Kol's feelings for you must be double what mine are for my mate, so I cannot imagine how he is able to force himself to be away from you."

I felt like I was suddenly sucker punched, and I lost my smile.

"It's my fault," I admitted. "I told him to give me space, or he'd never see me again."

The Revered Father nodded. "May I request why?"

"Because," I said, my shoulders slumping. "I didn't want him to want me just because the glow in his eyes was telling him to. It's like he craves my body, but not me. Does that make sense?"

"You wished to test his restraint?" he quizzed. "To prove that his heart wants you and not his body?"

"Yes, exactly."

"And do you not feel he has done that already?"

"I do. I truly do," I instantly answered. "But it's not that simple now that I'm pregnant. Things changes things, and I don't want *him* to think *I* want us just to be together now because I'm having his babies."

"He will not think that," the Revered Father assured me. "Maji do not think like you humans."

"I know." I sighed. "I guess … I guess I'm just nervous. We've been apart for weeks, and I'm now about to hit with my pregnancy news."

"He will rejoice," the Hailed Mother said, and Surkah nodded in agreement.

I looked back at the Revered Father and then at his mate.

"Congratulations," I said to them. "You're going to be grandparents."

"Grandparents." The Hailed Mother trembled.

"I'm going to be a grandfather." Her mate beamed.

I felt almost as happy for them as for me and Kol. "You are."

"Thanas blesses us," he said.

I jumped when the Hailed Mother suddenly growled. "Kol has rejected to come and see his female; he said he informed her that when he saw her next, she would have to come and seek him."

I paused, remembering that he said those very words.

"That's fine," I told her. "He wants me to be sure about when I come to him. I am very sure, so tell me where he is and I'll go to him."

"He is in the dining hall with his brothers."

I raised a brow. "All of them?"

The Hailed Mother nodded. "They were sparring, and after they cleanse, they eat, so they're all together."

"Perfect," I said. "Everyone can find out together about the babies. Will you bring me to him?"

The words barely left my mouth before the Hailed Mother took my hand and whisked me out of Surkah's wing, down multiple hallways, and eventually into a huge dining hall. I was thankful to my mother-in-mate for not pausing on our journey here; it meant I didn't have to focus on what I was about to do because I knew if I overthought it, I would freak out. I wouldn't run, though; I was done running. I would just probably freak out in the one spot.

My eyes found Kol right away; he was sitting at a huge table with his back to me. All his brothers were seated at the same table. Some saw us enter the room, and some didn't. Other tables in the hall were occupied by servants who were retaking their seats and continued to eat their food after they bowed to me and the other royals behind me.

Kol.

Silence then a quiet, *Yes, my shiva?*

My heart warmed. *Come to me.*

No, he replied. *If you want me, you come to me.*

I smiled as I stared at the back of his head.

"Kol," I called.

He didn't turn around, and that ticked me off because I *knew* he could hear me. I knew he sensed me the second I stepped into the dining hall. He always told me how attuned to my body he was, so I didn't believe for a second that he couldn't hear me.

"Kol," I called out again. "I will go to the nearest *male* and request his assistance if you do not give me yours in the next *five seconds.*"

He didn't budge.

"Are you going to make me count?"

When he remained still with his back to me, I deadpanned and opened my mind to him.

You're going to make me count. Fine.

"Fine," I huffed. "Five, four, three, two and a half ... two ... one ... one and a quarter... one ... half of one ... I'm getting *really* close to zero, sweetheart."

I saw Mikoh, who was next to Kol, grin at him, clearly amused by my actions.

With a grunt, I turned, and locked my eyes onto the male closest to me, and it just so happened to be Aza, Kol's younger brother. The male was walking towards his parents, but he froze to the spot when he realised I was approaching him with a bright smile on my face. He kept flicking his eyes back and forth from me to Kol who I knew was now standing and walking in my direction based on Aza's behaviour. The closer he got, the more nervous Aza became.

I slowly reached out with the intent to place my hand on Aza's shoulder, but a hand came from over my shoulder and clasped my wrist, halting my movements.

"You'd touch another male in *front* of me?" Kol growled from behind me, and I'd be a no-good liar if I said his vibrations didn't go straight to my clit.

"Didn't leave me much of a choice, did you, *mate*?"

He moved closer to me, and the second I felt the hardness of his chest brush off my shoulders, I shuddered as tingles broke out over my body. Kol inhaled then growled violently.

"My torture arouses you?"

Oh, damn.

"No," I said firmly, "your bossiness does."

Aza snorted but looked down when Kol growled in his direction. His lips were still turned up in a grin, though, and it made me chuckle. He respected Kol, and I knew he knew deep down that Kol would never truly harm him.

"Nova," Kol almost snarled. "I have *not* got the patience for you right now. I cannot be rational. Your arousal is making things *very* hard."

I reached back and grazed his very hard cock with my hand.

"I can tell."

He hissed as he turned me in his direction. I knew what he was about to do, but I stopped him from flinging me over his shoulder just in time, and he glared down at me because of it.

"What are you—"

"I don't want to go over your shoulder, not for a few more

months anyway."

Kol's brows furrowed. "Explain."

I glanced around the room and saw we were the focus of everyone. I wasn't going to hide it from them; it was just as much their news as it was mine. I reached down, gripped the hem of my top, and pulled it up, exposing my barely swollen pregnant belly to Kol and everyone else. I heard gasps, but I didn't smile until Kol's eyes widened. He staggered back a little, the shock of what I revealed clearly overwhelming him.

"Nova, you're ... you're ..."

"Pregnant," I finished with a nod. "Yep. It's *your* fault, too."

"My fault?" Kol repeated, his focus on my belly.

He blinked his eyes a couple of times as if they were tricking him. I reached for his hand, and he absentmindedly gave it to me then stumbled forward a little when I took hold of it and tugged. I flattened his hand over my small but hardened tummy and looked up at him.

"It's kind of a double whammy pregnancy."

"What does *that* mean?" he asked, his eyes locking on mine.

"It means," I said with a little shrug, "you've got super sperm."

Kol continued to look at me in confusion, so I laughed and said, "There are two of them in there. *Twins*. A boy and a girl, to be exact. Surkah confirmed it."

Kol's eyes filled with emotion, but he quickly blinked any evidence away.

"This is a gift," he breathed. "Thanas has blessed us."

I smiled. "It appears so."

"The three of you," he rasped, "are *mine*."

"Is that so?" I mused.

He growled, his hold on me tightening. "It is."

"Good." I smiled. "Because if there is ever an inch of space between us ever again, it would be too much."

Kol swooped me up in his arms, and with the laughter and

cheers of our family, he ran from the room and didn't stop until we entered our wing and eventually our bedrooms. A room we had not shared together for too long.

"I feel like I am dreaming," Kol blurted when he set me down gently on our bed. "This is everything I have ever wanted."

"Me too," I said, my voice tight with emotion. "I never believed I'd have what I have with you."

"What do we have, Nova?"

I leaned my forehead against his after he kneeled before me.

"We have love, my mate."

Kol squeezed his eyes shut. "You accept our mating? You believe I love you truly?"

"I do, and I am so sorry for doubting you. I thought our love, for you, was because of your physical reaction to me. I didn't understand."

"It is hard to explain, so I know it is hard to understand," Kol said, brushing hair back from my face. "I want you, Nova. My heart wants you, my body wants you, all of me wants you. I breathe for you, my heart beats for you, blood runs through my veins and cock for *you*."

"You're so romantic."

"Nova!" Kol growled, not amused.

I chuckled. "I love you, Kol."

He blinked. "Repeat that."

"I love you, Kol."

I felt emotion surge through him, and he growled.

"I tell you I love you, and you growl at me?" I teased.

His face was still a mess of emotion, but his eyes gleamed with amusement.

"You like it when I growl at you," he said, growling for good measure.

My clit pulsed with an empty ache.

"I definitely do," I groaned. "Good, I hurt so bad for you."

Kol almost snarled as he plastered himself against me.

"You truly love me?" he asked. "And not just because you're carrying my young?"

"I loved you before I knew I was pregnant, and I love you now that I know I'm pregnant.

"Before?" he growled. "You truly loved me but wished to stay away from me. *Why?*"

His anger was expected.

"Because"—I frowned—"I didn't want this whole fated mate thing to be your focus. I wanted you to love me for me, not because some instinct was telling you to."

Sadness lurked in Kol's eyes.

"It does not work like that," he said. "I could hate you, but as my true mate, I'd still crave your touch. Having a true mate does not mean instant love; it means an instant bodily bond. Love is an ... extra to being a mate. If you love your mate, you will love them until you breathe your last breath. It is forever binding, both body and soul. I will never look at another female and feel sexual desire. I will never consider any other female for anything other than friendship, and if you do not want that, then I will never speak to another female ever again."

My heart thudded against my chest.

"What about your sister?" I tested.

I'd *never* go through with asking him not to talk to other females; he could befriend whomever he wanted to because I knew he'd be coming home to me. I was curious to see if he was serious, and testing him with his sister was my go-to card because I knew he adored her. Surkah was precious to him.

Kol eyes widened, and I saw his pain as he said, "If you wish it, I will not speak to my sister again."

I felt my jaw drop. "You're serious?"

He nodded.

"I love Surkah with all my heart, and you love her with all of yours. I'd never come between you, and you don't need my permission on who you befriend, Kol. You're my mate, not my property."

Tears filled Kol's eyes.

"I'm your mate?" he whispered. "Truly?"

"You're my fated mate, my male, my pain in the ass." I smiled. "You're all mine."

He closed his eyes and began to breathe heavily.

"I'm sorry I've been so ... difficult," I said, "but I had to know for sure. I was afraid what we had wasn't real. I was so scared this mate bond was just about sex, and I couldn't be with you when I loved everything about you while you just loved my body."

Kol cupped my face in his hands, and he reopened his eyes.

"Our love is very real," he assured me. "You're my everything."

I smiled and reached up and took hold of his wrists. I placed his hands on my belly and covered them with my own.

"*We* are your everything."

"Yes," Kol rumbled. "The three of you are *mine*. I just cannot believe we're going to have little ones."

I kissed him before he broke it seconds later.

"I promise not even death will part us, Nova. You own my heart and soul for all of eternity. I am yours."

"Mine," I whispered. "And I am yours."

"Forever."

I intertwined our fingers. "Forever."

I had never felt happier, and from the look on Kol's face, neither had he ... but then his face fell.

"What?" I asked, knowing he heard something through his comm. "Kol, what is it?"

"The Earth," he began, nervously flicking his eyes towards me. "It has imploded."

I sucked in a sharp breath, and with a strangled cry, I leaned into Kol's embrace and wrapped myself around him, taking the comfort he offered. I felt my heartbeat in my ears and pain in my chest.

"I am so sorry, *shiva*."

I hugged him tighter. "It's really gone?"

"Yes," Kol answered, pulling back slightly to look at my face. "It is gone."

Tears fell from my face.

"I don't know why I'm crying so much; I had a horrible life on Earth."

My mate brushed away my tears. "You still had some good times on Earth. You had a good family there, and the life you led turned you into the brave female you are today."

"Ealra is my home now." I pressed my forehead to his. "*You* are my home."

"And you are my everything, my *shiva*."

Kol pressed his hands against my stomach, and I covered them with mine, and together, we basked in the news of our pregnancy. My mate was right; Earth made me into the woman I was today, and in a way, I had Earth to thank for bringing Kol into my life. Myself, other human women on Ealra, and even on Terra, would represent Earth always … and we now had a chance to clear her name and restore honour to our planet with our future actions.

Earth might have been no more, but out of the ashes, a new generation of Maji and humans would be born.

ACKNOWLEDGMENTS

Book number eleven finished? Check!

What a rollercoaster of emotions writing *OUT OF THE ASHES* was! This was my very first book in the Science Fiction Romance genre—a genre that I *love* to read—and I hope that you guys have enjoyed it, because I *loved* writing it.

I have to thank my girls, Yessi and Mary, for being the best friends, and best support system, a person could ever ask for. I love you ladies all the way to Ealra and back.

Jill, my superwoman, thank you so much for your patience with me. It's not easy being my PA, but you're so awesome at your job that it makes me incredibly glad that you stick around and put up with me.

Editing4Indies, thank you for dealing with my pretty shocking schedule when it comes to sending you manuscripts. You're one in trillion, Jenny. I appreciate you so much.

Mayhem Cover Creations, thank you for creating a cover that is truly out of this world.

JT Formatting, thank you for making my words look pretty. You're a star, Julie.

Mark, for being a brilliant agent, and not losing your mind when it took me forever to send you the manuscript for *OUT OF THE*

ASHES.

My readers, from the bottom of my heart, thank you for taking a chance on Kol and Nova's story. If you liked their journey, stick around for future books in the Maji series, because I've *whole* lot in store for these two species. :)

ABOUT THE AUTHOR

L.A. Casey is a *New York Times* and *USA Today* best-selling author who juggles her time between her mini-me and writing. She was born, raised and currently resides in Dublin, Ireland. She enjoys chatting with her readers, who love her humour and Irish accent as much as her books.

Casey's first book, *DOMINIC*, was independently published in 2014 and became an instant success on Amazon. She is both traditionally and independently published and is represented by Mark Gottlieb from Trident Media Group.

To read more about this author, visit her website at
www.lacaseyauthor.com

Printed in Poland
by Amazon Fulfillment
Poland Sp. z o.o., Wrocław